only for you

BY SAMANTHA LEIGH

Valentine Bay Series
Ready For You
Meant For You
Perfect For You
Only For You

Aster Springs Series
Wallflower
Sunshine

only for you

samantha leigh

*For incoming members of the (non-problematic)
Daddy Will Fan Club.*

Now taking nominations for president.

AUTHOR'S NOTE

My books are low on angst and big on feel-good vibes, but they occasionally touch on topics that may be difficult for some readers. To access a complete list of content warnings for all my books, including *Only For You*, please visit my website at samanthaleighbooks.com or use the QR code below. And most importantly, take care of yourself.

1

ABBIE

"OKAY, EVERYONE." I used my sing-song instructor tone as I flattened myself on my mat and closed my eyes. "Let's move into corpse pose."

"Hey!" Burt the Third barked over the gentle notes of meditative music floating in the air. "Thought we told you not to use that word anymore."

My lips quirked as an annoyed murmur rolled through my seniors' yoga class. I shouldn't tease them, but when twelve geriatrics tell you not to imply they're already dead, it's hard not to laugh.

"My apologies, everyone," I intoned. "Let's move into *savasana*. Settle yourselves on your mats, face up with your arms by your sides, palms open if that feels good, and eyes closed."

I waited for the shuffling to ease and silence to fall, paying close attention to the sound of measured breathing over the light yoga track. A faint but insistent hissing sound underpinned the music, and I made a mental note to remove this song from my play list.

"Breathe in through your nose." I followed my own advice, then emptied my lungs with a small sigh. "Now let it go. Sink into the floor, releasing all tension from your body."

A chorus of exhalations answered me, and I fell quiet, leaving the class to their own meditation. Everyone was a regular participant with a good understanding of their practice.

Who was I kidding? Most of them would be snoring inside a minute.

My eyes grew heavier, and my muscles looser as I released another long breath. I'd been a yoga teacher for three years and a serious student for five before that, and I still didn't take these pockets of rest for granted. My life off the mat was what some people might call... vibrant... and my practice was my stabiliser. I did hours and hours of yoga every week, in class and on my own time. If anyone asked, I told them the best thing about it was it kept me in shape, but that wasn't the reason I'd never give this up.

Yoga required me to check in with myself every day. It was a reminder that the Abbie Ellison people thought they knew wasn't always the same Abbie Ellison who went to bed alone every night.

Yes, alone. Every night. It had been a long time between drinks, and this girl was thirsty.

The hissing sound grew louder, and I wondered if the

noise might be air whistling through Irena Kowalski's false teeth.

I did my best to clear my mind, letting my thoughts pass by like cotton clouds in an empty sky, but for whatever reason, today was not my day. *Something* nudged at me, an uneasy sensation of waiting without knowing for what. I didn't ignore it or try to fight it—I'd long accepted I had a sixth sense for certain things. For one, I could tell when my friends got lucky just by looking at them—their auras took on this kind of post-coital glow that was hard to miss. And for another, I could feel when change was coming, a sensation of waiting like standing under steel-coloured clouds carrying fat drops of rain.

The hissing grew louder and more urgent. I sat up, looking around for the source.

"What *is* that?" Burt dragged himself to standing and slapped his faded old baseball cap on his head. "Been getting noisier for the last half-hour."

"I'm not sure," I admitted as I climbed to my feet. The sound seemed to come from the ceiling, and I rounded the room slowly, ears straining as I tried to figure out where it originated.

Lorraine Langley, my old history teacher, mirrored my movements on the other side of the room, her knotted feet creaking on the polished floorboards as she passed racks of luscious indoor plants, hunting for the hiss. "Sounds like the time a water pipe broke in my classroom."

"I hope you're wrong, Mrs Langley," I muttered, passing the wall of shelves and hooks that housed my extensive collection of yoga mats, blocks, belts, and bolsters. "I have no interest in dealing with a leak today."

Around us, all but two of my students were upright. After asking Irena to gently wake the ones still sleeping, I rounded the last corner of the room and still wasn't any closer to finding the source of the sound.

"I think it's loudest over here," Burt called, standing almost directly in the centre of the large room, head tipped back and hands on hips. "What do you think?"

"I think—"

With a soggy crack, the ceiling over Burt sagged, and every chin in the room jerked in that direction. Like a slow-motion horror scene, the hissing grew louder—and wetter. The plaster around the bulge split and flaked, sending specks of white paint and dust raining down on our heads.

I took a few fast, worried steps forward as, with torturous inevitability, the ceiling gave way.

Someone screamed—me, I think—as an explosion of ice-cold water pelted down over my head.

"Holy fuck!" I skipped out from the gush of water, which was steady but slowing. My feet slipped a little on the wet floor, and I righted myself easily enough before panicking about everyone else's footing. Not everyone here needed new hips, and I didn't want to be the reason for a sudden uptick in the sale of bionic joints.

"Nobody move," I ordered as I sloshed my way to the stack of rubber mats on the opposite side of the room. The water had pooled from wall to wall to a depth of an inch, maybe less. I tried not to worry about that now. Stressing over my business could come after I made sure my clients were okay. "I'm going to set down a row of mats from here to the door, and then I'll help you down the stairs one by one, okay?"

"I don't need help getting down a darn flight of stairs," Burt grumbled, though he did me the favour of not moving.

"For me, Mr Spies?" I threw him a pleading look as I stamped down a rise of panic. "Please? I don't want anyone to get hurt."

He muttered something under his breath but stayed put, hands shoved into the pockets of his tracksuit pants, and I mouthed him a silent thank you.

It took me a few minutes to arrange a path of safety from sodden rubber mats before I could escort my students from the studio to the street outside one at a time. After that, I went back for their belongings. I lived in a cute little two-bed apartment underneath the studio, and though I was tempted to pop my head in and make sure everything in there was dry, the bright green door remained closed no matter how many times I walked past it. One problem at a time.

Someone was sensible enough to call the fire brigade while I was busy, and by the time a couple of firefighters with hoses and water vacuums had been in and out of the building multiple times, a decent crowd of busybodies had gathered on the street to get a look at today's gossip.

A man in uniform pulled me aside. "Abigail Ellison?"

"That's me," I confirmed, scraping my soaked hair back from my face. Jesus, what a moment to meet this guy. He was just my type—tall, lean, and toned with a boyish light in his blue eyes. Meanwhile, my long blonde waves hung in wet, ratty lengths stuck to my face and back, an icky stale water smell had washed away my coconut-scented body lotion, and my workout wear was sticky and wet in all the wrong places. Well, perhaps not *all* the wrong places. One quick check confirmed my nipples felt the chill. Excellent.

"The water damage is extensive across both floors," he confirmed, glancing back at the old, narrow building I'd bought two years ago. "We've turned off all power to the property, and your insurance company will need to do an assessment, but nobody should enter the premises until an electrician completes a safety check and gives you the all-clear. We can assist you now with extracting any personal items you need to take with you—"

"Hold up." I frowned up at him, his face not nearly pretty enough to warrant a smile right now. "What do you mean, *take with me*? I live here. I'm not going anywhere."

Mr Sexy Firefighter's grimace was apologetic. "I'm afraid that's not possible. At least, not for a while. Why don't you come in and take a look?"

2

ABBIE

—————————

THIRTY MINUTES LATER, after a depressing tour of my flooded studio and the soaking mess that was my apartment, I'd packed my bags, loaded them into my hatchback, and set off for my parents' house. That waiting sensation still lingered around my solar plexus, and after I turned into their familiar driveway, I activated the handbrake, cut the engine, and completed a deep breathing exercise that eased some of the tension. Only then did I open my eyes.

"Hey, Universe," I muttered as I climbed out of the car. "I don't know what else you've got lined up for me today, but I'm listening, okay? No need to drop the entire sky on my head."

I let myself into my parents' house and dropped my half-dozen bags in the hallway. The place was quiet, faint classical music playing from an ancient stereo system in the living room, and I knew better than to call out for someone. At this time on a weekday morning, Arthur and Nancy Ellison always shared tea and toast over the morning papers. The old-fashioned printed-in-ink kind. The kind nobody bought anymore. But Mama and Dad had me late in life—I was the miracle baby who arrived fifteen years after their only son, my forty-four-year-old doctor brother who lived in the city—and they were in their seventies now. Nothing I said would ever convince them to ditch the black smudges on their fingertips for a digital version of the daily news.

"Morning, Mama," I said, planting a kiss on her greying crown.

She startled and dropped her last corner of jam toast just as Dad looked up from the sports pages, moving his glasses to the end of his nose.

"Abigail," he said as I pressed a kiss to his creased but freshly shaved cheek. "What are you doing here, Pumpkin?"

I took a chair and straightened, even though I wanted to drop my head onto the table and stay there until my problems had magically solved themselves. I had no idea how long it would take to fix my studio or apartment or how I was going to keep teaching my classes without a venue, but I wanted my parents to believe I had everything under control. Their worries, added to mine, wouldn't solve anything.

I wasn't hungry, but I reached for a slice of melon and chewed on it like I didn't have a care in the world.

8

"A water pipe burst in the studio and flooded the building. My apartment, too."

My mother gasped, hand flying to her chest, while my father shook his head and set his glasses on the table. "I've always worried that building was too old."

I set the half-nibbled melon slice on an empty plate and lifted Mama's hand to reassure her. "It's not too old," I said to Dad. "I had all the proper assessments done when I bought it. The burst pipe could have happened anywhere, to anyone. It's just bad luck."

"Well, I can always come by and take a look at it if you need some help."

My heart grew a little bigger, and I leaned over to give his cheek another kiss. "Thank you. I think the insurance company will take care of everything, but I need to stay here while I sort out the repairs."

Mama withdrew her hand from mine to pour me a cup of tea from the pot she always brewed for brunch. She slid it in front of me as she threw a furtive look at my father that he completely missed.

"What?" Mama was about to give me trouble, though I wasn't sure why. I'd just announced their little girl was coming home for a few days. I'd anticipated some kind of parade and my favourite dinner on the table by six. Not a hard time. My eyes bounced between the two of them, but Dad was oblivious. "What is it?"

Mama smiled apologetically. "You know we'd love you to stay with us a while, sweetheart, but the church is using our extra bedrooms for storage while they prepare for the biannual charity markets. We're overrun with boxes and bags of old clothes and books, and there are people in and out almost every day. It's a madhouse here."

The knot in my stomach loosened, and I relaxed back into the chair. I should have known Mama's problem would be something trivial. Small inconveniences were always large, life-altering events for Nancy Ellison.

I popped the last of the melon in my mouth and spoke around it. "A madhouse, you say?"

Mama nodded gravely as the sounds of birds chirping and butterfly wings floated in through the open kitchen window, audible even over the tinkle of elevator music in the next room.

I lifted an ironic brow. "I'll risk it."

Mama fiddled with the pearl buttons on her cardigan, a pretty pale blue garment she'd knitted herself fifteen years ago. "I don't know, sweetheart."

A pang shot through my chest as I tried not to let on that her rejection stung. I adored my parents, but they had been old for as long as I could remember. Mama reminded me of those well-to-do biddies in the movies, the ones who wore their white hair curled and sprayed, pearls around their necks, and colour-matched twin sets well before they qualified for a seniors' card. More than once, Arthur and Nancy had been mistaken for my grandparents. I knew that made them sad sometimes, and it might have bothered me when I was young, but I'd learned a long time ago not to care about what other people thought. In fact, I took great pride in taking people's judgements and shoving them in their faces.

"Well, what would you have me do?" I asked.

"Have you spoken to Will?" she replied. "This might be the perfect opportunity to take your relationship to—well, you know, the next level."

Ah, shit. I tried to smooth my expression even as I blinked a little too quickly. Will Kidd was the owner of Valentine Bay's best bar, The Salty Stop, as well as our small town's resident playboy. He was my best friend, and there was an undeniable undercurrent of sexual chemistry between us, but I wasn't in a relationship with him.

That wasn't the story I'd told my parents, though.

My eyes cut to Dad, who was still engrossed in his paper, and back to my mother.

"I'm not sure what you mean… exactly."

Mama's cheeks flushed with rosy self-consciousness. "I mean, you've been dating that boy for quite some time now, and I know you aren't, ah… *exclusive*… but I can see how much you adore him. Your closest girlfriends have good men and are settling down, and I worry about you leaving it too long." Her smile was small and a little sad. "I don't want you to wish you'd started your family earlier."

I shifted uneasily on the chair, even as I stifled a groan. I understood why they worried, and I hated lying to my parents, but it was for their own good. Nine days out of ten, it also made my life easier. Just not today.

"I'm not even thirty yet," I reminded her for the thousandth time. "There's plenty of time for marriage and babies." *Assuming I even want them.*

Mama nodded slowly. "You think that now, but we never know what life has in store for us, and your father and I will feel better when you're settled."

Will was always a tricky topic—and thanks to my little white lie, I only had myself to blame—but Mama had double-whammied me by bringing up Will *and* a subject that made my insides wind up so tightly it hurt: the fact my parents were as old as they were. They wouldn't be around forever, and both Mama and Dad wanted nothing more than to see me married with kids as soon as possible. On the one hand, they'd found it difficult to be older parents and didn't want me to face the same challenges. On the other, they'd quietly given up on my brother Adam ever giving them grandchildren so that burden had now fallen completely on me.

I understood their dream on a theoretical level. They'd had such a happy marriage they only wanted the same for me, and knowing I had someone to share my life with would give them both a sense of peace—the knowledge that even when they weren't around anymore, I'd have someone to look after me. Thinking about that made me sad, and I'd do almost anything to alleviate their concerns, but the truth was I'd never dreamed about a husband, two-point-five kids, and a house with a white picket fence. I'd spent my twenties convinced I wasn't cut out for monogamy, let alone marriage.

That made Will my matrimonial beard.

One morning about eighteen months ago, when we were hungover and nursing sore heads and coffee on the way

home from our respective walks of fame—not shame—
both of us agreed that neither of us was the marrying type.
Did that mean we wanted to grow old alone? Hell, no.
So, we made a pact. We promised to be lifelong friends
without benefits—each other's emergency contact person
and the partner we always took to weddings and awkward
family functions. We understood each other's need to enjoy
ourselves, and the more we thought about it, the more our
wacky plan made sense.

I didn't think far enough ahead to the day when watching
a line of women parade in and out of his bedroom might
make me want to claw someone's eyes out—theirs or mine.
Take your pick.

Mama reached over to rub my forearm the way she'd
done since I was a little girl. To soothe me. To broach a
difficult subject. To convince me to do something that she
believed was for my own good. "So, what do you think?
Wouldn't it be better if you stayed with Will? Isn't it time
you took the next step?"

Her eyes looked too hopeful for me to argue, and Will
would never say no, so I sighed dramatically and rolled my
eyes. "Okay, *fine*. I'll stay with Will."

Mama gave me a satisfied smile. "Good. Now, let me
tell you about this charity sale. You won't believe some of
the things people have tried to give us. Just yesterday, I had
to return…"

I nodded along as my mother rambled about dirty old
kitchen pots and odd shoes with no soles, but I was too in
my head to pay close attention. I lived a wilder life than

either of my parents knew, but not nearly so scandalous as I let everyone else believe. The real Abigail Ellison existed on the yoga mat, a woman somewhere between the compassionate, dutiful daughter my parents needed me to be and the reckless free spirit I presented to the world. And when it came down to why I went to all that trouble, the answer was simple. It was so the people I loved never had to worry about me.

My parents—who didn't want to leave me without a family of my own. My friends—who needed me to get back up after a cruel rumour in high school tore me down. And Will—who would always be a playboy and hate himself forever if I forced him to break my heart. Because when it came to Will Kidd, I refused to be one of the many. If we were ever going to be together, I had to be the one.

3

WILL

"IF YOU GO to page twelve," I began, flipping through my own copy of The Salty Stop Bar & Brewery Business Plan, "you'll find income forecasts and a comprehensive repayment plan." I ran my forefinger over a printed chart, stopping at the end of a descending red line and tapping the point marked "zero". "You've seen my savings records. That money, combined with the additional revenue I'll gain from expanding The Stop's opening hours, means I can purchase the warehouse space next door and fit it out with the necessary brewing equipment and repay your loan within two years."

Sitting opposite me in a booth at the back of Valentine Bay's best bar—my bar, The Salty Stop—Birdie Maxwell bowed her head over her copy of the paperwork. Beside her, with one thick arm stretched behind her along the leather-upholstered seat, Birdie's boyfriend and one of my best mates, Sergeant Isaac Greene, leaned back with a small, amused smile.

I ignored it. The old advice was to never mix business with friendship, and if there was a bank within a hundred miles that hadn't already rejected my loan application, I wouldn't be sitting here after closing time in the bar I already owed a shit-ton of money on, asking my best friend's millionaire girlfriend for cash.

I was taking this seriously, even if Isaac thought it was a done deal—a favour between mates. I wasn't a charity case, and I didn't want a handout. Running my own craft brewery was my dream, sure, but it was also a solid business idea. I knew that in my bones, but I needed the capital to prove it.

Birdie raised her head, her copper braid glinting in the golden glow of the hanging overhead lamp, and I breathed a little easier at the seriousness pinching the corners of her mouth. She, at least, was treating this like the business transaction it was supposed to be.

This woman was smart—like, real-life genius-level smart—not to mention a pro poker player who was always up for a gamble. I was betting on that fact to work in my favour.

"Why now?" she asked, turning back in the report until she reached my statement of savings. She twisted the page to face me and stabbed one finger at the total near the bottom. "If you keep putting away money at the rate you have been the last three years, you'd have enough to do this on your own in eighteen months. Maybe less."

I grimaced and ran a hand through my hair. "That was the plan, but the space next door became available unexpectedly, and it's too good an opportunity to pass up. Frank Murphy is a sullen old arsehole, and he swore black and blue he'd die before giving up the deed. Turns out his daughter needs the money now, and he promised to hear my offer before officially putting the place on the market." No need to mention that the guy insisted that the offer be made before the end of the week, and he wasn't interested in negotiations.

Birdie closed the business plan with a smack and pursed her lips to one side. "Don't suppose we could take a look at the property before I make my final decision?"

I leapt to my feet, the keys Mr Murphy had given me already free of my pocket and jingling in my hand. "I can give you a tour right now."

"It's nearly midnight," Isaac grumbled, begrudgingly getting to his feet. Birdie took his outstretched hand, and Isaac slid her out of the booth and against his side.

"Which is when I do my best work." Birdie elbowed Isaac in the thick muscle around his ribs and gave him a wink. "You know that. This won't take long, and then we can sign the paperwork. Put Mr Kidd here out of his misery."

She offered me a grin, and I returned it as professionally as I could. So close, but not there yet. And definitely *not* a favour.

I led Birdie and Isaac through the bar to a back door that led out into the service alley, and they followed the half-dozen steps to the warehouse next door. I unlocked the entrance and was the first one in, switching on the blinking fluorescent lights before moving further into the space. Birdie and Isaac followed close behind.

"It's not much to look at now," I said, striding to the centre of the room, my shoes leaving prints in the thick layer of dust covering the old timber floors. "But it's the perfect size for a microbrewery. Grain mill will go here"—I gestured to one side of the warehouse, then began to pace as equipment materialised before my eyes, creating a state-of-the-art brewery that was going to be the foundation for my entire future—"hot liquor tank there, the brewhouse system, fermentation vessels—"

Birdie sniffed and then sneezed, and I snapped my mouth closed. Nobody could possibly look at this dilapidated old building and see what I saw, but the details were in the business plan anyway, and Birdie had already read it. I stuffed my hand in my pocket before I could run it nervously through my hair again.

Birdie did a quiet circuit of the warehouse, eyes roaming over the dirty windows covered with torn pieces of canvas nailed to the frames and the old buckets and broken barrels stacked in the corners. I watched her as Isaac watched me.

"Stop fucking looking at me," I muttered under my breath.

Isaac chortled, then raised his hands. "Sorry, but you look stressed. It's going to be fine."

"I don't want to take Birdie's money unless she believes in this place, okay? I'm serious."

"I'm sorry," Isaac repeated, only this time he sounded like he meant it. "I didn't mean to bug you, but if it's any consolation, Birdie's as honest as she is smart. She's not going to agree to anything unless she thinks this place is a good bet, and she'll tell you what she thinks whether you want to hear it or not. I'm not the business type, but your report looked thorough. You answered all of Birdie's questions, and it sounded to me like you knew what you were talking about." Isaac grinned again. "Good thing you've got your act together. No way you're getting into her pockets on those dimples alone, Kidd. Trust me."

The corner of my mouth ticked up. It felt good to know one of my oldest friends could see how hard I was working at making something of myself. Still, old habits died hard. "These dimples have never failed to get me into a girl's pants before, Greene."

Isaac rolled his eyes, but his punch on my arm landed with enough impact to make me grunt. "You're lucky we go back as far as we do, Kidd, and I know not to listen to you talking shit like that."

I chuckled quietly. "Noted."

Birdie had completed a round and was going back for a second. Isaac crossed his arms over his barrel chest and watched, still as a statue, while I kicked absently at the dust on the floor. The two of them—him the gentle, giant, small-town cop and her the globe-trotting pro poker player— were an unlikely couple, but they fit like they were made for each other. And following a totally unconventional agreement that involved sex coaching, they were the latest to give in to the love bug plaguing Valentine Bay. One by one, my best mates had all left bachelorhood behind, and I was happy for them, but right now, I only had eyes for the brewery. If Birdie agreed to this loan, I'd be staring down years of more work, more responsibility, more debt. That was enough commitment for me.

"I've got a counteroffer for you," Birdie said from across the room, her voice jolting me out of my thoughts. She walked back our way and stood behind Isaac. "One that I hope you'll take up because if we can pull it off, it'll mean you should easily make enough to repay my loan. You might even make enough to clear some of your debt on The Stop as well."

Birdie was smart, but she was also a risk taker, and whatever could make me double my money sounded like a huge gamble.

My stomach rolled with anticipation. "I'm listening."

Birdie nodded once. "Good. There's a local poker tournament scheduled for the weekend before Valentine's Day—a smaller event in Scarborough Cove—but two days ago, the venue pulled out. The organiser has until the end of the week to find a suitable alternative, or the entire event will be cancelled."

I glanced disbelievingly around the dirty warehouse. It was large enough to fit dozens of people, but it wasn't what anyone would call hospitable. "Valentine's Day is barely a month away."

"Yep."

"And you think they'd want to do it *here*?"

"I know they would because I'm the organiser." Birdie crossed the floor and stopped in the middle, then turned to face me. "Here's my deal: *I* agree to the loan, and you delay your plans to set up the brewery. I'll need you to clean the place up—tidy it, of course, but also arrange any repairs or refurbishments well before the big day. I know all the costs for that were included in your business proposal, but if you need more to get it done fast, I'll cover the extra overheads. I'll also need you to be here to receive deliveries and manage the hired furniture and equipment."

I rubbed my eyes and tried to keep up. The relief that Birdie wanted to give me a loan was swamped by my scramble to understand where in this plan I'd make enough at just one event to clear so much of my debt. "I'm not sure I follow you."

"That's because I haven't got to the part about the money." Birdie lifted her hand and unfolded her fingers along with her list of perks. "One: I'll hire The Salty Stop to provide all catering and beverages. Two: We charge a cover fee and split it between us. Three: You're free to display any kind of branding you want in here and market yourself to patrons on the day." Birdie cocked her head and considered me for a moment. "And four: I've pulled some strings, and it won't be a strictly small-town crowd for this one. There might even be some deep pockets interested in investing in a local, up-and-coming craft brewery. Money like that will cut your five-year business plan in half—at least."

My pulse jumped as the possibility of finding an investor fired up the adrenaline. "Seriously?"

Birdie shrugged and gave me a smile. "You never know."

It was all happening so fast… But what the fuck was I afraid of? I'd owned my bar for five years and spent most of that time coasting—surfing and sleeping around while doing just enough to keep the bills paid and the beer flowing. On a whim, I'd started small-batch brewing last year and loved it so much that suddenly, owning a bar and pouring other people's ale wasn't enough. It took me a long time to get here, and now that my dreams were within reach, why should getting everything I wanted not sound like the best thing in the world?

In the back of my head, the rough soundtrack of my childhood played like clockwork, the legacy of having a deadbeat dad who only ever drifted into your life long enough to tell you what a disappointment you were before he drifted right on out again.

You fucked it up again, Will. Don't know why you even try. No way you'll ever measure up to your old man.

I thrust out my palm before doubts about the work, the risk, or the commitment—or the memory of my father—could scare me into second thoughts. "It's a deal, Maxwell."

Birdie's grin split her freckled face in two, and she took my hand in a firm grip. "I'll have my lawyers draw up the paperwork," she said. "Pleasure doing business with you, Kidd."

Isaac, on the other hand, threw his arms around me and squeezed so tight my ribs cracked. "Proud of you, Kidd," he said quietly, and when he pulled back, I nodded to let him know I'd heard.

It was nice to know Isaac was proud of me, but it wasn't enough.

4

WILL

———

I LIVED IN a loft above the bar, a tiny place with the master bedroom at the top of a set of stairs, a smaller bedroom down below that I used for storage, and barely enough room outside of the kitchen and bathroom for a small round dining table, two-and-a-half-seat sofa, coffee table, and wide-screen television. The loft was included with the title when I bought the bar, and it suited the life of a bachelor. All I had to do was stumble upstairs after a late night at work, and saving on rent didn't hurt either.

The loft faced east and, depending on how sore my head felt from the night before, I kind of liked the way the sun streamed through the windows as soon as it rose over Valentine Bay. I tried to surf more mornings than not. Early sessions weren't necessarily compatible with a job that kept me up late at night, but surfing was non-negotiable. It kept me sane. That said, after a night that delivered the answer to my prayers in a Birdie-sized package, I was in the mood for a sleep-in. When I finally rose, the sun was twice its height above the horizon. I glanced out the windows at the waves on my way to the kitchen, fixed myself coffee and cereal, and scrolled the bar's social media feed.

Since Emily Jones had moved to the Bay, fallen in love with my best mate Josh, and revamped her photography career, she'd taken over most of my marketing. Jones had a good eye and mind for socials, and her images were a big reason the bar did so well. I was what she called a micro-influencer, and the extra money I made from tourists— okay, single women—visiting Valentine Bay just to drink at my bar—okay, slip me their numbers—was a big reason I was ready to take that next step with the brewery.

Yep, life was lining things up just right. I'd called Mr Murphy, and he'd accepted my verbal offer on the warehouse. Birdie's solicitors were fast-tracking all the paperwork. My good luck was nothing less than fucking miraculous, and now that I'd agreed to Birdie's big scheme, I wasn't about to waste any time feeling nervous.

Abbie, my quirky best friend with a fast-and-loose philosophy on life like my own, would tell me to direct all that energy into positivity or some shit like that, and that's exactly what I was going to do.

I'd just picked up my phone to call Abbie and tell her about Birdie's offer when a light tap sounded on my front door. I pulled my phone from my pocket to check the time and waited for another knock. Mine was the only loft in this building, and I rarely had guests, so perhaps someone was lost. When the knock sounded again, louder and more insistent, I hurried over and swung open the door.

A woman stood with a bulking tote bag on one shoulder, and weirdly, a baby in a bulky plastic carrier sat at her feet. She looked a little familiar, but I couldn't place the face or give her a name.

"Hi," I said. "Can I help you?"

She ran her bottom teeth over her top lip. "You don't remember me."

She said it like a statement, not a question, and I frowned. My eyes flickered to the baby, squirming and smiling in the carrier. Involuntarily, I smiled back, and the baby grinned harder, flashing tiny dimples in his fat pink cheeks.

"I'm sorry." I returned to the woman's face, scanning her features and trying to place her as I took a deep breath. Something about her was kind of familiar…

My heart started racing, and I wasn't sure why. "If you could give me your name?"

She hitched the bag higher onto her shoulder and crossed her arms over her chest, eyes dropping to the carpet. I noticed then the dark roots lining the perfect part in her blonde hair, the small hole in the sleeve of her shirt, the frayed edges on the bag she carried and the worn toes on her scuffed-up sneakers. I checked the baby again. The knees of his jumpsuit were a little worn, but he looked happy enough. Healthy. Then again, what did I know?

My gaze volleyed back to the woman, who was looking at me now, her rich brown eyes underscored with tired shadows, and something clicked. From the depths of a forgotten night when this girl lay tangled in my sheets, a name swam to the surface.

She opened her mouth, and I answered my own question at the same time she did.

"Heather."

Heather nodded, then set down the bag. It hit the ground with a heavy thud, and I suddenly recalled my manners.

I shifted to the side. "Do you want to come in?"

She glanced into my apartment. "No. Thank you." Her hand waved towards the baby, but she didn't look at him. "This is Sebastian and— Look. There's no easy way to say this. He's yours."

A choked laugh sounded from my mouth, not that this was funny. "Huh?"

"He's yours."

Whatever was stuck in my throat grew a few sizes bigger, and all coherent thoughts fled. "You're having me on."

Heather shook her head. "We met last year, remember? Downstairs at the bar. I spent three days in this loft. We—"

"I remember." I raised a hand to stop her and glanced at the baby. His dimples landed differently this time, and I quickly looked away. It was so fucking hot all of a sudden that I was sweating through my shirt. "But we were careful."

"Not careful enough," she replied. "A few weeks after I left the Bay, I found out I was pregnant."

"And it didn't occur to you to call?" My tone was harsher than I intended.

She narrowed her eyes. "How many women have you had in your bed, Will?"

My stomach sank, and I opened my mouth—but nothing came out. We both knew the answer, and it wasn't going to help to say the number out loud. I scrubbed at the moisture on my forehead and muttered, "I don't believe this."

Her eyes flashed as her nostrils flared. "You think I'm lying?"

"I—" I didn't need to glance at the baby again to confirm how much of myself I saw in his features. "No. I didn't say that."

Heather shook her head, and her shoulders fell. "Look, you were the only man I was with that month and the first in the three months before that. And maybe I should have reached out at the time. For a hundred reasons, I didn't, but I'm here now." She hefted the baby carrier, and he reached for her fingers wrapped around the handle. Heather ignored him. "This is your son."

This must be what people meant when they talked about out-of-body experiences. I took a few wooden steps backwards, falling onto the sofa when my legs hit the fabric. Heather rolled her lips, then stooped to collect the tote bag. She followed me into the apartment and set her baggage at my feet. "I need you to take him."

"Take him?" My echo was hollow. Her words made sense to my ears but not my brain. *Take him where?*

Again, because I couldn't help it and because I could feel his eyes on me, I looked at the baby. Sebastian. He wore a navy cotton onesie, and a soft toy rabbit was stuffed into the side of the padded seat. His cheeks were rosy, thin wisps of light brown hair dusted his scalp, and his eyes were so blue they were almost purple—a sapphire colour like the one I'd inherited from my father and always hated. Sebastian was still smiling, a trail of drool crawling over his chin, dimples dancing. Those were from my father, too.

"Yes." Heather opened the bag and riffled through some things before extracting a fat envelope and trying to hand it to me while I fixed her with a blank stare. "Birth certificate. Doctor's records. Sleep and feeding schedule. And a contract transferring all parental rights to you."

I didn't realise I was on my feet until Heather took a step back.

"You need to slow down," I said, taking handfuls of my hair and tugging hard enough to hurt. "I don't *understand*. Why the hell would you come here after all this time— how long has it been? A year? Fifteen months?—and give me your baby? You don't even know me!"

"I'm giving you *your* baby."

Her neck was stiff, and her chin raised with so much determination that her refusal to look at Sebastian had me feeling irrationally pissed off. What kind of parent refused to look at her child?

My child.

"What kind of person walks away from their own son?" I demanded, though I already knew what kind of person did that. The kind of person like my dad, which is why I didn't for a second doubt that Heather was serious.

Her chin trembled once, and regret at my tone fleetingly replaced the anger burning my skin, but then she spoke again.

"I've met someone, and—"

"He doesn't want a kid?" I opened and closed my fists slowly and deliberately, hanging onto reason by my fingernails alone.

"He doesn't *know* about the kid."

Jesus. I sank down again and dropped my face into my hands. I was going to throw up.

Heather waited in silence, but when I didn't raise my head, I heard her place the paperwork on the coffee table and step back again.

"He's formula fed—the directions are in the paperwork. I've signed all the contracts, so when you're ready to file, all you need to do is add your name to the tabbed pages. My phone number is in there, but—don't use it. Please. It's just… It's just in case I've missed anything in the legal documents. I don't need complications. I want to settle this quickly and move on with my life."

I raised my head and stared at her in disbelief.

"What about my life?" I pointed at the baby. "What about *his* life? You're the only parent this boy has ever known."

Heather cleared her throat, feet shifting, but she didn't back down. "He's an easy baby. Happy. Good sleeper. He's used to being cared for by new people, so he won't give you any trouble."

The inference that I'd ever think of my own son as *trouble* set muscles firing in my clenched jaw, and I swallowed the bile rising up at the thought that at less than a year old, this little boy was comfortable around strangers.

"His next bottle is due in half an hour, and he'll probably need a change. I've packed enough supplies to last you two days, then you'll need to buy more." Heather backed away two steps, and for the first time, she set her eyes on the baby. "I know we only spent a few days together, but you were sweet to me, Will, and I'm certain this is the right thing. For Seb."

"For you," I snapped.

Heather blinked a few times as she rolled her lips again, and then she walked out, closing the door behind her.

I stood staring at the closed door for a few seconds, waiting for the dream to end and for Heather to return, but she didn't, so I sank into the sofa again, hands tugging at my hair, staring at this child who was now my responsibility.

This was a fucking joke, right?

Sebastian sat snug in his cushy little seat, blowing raspberries and blissfully unaware that his world had just changed forever. That his very life was now in my hands. A man he didn't know and who had no idea what he was doing. Tentatively, I reached out to Seb the way I might a strange animal, offering the backs of my fingers first, slowly so I wouldn't scare him.

He squealed and stretched his pudgy little fingers towards me and latched onto my thumb. When his soft, warm skin hit mine, my heart exploded, and I was gone.

5

ABBIE

I PASSED A woman in the hallway outside Will's loft. She was pretty, if a little pale, and she moved with her eyes downcast, arms wrapped around her body. Not everyone was built for walks of shame, and that's exactly what this was. I knew where she'd come from—there were no residents here aside from Will, living in the single apartment above his bar.

The fucking irony of me turning up on Will's doorstep begging for a place to stay while his bed was still warm from the body of another woman.

I almost turned around, but where the hell was I supposed to go? My parents would ask too many questions if I refused to move in with Will. Plus, my closest friends in the world were shacked up with men they loved, and I didn't fancy being a twenty-four-seven third wheel. Will was my only option, and I'd spent many nights in his bed—usually after I'd had one too many margaritas downstairs and always with him shunted to the couch—so I didn't think this latest favour was that big a deal. It didn't even occur to me to text first until I'd knocked on his door, and it was already too late.

It swung open almost instantly. Will slumped on the other side, a look of relief on his boyish, sun-tanned face. My stupid stomach flipped, and my neglected lady parts sent up a desperate SOS. I didn't know many times I'd begged the Universe for the day those blue eyes, that unkempt light brown hair, the long, lithe surfing-is-my-workout muscles, and sexy freaking dimples would stop doing things to me, but today—like every other—was not that day.

"Oh, thank God, you— Ellison." He straightened and glanced past me down the hallway as if looking for someone. "What are you doing here?"

"Nice to see you too, Kidd." I elbowed him aside and pushed my way into the loft, dragging my bags behind me. I had intended to ease into it—I'd practiced a little speech on the way over and everything—but slow and steady really wasn't my style. "I'm moving in."

"You—" Will dragged a hand through his hair, scanning my gear as if seeing it for the first time. "You're what?"

"A pipe burst at my yoga studio and flooded the entire building, including my apartment. I'm homeless." I grimaced before I could stop myself. "And unemployed until I can find a temporary space to run classes."

Will blinked at me as if my words didn't compute. There was no roll of the eyes, no sarcastic quip, none of the sexually repressed flirting-like-we're-fighting that was the backbone of our relationship.

I moved closer and waved a hand in front of his eyes. "Hello? You feeling okay?"

A wet, gurgling noise sounded on the floor behind me. I spun and my heart skipped at the sight of a tiny smiling baby squished into a carrier half-hidden behind the coffee table. "What the f—?"

I carefully lowered the last of my bags to the floor—nice and easy, like there was a poisonous snake coiled up behind me—and turned to Will with wide eyes. "Why do you have a *baby* in here?"

Will rubbed two open hands over his face, then dragged his feet to the sofa and fell onto it, close enough to the baby to put him right at Will's feet. I chanced a glance up to the loft but couldn't tell if there was a woman in the apartment, which was the only explanation I could come up with.

"His name's Sebastian," Will replied, "and... Jesus, Abbie. He's mine."

My spleen jumped into my throat, though there was no good reason for it. Nobody had just announced that *I* had a kid. I lowered myself to the sofa beside Will. "What do you mean, he's yours?"

Will huffed out a humourless laugh as he placed his forefinger in the baby's outstretched hand as if he'd done it a hundred times before, but the look he gave the baby was ironic. "Ten years of sleeping around... You think I've got a hundred of these out there?"

"Will, for fuck's sake. What's going on?" At his brief, disapproving frown, I rolled my eyes. "I'm sorry but help me out here. What the hell happened?"

"A woman I was with more than a year ago just knocked on my door, handed him over, and walked away."

"Do you mean the one who was leaving as I arrived?" At Will's slight nod, a weird kind of anger came over me. I was pissed off not only on his behalf but the baby's as well. I didn't care who she was or why she'd done it, but she couldn't turn up out of nowhere, abandon her son, and leave Will all alone to clean up the mess.

I jumped to my feet and started for the door. "She can't have gone too far, and someone must have seen where she went. I'll find her and—"

"Abs, no." I stalled, and Will shook his head at my incredulous stare. "Heather knew what she was doing when she came here. I tried to convince her to stay— believe me—but her mind was made up. There's nothing you can do."

I hesitated, wondering if this was a time to ignore Will for his own good, but then the baby—Sebastian—released Will's finger. Will set his elbows on his knees and hunched over to latch onto handfuls of his hair, tufts of it sticking out between his fingers. "In what twisted world do I have a child with a person who'd just leave him behind and never look back?"

I knew instantly that Will was thinking about his father—a good-looking but bad-tempered grifter who had charmed his mother into leaving her family behind in California, married her and fathered her child, then left her with the baby when he disappeared for weeks and months on end. When we were young, Will would come to school beaming with the news that his dad was home after a time away. As we grew older, we only ever found out Will Senior was back when our friend grew withdrawn and we spotted the reason strutting around the Bay like he owned the place. He walked out for the last time ten years ago, and Will hadn't heard from him since. It was for the best, and Will knew it. Even though he pretended like it didn't affect him anymore, their toxic history still caused him pain. We hadn't talked about his dad in a long time, but there were some things he never had to say.

I sighed as I sat beside him and set a comforting palm on his back, brushing my thumb back and forth. Will and I were all about casual touch, but the warmth of his skin against mine, even through his shirt, never failed to make my pulse jump.

"Not twisted," I told him. "Kismet." Will turned his head and met my eyes, confused and a little spooked. I gave him a crooked smile and rested my chin on his shoulder. "If there's a baby out there in desperate need of a parent, he couldn't do better than you."

One corner of Will's full mouth turned up in a grateful smile, setting off a dimple in one cheek. With a face like his, it was a wonder Will hadn't found himself in this kind of trouble years ago. I leaned away and hoped distance would dilute its panty-melting power, but no luck. Like magic, nerve endings lit up in all the right—I mean, wrong—places.

I crossed my arms to cover my traitorous nipples and glanced down at the baby. He was tiny but plump, with smooth cheeks and big blue eyes. Objectively cute, like those babies in laundry detergent commercials. He'd also kicked off one sock and was sucking noisily on his big toe.

"I don't mean to be insensitive, but…" I hesitated, but now or later, I had to ask the question. "I'm just going to say it. Are you sure he's yours?"

"Have you seen the colour of his eyes?" Will reached down and curled a finger under the baby's chin, tickling the creases of his neck. Sebastian squirmed and giggled, and little divots fired in his chubby cheeks. "The dimples?"

"Not sure that'd stand up in court," I quipped.

Will stood up, and while his back was turned, I reached for the place on Sebastian's neck that Will had tickled. I didn't know the first thing about babies—never cared enough to learn—but I could stand to listen to that little laugh again. I crooked my finger against the baby's warm, damp skin, and though he smiled a little, I didn't get the infectious giggle he'd given Will. I sat back on the sofa and watched the little guy from the corner of my eye until Will thrust a piece of paper in my direction.

"Birth certificate," he announced. "My name is right there in black and white."

I scanned the document. It said that Sebastian was a little more than six months old and listed William Kidd as the father. "Will," I said gently. "This doesn't mean—"

"He's mine." Will snatched the paper and stuffed it back into the envelope. "No question."

I bit my lip and let it go. Not because I thought Will was right, but because the defensive daddy energy was new. And unexpected. And bloody hot.

We both looked down at the baby at the same time. Sebastian had stuck his big toe in his mouth again, and slobber dripped down his foot and along his wrist.

"What is he *doing*?" I asked.

Will frowned. "I don't know… Hang on a minute. Heather said there was a schedule in here somewhere." He turned back to the bundle of papers and started pulling everything out.

Then Sebastian opened his mouth—and let out an ear-shattering scream.

6

WILL

_____

ABBIE JUMPED TO her feet, flapping one hand at Sebastian. "What's wrong with him? What's wrong with him?"

"How am I supposed to know?" I fumbled with the papers, the urgency of Seb's cry making my fingers clumsy. "Let me check the instructions."

"The *instructions*?"

"You know what I mean."

"How about *I* check the instructions, and you try to switch him off?"

I looked up from the wad of crushed papers in my hands, and even with the blaring wail of a baby-sized siren, I grinned. "You look terrified, Ellison."

"I am." She snatched the documents from my grip. "Now, do your thing, Daddy."

We froze. Holy fuck. Hearing that word on her lips sent a lightning bolt to my dick. And the way Abbie's wide, honey-brown eyes rounded a little more, she heard—and felt—it too.

Seb cried louder, so I tore my gaze away and dropped to my knees in front of him. His scream decreased a decibel or two now that we were face to face, and as I yanked at the straps and buckles that kept him restrained, he seemed to sense I was there to help. The yowling deescalated into frustrated wails.

I could count on one hand the amount of times I'd held a baby. I could also count on the same hand the number of minutes they'd been happy in my arms. Apprehensively, I slipped my hands underneath Seb's soft body—under his bottom, around his head—then stood up and snuggled him awkwardly against my chest. He twisted his face and wiped a wet stripe of something over my shirt, but the crying stopped.

I looked at Abbie, who watched me with something that might have been fascination, but then she shook her head and read from a sheet of paper.

"Looks like he's due for a bottle soon, and he'll also need to be changed. Then he needs a nap." Abbie looked around at my tiny loft with barely room to swing a cat. "He's going to need a bed, Will. There's some formula in here, but you'll need more soon. Same goes for the nappies." She plucked a plastic rattle from somewhere inside the enormous tote bag and shook it in Seb's face. He reached for it and stuck one end straight in his mouth. "Doesn't look like there's a list of supplies in here, but I'm sure we can Google it."

My chin jerked up. "We?"

Abbie released a dramatic, put-upon sigh. "Yes, we, unless you missed the part about me moving in?"

I hadn't missed it, but it hadn't really sunk in either. Now, I latched onto it like a lifeline. "You're serious?"

She rolled her eyes towards the ceiling. "Can't believe I'm saying this, but yes." Her chin dropped, and her honey-brown eyes were sincere. "I'm here for you, like always, and I want to help if you'll let me."

I glanced down at Seb with my first little flare of hope. I'd take care of him by myself if I had to—I'd made that decision, and nothing would change my mind—but I'd be a lot less freaked out if Abbie were around to keep me from making too many mistakes. I didn't have to do this alone.

Thank fuck.

I tried to sound cool about it. "Yeah, sure. Of course, you can stay."

"Good." Abbie retrieved a baby bottle full of water from the bag, followed by a can of baby formula. She took them to the kitchen, set them down, and opened both lids. "Where am I going to sleep?"

"Huh?" Seb started to fuss, twisting and arching in ways that made holding onto him feel like wrestling an eel. It took all my concentration to not drop him, and I started to sweat again. Could I hold him *too* tightly? I didn't want to lose my grip, but I didn't want to squash the little guy either.

"Sleeping arrangements?" Abbie tipped four plastic scoops of formula into the bottle of water, returned the cap, and shook it up before running it under a flow of hot water from the tap.

I watched in confused relief as Abbie dried off the bottle and handed it to me. Seb twisted towards it and opened his mouth, snuffling at the air like he could smell the milk.

"How did you know how to do that?" I asked as I dropped back onto the couch.

"It was in the notes."

I pretended not to notice how Abbie watched me with a tilt to her lips as I self-consciously arranged Seb in the crook of my arm and plugged his cries with the rubber teat. The complaints cut off immediately, thank Christ, and the little sucking noises he made were… kind of cute.

Abbie nodded to the half-open door of the spare bedroom. "I'm guessing you'll make that the baby's room, right?"

As Seb snuggled in against my chest, I frowned at the small room, barely more than a glorified cupboard. I hadn't used anything stored in there in over two years, and I'd been meaning to clean it out. Safe to say almost all of it was destined for the garbage heap. "I suppose that makes sense."

"That leaves your bed and the sofa," Abbie added.

I flashed her the type of suggestive grin that made lesser women giggle, and Abigail Ellison narrow her eyes. "Not going to happen, babe," she said.

No surprise there. I propositioned her all the time—joking, of course, so she couldn't see how badly I wanted her—but Abbie was too good for me, and we both knew it.

"Guess I'm on the sofa, as always, *babe*."

I reclined onto the couch as Abbie pursed her lips and leaned her hip against the dining table. "This vibe... It looks good on you."

I tucked Seb closer to my body and leaned forward a little so he could latch onto the collar of my T-shirt. He was soft and warm, and his wide blue eyes stared up at me in a way that made it difficult to look away. "What vibe is that?"

She laughed and pushed upright, turning to dig through the baby's bag. "Responsibility."

I winced. *Ouch*. It was a good thing Abbie had her back to me, so I didn't have to hide how deep that cut.

Abbie spun back to me with a small waterproof mat in her hand. "The manual says we should change him after his bottle, then he's supposed to sleep, but perhaps we should go shopping for a few basics."

Seb had drained the last mouthful of milk, and he grinned up at me around the plastic teat. There was so much trust in his eyes—so much innocence and faith, not a trace of fear—and it struck me that this little person was entirely dependent on me for everything. Food, shelter, safety, and stability. Love. The first few were things I could research and learn how to do right. The last one, however... If the way my heart already felt too large for my chest was any indication, the love part was out of my control.

"Shopping," I agreed absently until I registered what that meant. My head jerked up. "You mean, taking him outside?"

Abbie nodded, but her expression was sympathetic. "Afraid so."

I set the empty bottle on the coffee table and shifted Seb until he was a little more upright. A loud, wet burp slipped out of him, and I swear the little guy looked proud. "Nice work, buddy," I congratulated him, and Abbie chuckled.

I stood and glanced at the door, dreading everything that waited for me on the other side. The small-town gossip. The whispered judgements. Admitting to the people I loved that I'd fucked up and gotten a stranger pregnant. Pretending I didn't hear it when people said I wouldn't be able to raise a child, that I wouldn't *want* to do it—and there'd be plenty of arseholes who believed just that. An hour ago, I was one of them.

"Half the Bay will know about him before we reach the car," I said.

Abbie's plump mouth pressed into a thin line. She knew what was coming as well as I did. "Probably."

I stuck out my hand, and Abbie handed me a plastic mat, a surprised curve to one eyebrow. *Yes, Ellison. I'm going to change this kid's dirty nappy. That's what responsible dads do.*

There was something else responsible dads did, and that was own up to the choices they made that led to them becoming parents in the first place.

I arranged the mat on the rug and knelt to deposit Seb in the middle of it. He tried to wriggle away the second his back hit the floor.

"Not so fast, little man." I flipped him over and pressed an open palm to his stomach, and he blew a wet raspberry in reply.

It was frustrating work getting Seb undressed. Abbie echoed my sigh when we both saw the nappy was only wet, but she didn't offer to help, and I didn't ask. I could feel her watching me, and we both knew I had no idea what I was doing, but I was going to change this kid without asking for help. Then, I was going to face the music.

"Before we go shopping," I said, fumbling at the sticky tabs on the clean nappy before finally getting the thing secured around Seb's middle, "we need to make a stop."

"Okay. And I think I know where."

I was quietly confident she'd be cool with it—eventually—but the gossip in this town moved faster than cold beer on a hot Friday night, and I couldn't let my mother find out she had a grandson from anyone but me.

7

WILL

———

I LEFT ABBIE with the baby so I could move my car
from the street outside to the service lane that ran behind
the building. In an operation any criminal would be proud
of, I texted her when the coast was clear, and she came
through the back door with her long blonde waves tucked
into one of my old baseball caps and dark glasses on her
nose. She held Seb's bag over one shoulder and the carrier
in the other hand, a light cover draped over it, and slid it
straight into the back seat before climbing in after it and
slamming the door.

I smirked at her in the rear-vision mirror. "This isn't a
kidnapping, Ellison."

"Hey, smart arse," she retorted. "You want to tell your
mother about Seb on your own?"

I grinned and glanced down at the skin-tight yoga gear
she wore. Abbie had always had a body that made me

hard, but in the years since she'd become a yoga instructor and adopted Lycra as her official uniform, I'd been in and out of blue ball hell. Her long muscles had grown leaner and tighter, her arse was hard enough to break rocks, and her tits were always on show. Barely a handful, I estimated, and just enough.

Maybe I should have felt bad thinking of her in that way, but I didn't. Abbie knew she was gorgeous, and it's not like she didn't get an eyeful of me every chance she got.

"Have I told you yet how hot you look today?"

"You should have seen me just after the pipe burst," she muttered, then her nose scrunched up. "And don't change the subject."

I winked, then turned my head to check on Seb. "We need to belt the carrier in, right?"

"Right." Abbie scrunched her nose as she ran her hands over the plastic frame, looking for instructions or an obvious way to secure the seat. "I've got no idea how. Can you Google it?"

It took five minutes to locate a how-to guide on the internet, then another fifteen to get everything secured properly. Seb didn't object to the jostling, and he might have even liked it because he eventually fell asleep.

"Parenting isn't really so hard, is it?" Abbie said once Seb was settled in. She slouched in her seat and took a swallow from the water bottle she'd tucked into Seb's tote bag.

I gave her an unimpressed look from where I hunched awkwardly into the car, checking the straps on Seb one last time before wiping a line of perspiration from my brow.

But Abbie wasn't all wrong. Seb was asleep, wasn't he? His stomach was full. His pants were clean. Two hours into this gig, and I hadn't screwed it up yet.

Abbie chuckled at my pointed look. "You want me to ride in the back with him, just in case he needs something?"

I blinked in surprise. "Uh, yeah. Thanks." I closed the door gently and returned to the driver's seat, a little surprised about the relief I felt knowing Seb wouldn't be in the back seat alone.

I turned on the engine and rolled out of the service lane, my hands tighter than usual on the wheel.

"You can go a little faster, you know," Abbie mumbled as we approached the first corner. She'd ducked her head a little, and I had a dark tint on the windows, but the back seat earned a few curious looks from nosey pedestrians crossing Main Street. As much as I wanted to fly through the busiest part of town, I stuck to a speed just a little slower than the limit.

I finally flicked on the indicator and pulled onto the next street, and Abbie sighed. I could *feel* her eyes rolling. "At this rate, we'll be able to drop Seb off at kindergarten before we reach your mother's place."

I pressed harder on the accelerator—but only a little.

My mum and her new husband lived in the house I'd grown up in, a small two-bedroom bungalow six blocks back from the ocean. I pulled into the drive and got out of the car without looking directly at the place. I didn't avoid visiting exactly, but it had been months since I'd dropped by. Mum and Ray came down to The Stop once a week for dinner instead, and I preferred it that way. Even better would have been Mum selling this dump and starting fresh somewhere else, but for reasons that remained a mystery to me, she didn't look back on our life with my father with the same bitterness I did. Lori Kidd—now Lori Allen—always saw the bright side of things. Always believed in the good in people, even the man she'd chased halfway around the world to marry, only to be left alone with a child at the end of it.

"William!" Mum burst onto the front porch, and my stomach clenched nervously as she skipped down the stairs and ran straight into my arms. I returned her hug even as I winced at my full name. She was the only one who got away with calling me that, and it hit certain buttons delivered in her American accent. The only other person she called *William* was my father, and I could have done without the reminder that I shared so much as a name with that man.

Mum held me at arm's length. "What a nice surprise. What are you doing here, honey?"

"I, uh…" My mouth went dry, and the words stuck in my throat, but Abbie rescued me by popping out of the back seat and skirting the car to give Mum a hug.

"Good to see you, Mrs Kidd," she said.

"Abigail, sweetheart!" The hug Mum gave Abbie looked tighter than the one she'd given me. "How many times do I have to tell you to call me Lori?" Mum gave me a sly look. "Unless you want to start calling me *Mom*?"

A couple years ago, Abbie and I made a promise that we'd grow old together—platonically. A kind of insurance policy against infirmary and loneliness so we could have fun now and not worry about who'd be there to put up with us in our old age. The deal also meant I was Abbie's fake boyfriend at family events, so her parents didn't give her such a hard time about *finding someone*. I think I was half-drunk when I agreed to do it, but it hadn't been so bad. Abbie's mother thought I was adorable, and it gave me something to annoy Abbie about when I felt like being extra obnoxious. Plus, I kind of got off on being referred to as *Abbie's boyfriend*. It had a nice ring to it.

Mum knew all the details of our pact, but no matter how many times I told her there was nothing more to it, she'd always behaved like there was—like she knew something we didn't. Most people in the Bay did that—looked at me and Abbie like they saw a secret. We didn't fight it. People would think what they wanted to think and say what they wanted to say—nobody had learned that lesson harder than Abbie—and I didn't need the constant reminders that Abbie wasn't interested. She was too smart to let me or sex screw up the good stuff we had. Message received loud and clear. And repeatedly.

So, Mum's teasing was standard, and I didn't usually snap at it, but knowing I was about to spring Seb on her made it impossible to think straight.

"I've got a kid," I blurted.

Abbie widened her eyes, then dropped her face into one hand, head shaking.

"You've..." Mum glanced into the backseat of the car,

squinting at the outline of the baby carrier through the tinted window. "What?"

With the hard part out of the way, I opened the door and unclipped the carrier from its restraints. Seb was sound asleep, thick dark lashes resting on his pink cheeks, and at the sight of him, I was suddenly kind of excited to tell Mum he was mine. As I extracted Seb from the car, Mum gasped, and I turned to see her with her hands covering her mouth. Abbie had her arms around Mum's shoulders.

"An old... friend... came by this morning," I began, concerned at the sight of tears welling in my mother's eyes. I cleared my throat—no way was I about to fucking cry—and ignored the sharp catch when I tried to swallow. "I didn't know about him before today. Otherwise, I would have told you earlier, but..." I looked to Abbie for reassurance, and she nodded reassuringly. Her honey-brown eyes were glassy with emotion, and I dropped my head back to make more room in my chest. Jesus. I blinked a few times, and when I had my shit together, I turned the carrier to give Mum a better view.

"Mum, this is your grandson, Sebastian." Seb was sound asleep, but I completed the introductions anyway. "Seb, this is your grandma, Lori."

Mum reached for him, and I set the heavy carrier on the ground between us. She bent down to get a better look at him, and as I watched my mother drink in the face of her only grandchild, joy brightening her face more and more with each passing moment, Abbie came over and looped an arm around my waist. The gesture was warm and familiar and comforting—all the things Abbie was to me—and I took my first full breath since we'd pulled into the driveway.

"You did good, Kidd," Abbie whispered as we watched a bond bloom between my mother and her grandson.

I slung an arm around Abbie, pulling her against my side so I could press a kiss on her temple. "Thanks, Ellison."

ABBIE

———

LORI LED THE way down the centre aisle of the baby supply store, little Sebastian propped happily on her hip. "We've got the crib and the stroller—"

"The cot and the pram," Will mumbled.

"And you'll need diapers."

Will scanned the boxes and pulled out two marked with Seb's age. "They're called nappies."

We'd driven out of Valentine Bay and into Scarborough Cove to do the shopping, hoping we could avoid the town snoops for a few more hours. Word of Will's baby would be on everyone's lips soon enough, and he still hadn't had time to wrap his head around it. He also wanted to tell our closest friends before rumours reached them, and he had plans to break the news that afternoon. Afterwards, Will would go to work downstairs at the bar, and I'd stay in the loft with Seb. It made the most sense, and I hadn't thought twice when I'd volunteered to do it, but as we loaded the shopping trolley with the mountains of stuff Lori insisted Seb needed, I'd started to think my generosity was more like idiocy. What the hell did I know about taking care of a baby? Nothing. But what did Will know? Just as little, and I wasn't about to let him struggle with it on his own.

"Does he take a pacifier?" Lori asked.

"A dummy," Will corrected her absently as he unfolded Heather's notes and scanned them for the answer. "There's nothing in here to say either way, so I don't think so."

Lori abandoned the display she'd been perusing and kept walking, bouncing Seb and cooing at him constantly, eliciting rounds of sweet little laughs. She was a natural, all maternal instinct and easy confidence, and an uncomfortable lick of inadequacy flickered in my gut. Were some women born with a baby gene and others weren't, or had I spent so many years telling everyone I didn't want to be a mother that I'd erased that particular evolutionary program from my system? It never bothered me before, but now I wondered if something about me was broken.

Lori paused and shifted Seb to her other side. "Oh, my. You're getting heavy, little guy." She lifted him under the arms and offered him to Will. "You take him for a while, honey, and I'll push the cart with Abbie."

Will wrapped his large, tanned hands around Seb's tiny torso and settled the baby in the crook of his arm. Seb looked so small and safe tucked in against Will's muscular frame that I froze mid-step before remembering how to walk. One foot in front of the other and ignoring how Will with a baby did something to my dusty ovaries—things that made other parts of my body tingle in more familiar ways. My stomach fluttered, my nipples tightened, and I had to remind myself to breathe.

Without meaning to, I flashed back to the way Will looked at me when I'd called him daddy at his loft. He'd been surprised. Pleased. Aroused. The memory wasn't helping me keep cool now.

Lori took Will's place beside me, and we followed him down the aisle. Without a word, Lori pulled a baby monitoring system from the shelf and transferred it to the trolley.

I poked at the growing collection of linens, electronics, bottles, creams, and toys. "Babies really need a lot of crap, don't they?"

"They need less as they grow older," Lori agreed. "It's just one of those things."

She stalled at a discount bin full of baby socks, and I waited while she sorted through the pairs to find half a dozen in sizes that would fit Sebastian. It took long enough that by the time we started moving again, Will had wandered out of earshot.

"I'm glad he has your support," Lori said, one eye on her son to make sure he couldn't overhear as we followed him towards the back of the store.

I grimaced and shook my head. "I don't know how much help I'm going to be. I know as much as Will does about babies. Maybe even less."

"Oh, none of us know what we're doing when we become parents. They send us home from the hospital with this tiny, helpless thing in our arms, and you walk out of there wondering who on Earth decided you were capable of keeping a child alive. It's terrifying."

I chuckled. "That's good to know, I suppose. I guess the Universe had a plan when it burst a pipe at my apartment. I'll be around to get Will through the first few days of fatherhood, at least."

"You— What? You're moving into Will's place?"

Shit. Lori loved me, but she loved the idea of me and Will together even more. Luckily, I didn't need to wrap her in cotton wool the way I did with my parents. Lori was the kind of woman who could handle the truth—and I'd told her the truth about a lot of things over the years, including the way I felt about Will and why the chances of us being together were non-existent. Growing up so close to Will, I'd come to think of Lori as something like a cool aunt. She was accepting of everyone—there wasn't a judgmental bone in her body, and I'd always done my best to emulate that—and I'd never been so honest with anyone, even my best girlfriends or big brother. Lori had never betrayed my trust, and she insisted she understood, but it didn't stop the smug twinkle in her eye.

"Yep," I confirmed. "I tried to crash with Mama and Dad, but they're of the opinion that it's time for me and Will to take our relationship to the next level. They practically shoved me out the door."

Lori gave me a loaded sideways look.

"What?"

"Oh, I just find it amusing that this little pact you two concocted to keep yourselves free of commitment and kids for the rest of your lives is the only reason you're now living together with a six-month-old baby to care for."

Holy fuck, she was right.

Lori laughed at whatever she saw on my face. "I think it'll be a good experience for both of you. And who knows? Maybe you'll enjoy it."

I dropped my chin and gave her a sceptical look. "What's there to enjoy? A crying baby? Sleepless nights? Early mornings and dirty nappies and spit-up? No, thanks. A few days of this—a week max—and I'm out of there."

Lori smirked. "We'll see."

"Lori—"

"Forget I said anything." Lori raised a placating hand. "I know how you both feel about these things. I'll keep my opinions to myself from now on."

She mimed zipping her lips, and I huffed out a laugh.

"And Abbie, I know he was worried about how I would react to finding out he had a child he never knew about—and I won't lie, this is not the way I'd have chosen to become a grandmother—but I'm happy for William. Parenthood will be good for him." She gave my hand a quick squeeze. "It's time he grew up a little, and that boy has a lot of love to give."

I knew the meaning Lori wanted me to take from her words. Maybe Seb would be the reason Will moved on from his thoughtless, bedhopping lifestyle, but I wasn't so sure. Will *did* have a history of irresponsibility, and yes, he had a lot of love to give, but the problem was where these two facts intersected. He'd never been shy about sharing the love whenever and with whoever caught his eye, and there was no guarantee a baby would change anything. It was just as likely to have the opposite effect and make Will's allergy to commitment permanent.

And let's face it—it wasn't as if I'd ever had a long-term relationship either. That's what made the pact so perfect. That's why it made sense for party girl Abbie Ellison. And that's what made re-thinking it so freaking terrifying.

9

WILL

_____

WE ARRIVED HOME with a truck full of baby furniture and equipment, bags and bags of clothes and linen, and one very hungry baby boy. The little guy had slept on and off for the three-hour round-trip to the baby supply store, but according to Heather's schedule, he was due a bottle fifteen minutes ago, and he wasn't shy about letting us know it.

Mum had generously bought a couple of the big-ticket items, but my savings account had taken a hit. I tried not to think about what couldn't be helped, but I'd spent the last twelve months stashing away every last cent to expand my business, and I was *this close* to realising my dream. As the costs had tallied up at the register, I'd begun to wonder if agreeing to Birdie's plan was worth the risk. What if the gamble didn't pay off, and I was left with more debt than I already had? What if I couldn't deliver all the things

I'd agreed to—the repairs, the set-up, the food, the beer, the service? Raising a kid wasn't part of the plan, and it hadn't been considered in the figures. I couldn't work my arse off the way I had been the last twelve months, and I couldn't extend my opening hours without worrying about childcare first. Fuck. I couldn't make *any* decisions now without thinking about how they'd impact Seb.

Mum had gone straight home after the shopping spree, wanting to wait for Ray and tell him about Seb in person, so Abbie and I were on our own. Once we were inside and Seb was guzzling happily on a fresh batch of warm formula, Abbie looked around at the state of my place. That was the same moment my eyes darted to the clock on the wall. The morning was gone, the afternoon was slipping away, and I had to open the bar in less than four hours. There was no way we'd be able to clear out the spare room and build the furniture in the time we had. Not alone, anyway.

As if she'd read my mind, Abbie pulled her phone from her back pocket. "You want me to text the crew and ask them to come around?"

Seb noisily finished the last mouthful of milk and started to squirm, and I sighed with resignation. I wanted my mates to meet Seb and know he existed, but I wasn't looking forward to having the conversation. I didn't know it was possible to want to share a piece of news as badly as you never wanted to say the words out loud.

"Yep. We're going to need them. Just keep the message vague for now, okay?"

"No problem."

As the tap-and-whoosh of an outgoing text message sounded from Abbie's phone, I tucked Seb against my body and started pulling things out of the shopping bags. When I found the fabric baby carrier, I tried unsuccessfully to unpack it with one hand until Abbie laid a blanket down on the floor and then took the baby from me.

I pressed my lips together as she deposited him on the floor, then stood back to give him a little room. He looked so small and... kind of abandoned.

"Is he all right down there?" I gestured to one of the boxes stacked near the front door. "Should we put him in the bouncing chair thing instead?"

Abbie glanced at the box, then back at Seb and set her hands on her hips. "We could, but I think this is okay too. He's been in a chair all day, and I'm pretty sure babies are supposed to spend time kicking their legs or whatever."

Seb stared up at the ceiling for a moment before squealing and twisting his body. I worried if it was normal for him to want to curl up so tightly, but then Seb tucked his legs and flipped himself onto his stomach, and I exchanged a startled look with Abbie.

"Is he old enough to be rolling like that?"

"How the fuck should I know?" Abbie rolled her eyes at my disapproving frown. "What? When his first word is 'fuck', then come at me. Until then, I reserve the right to use the word when required."

"That was not required," I muttered, returning to the fabric baby carrier. I lengthened a few straps to get it to fit over my shoulders and back, then slipped it onto my front.

The fabric sagged in the middle even after I tightened it, so I pulled on a different set of straps. It was lopsided then, and when I couldn't get the clips around my waist to connect, I swore under my breath and snatched up the instructions.

"Not required," Abbie murmured, and when I scowled at her, she clicked her tongue and planted herself in front of me. "Oh, come here."

She tugged at the carrier, and I focussed on the top of her blonde head as her familiar coconut fragrance filled my nostrils. I let my eyelids close while I breathed it in, wrapping myself in the comfort of her closeness, and my nerves began to settle. I wasn't all that frustrated about this stupid baby-wearing sling thing. Things were moving so fast and changing before I could understand them, and wrapping myself in a fucking baby harness was just one challenge too much.

Abbie made a little noise as she frowned at the carrier. I watched her fingers dance across my arms and chest as she readjusted it and smiled a little when her hands jerked with irritation. I loved the feel of Abbie's skin on mine. She touched me like she owned me—never asking first, never hesitant or shy or unsure if she should. I'd always loved the way she did that, and if all the years we'd known each other hadn't dulled the thrill, nothing ever would.

When she was satisfied with the results, Abbie smoothed my shirt underneath and gave me an approving nod. "Done."

I tugged at it to settle it better across my chest. "Thanks."

I scooped up Seb from the floor and tried to slide his legs through the spaces in the carrier, but he got a little stuck. He protested, wriggling and whining, and Abbie clicked her tongue as she adjusted the straps again.

"Is he going to fit?"

I grunted as he finally slid into place. "He's solid, that's for sure."

I preferred holding him like this—less chance I'd drop him—and once Seb was secured, Abbie stepped back. She had a small, amused smile on her face.

I spread my arms and turned around to give her a proper look. "What do you think?"

"Very cute."

I gave her a crooked smile—the one that made the dimple in my right cheek pop. "Me or the baby?"

"What do you think?" I opened my mouth, and she smacked her hand over it. "Don't answer that. I already know what you're going to say."

I grinned wider against her palm as she fought a smile. My eyes dropped to her lips, full and pink with a shape I could draw with my eyes closed. For the millionth time, I wondered where Abbie and I would be today if she'd ever let me kiss those lips, but she hadn't. Probably because she already knew the answer.

I'd have found a way to fuck us up.

Abbie dropped her hand just as her phone pinged with a message. She picked it up and swiped to unlock the screen.

"So, what did you tell the crew?" I asked, playing with Seb's little feet as I waited for Abbie to read the text.

"I sent out an SOS and asked anyone who was available to get here ASAP." Abbie faced the screen out towards me so I could read the replies. "Looks like all the boys can make it. Jess is at work, but she'll join us later." Abbie gave me a sympathetic smile. "You ready?"

My stomach rolled uneasily. I knew my mates would be there for me—and Seb—no matter what, but I still wasn't looking forward to their reactions. They wouldn't judge me exactly, and I wouldn't get pity, but there'd be jokes. A nudge and a wink because if single fatherhood were ever going to happen to one of us, of course, it'd happen to me.

That was probably the part that had me dreading the next half-hour. Pretending like it didn't bother me that I'd lived up—or down—to everyone's expectations and that nobody was going to be surprised.

10

WILL

_____

I WAS PACING the floorboards inside The Stop when a knock sounded on the bar's closed front door. Abbie hurried over but looked back at me before she unlocked and opened it.

"You ready?"

"No?" She hesitated, and I shook my head. "Yeah, I'm ready. Go ahead."

Abbie heaved open the heavy door, and I stood front and centre with Seb hanging off my chest. My mates filed in, talking among themselves at first, then quickly piled up just inside the doorway as Isaac and Birdie drew up short. Josh and Emily were next, then Logan on his own—Jess would join us later that afternoon—and Luca with Tash last in line.

"What the—" Isaac dragged a hand over his beard, visibly collecting his thoughts. "Is that what I think it is?"

"A baby?" I rubbed my palms nervously over Seb's cotton-covered thighs. He kicked his legs in reply. "Kind of. Yeah."

Josh whistled under his breath at the same time Logan frowned and asked, "But where'd he come from?"

"Uh, well, about that..." I ran one hand through my hair and ducked my chin, giving them my best shamefaced grin—the one that said I knew I'd done something naughty but was too cute to pay for it. I'd used the same face a lot over the years—on my mother, teachers, women I didn't want to see again—but not once had my heart raced as hard or fast as it did now. "Me?"

When nobody moved and she couldn't get in the door, Abbie elbowed her way through our friends with the brash, no-nonsense confidence she used in situations like this.

"Okay, so now you know. Will's a daddy. Now get your butts inside and close the door before the whole town finds out."

Abbie flicked a quick look my way, brushing me with her gaze like she was watching for a reaction to *daddy*. I tried to give her a standard-issue Will Kidd smoulder in return, but I couldn't find it. Abbie and I flirted all the time. Innuendo was our love language. But the sexual tension underpinning *that* comment was new... and right now, fucking confusing.

Abbie herded everyone to our usual booth at the back of the pub, and I followed, standing at the open end when I figured out that sitting with a baby attached to my front was too difficult. I tried to catch Abbie's eye again, but she was talking quietly with Emily, so I gave up and waited for everyone to settle in, then scanned the faces looking up at me instead.

"Everyone, this is Sebastian." I tugged on Seb's toes. "Seb, this is... well, everyone."

Emily reached up and brushed Seb's cheek. "Hey, little man. Nice to meet you."

Logan raised his hands to get everyone's attention, then gave me a pointed look. "What the fuck is going on, Kidd?"

Abbie smacked Logan over the back of the head. "Language, Reeve."

He glared at her and rubbed his head. "Can you blame us for being confused? What's going on? How did this happen?"

Josh cleared his throat. "Well, the way it works is when a man and a woman love each other very much, they take off all their clothes and—"

I slapped Josh on the back of the head. "Smart arse."

He laughed as Emily smacked him disapprovingly on the chest, but she was biting back a smile.

"Do you guys remember a woman named Heather? She travelled through the Bay a little over a year ago."

At their blank looks, I rolled my eyes and explained how we'd spent a weekend together fifteen months earlier, and I'd never spoken to her again until she appeared at my door only hours ago with Seb and a bag of baby supplies.

Tash looked troubled, and her chin quivered when she asked, "So, she's gone? She gave you this beautiful little boy and disappeared?"

I clenched my jaw, feeling Tash's horror bubble up in me as quiet rage. "Pretty much. She left me a contact number but asked me not to use it for anything other than legal reasons."

Moisture welled in Tash's eyes, and Luca wrapped an arm around her shoulders as Abbie slipped out of the booth. She took Tash's hand, gently coaxing her out beside her.

"Are you good here?" Abbie asked me quietly.

Tash's tears were a little overwhelming, and some of that must have shown on my face because Abbie added, "How about I take Tash and the girls upstairs while you guys talk some more?"

My next exhalation escaped as a sigh. "Okay. Thanks."

"Do you want me to come with you?" Luca asked Tash.

"No, you stay." Tash dropped a kiss on Luca's cheek. "I might go lie down."

It was another moment before I remembered that Tash was pregnant. Luca had told us that she was extra sensitive these days, as well as suffering from all-day morning sickness. I guess that explained why she was so affected by Seb's story and why Luca was a little more protective.

When Abbie, Birdie, Emily, and Tash had disappeared, Luca got to his feet and held out his hands towards me.

I raised my eyebrows. "You want to hold him?"

He shrugged with one suited shoulder, though it seemed to me he was feigning his indifference. "I'm going to have one of my own soon enough. I should probably learn how to do this."

The realisation I wouldn't be alone in this parenthood thing forever lifted my spirits, and I grinned as I unclipped the buckles of the baby carrier. "He's all yours."

It took a few awkward seconds to settle Seb in the curve of Luca's arm, and when he looked comfortable and secure, I slipped off the carrier and sank into the seat of the booth. The sensation that something was missing bugged me a little as Luca strolled away to show Seb around the bar, and I told myself to stop being ridiculous.

"Can I get you guys a drink?" I asked.

"In a minute." Isaac thumbed his earlobe, watching me warily. "Look, the timing couldn't get much worse, and I'm sorry to add more to your plate, but there's something you should know."

Logan groaned and dropped his head back on the seat. "Fuck. He got you pregnant, too."

Josh flicked a paper coaster at Logan's head, and they both chuckled, but I couldn't laugh. Isaac looked too serious for this to be good news.

Shit. Birdie must have changed her mind about the loan. She'd slept on it and decided I was a bad bet. I was going to lose the warehouse, which meant losing the brewery. Losing my dream. Losing a future that I'd be building not just for me but for Seb now, too.

The weight of that responsibility hit me from nowhere, hard enough to take my breath. I was a father now, and fathers provided for their families. Good fathers did, anyway. Not loser fathers. Not fathers like mine.

"Oh, yeah?" I smoothed the edginess from my face and prepared to add a point to the Loser Dad column on my mental tally card. "What's that?"

"It's about the poker tournament."

I knew it. But better to fail small now than big later, right? I swallowed the lump in my throat and braced myself.

"Birdie was going to call later today and fill you in, but I may as well tell you now. Bottom line is she met with the local tourism council this morning to let them know about the event. Kidd, they're frothing at the mouth over it. They want to expand the Valentine's Day in Valentine Bay Festival so they can market the tournament at the same time." He grimaced in apology. "She had to tell them where she's holding it, of course, and that she's hired you to manage most of the logistics. Sorry, bro. The council's going to be up your arse from now until it's done."

I said nothing at first, staring through Isaac and turning his words over in my head until I understood what that meant. That was... not the news I was expecting.

It was worse.

All eyes would be on me while I tried to pull off the biggest shift in my career. An important tourism campaign hinging on me and my little bar. Oh, and the small matter of proving to everyone in the Bay that I was more than a playboy who couldn't keep it in his pants—recent developments notwithstanding—and that I was capable of raising a child.

Pfft. No sweat.

I wiped my forehead, and Isaac's brow furrowed as he shared darting glances with Josh and Logan. "Look, maybe it's not too late to get out of this. The deal's less than twenty-four hours old, and you didn't have a baby to think about when you agreed to it. I'm sure if you explain the situation to Birdie—"

"No." I forced myself to smile. "It's fine. I can manage it."

Isaac looked dubious, which did nothing for my shaky confidence, so I sprang to my feet. "Let me get you something to drink."

The five-minute breather from the boys did me good. The ritual of working behind the bar calmed me a little, and I felt more in control. There'd be more publicity around the poker tournament now. So what? It didn't change the commitment I'd made when I shook Birdie's hand, which was to work hard and keep my eye on the prize, and I could do that. I wouldn't worry about who was watching me or what they were saying. That shit wasn't important.

I cast a quick look across the room at Luca and Seb as I picked up the tray of drinks, then put it down almost immediately as Seb squirmed and made a little crying noise. Before I was able to clear the bar, Luca had managed to shift him a little, giving him more room to stretch out and turn his face into his chest. I paused a moment longer to be sure Seb was okay, but the little guy stayed quiet, and Luca resumed his measured pacing.

Back at the booth, I handed out the drinks and took my seat. Josh shook his head and wrapped both hands around his glass. "I can't believe you've got a kid."

Logan lifted his water to his mouth and grinned at me over the top of it. "I can't believe one's all you've got."

"Fuck off, dickhead."

Logan snickered, and I shifted uncomfortably. I wasn't about to admit I'd had the same thought.

"But seriously." Isaac frowned at the ginger ale in his glass. "How the hell are you going to run The Stop and manage Birdie's event with a baby to look after?"

Luca approached us with a sleeping Seb in the crook of one elbow and a chair in the other. He set it down at the end of the booth and took a seat, shifting a little to make sure Seb stayed asleep. We sat in silence, and the longer I gazed at Seb, the tighter my chest became, and I realised failure wasn't an option.

I took a long swallow of water and returned the glass to the table with a smack. "First, I have to get the loft sorted. I've got flat-packed furniture to build—"

Logan, a qualified carpenter, raised his hand. "I can help with that."

I gave him an appreciative nod. "Thanks, mate. And there's a bedroom I need to clean out."

Isaac, Josh, and Luca exchanged nods. "Consider it done," Josh said.

A little of the tension between my shoulders eased. With the boys' help, Seb might have a room and a bed to sleep in that night. "I appreciate it. For now, let's move everything into the small function room over the bar. It's not booked for any events over the next month or so, and I'll worry about sorting through everything when things settle down—"

"In about eighteen years?"

I gave Logan a flat stare. "Has anyone ever told you you're fucking annoying?"

Logan grinned. "Daily."

"And then what?" Luca looked down at the sleeping baby in his arms. It was a weird picture, the five of us sitting around like we always did, only now a baby had been dropped into the middle of us. "These next few weeks are going to be busy, Kidd. We'll all pitch in as much as we can, but..."

"You've got your own jobs to worry about." I leaned back in the seat and rubbed my palms over the tops of my thighs. "I know, and I get it. Having you here today is already enough. Don't worry. I'll work something out."

"You've told your mother?" Josh asked, and when I nodded, he added, "Bet she'll be happy to take the little guy off your hands once in a while."

"Uh, yeah. I suppose she could."

"And the girls can help, too," Luca added. "I'm sure Tash would love it—as soon as the exhaustion and morning sickness passes."

"I appreciate that," I mumbled. "Thanks."

Talking about Seb like he was an inconvenience made me uncomfortable. He wasn't a community project or a problem that needed a solution. He wasn't anyone's responsibility but mine, and I didn't want him to ever feel otherwise. I had to make sure my mates knew how determined I was to make space for this little person in my life. We were a family now.

"Abbie moved in with me," I announced, as stunned as everyone else when the words came out of my mouth.

That was not what I'd meant to say.

Isaac blinked a few times. "She... Huh?"

Josh frowned. "Are you... together? Like, for real?"

"How many times do I have to tell you idiots that Abbie and I are just friends?"

Josh rolled his eyes and took a long draw of his beer. "Yeah. Right."

I scowled at Josh, who kept smirking like he knew better. "She's not *moving in* exactly," I explained. "There was a problem with a water pipe at her place. Flooded her studio and her apartment underneath, and she needs a place to crash while she sorts out the insurance and repairs." Josh and Logan exchanged smug glances, and I elbowed Logan in the ribs. Hard. "It's just for a few days."

"The timing is kind of perfect," Isaac said with a small wince. "I guess?"

Logan snorted. "Ellison with a baby? Kidd—you'll have twice as much work taking care of those two than you would with just the little guy." He dropped his chin and chuckled to himself, head shaking. "Ellison with a baby."

A week ago, if someone had told me to picture Abbie with a child, I'd have laughed too. She'd made a point of telling anyone who listened that motherhood was not for her, but something about the way Logan had phrased it put a fire in my belly—an explosion of purpose that made the hair on my arms stand up. *You'll have twice as much work taking care of those two...*

Images I'd replayed a thousand times before spun through my head. Abbie waiting for me in my loft in nothing but her panties. Abbie sighing at my touch. Her skin warm and soft under my tongue. Her mouth pliant. Her knees open, and her thighs wet. Abbie in my bed every night. My bed and only mine. No more of the arseholes she'd been fucking all these years. Abbie choosing me because she was the only one who *saw* me, and finally, she saw something she believed in.

A new one. Abbie arching her back and clawing the sheets. My ring on her finger.

Where the fuck did that come from? The idea of commitment was as big a turn-on as the image of Abbie writhing underneath me, and I wasn't strong enough to look too closely at that. My cock swelled, and I pressed my eyes closed to shut it all down. Now wasn't the time to fantasise about Abbie. I saved that stuff for the shower.

I nudged Isaac with my elbow, leaning into it to shove him out of the booth, and I slid out after him. "Just forget about Abbie, okay? I've got less than half a day to make my place fit for a kid, and I need to get to work."

11

ABBIE

WILL, WITH THAT baby strapped to his hard, broad chest... Smooth, tanned biceps bulging underneath his dark cotton T-shirt... His light brown hair falling across his earnest, boyish blue eyes... The way he fumbled nervously at the buckles and furrowed his brow when testing the weight of Seb against the restraints... The fucking dimples that had dropped a thousand pairs of knickers...

Metaphorically speaking, mine were closer to my ankles than they'd ever been, and I'd always had perfect self-control where Will Kidd was concerned. What the hell was wrong with me? Will was like a planet. His daddy energy was gravity, and as long as I stayed in his orbit, I was at risk of crashing in a blaze of sexual glory.

Don't think I wasn't tempted because, mark my words—the collision would indeed be glorious. It'd also be plain stupid. I was a strong woman, and I never equated sex with love, but I never wanted to wake up the next morning and have to pretend that sleeping with Will meant nothing to me.

"All right," Birdie said, following me into the loft. "Tell. Us. Everything."

"Oh, just try to stop me."

I closed the door behind Emily and Tash, who made her way to the sofa. She stretched out on it and flung an arm over her face with a groan.

"Can I get you anything, sweetie?" I asked.

"A bucket would be nice," she mumbled.

"On it."

I raided Will's laundry cupboard for something appropriate and handed a large plastic bowl to Tash. "Anything else?"

"No, thank you. It feels better when I'm horizontal."

"That's what he said," Birdie quipped.

Her joke released the knot of nervous energy in the room, and I laughed in disbelief. "Oh, my God, you guys. Will has a baby!"

Birdie folded herself onto the floor at the foot of the sofa. "Sit and give us the details."

"Okay, but first—snacks."

Emily ran her fingers through her short dark hair, making it stick out at awkward angles now that she'd decided to grow out her pixie cut, and sat down on the other side of the coffee table while I raided Will's pantry. I returned with a selection of random packets plus four bottles of water.

Emily took a drink and shook her head. "I still can't believe it. A woman Will used to date knocks on his door, drops off a baby, and leaves?"

I lifted my shoulders and let them drop with a sigh. "That's about it."

"And then he called you for help?"

"God, no. A pipe burst at my studio, and I'm officially homeless for a few days. I arrived right after Seb, looking for a place to live."

The silence was deafening. The careful expressions were even louder. Even Tash uncovered her face and raised her head, though she avoided looking at me directly. I knew they'd react like this.

Emily's big green eyes widened in pretend innocence. "So… you're moving in?"

I glared at her. "We're just *friends*, you weirdos."

Emily raised her palms. "I didn't suggest anything."

I picked up a chip and threw it at her. "You didn't have to. I know how your freaky little mind works."

Em ducked her head to hide a smile. "I just think it's odd you find yourself in this position with Will, of all people—the man you're going to marry one day."

She was referring to the deal Will and I had made to grow old together. Emily—a relative newbie to the Bay who fell in love with my high school friend Joshua Ford about the same time the whole town fell in love with her—was late to the pact party. She deliberately misunderstood the details over and over and thought it was fun to tease me about it. Spoiler: it was *not* fun.

I scowled. "I swear, Emily Jones. If you make that joke one more time—"

"All right, all right. I'm sorry." She grinned as Birdie chortled but changed the subject. "Truthfully, I'm kind of surprised you didn't run screaming in the other direction as soon as you saw the baby. We all know how you feel about procreation." Emily flinched and threw Tash an apologetic look she couldn't see with her arm back over her eyes. "No offense, Tash."

Tash flapped her hand in our direction, her reply muffled. "I'm not exactly a poster child for the joys of motherhood right now. Go on."

I shook my head and twisted the cap on my water bottle back and forth. "You should have seen the look on Will's face when I walked through the front door. I think he was in shock, and when I dared to hint that maybe the baby might not be his..." I recalled his surprisingly protective vibe, then pictured him with Seb curled up in his muscled arms, and a shiver ran up my spine.

Tash raised her head again and squinted at me. "When you hinted the baby might not be his... what?"

"He shut me down. Hard. As far as Will is concerned, he is that baby's father, and the birth certificate says as much. He's taking responsibility for Seb, and he's going to need help. I'd do the same for any of you."

Emily leaned over and gave me a side hug, her head on my shoulder. I'd been there for her when she was faking an engagement with Josh to get rid of her slimeball ex-fiancé. She knew the lengths I'd go to for someone I cared about. "Will's lucky to have you."

"Oh, sweetie. You're all lucky to have me." Emily chuckled as she straightened, and I added, "And anyway, it's only for a few days. I'm sure the insurance assessor will tell me I can move home in a day or two. That'll give Will a chance to get the baby stuff under control, and it'll be back to business as usual."

It was best to make it clear right from the start that there was nothing more to my temporary stay at Will's place. The fact I was here at all was circumstantial—forced to move in by a broken pipe and a meddling mother— and a baby wouldn't change that. Will needed forty-eight hours of support—three days max—and I could survive that, sexual tension or no sexual tension.

Em appeared to believe me but the more adamant my thoughts became, the less sure I was about who I was trying to convince—my friends or myself.

It looked like Birdie was going to be a harder sell. She tapped the lid of her water bottle with her fingertips and pursed her lips to one side like she had something to say.

"What is it?" I asked.

Birdie glanced up and away immediately, meeting Emily's eyes instead. Something passed between them, and Emily, confused at first, suddenly closed her eyes and groaned.

A little snore escaped from under Tash's arm.

"I can't decide if I'm worried or irritated," I whispered. Not true. I was irritated. "What's with the eyes?"

Emily screwed up her nose in Birdie's direction. "Do you want to tell her, or should I?"

"Somebody better tell me something—and fast."

"I had a business meeting with Will last night," Birdie explained.

That's what this was about. I kicked myself for having let it slip my mind.

"About the property next door, right?" I asked.

I knew all about the meeting. It had been my idea. Will had been so freaking excited when the old warehouse became available out of nowhere, and he'd beaten himself up so hard over his rejected bank loan applications. I'd had to talk fast to convince him to approach Birdie with his proposal, and amid all the drama, I'd totally forgotten to ask how the pitch went. It had to have been the last thing on Will's mind as well. Otherwise, it would have been the first thing we talked about...

Unless the news was bad. *Fuck.*

My stomach flipped, and I crossed my fingers where Birdie couldn't see them. "How did it go?"

Birdie shook her head a little and smiled. "He had a fantastic business proposal, and I was impressed by the numbers. I think he's onto a good thing, and I agreed to loan him the start-up funds—on one condition."

My heart, which had leaped at the good news, plummeted at the mention of a *condition*.

"Will agreed to let me use the space to host a poker tournament first," Birdie went on. "I'm the organiser of an event that was supposed to take place in Scarborough

Cove, but the venue pulled out, and without an alternative, I'd have to cancel. Will agreed to take the loan and host the tournament, so this morning, I had my solicitor draw up the paperwork."

She exchanged that loaded look with Emily again, and my glance volleyed back and forth. "This sounds like a lot of work, and he agreed to it before finding out about Seb, but I know he can do it." I chewed on my lip for a second, sweeping my finger between my two friends. "I still don't understand what this is about."

Birdie sighed. "I also called the local tourism council to apply for the necessary permits."

I groaned and dropped my head back. The tourism council was a pain in the arse at the best of times, and a big event like a poker tournament was going to drive them wild. I knew where this was going.

"They called me straightaway," Emily hurried to add. She was employed by the council as a professional photographer and social media advisor, so contacting her made sense. "The thing is, Abs... The poker tournament is scheduled for the weekend before Valentine's Day—"

My head jerked up in horror. Valentine's Day in Valentine Bay was the biggest event on our community calendar. The tourism council abused the town with layers and layers of pink and red, and we welcomed thousands of people to our stores, night markets, and bonfires to celebrate. It grew bigger, brighter, and more vulgar every year, except for one lone, reliable black spot: Will and The Salty Stop. The only venue that resisted the council's Valentine's Day madness. Will and the council clashed about it every year, but Will always stood his ground, to the huge relief of the humbug locals like me (and there were a lot of us) who needed a place to wait out the weekend. But if this poker tournament was happening the same time as the festival and Will had agreed to host it… They'd make his life hell from now until it was done.

"Oh, no," I whispered.

"Oh, yes." Emily looked uncomfortable. "The council's already gone a little wild over the possibilities."

"I bet." I huffed in disbelief. "I'm stunned Will agreed to it."

Birdie shrugged guiltily. "Will doesn't know about the Valentine's Day twist yet. I planned to break it to him today."

Will was going to fucking freak, and I didn't blame him. I patted Birdie on the shoulder and gave her a flat smile. "Good luck with that."

"Yeah. Thanks. But it's not all bad news. If this poker event is a success, there's the potential for Will to make enough money to repay my loan quickly. It'll be great publicity for The Stop, and there might even be investors interested in helping him establish the microbrewery."

I let myself consider the opportunities this would give Will rather than the ways it'd challenge him—just as soon as he'd pushed through the freak-out phase and figured out a plan. "This could make a huge difference to Will's business, Birdie."

"If we can pull it off, it'll *make* his business," she confirmed.

Emily leaned back on her hands. "We're talking about managing more than just the one event here. There's his bar. There's Seb. There's getting the warehouse ready for a poker tournament, then transforming it into a brewery and launching a new business. What if he *can't* pull it off?"

"He can," I replied brusquely, dropping the chips I'd been nibbling on and dusting the salt from my hands. "No doubt in my mind."

"I agree." Birdie's face was full of determination. "Not if—when. *When* we pull this off, it'll be the best thing that ever happened to Will—surprise babies aside, of course."

I returned her nod and tried to look positive, but everything was happening so fast, and none of it was low stakes. Will discovered he had a son less than twenty-four hours after taking on more debt and the significant commitment of hosting Birdie's poker tournament. The entire town would be watching him for the next three weeks, not only as a new father but as a business pillar of the community. He was about to go from one extreme to the other—lovable rogue to single dad and upstanding businessman—overnight and under a microscope.

If I knew Will—and I did—the first thing he'd want to do when he found out about this would be quit. He'd doubt himself. He'd think it was too hard and that he wouldn't succeed. Well, he could do it, and I wouldn't let him do it alone.

A plan started to come together, one that would let me stay in the loft and help take care of Seb without Will realising that's why I was there. In fact, if I managed this right, I might even be able to convince Will that *he* was the one helping *me*.

12

WILL

———————

AS A GROUP, we did more in three hours than I could have done on my own in three days. We moved every box and piece of furniture from the spare bedroom into the rarely used function room above The Stop. I helped Logan unload and build the baby furniture—a cot, a change table, a dresser, and a shelving unit—and we cleaned the room before setting it all up. Abbie plugged in the baby monitor to charge, washed Seb's new clothes, and found places for his bottles and sterilising equipment in the kitchen. Everyone took turns with Seb—feeding him, playing little games, reading to him, and passing him over to me when he soiled his pants.

I handled it like a man, of course.

Jess, a schoolteacher with a natural knack for interior decorating, arrived just as the last of the grunt work was done, bearing bags of rugs, cushions, books, posters, and stuffed animals. Logan had filled her in on the details over the phone, thank fuck because I was too exhausted to go over it all again, and the first thing she did when she walked into the loft was wrap me in a hard hug.

"I can't believe it, Kidd," she murmured in my ear. "I'm happy for you."

I folded my arms around her and held on tight. Jess was one of those friends I'd known for so long, and she was as good as a sister.

"Thanks, Frost." She stepped back, and I smiled at the emotion in her eyes. "You want to meet him?"

"Only immediately."

By the time we were done, I didn't recognise the space. It was a little boy's bedroom. *My* little boy's bedroom. All white and grey and pale blue, smelling like soap and baby lotions, stocked with piles of nappies and wet wipes and jumpsuits, a pram tucked away in the corner.

Maybe the sight of it should have freaked me out, and part of me did wonder how the fuck I'd found myself in this situation, but mostly I was relieved that there was one thing I could cross off the list of things I needed to get done.

Fifteen minutes before I needed to head downstairs and open the bar, I waved my mates off with promises of free drinks and a lifetime of favours, then stood in the middle of the quiet loft with Abbie at my side. Seb was tucked into his bed, sleeping in something other than the car or someone's arms for the first time that day.

As I scooped up my phone and keys and prepared to leave, an unexpected heaviness settled in my stomach.

I'd spent the afternoon not thinking much about the fact that I'd have to leave Seb to go to work, but now that it was time for me to go, it felt weird letting him out of my sight. I glanced over Abbie's shoulder to Seb's closed bedroom door and hesitated.

Abbie crossed her arms and jutted her hip, looking up at me with knowing eyes. "We'll be fine."

Would they? Abbie knew nothing about babies, and I was about to leave her alone with mine for at least six hours. As quick as the doubt came to me, I pushed it away again. It wasn't fair. Abbie knew at least as much as I did, probably more, and I trusted her.

Worst case, I was only a flight of stairs away.

"You've got the feeding and sleeping schedule?" I asked.

She pointed towards the kitchen. "It's on the fridge."

"And the baby monitor—"

She lifted a glowing screen towards me, lights flashing on the side. "Fully charged."

"Right." I scratched my cheek, the coarse shadow reminding me that I'd forgotten to shave that morning. "Just call if you need anything."

"I will." She turned me around and pushed me towards the door.

"Or just bring him downstairs if you have to."

Abbie opened the door and gave me an exasperated look when I didn't walk through it. "I won't need to, but okay."

"I'll send up some food from the kitchen around dinnertime."

"I appreciate that. Thank you." She shoved me hard enough to move me half a step into the hall. "Now *go*."

A mewling sound escaped from the monitor in Abbie's hand, and my heart lurched. Both Abbie and I paused, our eyes locked on the buzzing green lights. A long second passed, then a few more, but Seb was silent.

"See?" Abbie didn't look so certain anymore, but she set a hand on my chest anyway and tried to push me the final step through the door. "Everything is fine, and I'm perfectly capable of taking care of a baby for one night. Now get out of here."

I cocked a sceptical eyebrow her way, and she poked her tongue out at me. She meant it to be playful, but it was so fucking sexy.

"I'll go if you call me *Daddy* again."

Abbie froze with a hand on my pec and pressed the tips of each finger a little harder into the muscles. She gazed up at me, eyes wide and lips parted, and my pulse thundered. Her eyes dropped to my mouth, and her teeth caught her bottom lip, and there was no mistaking the sexual tension now.

If Abbie were any other woman, I'd have slipped my hand behind her neck, slammed her against the wall, and rolled my hips against her so she knew exactly what she did to me. But this wasn't any other woman. This was Abbie, and I'd never get a second chance at our first kiss. If I tried that shit on her, I'd probably end up with a knee to the balls.

Slowly, I turned so we were chest to chest. I reached

for the hand at her side and brushed her fingers with the backs of mine. "Abbie…"

She shoved me into the hall with a grunt. "Go to work."

The door slammed in my face, and I stood in the hallway looking at it for a good thirty seconds, wondering if I should storm back in and just freaking kiss her.

And wouldn't that prove what a fucking idiot I was?

I adjusted my pants before jogging down the stairs to the bar, reminding myself why Abbie and I had gone ten years without ever crossing that line.

Because sex was the only thing I was good at. Because sex was all I had to offer. Because sex would change everything, and neither of us had ever wanted that.

Jesus fucking Christ, this had been the longest day in the history of the fucking world.

I'd closed The Stop half an hour ago, and I'd been on my feet for six straight hours before that, not counting all the work I'd done in the loft throughout the afternoon. Weekdays were quiet enough that I could man the bar by myself, and my chef, Noa, made do with a single assistant in the kitchen. Once happy hour passed and the dinner rush was done, I'd pulled them aside and explained about Seb.

I was surprised at how little fuss they made. Noa had three daughters of his own, the youngest barely a toddler, and when I'd told him Seb was six months old, Noa had stayed for an hour after his shift to steam, boil, process, and puree about a hundred little labelled pots of fruits and vegetables. Apparently, Seb was at an age when he'd soon want to start eating more than just formula, and when I tried to pretend I already knew that, Noa took pity on me and shared a few websites I could use to track Seb's upcoming milestones. I went a step further and ordered half a dozen parenting books online but knowing that Noa would be a willing source of information over the next few months loosened another knot in my stomach.

I left most of the baby food in the commercial freezer downstairs, but I carried a small bag of the little containers up to the loft in case Seb wanted to give the apple or pear a spin for breakfast. I dragged my exhausted arse up the stairs, not even caring that I was on the sofa for the foreseeable future. A soft place to pass out was all I needed.

I opened the front door, pulled up short, and blinked my dry eyes at the destruction. What the actual fuck?

The space was dark, but enough light glowed from my bedroom overhead to make out the half-dozen milky bottles, the open can of formula, and takeaway boxes tossed to one side in the kitchen. The baby bath on its plastic frame was tucked into a corner in the dining space, three towels were flung across the dining chairs, and open bottles of soaps and creams littered the table. A large blanket had been laid out on the floor, and a mix of soft toys, building blocks, and books tumbled across it.

I set the bag of baby food down and scanned the loft once more, trying to wade through a fog of exhausted confusion. That's when I noticed the baby monitor in the kitchen, switched off or the battery dead, and alarm flared. Where was Seb?

I went straight to his darkened bedroom and opened the door, two more steps taking me to the side of his cot. It was empty, and the alarm in my chest escalated to panic. Spinning around, I bolted through the living space and took the stairs to the bedroom two at a time. The stand lamp in the corner was switched on, so it was clear straightaway that neither Abbie nor Seb was there.

Fuck. Heart racing, I patted my pockets, looking for my phone, but I'd left it in the kitchen with the baby food. In my rush to get to it, I practically fell the first few steps down the stairs, but from that vantage point, I noticed something I hadn't seen before. The shape of someone on the sofa, invisible in the shadows. As I squinted into the darkness, relief leached the tension from my muscles. It was Abbie, and on her chest was the smaller shape of Seb, his little legs tucked underneath him and his bulky bottom high in the air. I took a moment to collect myself, sucking in a lungful of air and rubbing my exhausted eyes, then approached the couch quietly so I wouldn't disturb them.

Abbie was propped up a little, a couple cushions behind her head and shoulders, but her eyes were closed. Her arms curled protectively around Seb, who had snuggled in under her chin, his lashes brushing his rosy cheeks and his hands tucked away somewhere I couldn't see them. They smelled like soap, and I stared at them for a moment, stunned at how this picture made me feel.

So deep in love I had no idea how I was going to dig myself out of it.

Seb stirred, turning his head and rubbing his little nose against Abbie's neck. Not wanting him to wake her if it could be avoided, I lifted Seb as gently as I could. He yawned adorably and snuggled against me, and I couldn't believe that something so small could make me feel such big things. Awkwardly and with two open hands, I cradled him against my chest as I carried him to his bed. He whimpered when I laid him down, and even though his eyes remained closed, I panicked and laid a hand on his stomach, trying to keep him still. The warmth of his body radiated into my palm, and I waited with unusual patience until, miraculously, he quieted again. Then I tiptoed from the room, leaving the door slightly ajar behind me.

I found the baby monitor and plugged it in to charge, then returned to Abbie on the couch. She'd burrowed deeper into the cushions, turning onto her side, and her chest moved with the steady, even inhale and exhale of sleep. She wore long-sleeved white linen pyjamas that buttoned down at the front, and I'd never seen her in pyjamas before. She'd only ever crashed here unannounced after a big night, arriving in the dark and climbing upstairs wearing a dress that showed off her figure before coming down in it again the next morning. Tonight, she was covered from neck to ankle, and I'd never seen her look so pretty.

I crouched and slipped my hands under her back and knees, then rose and tucked her against my body, reminding me of the way I'd held Seb. She turned into me without waking, and I buried my nose in her hair, inhaling its clean coconut scent. Abbie had smelled that way since high school, and I'd never get my fill of it.

I'd carried her to the top of the stairs before she jolted awake, and my arms tensed around her, not wanting to put her down just yet.

She looked around in a groggy fright. "Where's Seb?"

"Shh. He's fine." I pressed a calming kiss to her forehead. "I took him to his own bed."

"Oh." Her body relaxed again, her head dropping onto my chest, and she didn't seem to notice my arms around her. "Okay."

She let me lay her down on the near side of the bed while I went around to the other side to pull back the covers. Abbie shifted to put her elbows underneath her and squinted at me in the dull light of the lamp. "He's asleep?"

"He is."

She collapsed onto the bed with a relieved sigh and didn't protest when I dragged her over to the other side of the mattress and then pulled the blanket up to her chin. I considered asking how the night had been—though given the state of the loft, I could probably guess—but Abbie nuzzled into the pillows, already asleep again. Probably for the best. I was too tired to talk anyway.

I stood up to leave, but Abbie's voice stopped me.

"Will?"

She reached for me, her face half-hidden in the pillows, and I put my hand in hers. She pulled me down to sit on the side of the bed.

"I did good, didn't I?" she mumbled.

I brushed a strand of hair from her face, and she turned her face towards my hand like a flower following the sun.

"You did better than good. You did amazing."

She smiled crookedly before her face relaxed. I brushed her forehead again, then her cheek.

I was tired, but I still sat there for an hour and watched her sleep.

13

ABBIE

I WALKED THE insurance assessor to where his sensible white sedan was parked on the street in front of my apartment and shook his hand before he drove away. Tucking his business card into the waistband of my yoga pants, I sat on the edge of the gutter and pulled out my phone.

A deep, harried voice picked up after a single ring. "Dr Ellison."

"Hey, brother."

I could sense the long, silent exhalation on the other end of the line and heard Adam dropping the patient file in his hand onto the desk. I stretched my legs onto the warm bitumen of the empty road and imagined my tall, broad big brother relaxing in his high-backed leather chair, rubbing the heel of his palm over his eyes, and putting the doctor part of his personality on hold for as long as I needed him. He'd always said a little Abigail was as good as a holiday, and my brother took none of those. He never forgot he was a doctor for anyone but me.

"Hey, Little Bug." There was a grin in his tone. "I was wondering when you'd call."

"I—" I groaned and fell back onto the soft grass behind me, closing my eyes as if that would make the inevitable easier to bear. "What do you know?"

Adam chuckled. "I know about the flooding at your studio and apartment." His tone turned serious. "Do you need money?"

I couldn't help but smile. "Thanks, but no. The assessor from the insurance company was just here. My policy will cover all the damages."

He grunted. "Good."

Next, as always, he'd ask what was new in my life, which was my cue to tell him about Will and the baby. When he remained quiet, my intuition tingled. "You know, don't you?"

"Know what?"

"Adam!"

"God, I miss that little sister whine."

I stomped my foot on the road as he laughed, a reflex to the big brother torment. "Tell me now, or I'm hanging up."

"No, don't hang up," he ordered between chuckles. "I know about Mama manoeuvring you into Will's place."

I paused, unsurprised that my secret was out but unsure how Adam would take it. "She told you?"

"Yep. She also told me that you're helping Will with the baby."

I sat bolt upright, heart pounding and all thoughts about how protective my big brother would be flying out of my head. "Mama doesn't know about Seb!"

There was the laugh again, the one that came from deep in Adam's gut. I heard it so rarely that I usually loved listening to it, even if it meant Adam was laughing at me, but I was too stunned at the speed of the Valentine Bay rumour mill to spend any time basking in the sound.

"I assure you, she does." Adam had left the Bay straight after high school, studying in Sydney and going on to practice there. He insisted he hated living in Valentine Bay, where everyone knew everyone else's business, but I could tell from the smile in his voice that he got a kick out of the gossip. You could take the boy out of a small town, but not the small town out of the boy. "She's already knitting him cardigans for the winter."

My heart settled a little, still beating hard, but now back in my chest instead of my throat. "She's... happy about it?"

Adam snorted. "Are you kidding? I spoke to her about an hour ago, and she called herself *Grandma* at least twice."

"Oh, Jesus." I collapsed back onto the grass and slung an arm over my face. "What the hell am I going to do?"

Adam's chuckle faded into a sigh. "I've told you a hundred times this arrangement between you and Will was an idiotic idea."

"Harsh," I mumbled.

"But true."

"Maybe." I flopped my arm down by my side and sighed loudly. "But what else was I supposed to do?"

"Tell him how you feel? Have a real relationship for once?"

I scowled at the sky overhead. "You're one to talk, Mr Married-To-His-Career."

"Touché."

I fiddled with the grass underneath my fingers. "Do you know who told Mama about the baby?"

"Dawn Linley."

"How the hell did Dawn find out about it?" I demanded.

"Direct from Lori."

"Ah." I nodded, appreciating the genius move by Will's mother. "Smart. Get in first and control the narrative. So what's the story doing the rounds?"

"Minimal details. A previous *acquaintance*—"

"Smooth."

"—knocked on Will's door early yesterday morning and left him with a little boy."

"And how do I figure into all of this?"

"Burst pipe. Flooded apartment. Moving in with Will on the same day he found out he's a father was pure coincidence."

"Oh. Good." I scraped my teeth across my bottom lip as I worked around a flutter of disappointment at the generic description of my role in Will's life. "I shouldn't get too much grief about it then."

"Abigail."

"*Adam.*"

A sigh sounded through the speaker on my phone. "You're almost thirty—"

"Rude."

"Isn't it time you stopped worrying about what other people say about you?"

I closed my eyes and tried to extinguish the flash of ancient mortification roaring in my ears. That helpless, hopeless flush of shame as the people who loved me and barely knew me judged me and laughed at me whenever my back was turned. Adam was a man. Nobody had ever called him easy or asked him to justify the number of women he'd been with. No one had labelled him a slut because he'd been pressured into giving his virginity to an arsehole with a big mouth at an age where that kind of thing could make or break a girl. He hadn't seen Mama crying in the kitchen while she peeled potatoes over the sink or found Dad hiding in the garage while everyone whispered about his daughter and *what she'd done*. Adam never had to pick himself up and own his pain like he chose it.

"I *don't* care what other people say," I mumbled. "I've made it my life's purpose to not give a shit about rumours."

Adam was silent for a beat too long, which meant there was something he wanted to say, and I wasn't going to like it. I rolled my eyes. He probably had his doctor's face on.

"I say this with love, Little Bug."

"Okay?"

"Nobody knows you like I do."

"I know."

"And I get why it was important for you to control the

narrative after high school. It was about self-esteem and self-respect and girl power and all that."

He was such a dork. I smirked with affection but said nothing. I'd let him finish his case before I started arguing.

"But you don't have to keep pretending that the things you wanted ten years ago are the same things you want today."

Pfft. Adam had zero idea what he was talking about. I opened my mouth to tell him I wasn't pretending anything, but no words would come out, and I closed it again.

"Nobody's going to think less of you if you storm onto Main Street tomorrow and declare you want to spend the rest of your life with one man."

I pictured it. For a split second, I imagined announcing to Valentine Bay that I was ready to give up my bedhopping ways and settle down. The idea of admitting I wasn't who everyone thought I was made my stomach twist.

"They'd think I was an idiot, and they'd be right."

"Why?"

"Because I'm Abigail Ellison: Man Eater, remember? I'm not interested in monogamy or marriage or babies." I tossed my head and recited my mantra. "A man is for now, not forever."

The click of a pen floated through the phone before Adam asked, "And that's what makes you happy?"

"I'm happy knowing my heart's safe," I retorted.

"Abbie—"

"It's getting late, and I've got to get back to the loft." I got to my feet and brushed the dust from the back of my legs. Adam knew all about the rumours I'd faced in high school. He understood why it was important that I write the rules for my own sex life, and there wasn't any point rehashing it now. "Will needs my help with the baby again tonight."

Adam sighed but let me change the subject. "And what did the insurance company say about your apartment? How long until you can move back in?"

My fingers strayed to the card tucked into the waist of my yoga pants, the assessor's name and number printed on one side. He'd said to call him late the following day to confirm that my place would be habitable again. It would take more time to repair the yoga studio, but my apartment wasn't too badly damaged, and I could be sleeping in my own bed again in as little as forty-eight hours.

"Seven days, at least," I replied, hating myself for lying to one of the few people in the world who always got the truth from me.

But the damage to my place was the perfect cover story. This way, I could stay at Will's loft while he prepared for Birdie's event. He'd never come right out and ask for my help, and if I was homeless, he'd go on believing he was the one supporting me.

I couldn't admit, even to my brother, that as much as I wanted to be there for Will while he learned how to be a dad, more than anything else, I just wanted to be *there*.

14

ABBIE

I WENT TO see Mama on the way back to the loft. The front door to the house was open, and people swarmed in and out with boxes and bags of stuff to sort through for the charity sale. That should have set off alarm bells, but it wasn't until I ran into Dawn Linley in the hallway that I realised my rookie error.

"Abigail!"

Dawn stalled in the middle of the tight hallway, blocking traffic behind her. Her blonde hair was loose around her shoulders, a few of her trademark plaits peeking out here and there, and she was in linen overalls today. I leaned into one wall to give the grumbling old man behind her space to squeeze past with a bulky old ice-cream churner in his arms, but Dawn beamed up at me, oblivious.

"Hey, Dawn." I gave her a genuine but quick hug. I adored Dawn most days… and in small doses. "I wish I could stop and chat, but I need to talk to Mama—"

"Nancy's out back in the dining room. She runs a tight ship, your mother."

I smiled at Dawn's roundabout complaint. "She definitely likes things to be organised."

Dawn sidled up closer and dropped her chin as well as her voice, and I was forced to duck my head to hear her. She had a gleam in her eyes I knew all too well. The gleam of a bird who got the worm and wants the whole world to know about it. I gave her a blank look like I didn't know what was coming. I'd learned that playing dumb with Dawn was the fastest way to wrap up a conversation.

"Lori called me late last night," she murmured. "Told me all about you moving in with Will and the baby."

"I'm not moving in exactly. I'm staying at his place while my apartment and studio are out of action."

"Of course, of course." Dawn tilted her head to one side and gave me a speculative look. "It's just fortuitous, don't you think? The baby and the flooding happening on the same day."

I spared a smile for Burt the Third, who lurched past us, dragging three bulky striped plastic bags. He returned it with a nod and kept on moving.

I looked at Dawn blankly. "Sorry. What?"

"You know I don't like to gossip," Dawn went on, "but Nancy tells me things are starting to get serious, and if you ask me, it's about time. I mean, we all know Will has a history of, ah, playing the field—"

"You don't believe everything you hear, do you, Dawn?"

I widened my eyes innocently as Dawn blinked uncertainly, then bit my lip to stop a chuckle.

"Of course not. No. But you know how much I dislike a mystery."

"No mystery," I said, "and nothing more to tell you. I'm sure Lori gave you all the details."

"Oh, yes. She did. I also heard from the tourism committee that Will's hosting Birdie Maxwell's poker tournament in a few weeks. And on the weekend before Valentine's Day! Did you hear that they're thinking about extending the annual festival to run for an entire week, not just a weekend? It's going to be the best one yet!"

I ran my teeth over my bottom lip, concerned again about the responsibilities piling up on Will's shoulders. I was suddenly anxious to get back to the loft and take Seb off his hands so he could get back to work.

I squeezed Dawn's arm. "You know I always love talking to you, but I need to say a quick hello to Mama, then head back to The Stop."

"Of course, honey. It was lovely to see you. You let me know if you need help with the baby or the tournament. I'd be happy to pitch in."

If there was one thing Dawn was good for, it was corralling the troops, and it was always smart to keep her offers of support in your back pocket. "You know what? I may just take you up on that."

Dawn moved aside so I could move into the house, and I found Mama set up at the dining table with a clipboard and stacks of papers, ordering people and things like a grey-haired dictator. There was nothing like a list to get Nancy excited about life, and I loved that about her.

A flutter of nerves twirled in my stomach as I pulled out a chair. I should have been the one to tell her about the baby, and finding out from Dawn must have hurt her feelings. "Hey, Mama."

"Abigail!"

I took a seat and leaned over to press a kiss on her cheek. "I just spoke to Adam. He filled me in."

"Oh, darling. I wish you'd called me."

"I know. I'm sorry. I thought today would be soon enough, but—"

"It's okay." Mama leaned in and lowered her voice. "Lori called me last night and filled me in before Dawn could break the news."

"But Adam said—"

Mama pursed her lips and whispered, "Dawn was here when he called, so I couldn't give him the details. She was so thrilled to be the one to tell me."

I closed my eyes in awe at the sheer scale and complexity of the Valentine Bay grapevine.

Mama latched onto my hand, and when I opened my eyes, she'd removed her glasses, and her eyes were shiny with tears. "A *baby*. What a blessing!"

I smiled crookedly as I plucked a blank white sticker from a stack of labels and started picking at one corner. "A blessing that breaks the sound barrier when you can't read his mind. I don't think I slept more than five hours last night."

Mama patted the back of my hand, then let it go. "You'll get there."

Did I want to get there? No. I just needed to get Will through the next few weeks, and then everything could return to the way things were. A little voice in my head argued that the way things were didn't sound all that great anymore, but I refused to listen.

I set the paper aside and looked Mama straight in the eye so she wouldn't see the lie.

"I just met with the insurance company about my apartment and the studio. It'll take some time to repair the damage, so I wanted to let you know I'll be at Will's a little while longer."

"Oh." Mama pressed a palm to her chest. "That's great news."

I lifted one eyebrow in amusement. "The destruction of my home and business is *great news*?"

She clicked her tongue. "Oh, you know I didn't mean it like that. I'm just happy for you and Will. And little Sebastian, of course."

I rolled my lips as guilt and obligation twisted in my chest. "Mama, I don't want you getting too attached to this new arrangement. Nothing about this is permanent. I'll be moving back home as soon as I can, and things will go back to the way they used to be."

Mama shook her head and gave me a look that clearly said I was missing something.

"What?" I asked.

She took one of my hands in both of hers. People milled around us, waiting for directions, but Mama ignored them. "A baby is permanent, Abigail. *Sebastian* is permanent. Will is a father now, and *that* is permanent." She gave my hand a tight squeeze. "And is any of that such a bad thing?"

I smiled like what she said didn't land like a punch to the stomach, and I thought long and hard about it on my way back to The Stop. Mama was right. Sebastian was permanent. Daddy Will—gird my loins—was permanent. Will's new business venture and the life he was building for his little family were permanent. I was so freaking proud of him, and I'd always be the loudest, most obnoxious cheerleader on his team, but none of that meant Will was ready to make a permanent place for someone in his bed—or in his heart.

15

WILL

"WILL? WILL! WAKE up!"

I groaned and tried to roll over, but I'd forgotten I was sleeping on the couch and tumbled onto the hardwood floor.

"Ah, fuck." I grunted at the way my shoulder jarred a little, adding to the crick in my back. "What's the problem?"

Abbie sat back on her heels while I dragged myself upright, raising my legs and setting my elbows on my knees, then dropping my face into my palms. The past week was a blur of bottles and bedtimes, calls and emails about the poker tournament and warehouse repairs, and late nights behind the bar. Seb had woken at five a.m. I'd changed his nappy and given him a bottle, and he'd woken again an hour later. He didn't want his formula, didn't seem fussed with the applesauce—though when I'd texted

Noa about it, he'd told me to warm it up next time—and Seb had been wide awake and *smiling* the whole time. It was confusing as fuck.

I'd finally gotten him to sleep about five minutes ago, and then I'd closed my eyes for a minute before I had to meet a contractor downstairs to talk about fixing up the old warehouse. I'd hoped Logan could manage the job, but he was backed up with work of his own, so he'd called in a favour from a colleague in Scarborough Cove.

"There's a guy on the street downstairs asking for you." Abbie picked my phone up off the coffee table and flashed the screen at me. "He said he's called you three times, and he's not wrong."

I scrambled to my feet, snatching my phone and hunting for my shoes, hopping around while I tugged them onto my feet. "Shit. Shit. Shit. Is he still there?"

Abbie collected my keys from the little table by the door and shoved them at me as she pushed me towards the door. "I said you'd be right down, and he promised to wait another five minutes. Go!"

I stalled in the doorway, rubbing my eyes as I tried to think. "Um, Seb's asleep. He had a bottle about"—I checked the time on my phone before sliding it into my pocket—"ninety minutes ago. I have no idea when he'll wake up."

"Don't worry." Abbie shoved me into the corridor. "I've got it under control."

I hesitated. "Are you sure? *Fuck.* I feel awful. I have to meet with this contractor or I'll lose him, but I hate running out on you like this."

"Would you just go already? Seb and I know what to do. And I like the little guy. He's cute, and he's got a great attitude. A lot like his dad."

Jesus, I was lucky to have Abbie in my life. I'd always known it, but she was saving my arse right then, and even in my panic, I had to pause to take in the familiar lines of her face, the warmth behind her eyes, the tilt of her perfect cheekbones, the graceful slope of her neck.

She dropped her head to one side, a questioning furrow on her brow. "What—"

My phone rang in my pocket, jolting me out of reflection and re-agitating my frayed nerves. I had to move. Fast.

I slid my hand behind Abbie's warm, supple neck, pulled her towards me, and kissed her full and fast on the mouth. "Thanks, Abs."

Racing down the stairs and praying I hadn't already screwed up my new business, I burst onto the street and spotted the contractor standing out front of The Stop, his truck pulled to the kerb. I hurried the last few steps to close the distance between us, my hand stretched out towards him.

"Sorry to keep you waiting. I'm Will."

The contractor—an older, rounder guy short enough for me to spot the bald patch in his dark hair and with a red pencil balanced over one ear—shook my hand with a tight smile. "Ramoun. Nice to meet you. Your wife explained that you've just had a baby. I've got four of my own, though they're old enough that the youngest asked for my car keys last night, so I understand what you're going through. Congratulations."

"She's not my…" The words died on my lips. That was the first time a stranger had congratulated me on becoming a dad. Running a hand through my hair, I glanced up to the loft window where Seb was sleeping inside, and a swell of pride rose in my chest. I couldn't explain it, but Abbie was part of that feeling, too. "Thanks. It's a steep learning curve for both of us."

"But worth it." Ramoun hitched at his pants and pointed his thumb at the building. "So, you want to show me what we're dealing with here?"

I dug the warehouse keys out of my pocket and led the way to the entrance, my phone buzzing again as I worked on the locks. I gestured for Ramoun to go in first, and when his back was turned, I checked my notifications to be sure Abbie wasn't trying to get a hold of me. It was my mother calling—for the second time. I sent her call to voicemail and dropped my phone back into my pocket.

It took about forty-five minutes to do a thorough assessment of the building, and my phone rang twice more—both times my mother, and both times without a text to let me know if whatever she needed to tell me was important. I fired off a quick text to make sure she was okay—she responded with a thumbs-up emoji—then I followed Ramoun as he recorded measurements and made recommendations that seemed reasonable. Given the tight turnaround I required and no interest in making concessions on the quality of materials, I was anticipating a significant investment, and still, I had to suppress a wince when he gave me a ballpark figure to prepare me for the final quote I'd receive later in the day. I assured him cash flow was no problem, but the amount settled heavily in my stomach. The more I borrowed, the more money I needed to make at this tournament. Otherwise, God knew how long and hard I'd have to work to clear the debt. And the success of the event would come down to me and how I managed my life over the next few weeks.

But I could do it, couldn't I?

That old recording started up in my head again, the one that told me even if I tried my hardest, it wouldn't be enough. But then I thought about Seb, and the voice faltered. I had to work harder. That was all there was to it. Smarter. Learn to delegate. Set my fucking alarm. And I had Abbie—

Holy fuck. I'd kissed Abbie.

"I'll send the quote through in the next few hours, and if it all looks good to you, we can get started as early as tomorrow."

I raised my head and blinked at Ramoun, who stood across the doorway where I waited to say goodbye. "Huh?"

"The quote?" Ramoun clipped his measuring tape onto his belt and stuck his stubby pencil back behind his ear, then clapped me on the shoulder. "Go get some sleep, buddy, and I'll call you later with the numbers."

I watched as he climbed into his truck and pulled out onto the road, then I followed the glow of his taillights as he disappeared down the street. The same three words floated through my brain in a nonsensical loop.

I kissed Abbie. I kissed Abbie. I kissed Abbie.

My phone rang again. Assuming it was my mother, I fished it out of my pocket and hit the green Accept button without checking the caller ID before holding it to my ear.

"I kissed Abbie."

A deep grunt rumbled through the speaker. "Yeah, that's the kind of shit that'll get you in trouble."

I frowned at the voice—and the accent—and checked the screen for the caller's name. *Dylan.*

"Fuck, sorry, bro." I glanced up and down the street to make sure nobody had been close enough to hear my confession. "Just give me a second. I need to get inside and hide."

Dylan was my cousin on my mother's side. He was my age, and he ran a restaurant on his family's estate in California wine country. Even with the distance between Valentine Bay and the States, we'd travelled back and forth a lot over the years and managed to stay close. Ironically, Dylan was a single dad with a story not unlike my own, a fact only occurring to me now that he had me on the phone. It had been a fucking long time since we'd spoken.

Dylan waited while I unlocked the door to The Stop, and when I'd collapsed into the closest booth, I set the phone on the table and set it to loudspeaker. "You still there?"

"Yep."

Intuition niggled, so I asked, "Did Mum call you?"

"About an hour ago," Dylan confirmed. "She asked me to talk to you but said she'd let you know about it first." He paused. "I take it from your silence this is news to you?"

I set my elbows on the table and stared at the whorls in the wood, dragging my hands through my hair. "She's tried to reach me four times in the last hour, and I couldn't pick up. But it's cool. I'm glad you called."

"Thought you might be."

"Got any advice?"

Dylan huffed out a laugh. "Buckle up?"

I groaned and sank back against the leather of the booth. "Thanks, mate."

"Sorry. I'm not trying to be a dick about it, but single fatherhood is a fucking ride."

"I'm barely a week in, and I believe you."

"Aunt Lori gave me her version of the story, but I wouldn't mind hearing it from you."

I sighed and explained everything. I was more transparent with my cousin about how I'd freaked out when Heather first showed up and the pressure I was under, given all the balls I had in the air: Seb, the bar, the loan, the poker tournament. If anyone could understand what I was going through, it was Dylan. And he wasn't much of a talker, so I knew my secrets were safe with him.

16

WILL

———————

AFTER I BARED my soul, I braced for whatever wisdom Dylan had to share. His little girl, Isobel, was three years old now, so he'd been doing the single-dad thing for a while, and he'd had a father of his own who was actually good at the job. Dylan had to have a few secrets to raising a kid and running a business without dying from sleep deprivation or losing your mind.

"That's tough." Dylan paused, then said, "But where does kissing Abbie fit into all this?"

I dropped my head onto the table and banged my forehead against the wood a few times. Maybe it'd knock some sense into me.

"I just fucked up the most important kiss of my life."

"Oh, yeah?"

"I didn't even realise I'd kissed her until nearly an hour later. She was rushing in to take Seb off my hands. I was rushing out to meet the contractor. I'm sleeping on a couch that's too short to be comfortable, and I'm too fucking exhausted to think straight. And I just... did it. It wasn't even a good kiss. It was rushed. Ordinary. A 'ten-years-married-with-kids' kind of kiss. *Fuck.* Does she think that's how I kiss?" I straightened, pissed off by the thought that Abbie believed I was a bad kisser. "That's not how I kiss, all right?"

"All right."

"My first kiss with Abbie was supposed to be world changing. Earth shattering. The kind that curls her toes and leaves her gasping for breath."

"Your *first* kiss with Abbie?"

I was silent for a heartbeat. I hadn't meant to let that slip. "Yeah. So?"

Dylan chuckled. "Didn't know men who worked as fast as you believed in taking it slow."

"Abbie's different. Abbie's... Abbie."

"I get it. She's special."

Dylan had met Abbie many times on his trips to Valentine Bay. Flirted with her, too. She'd enjoyed his game but never took him seriously. We'd been young, and Abbie flirted with everyone, and it had bothered me less at the time than it did thinking about it now, which was stupid.

"Yeah. She is."

"And she's living with you now?"

"For a few days."

"So, this is your chance. Stop tiptoeing around the fact that you want this girl." He paused. "You do want her, right?"

"Yeah," I agreed softly. It felt good to finally say it out loud. "I do."

"And she wants you?"

I opened my mouth to say yes before I realised that wasn't technically the truth. Abbie might want me, but she didn't *want* to want me. I huffed out a dry, self-mocking laugh. "That's debatable."

"Fuck it. You'll never get an opportunity like this again, and you'll hate yourself if you don't make the most of it."

I rubbed the back of my neck. Dylan's suggestion made me equal parts uncomfortable and excited. "And how do I do that, exactly?"

Dylan laughed wryly. "My experience with women is limited these days. You know more about seducing someone than I do. I promise you that."

"Yeah, well. My moves don't work on Abbie."

"Then it's time to get some new ones."

I imagined trying something on Abbie. Something more than the teasing suggestions and overt innuendo we volleyed back and forth all the time. Something she'd have to take seriously. Something that would force her to take *me* seriously.

Then I pictured the swift rejection that would follow, and the wave of anticipation flattened. Even if my intentions were real—maybe, especially if they were—Abbie would rebuff any advance I made, and I was sick of playing games of *what-if* in my head.

Weariness washed over me. I'd never second-guessed myself as much as I had this last week—as a father, as a business owner, as a man—and the possibility I might not be good enough for any of it was wearing me down. In the past, I'd always consoled myself with the knowledge that at least I was a king in the sack, but when it came to Abbie, that didn't matter.

I rubbed my eyes and exhaled. "Yeah. Maybe."

"Listen, it's late here, and I've got an early start at the restaurant in the morning, so I've got to go. But call me anytime, okay? Baby advice. Business advice. Whatever you need. I'm here."

"I appreciate that, and I'm going to take you up on it."

"Good. And Will?"

"Yeah?"

"All jokes aside, fatherhood is the best thing that ever happened to me. It's hard, and some days it hurts, but Izzy is the reason I get up in the morning. She's the reason I work so damn hard at the restaurant and the reason we're busting our asses over here to save Silver Leaf. She's a miracle, and I thank the Universe for her every fucking day."

I smiled a little at the ferocity in Dylan's tone. "Yeah, I believe that. I kind of already feel that way about Seb."

Dylan grunted. "Good. The trick is to remember that the next time you're covered in throw-up at three a.m."

I chuckled lightly. "Noted."

In the end, I did feel better after talking to Dylan. I was still stressed, but I was more confident in my capacity to handle what was on my plate. My cousin had spent the last three years doing all the things I needed to do in the next three weeks, and it was kind of like the first four-minute mile. Once I had it in my head that raising a kid on my own *and* running a business were in the realm of possibility, it was easier to stop listing the ways it could go wrong and focus on the ways it could go right.

There was only one thing he'd been wrong about. Abbie. She was satisfied with the way things were between us, and for the most part, I had been, too. I'd had a lot of fucking fun over the years, and my few pathetic attempts at getting serious with a girl had always blown up in my face. I wasn't boyfriend material, and Abbie would be the first to confirm it. Sure, I'd hated every man she'd ever been with and believed she deserved better, but it's not as if *better* meant me. I just had to keep it in my pants—or my hand—and pretend like that kiss never happened. So what if Abbie thought it was terrible? I knew it wasn't my best work, and that's what mattered, right? My ego wasn't so needy I had to obsess over this.

I checked the time on my phone and dropped my head back with a groan. The bar was due to open in less than twenty minutes, giving me no time to rest and reset, let alone eat anything. I hadn't even extended operating hours yet, and I was struggling to keep up with my schedule. I ran the bar solo as often as I could, but I did have staff who were available for extra shifts when I needed help. And I did need help. Another expense I hadn't counted on, but one that I'd have to suck up along with all the others.

Dragging myself to standing, I headed for the loft. There was still time to check on Seb before I changed for another night behind the bar.

I smirked as I set my foot on the first stair, the hem of my shirt already bunched in my hands. Because the thing about my ego? It might not be needy, but it was bigger than my self-preservation instincts. And if sex was all I had to offer Abbie, I had no choice but to up my game.

17

ABBIE

———

I HAD MY Eyes on the clock and my mind on Will's mouth when he rushed into the loft fifteen minutes before opening time at The Stop. By the time the door had swung closed behind him, he'd crossed half the living room and pulled his dusty black shirt off over his head, so he was half naked when his eyes landed on me and Seb. Where did he get off looking so hot?

Will paused with an adoring smile tugging at the corner of his mouth. I'd pushed the coffee table to one side and set up Seb on a play mat in the middle of the living room rug, then stretched out beside him while he played with the frame of toys dangling over his head. Will came over and crouched on Seb's other side, offering him a goofy grin as he tickled his tummy.

I did not acknowledge Will's tanned, muscular arms or the way his forearms flexed as he rested them on his knees.

I paid no attention to his hands, his hard, carved stomach, or the V lines that led my gaze to the promised land. I ignored it all. The same way *he* was apparently going to ignore the fact he'd kissed me on his way out the door earlier.

He was probably ashamed about how bad it was. I would be.

And I wasn't going to be the one to bring it up. Denial made it easier to ignore how that one ordinary, boring, thoughtless touch of his lips had turned me to mush. Will kissing like a grandpa was his shame to bear.

That it could turn me into a puddle anyway was mine.

Will's blue eyes flickered up to mine. "You napping on the job, Ellison?"

"Not napping. Chatting." I turned my head towards Seb, and he reached out and latched onto my nose tight enough that my next words came out all nasally. "We're getting to know each other."

Will's mouth turned down at the corners, and he stood up. "I wish I could join you, but I have to get back downstairs."

Seb detached from my face, and my gaze travelled upwards, raking over Will's body from ankle to eye. When I reached his face, there was a knowing smirk on his mouth. Busted.

I rolled my eyes and threw a stuffed toy at him. "Stop showing off and put some clothes on."

He laughed and spun around, leaping up the ladder to the loft and taking the fuzzy bunny with him. I wiped the drool from my chin as his back muscles leapt beneath his

123

bronzed skin, and his impressive calves tightened as his toes sprung off each step.

"If I had more time, I'd let you look a little longer," he called over his shoulder. "Sucks to be you."

I squeezed my thighs together and sighed. He had no idea.

Propping myself on one elbow, I faced Seb and gave him my hand to play with. "Safe to say you're going to be as handsome as your daddy, but promise me one thing, will you? Don't torture women the way he does. No man needs an ego that size. It's unattractive."

Seb squealed and pumped his legs, babbling a response.

I huffed irritably. "Okay, *fine*. If you end up even half as hot as the man who made you, the overstuffed ego might work for you, too." I leaned in and whispered, "Just don't tell him I said that."

Will reappeared in a clean grey T-shirt, and he'd swapped his shorts for dark blue jeans that hugged his bum. I sat up and looped my arms around my knees as I watched him drop onto the sofa and pull on his sneakers.

His glance darted to me and away again as he tied his laces. "How are the repairs coming along at the studio?"

Yep, he was ignoring the kiss. I told myself it was a good thing and shoved the flicker of disappointment to the side.

It had been a few days since I met with the insurance company at my place. I'd told Will the truth about the studio needing major work but accidentally, on purpose, left out the fact that my apartment didn't.

I shook my head and pretended to be devastated. "Bad news."

Will straightened and gave me his full attention, concern on his face. "That bad?"

For a fleeting moment, I felt guilty about lying, but what was the alternative?

Hey, Will. Guess what? I can go home anytime I want, but then I'd have to leave you alone with Seb, and it's not like I don't believe you can do it, but it'll be almost impossible to get everything done on your own, and I know how you hate asking for help. Oh, and I like looking at you very much, and I haven't had sex in a really long time, and all this near-nakedness and bad kissing is giving me all kinds of naughty things to think about when I'm lying in your bed breathing in the smell of you on your pillow every night?

Jesus, Abigail. Get a fucking grip.

"I need to stay another week," I told him. "Maybe more. The damage is, uh, significant."

Will ran a hand through his hair as his shoulders sagged. "Shit. Sorry, Abs. I wish there was something I could do to help—"

"Actually, there might be." I scooted up on my knees, eager to reassure him that my staying here was about him helping me and not the other way around. "I've worked out a few ways to keep classes running while the studio is closed, and one of them involves Seb."

Will spared me a puzzled look before he glanced curiously at the baby, but then his eyes snagged on the clock on the wall, and he jumped to his feet. "I have to go.

Are you sure you're okay with Seb?" A frown danced across his brow. "I'm depending on you too much, aren't I? You've got your own problems to deal with, and I'm asking for so much of your time. I didn't even think…" Will rubbed his eyes with his thumb and forefinger. "Maybe I need to hire someone to help with the babysitting or start looking at daycare options."

"No!" I stood up and crossed my arms over my chest, surprised by how my body reacted so viscerally to the idea of handing Seb over to a stranger. "He needs stability right now. He needs to bond with you and get used to his new home, and I'm happy to be here when you're not. I told you. I like the little guy, and I'm starting to get the hang of things. We've got a little routine going, and you know what they say. If it ain't broke and all that."

Will looked at me funny, kind of like he was seeing me for the first time, then grabbed my shoulders and yanked me against his chest before wrapping me up in a hug. His nose burrowed into my hair. "You know I appreciate you, right?"

"It's always nice to hear it."

I looped my arms around his narrow waist and pressed my cheek against him. I knew this hug. It was from the old days, and it was perfect, but it made me wonder if Will wasn't ignoring our kiss after all. Maybe he didn't think there was anything *to* ignore. Maybe the increased sexual tension between us was all in my head.

I dragged my open hands down Will's back and breathed in the smell of him, pressing my breasts harder against his body and humming contentedly against his chest. When his muscles tensed, I paused and listened as he took in a ragged breath and tilted his hips away.

A satisfied smile twitched my lips. Nope. Not in my head.

Will let me go and reached down to pick up Seb. After giving him the sweetest goodbye kiss on the forehead, Will handed him to me, then hesitated. The look he gave me was lingering.

"I want to hear all about the yoga classes," he said, "but I can't stop now."

I shifted Seb on my hip, and Will followed as I crossed the room and opened the door. "It's fine. We can talk on the way to Aunt G's tomorrow."

Will paused in the hall outside. "What's happening at Aunt G's tomorrow?"

"Annual family reunion." His face dropped, and I winced. "I'm sorry. I'd get us out of it if I could, but Mama's told everyone about Seb, and she's so looking forward to showing him off. I promised her we'd be there. Plus, Aunt G's got the pool, and there'll be a barbecue. Seb can have his first steak!"

"Abs—"

"I know the timing is bad, but we don't have to stay more than a couple of hours. Just long enough to keep Mama happy and the rest of my family quiet about, well— you know. And this week has been a lot for both of us. I think it's a good idea to get away from the bar and the loft for a little while. We could use the break." I pouted and gave him my best puppy dog eyes. He never had the strength to say no to those. "Please?"

"Cheater," he grumbled. "What time?"

"Any time after eleven a.m."

Will ran a hand through his hair, and a little tension melted from his shoulders. "You're right. I could use the break—though I'm not sure I'd call an Ellison family reunion a *break*." He gave me an exasperated look that I returned with a shit-eating grin. Will rolled his eyes, but his lips twitched. "I can take care of my emails in the morning and let the tradespeople into the warehouse before we leave. And I'll call Stephanie to cover for me downstairs over the lunch service."

"Oh, babe." I gave him a patient smile. "You already did that when I told you about this six weeks ago."

"Did I?" Will covered a yawn with his fist and shook his head. "Good to know, *babe*. So, I'll send up dinner for you at about seven again?"

"Yes, please."

He saluted mockingly before closing the door behind him.

I turned to Seb, running my nose over the top of his soft curls and inhaling his soapy baby smell. "So, little man. What do you want to do today?"

The afternoon with Seb was easy and kind of fun. The nerves I'd struggled with to start had slowly given way to a sense of… not competence exactly, but at least a level of confidence that had shifted the energy between us, and Seb had begun to warm to me. I even got him to giggle.

I considered wrangling both the baby and the pram down the flight of stairs so we could take a walk before deciding that the first time Seb was paraded through Valentine Bay, Will should be there. Still, I put *sunshine*, *sand*, and *saltwater* on my list of things Seb needed to experience as soon as possible.

I used my phone to take about a hundred pictures and videos of him over the space of a few hours, wanting to capture as much as I could in case he did something cute or important that Will shouldn't miss. When Seb took his afternoon nap, I scrolled through my camera roll and sent the best snaps and clips to Will, but the baby was only asleep for forty-five minutes before he was ready to get up again. After a little time on the mat and a small dinner of pureed pumpkin, I bathed him, gave him a bottle, and read to him. He was in bed just before seven, snoring quietly, and as I stepped out of his room into the darkening loft, I was more than a little impressed with myself.

As I'd done the last few nights, I took the opportunity while Seb was asleep and I waited for food, to set up my yoga mat. Tonight, I also lit the candles I'd packed into my yoga kit before turning the music on low. I moved through the asanas slowly, focussing on the breath and meditative actions more than the pull and push on my muscles. Bridge. Downward-facing dog. Cat and cow.

I had settled into wide-legged child's pose, knees as wide as the mat, hips on my heels, arms extended and forehead on the floor, and was taking my last deep breath when someone cleared their throat behind me.

18

ABBIE

"HOLY CRAP!" I startled and flipped around. Will stood in the doorway, a bag of food in one hand, glass bottles wedged between his fingers in the other, and a flirty, dimpled smile on his face.

"Fuck, that's sexy."

I freaking *blushed*, for Christ's sake, but he'd caught me mid-practice—the only time in my life when my defences came down. I wasn't prepared for the banter right then. *Shit.* Twisting away so he wouldn't notice the roses in my cheeks, I rolled up my mat and reached for my phone to turn off the music.

"What are you doing here?" I asked with my back to him, still kneeling on the floor.

I listened as he moved into the kitchen and started pulling out takeaway boxes, plastic forks, and paper napkins.

"Logan and Jess came in for a drink, and when he saw

how beat I was, he insisted on covering the bar for me. I tried to say no, but then he got Noa involved, and that guy's too big to fight. Noa's going to close up for me so I can get a good night's sleep." Will snorted. "Should have told him about the sofa."

The heat in my skin cooled enough that I turned to face him, feeling a little guilty about how my extended stay was impacting his rest. The couch didn't look very comfortable, and I'm sure Will hadn't slept on it for more than a night or two before.

"Is it that bad?"

Will cracked the lid on a bottle of pink liquid and offered it to me. "Half-strength pink margarita?"

My mouth twitched as I accepted the drink. "You didn't answer my question."

"Would it buy me a ticket to the bed upstairs?"

Yes.

No! Bloody hell, Ellison. What happened to your self-control? Keep it in your freaking pants.

I gave him a sarcastic smile, though it took effort. "What do you think, babe?"

"I think you should drink your cocktail, *babe*."

I took a sip and hummed with pleasure. Will made the best cocktails, even weak like this one. He handed me the box of chicken salad he'd brought home for my dinner and pointed at the sofa. "You get started. I'm just going to check on Seb."

"Yum. Thank you." I craned my neck to see what else was waiting in the kitchen. "Did you bring any—"

"Samosas?" He picked up another box and handed it to me. "I was afraid not to."

I plonked myself on one end of the sofa and set my food to the side as I watched the monitor as Will crept into Seb's room and leaned over his cot to get a closer look. It was kind of phenomenal how quickly Will had slipped into his role as a father. Despite all his doubts—or maybe because of them—he was good at this.

I dragged the coffee table back into place and set the monitor on it as Will collected his meal from the kitchen and joined me on the couch. The room was quiet, and the candles flickered while we ate. When Will finally set his meal aside, he stretched out his long legs and dropped his head back onto the sofa with a groan.

"Long day," I commented, setting my empty cartons on the table and picking up my drink.

"Long week." Will dragged his open hands over his upturned face. "Fuck, Abs. I've got no idea how to use my time anymore. I'd sleep for a year if I could, but all the stuff with the bar and the warehouse has me itching in my skin even when I go to bed. There's too much to do and not enough time. I can't stop thinking about Seb—if I can be a good father and what it means for him not to have his mother around anymore. And I know I chose most of this, but it feels like everything has spiralled out of control. Nothing's going according to plan and..."

He motioned for me to swing my legs up onto the cushions and stretch out, so I did, setting my feet in his lap. "And... what?"

"Nothing." Will wrapped his hands around my ankles and brushed his thumbs lightly over my skin as he shook his head. "It's not important."

Goosebumps rippled north, lighting up every inch of my legs and setting off tingles between my thighs. I swallowed and reminded myself that I'd felt Will's skin on mine a thousand times. "Bullshit. And *what?*"

His jaw muscles feathered with tension. "I'm fucking *frustrated*."

You're preaching to the choir, Kidd.

There was a good chance Will wasn't talking about the kind of frustration he'd made me think about, but suddenly, I was curious about the last time he'd taken a girl home. "How long has it been?"

He furrowed his brow. "Since what?"

I lifted a coy eyebrow. "Since you weren't *frustrated?*"

"Ah." Will huffed out a laugh. "You want to know the last time I had sex?" I tilted my head expectantly, and he squinted up at the dark ceiling as if trying to work out the maths. "With someone other than myself... four months."

I choked on my cocktail, and he rolled his eyes as I coughed and wiped my mouth. "Will Kidd hasn't had a good time in four *months?*"

"I've been busy with the bar." He shrugged and took a sip of his beer before looking at me sideways. "When was the last time for you?"

I scoffed quietly and concentrated on the glass in my hand. "Let's just say I'm about twice as frustrated as you."

Will's eyebrows shot up. "You're joking."

"Shut up." I shoved at his thigh with my heel, and he captured my ankle again with a laugh.

"Sorry. Didn't mean to insult you."

I glowered at him. "It's not like I haven't had opportunities, all right? I've had plenty. I'm just more selective these days." I lifted my nose in the air. "Only the best from now on."

Will's fingers tightened around my legs, and he waited until I'd met his gaze before he lowered his voice and said, "You haven't had the best until you've had me."

The glass mouth of my bottle froze on my bottom lip. I needed a smart retort. *Faster, brain!* But the sex in his eyes broke me, and all I could do was stare.

Will grinned, then rested his head on the back of the sofa again and closed his eyes. "Christ, Ellison. I miss sex."

I took a sip of my drink as my heart raced. "Amen to that."

He rolled his head to look at me, and his smile set off his dimples. "You're frustrated. I'm frustrated. Seems to me there's an obvious solution to our problem."

I didn't know how much longer I could say no to this man. I was one proposition away from unzipping his pants with my teeth, but still, I summoned up my best withering stare.

"You couldn't handle me, Kidd."

Will wiggled his eyebrows. "Try me."

Please don't tempt me. Please don't tempt me.

"No."

He straightened and leaned towards me, a slow smile spreading across his face. "Did you hesitate, Ellison?"

I snorted, but a warm flush was creeping up my neck. "Ah, *no*."

"Oh, I think you did."

Will leaned forward, reached around to the back of his shirt, and pulled it off over his head. His dimple danced as he read the arousal on my face. "Ready to try me now?"

I swallowed and willed myself to look nowhere other than his eyes. "No."

"Hm."

He set my feet to the side and stood up. The lines and planes of his sculpted chest and stomach lit up with the golden, flickering light of the candles, and I barely stifled a moan. His hands went to his jeans, and he unbuttoned the waist before pausing.

"How about now?"

God, he was so fucking cocky. I hated it. I loved it.

I coolly drained the last of my margarita and set the bottle on the floor before I stood. I swept my gaze over Will's body, not bothering to hide my admiration, then took a step closer. "You wouldn't dare."

Without missing a beat, Will unzipped his jeans and pushed them over his hips until they were low enough to sit snug under his arse at the back and reveal the shape of his hard-on, straining the fabric of his dark boxer briefs at the front.

So. Will Kidd had good reason to be cocky. I'd never worked so hard at anything in my life to keep my thoughts off my face as I dropped my gaze and took it all in. What I wanted to do was drop to my knees and take it all in my mouth. Instead, I ran my teeth over my bottom lip as I met Will's eyes. Then, I took a step back.

"That's all I needed. Thanks for the donation."

Will looked at his erection, then back up at me. "That's all you *need*? Donation for what?"

"The flick list." Doing my best not to laugh at his stunned expression, I lifted my mouth in a crooked smile and softened my focus as I patted his cheek. Then I turned and walked up the stairs. "Don't forget to blow out the candles before you go to bed," I called over my shoulder. "Goodnight."

I wasted no time stripping off every inch of clothing before I slipped under the covers, so aroused that even the thought of my naked skin against Will's sheets drove me wild. But it was knowing he was downstairs listening that had me moaning the moment my fingertips hit my clit. I palmed my breast, tweaking one nipple the way I liked it, and I had to pace myself before coming too soon, but my clit was so swollen and my folds so slick that I was arching off the mattress and coming on my hand in no time at all. I groaned. I gasped. I panted and cursed my way to climax, then moaned my way out of it. I put on a real fucking show.

I lay there with my eyes closed, listening for movements downstairs. It was silent until a creak on the stairs told me Will was at least considering following me up here. But sixty seconds later, the lights went off, and I heard him settle on the couch.

Chicken.

Was it fair to torment him like this? Probably not. But was it fun? Absolutely. And Will could use a dose of his own medicine. Indulging in a full body stretch on the linens, I let out a satisfied sigh and smiled into the darkness. *Your move, Mr Cocky.*

19

WILL
———

I COULDN'T SLEEP. Not after that. I lay on the couch for what felt like forever, slipping my dick through my fist over and over, but the idea of coming on my own stomach with Abbie upstairs and me on the sofa gave me loser vibes I couldn't shake.

I wanted to go up to her, but there'd been no invitation, either implied or explicit, and the last thing I needed after Abbie's performance was a solid rejection. So, I stared into the darkness as the sounds of her orgasm echoed in the loft long after she was done. Those whimpers were going to haunt me to the end of my days.

I yanked my hand out of my underwear, stuck it behind my head, and scowled at the ceiling. Jesus fucking Christ. Abbie was better at this than me.

I finally dozed off and managed to get a few hours of solid sleep. Seb woke once a little after midnight.

I changed him and gave him a bottle, and he was still asleep when I woke with the sun a little after six. I rolled off the sofa with a wince and stretched to relieve some of the stiffness in my back and shoulders. Maybe tonight, I'd try sleeping on the floor instead.

As I waited for the coffee machine to power up, I stood in the kitchen with my phone in my hand, scrolling through the pictures of Seb that Abbie had sent me. I might have been biased, but he was a *really* cute kid. I caught myself grinning at the better shots, the ones that captured his big blue eyes or that sunshine smile. Abbie was in a few of them, too, which only made me grin harder—until suddenly, I was breathing through my anger.

It should have been Heather taking those pictures. Seb deserved to have his mother in his life the same way I'd deserved to have my father. I loved my mum, but she didn't do enough to keep her husband accountable. She never set expectations or boundaries on his behaviour. Never demanded he do better. Instead, she let him coast in and out whenever it suited him. She believed his bullshit excuses and had a bottomless well of forgiveness in her. I never gave voice to the rage or heartache my father caused because it would have achieved nothing except break my mother's heart.

Walking out on your family really screwed a kid's sense of worth, and I'd be damned if I was going to make the same mistakes my mother did.

I dug Heather's phone number out of the paperwork she'd left me, then selected three photos of Seb and attached them to a message.

Me: Seb is settling in at the loft. I introduced apple and pumpkin to his feeding schedule, and he's starting to enjoy it. Everyone who meets him adores him on sight. He's an incredible kid, and I'm going to be the best father I can be, but he needs his mother. I haven't signed the parental rights papers, and it's not too late to change your mind, so if you want to discuss joint custody, please call. From, Will.

The whoosh of the outgoing message tightened my stomach. I leaned with my elbows on the kitchen peninsula, staring at the phone as though I could conjure a response via sheer will alone, but the screen was still blank when I heard Abbie moving upstairs five minutes later.

Letting myself hope that Heather would get back to me at some point, I set the phone down and straightened. I wasn't stupid. I'd always enjoyed the way Abbie ogled me every time I had my shirt off, and I wanted to make sure my bare chest was in full view as she walked down the stairs. I was going to up the ante today. Nobody played me like that and got away with it. Not even Abbie.

Then she sauntered down from the loft wearing my clothes—an oversized crew-neck T-shirt with The Salty Stop's logo printed small on the front and larger on the back—and I forgot my own name.

Abbie was tall, and the shirt barely covered the curve of her arse. I stared at her long, lithe, sun-bronzed legs as she slowly walked down the stairs, putting on a performance she knew I'd buy a ticket to see. Her tight nipples poked through the thinning white fabric, and when her bare feet hit the floorboards on the bottom floor, she reached up and ran her fingers through her long blonde hair, teasing me with a glimpse of what hid just underneath the hem of my shirt as she tied her tresses into a sexy knot on the top of her head.

"Morning, Kidd." She strolled over to the kitchen and rested the heels of her palms on the edge of the peninsula, leaning towards me. "Sleep well?"

I swallowed, throat bobbing with the effort. "You know I didn't."

Her mouth curled up at one corner as she lifted one shoulder. "Well, I slept like a baby. Thanks for asking."

I opened my mouth before I knew what the hell I was going to say to that, but a cry from Seb's bedroom saved me from saying anything too pathetic.

I set down my coffee mug and rounded the peninsula. "I should get him."

Abbie raised her hand. "I want to do it. Is that okay?"

I hesitated. She'd surprised me like this the day before when she'd argued against taking Seb to daycare or hiring a babysitter. I appreciated Abbie's help more than I'd ever be able to tell her, but I'd never expected her to be so invested. That she appeared so attached to my son sent a wave of warmth radiating through my chest. "Sure."

She turned around, and I couldn't miss the red outline of her G-string panties underneath the white tee. The subtle glow inside me ignited into a red-hot fire, and at my strangled groan, Abbie glanced back at me over her shoulder and winked before disappearing through Seb's door.

No doubt about it. This woman had me by the balls.

The contractor was due to start work on the warehouse that morning, and I was paying him extra for the weekend labour, so after I'd fixed coffee for both Abbie and me and given Seb his breakfast, I slipped downstairs to let the tradespeople in the building and return a few business emails. I was relieved to find new messages about supplies and equipment for the poker tournament, and Birdie had supplied a list of competitors as well as confirmation that the event had almost sold out. I forwarded the relevant information to Noa, who had agreed to manage The Stop's catering obligations, and I was able to put in final beverage orders, too. In two hours, I'd ticked a half-dozen critical tasks off a list of things to do that was longer than my arm.

The burdens of those small things added up to a good weight off my shoulders, and as I jogged back upstairs to take a shower, I was more relaxed and almost looking forward to the barbecue at Aunt G's. Like all families, Abbie's relatives were equal parts challenging and entertaining, and I'd become a semi-permanent fixture since we made our pact of convenience. I suspected some of her cousins had put bets on how soon Abbie would dump her new "boyfriend", and it was a pleasure to keep showing up and proving them wrong.

Thinking about Abbie sent a rush of blood to my dick, and I had trouble thinking it away this time. I had to admit that while taking care of business responsibilities that morning had relieved a certain kind of pressure, I wasn't going to get to the end of the day without taking care of *other* business, too.

Abbie was carefully closing the door to Seb's bedroom when I walked into the loft. She was still wearing my shirt, her hair tied messily on her head, her smooth legs illegally long and sun-kissed against the white fabric. My cock got even harder at the sight of her.

"Seb asleep?" I asked gruffly as I passed her on my way to the stairs.

She flashed the baby monitor at me. "Yep."

"Great. I'm going to take a shower, then I'll pack his bag for the afternoon."

"Okay. I'll use the bathroom when you're done."

"No problem."

I had my shirt off before my foot hit the landing, my pants were gone as soon as I stepped inside the bathroom, and I was under the hot water in record time. Images of Abbie in my clothes and on my sheets with her hand between her legs ran through my head as I thrust the hard length of my dick against my palm.

It could have all been over in less than a minute, but after last night, it felt too good to rush it. I didn't worry about the volume of my grunts and moans as I jerked myself off, either. Abbie deserved to hear them. I leaned my forehead against the wet tiles and thumped my fist on the slippery wall as I pumped my cock, clenching my teeth and groaning as the urge to explode ebbed and flowed with the pressure of my hand and the remembered sounds of Abbie climaxing in the dark.

A flicker of motion caught the corner of my eye, and in the reflection of the mirror, I saw a shadow hovering outside the barely open bathroom door. As I watched, the figure stepped away and back again, like she wanted to come in but didn't know if she should. I fucked my hand, arse flexing with every thrust, until her eyes on me drove me to madness. I wanted to see her. I needed Abbie to know what she did to me. I had to give her a taste of what we could do together.

"Get in here," I ordered, my voice deep and husky.

I kept my head bowed, wondering if she'd do as she was told. In my peripheral vision, I watched as Abbie pushed the door open and stepped inside. Her wide eyes latched onto my dick, and she caught her bottom lip in her teeth. Her chest rose and fell with a deep breath.

"Tie the shirt around your waist," I commanded, closing my eyes and grunting as I pushed against the pain and pleasure of my impending orgasm.

Would she do it? I got off on giving orders in the bedroom, but Abbie wasn't the submissive type in life. This could backfire, but I couldn't help myself. I'd fantasised about having Abbie my way and on my terms for too long, and I was too wound up to back off now.

And then she replied, "Yes, Daddy."

I let out a strangled groan and eased my stroke as her

words pushed me all the way to the edge, and I could only look at her sideways as she pulled her shirt to the side and knotted it above one hip. She was still in those skimpy red panties.

Sweat mingled with the water training over my temples as I flattened one hand against the slippery tiles and pumped my dick with the other.

"Sit on the vanity."

Abbie's eyes stayed glued to my cock, and she didn't even hesitate as she lifted herself onto the bathroom vanity.

"Spread your legs."

Abbie obediently opened her knees.

My heart lurched at the first sight of her smooth pink folds, barely covered by a damp strip of sheer lace, and I changed up the pressure on my dick, working the crown. "Good girl," I panted. "Wider."

Abbie spread her legs, and I drank in the sight of her pussy. It was smooth and pink and wet enough to make my mouth water.

"Fuck." I grunted as I fought the urge to come. I never wanted this moment to end. "Go wider. I know you can."

Abbie leaned back on her hands and opened her legs, and the way she put herself on display for me sent me plummeting into oblivion. I growled and tugged as my orgasm tore through me, shooting white ropes of cum over the bathroom tiles, squeezing my eyes closed as I struggled to breathe. Struggled to stay standing.

A brush of cool air brought me back to reality, and when I opened my eyes, Abbie stood with the shower door held open. The T-shirt was still knotted around her waist, and while I couldn't read anything on her face, she couldn't hide the proof that she'd gotten off on whatever this was. It was shining on her inner thighs.

I smiled with one corner of my mouth, activating dimple mode, and tried to catch my breath. "Your move, babe."

Abbie stared at me blankly long enough that I started to wonder how badly I'd fucked up. My grin slipped, and I pushed my wet hair back with one hand as she reached around me to turn off the water.

Then she slipped one hand between her legs, inhaling sharply as she curled her hand and slid a single finger inside her pussy. I stared, dumbstruck, as she lifted that hand to my mouth and ran a wet fingertip over my bottom lip.

Impulsively, my tongue darted out to taste her, and as she pulled away, I leaned in for more. Fuck, that taste. I was already craving her. Abbie's pussy was more addictive than crack.

My heart pounded as she took a small step back, and one corner of her mouth turned up as she shook her head and walked away.

"Don't play with me, *babe*. You'll never win."

20

ABBIE

WILL CHECKED HIS blind spot before changing lanes on the freeway to Scarborough Cove, where Aunt G lived. We were running twenty minutes behind, thanks to a last-minute dirty nappy that required a full outfit change. Seb was gurgling in the back of the car, turning a ring of enormous plastic keys over in his little hands, and I was having a minor life crisis. Neither Will nor I had mentioned what happened in the bathroom yet, and the suspense was killing me.

"We're friends, and there's always been this tension between us, right?" I blurted out. "No point denying it. Things have been tense. We're stressed. We needed to release some of the pressure, that's all, and what better way than with a couple of innocent orgasms? When you think about it, it's surprising this didn't happen sooner. What's the big deal anyway? We're grown-ups. Let's just *talk* about it."

Will slid his eyes to me briefly before looking back at the road, his competent hands so freaking sexy wrapped around the steering wheel. "You sound a little nuts, Ellison."

I felt a little nuts.

"You just saw my lady garden, Kidd. Can't take that back."

"No, you cannot."

He grinned like he was remembering it, and I whacked him on the arm.

"Stop it!"

"Never."

I closed my eyes and made a humming sound. "Fine. I'm picturing your dick in my hand. Your hand!" My eyes flew open again. Will's broad shoulders shook with silent laughter, and I thumped him again, harder, this time on the chest. "*Your* hand, arsehole."

"You have my permission to think about my dick in my hand—or yours—anytime you like."

I huffed and crossed my arms, sinking into the seat. I would think about it, thank you very much. Often. With glee. And in high definition.

I couldn't believe I'd given in to temptation. Not once, but twice. Where was my rock-solid self-control?

"This wasn't supposed to happen," I mumbled.

Will frowned but kept his eyes on the road. "What do you mean?"

Wasn't it obvious? "I *mean*, we were never supposed to cross that line. *Not* having sex is the secret to our relationship."

The crease between Will's brows deepened, and the corners of his mouth turned down. "You don't think our friendship is solid enough to survive a slip-up or two?"

Our *friendship* was strong enough to survive anything, including this sexual uh-oh, but my heart wasn't nearly so sturdy. I was not going to end up bitter and twisted because I'd let myself become another notch on his bedpost. And I loved Will in a way that meant he could never be another one on mine, but it's not like I could tell him that.

"I just think that when it comes to sex, we're better off getting what we need from other people like we've always done."

Will scowled as another driver cut in front of us. "Yeah. Right."

"What?" I frowned at him. "What's wrong?"

"Nothing." Will smiled, but it looked forced. "So, what happens now? Like you said, we can't take it back, but it's not like we had sex, either. The line wasn't so much crossed as it was…"

"Redrawn?"

His smile softened into something more real. "Exactly."

I mimed wiping sweat off my brow and gave him a relieved grin that he returned with amusement. "Phew. So, we call it a glitch, appreciate the fact that we're both a little more relaxed now, and go back to the way things were?"

He shrugged. "I can if you can."

"And you'll never think about it again?"

He flashed his dimple and cocked one eyebrow. "Unlikely."

I had to bite back a smile. Will wanted to jerk off with the image of me in his head? I didn't hate the idea. I wouldn't give back the picture of him fisting his cock in the shower for all the money in the world or the way it felt to do what he said, no questions asked. Just the memory of his voice, all bossy and husky with lust, made me press my thighs together.

But it wouldn't happen again. It wasn't too late to save whatever we'd put at risk. What *I'd* put at risk. Because, let's face it, I'm the one who lost control first. I was the one who cracked. Will could put the moves on all he wanted, but I knew better than to fall for them.

"So, is now a good time to talk to you about my new yoga classes?" I asked.

"Shoot."

Seb whimpered a little, and I twisted in my seat to return the toy to his hands before facing forwards again.

"It was easy to relocate my seniors' yoga class," I explained to Will. "There's a space available at the community centre, and at first, I thought that was the answer to all my problems, but I can only get it for two sessions a week. It's forced me to get creative."

"Oh, yeah?"

"I've moved three of my morning classes to the park, which is fine as long as the weather holds, but when I sent out the invitation to my existing clients, I actually had some new enquiries, so I might keep doing that one even after the studio re-opens."

"And when will that be again?"

I glanced out the window. Now was the time to tell him the truth, get the hell out of his loft, and put myself beyond the reach of temptation. I swallowed a snort. I was never going to leave a minute before I had to. I was a masochist.

"Still no firm date. I'm sorry."

"Don't be. You can stay with me as long as you need to."

"Thank you."

"You mentioned that you had an idea that involves Seb?"

"Right." I shifted in my seat to read his face better. Nerves fluttered low in my stomach. "And before you say no, remember this would be a good solution for both of us because it means we can both work mornings."

I really wanted Will to love my idea, and I'd be disappointed if the answer was no. I was excited about it, but I wasn't sure if Will trusted me enough yet to take Seb out of the loft on my own.

Will smiled, but his brow creased with confusion. "I'm not following you."

"Mother and baby yoga classes."

His eyes flicked up to Seb's reflection in the rear-view mirror, then to me, and back to the road. Hesitation flattened the line of his mouth, and my nervous flutter turned to dismay.

"He's too young for yoga, isn't he?" Will asked. "I mean, what's he supposed to do? Are you going to twist him into weird poses? Is that a good idea?"

"What?" I shook my head. "No. Mother and baby yoga is for women or carers with young babies. They bring

151

their kids to class, and I adapt their poses to work around the baby, who lays or rolls around on the mat."

I glanced back at Seb, and a stab of regret hit me in the chest. I should have thought about it a long time ago, but it never occurred to me before now how hard it must be for mothers to find time in their schedules to attend a yoga or fitness class.

Will checked his shoulder again before he changed lanes and directed us towards the next freeway exit. I knotted my hands and tucked them between my knees as I waited for him to say something.

"I love the idea. I think you should do it."

"Really?" I grinned and clapped my hands under my chin. "Thank you!"

Will's smile was curious as well as pleased. "You're welcome. But where are you going to hold these classes?"

I settled back in my seat, more relaxed now that Will was on board with my idea. "Oh, the little hall behind the church. When I called to ask about hiring it, they said it was all booked up with a bunch of different things, including new baby playgroups. That's what gave me the idea in the first place, so I called the organisers and pitched my idea. They put the word out and got a fantastic response."

"Smart."

I waved my hand to hide the pleasure shimmering in my cheeks. "I know. And Will?" I looked down at my palms as I said the thing that made me nervous. "Thank you for saying yes. It means a lot, and I know how important this is. I won't let you down."

Will slowed the car and flicked on the indicator as we pulled onto Aunt G's street. When he'd pulled to a stop outside her white-painted two-storey house, he switched off the car, turned in his seat, and gave me his full attention. His eyes burned, and his freshly shaved jaw was strong and chiselled.

"You don't need to thank me. In all the years we've known each other, you've never disappointed me, Ellison. I trust you."

Silence fell, and the car grew small. My pulse hitched as Will watched me with his deep blue eyes, his gaze travelling over my face and dropping to my mouth. I licked my lips as he leaned over the centre console. He was going to kiss me... For real, this time. A kiss that meant something. A kiss we couldn't ignore. I should draw back. I should make a joke. I should...

Seb's scream made me flinch, and Will opened the door with a rueful smile on his face. He was the first to get out of the car, and he unclipped Seb from his car seat while I took a shaky breath and retrieved the baby bag from the back. We avoided looking at each other the entire time.

I should have been relieved the kiss didn't happen because it would have been different from the Kiss We Did Not Mention. This one would have been intentional. It would have said something. Meant something. It wouldn't have even compared to what happened in Will's bathroom because a real kiss wouldn't just redraw the line we knew we shouldn't cross. It would obliterate it.

As I followed Will's strong, broad back up the drive to Aunt G's door, I had to remind myself that would be a very bad thing. The line between us had to stand. The line was what kept us safe.

———

Aunt G—short for Gloria—was my father's eldest sister, and she hosted a family reunion every year. It was always sometime in January when the weather was hot, so we could barbecue and swim and stay until late. Dad was the second of seven siblings, and Aunt G's place was the only one big enough to accommodate my dozens of cousins and their families. At last count, there were sixty-seven Ellisons on the family reunion guest list, and we all made an effort to attend. Adam had promised me he'd make it this year—the first time in the last three—but when my phone pinged with a message from him an hour before we were due to arrive, I knew it would be to say he wouldn't be there.

Me: I miss you, big brother, and I know you've got nothing on for Valentine's Day, so why don't you visit for the festival? There aren't nearly enough cynics in this town to keep me from committing violence.

Adam: I'll think about it.

It took an hour after our arrival for the fuss over Seb to settle. Mama scooped him up almost the moment we walked through the door and completed a full circuit of the party to make sure everyone got a personal introduction. Will kept one eye on them from where we trailed a few paces behind.

"Oh, no," Mama said in response to a question I didn't catch. "Sebastian's mother isn't in the picture anymore. It's just Will and Abigail and this beautiful baby boy, and I couldn't be more pleased about it."

"I'm sorry about this," I muttered, and Will ducked his head to hear me better. "She's excited if you couldn't tell."

"You think so?" He smiled easily. "I'm not going to complain. I was half-expecting your parents to corner me at some point and demand to know how I got another woman pregnant while I was supposedly dating their daughter."

The blood drained from my face, and my eyes widened at Will's amused expression. "Oh my God. Why didn't I think of that?"

Will chuckled. "It only occurred to me when we walked through the door, and Nancy came barrelling at us down the hallway. I thought for sure she was going to murder me until she claimed the baby."

I nibbled at my lip. "Maybe she hasn't thought of it?"

Will scooped up a handful of peanuts as we passed a trestle table laden with snacks and gave me a doubtful look.

I glanced at Mama, and the expression on her face was so bright I stopped worrying and waved my hand at Will. "I don't think we need to stress about the maths. I told Mama from the start that we weren't strictly exclusive, so—"

"You what?"

I blinked at Will's harsh tone. "Uh, I told her we weren't exclusive?"

He clenched his jaw and his nostrils flared, and I pointed at his face.

"Excuse me, what is this all about?"

He sucked a breath in through his nose and tossed the peanuts in his hand into an empty bowl. "Nothing."

I rolled my lips, puzzled by his reaction. "Come on, Kidd. You know the way people talk. It was either you're my non-exclusive boyfriend, or you're cheating on me. No, correction. We're cheating on each other." I elbowed him in the ribs as if his irritation was a joke, but his eyes were hot enough to burn through leather. "It's not that big a deal. Mama was thrilled I was even in the realm of commitment. She's convinced it's just a matter of time before we take things to the next level, and she never passes up an opportunity to ask me if we've decided to *get serious*."

"Next time she asks, tell her yes."

My stomach flipped at the way he said it like this was his decision to make. Bossy looked very good on him, and I bit back the impulse to call him *Daddy* again. "Why are you being so weird about this?"

"I'm not being weird."

He was. Will was the most even-tempered, easy-going guy I knew, and aggression was out of character. Hot enough to make me want to run my nails down his back, but that wasn't the point.

I came to a stop and planted my hands on my hips. "What is—"

Will took one of my hands and tugged me forward. "Come on. Food's ready."

21

WILL

———

I GRABBED ABBIE'S hand and twined my fingers through hers, leading her to the table like a boyfriend would. Not a freaking fuckboy.

I wasn't the kind to snap, and I didn't get mad often, but I had a tight leash on my irritation right then. She hadn't meant to do it, but Abbie had hit too many sore spots today, starting with our conversation in the car.

She insisted that there was an uncrossable line between us, an invisible boundary that made it possible for us to be in each other's lives, and that line was sex. Sex would be the end of us because I wasn't the kind of guy who'd sleep with a girl and stick around, was I? I wasn't the man girls went to for a long time. I was the guy they called for a good time, including Abbie, apparently. Mr Phone-A-Fuck. Not much more than a mouth or a hand or a cock to relieve her pressure.

I wasn't sure what I thought would change after the scene in my bathroom but pretending that it never happened wasn't on the list.

And *then* I find out that Abbie had let her family believe I was just one of a bunch of guys she was sleeping with. Her parents thought I was the kind of man who would let the woman he loved sleep with other people—that I was the kind of man who would tell Abbie I loved her and then fuck someone else!

And the joke was on me because nobody had trouble believing it.

I could be man enough and admit that part of my problem was the blow to my ego. There were people out there who probably laughed and said I wasn't man enough for Abigail Ellison. But more than that, I was mad at myself for being such an idiot and not thinking things through when I agreed to this stupid pretend-boyfriend plan.

The pact was Abbie's idea. She pitched it as a way for us to stay single in practice but committed on paper. It'd make her parents happy, she said, and who better to grow old with than a best friend who encouraged you to go out, have fun, and forget about the consequences? It sounded harmless at the time, and it wasn't such a stretch to imagine us doing what we'd always done for the rest of our lives.

How many times had Abbie knocked on my door late at night because the loft was more a convenient place to crash after she'd hooked up with someone at the bar? I'd been taking off her shoes and tucking her into bed for years. We'd shared sore heads and stories about the night before over morning coffee dozens of times.

Did I hate that she was screwing a list of losers when I knew she deserved better? Fuck, yes. But I'd been there when that arsehole in high school told everyone that Abbie was easy and watched her pick herself up and own her story. And she kept on owning it long after everyone forgot about why it was important for her to be a cheerleader for sexual liberation. I respected the hell out of Abbie and supported her sex positivity, and given the kind of life I'd been living, who was I to judge?

I was a lover, not a fighter, so why did the idea of Abbie as something other than mine and mine alone suddenly make me want to punch something?

As we approached the long table set out on the lawn for lunch, I smoothed the annoyance from my expression. We found two chairs beside Nancy, who had Seb on her lap. She looked so happy, pressing her cheek against his soft curls, and Seb appeared so content that I had no intention of taking him from her. But when my son set eyes on me, he immediately stretched out his fat little arms, and something like sunlight exploded in my chest.

Seb recognised me, and he wanted to be in my arms more than anyone else's. Someone needed to make a greeting card for this moment because I could never put into words how fucking fantastic it felt.

In my peripheral vision, I noticed Abbie watching my reaction. I lifted Seb from Nancy's lap as though my boy always reached for me when I got close, but it was hard work to stop the smile, so I kissed the top of his head to hide my mouth before pulling out Abbie's chair, then taking the seat next to her, Seb settled into the crook of my arm.

Abbie's cheeks looked close to bursting with joy, and she was so beautiful I had to remind myself I was annoyed with her.

Across the table, one of Abbie's uncles helped himself to a spoonful of potato salad as his eyes bounced between Abbie and me. "So, Nancy tells us you two finally moved in together."

"Oh, well," Abbie replied, "Uncle Darren, that's not exactly—"

"That's right," I interrupted, picking up Abbie's hand again and setting our interlocked fingers on the table where everyone could see. "We did."

Abbie shot me a questioning look, but I ignored it. Instead, I pulsed my fingers once against hers, a silent signal to keep her mouth closed, and miracle of miracles, she did.

Next to Darren, his son Kyle scoffed quietly and took a deep swallow of his beer, pretending he didn't see my glare. I'd met Kyle a few times over the years— he was about the same age as me and Abbie, and he'd visited the Bay on weekends and in the summer—and he was a dick. Beside me, Abbie swept her thumb over the inside of my wrist, which she probably thought was soothing, but it only added to my heightened emotions as I registered the condescension in Darren's eyes. Darren's and almost everyone else's looking at us around that table. And suddenly, I wasn't only angry, I was riding a rush of protectiveness—*possessiveness*—for Abbie and my child.

"Nice to see you again, Kyle." I nodded in Kyle's direction, but the flatness of my voice didn't match my polite words. "Keeping busy?"

Kyle shrugged in a phoney way that made my lips twist. "My property portfolio made a quarter of a million last year. Life could be worse."

I jerked my chin and forced a tight smile. "Good for you."

On Kyle's other side, his mother Melody smiled uncertainly at me, then at Abbie and the baby. "So, things between you two are serious now?"

"We've always been serious," I answered before Abbie could tell everyone I was her piece on the side.

"Abbie's never been serious with anyone in her life, have you, Abs?" Kyle shot me a look like we were in on a secret, and I threw up a little in my mouth.

"Now, Kyle," Nancy said, a whisper of impatience in her voice. "That's not true."

Kyle shook his head and set his beer on the table before cutting into his steak. "Never thought I'd see the day when Abigail shacked up with one man, not to mention a baby that's not even hers."

"Kyle!" Melody hissed.

Kyle looked surprised. "What?"

My blood boiled. Where did this arsehole get off degrading Abbie in front of everyone? In front of me? She was tough enough not to let comments like this bother her, but when I glanced her way, the expanse of skin beneath her collarbone was mottled with a gentle pink flush, and that impulse to protect her surged again.

I gritted my teeth instead of reaching over the table and decking the guy like he deserved. "Not that we owe anyone any explanations, but Abbie and I have been serious for a while. I met Seb's mother more than a year ago, and Seb's just come into my life. I wasn't expecting it, but I wouldn't change it for anything." Abbie's grip on my hand grew tighter, and I turned to make sure she knew my next words were for her. "And I couldn't do it without Abbie. She's fantastic with him. Caring and capable and confident. Watching these two together is one of the most incredible things I've ever seen."

Her honey-brown eyes widened a little, and her tongue slipped over her bottom lip. And although my irritation with her still flickered in my chest, it was nothing compared to the disgust I felt for her family or the urge I had to defend her. I clung to her hand and willed her to believe me.

Kyle snorted, and his mother hit his arm with the back of her hand. "I think what Kyle means to say is, we never imagined Abigail as the nurturing type. She's never been what anyone would call maternal."

"Or monogamous," Kyle muttered under his breath.

I ignored the weasels on the other side of the table because Abbie was still lost in my eyes. My gaze traced the lines of her exquisite face, and something about this moment felt too honest to take for granted. I squeezed her hand again. "Abigail is the best thing to ever happen to me and to Seb. He adores her. We both do."

———————

I wish I could say the moment at the table solved everything, and I left all the emotional bullshit at Aunt G's house, but the sideways looks and not-so-subtle digs about our relationship kept coming well into the afternoon, and by the time we got in the car to go home, I'd hit my limit. I was too pissed off and too wrapped up in my own stuff to put two civil words together.

"All right," Abbie declared ten minutes into the silent drive. "I could do without all this"—she waved her palm at me—"*energy*. Are you going to tell me what your problem is or not?"

I flexed my fingers on the steering wheel. "Not."

"My family are pains in the arse, and they were worse than usual today. I get that. I'm sorry."

"That's not it."

"Then tell me what's wrong."

I clenched my jaw and concentrated on the road. There was too much to say, and I didn't know how to articulate it yet. I couldn't even get it straight in my own head, and if I tried to explain it out loud, I'd only make a fool of myself. I wasn't up for more humiliation.

When Abbie realised I wasn't going to answer her, she crossed her arms and looked out her window. "Fine."

Seb slept for the entire half-hour drive, so the car was tense and quiet. When we got back to the loft, we unpacked and took Seb upstairs in silence.

By the time I was due to head down to the bar, irritation still churned under my skin, only now I was feeling foolish about it. Two hours of thinking had taken me nowhere other than back to a truth I'd known for years. Abbie didn't think I was capable of being anyone's partner, let alone hers. That was why we'd made the pact in the first place, and that was why she told her family our relationship was barely more than casual. Who'd believe that Will Kidd would settle down? And if they did, who in their right mind would believe that he'd managed to land someone as unattainable as Abbie?

"I'll be back late," I said as I collected my phone and keys and got ready to leave.

"No problem." Abbie looked up from where she was sitting across from Seb in his highchair, spooning pureed pumpkin into his open, eager mouth. "See if you can find a better mood down there, will you? I'm not vibing with this one."

"I know." I dropped a kiss on the top of Seb's head. "See you later, buddy." And because I had to touch her, had to let her know everything would be okay even if right now it didn't feel like it, I scooped my hand around Abbie's cheek and pressed my lips to her forehead. "I'll try."

Saturday nights were always the busiest at The Stop, and tonight was no exception. I was run off my feet, so I didn't even notice Josh and Emily had taken a table for dinner until he was at the bar to order drinks. I retrieved a white wine glass for Em and began to pour before Josh said a word.

"Hey, man. The usual?"

Josh frowned at me and then at three women with cocktails in their hands who were moving away from the bar, and I followed his gaze. Their heads were bowed together until one of them looked back at us, but when she saw we were looking, she shifted her gaze and started whispering.

Josh shook his head. "You know more than half your clientele only come here for the dimples, right?"

"Huh?" I screwed the cap back on the chilled bottle of Emily's pinot grigio and pulled Josh a pale ale from the tap.

Josh tilted his head towards the disappearing women. "They come here for the grin and the flirt and the possibility of being *chosen* when the lights go out."

He didn't know it, but Josh was picking at open wounds I'd been nursing all day. "What the fuck are you on about, Ford?"

Josh's brow furrowed, and the tilt to his mouth pinched downwards. "I was trying to make a joke about the fact you look ready to punch someone. You haven't smiled once since I got here."

I set his drinks on the bar in front of him. "Am I not allowed to have a bad day?"

"Sure." Josh hesitated, and instead of picking up his drinks, he perched on a stool and set his elbows on the bar. "Seriously, Kidd. What's up?"

I dragged a hand through my hair and slung a dish towel over my shoulder, releasing a heavy sigh. I knew better than to be an arsehole to my mates, and at the invitation to talk, some of the pressure eased. "It's been a big week."

Josh blinked with concern. "Is everything all right with Seb?"

Even in my bad mood, I couldn't stop smiling when I thought of my little boy. "Seb's a dream. I mean, I'm fucking tired, and the little guy's got a good set of lungs, but he's awesome." I shrugged and crossed my arms over my chest. "It's hard to explain."

"So, it's the business side of things? The warehouse and the bar and—"

"I mean, that's not helping, but it's under control. Noa's a huge help, and Birdie's more hands-on than I thought she would be. The emails never stop, and I have to be in the warehouse every morning to talk to contractors and accept deliveries, but it's manageable."

"Okay." Josh rolled his lips to hide a grin. "That leaves Ellison."

I shot him a sardonic look before I rolled my eyes. "That leaves Ellison."

"Are things not working out?" Josh chuckled and shook his head. "Be patient. Abbie's heart is always in the right place."

"No, I know. It's not that. Things are working out well, actually." I tucked my chin and glanced up at him. "A little too well, if you get my drift."

"Ah." Josh gave me a shit-eating grin as he stood. A line

167

of customers had started to form at the other end of the bar, and Josh bent his head towards them. "You take care of that, but are you free for a surf in the morning? I can give you my unsolicited advice then."

I huffed out a dry chuckle. "Care to drop it on me now? Five words or less will do. I'm in a rush."

Josh picked up his drinks. "Talk to her."

"That's it?" I flicked my towel at the bar. "Talk to her?"

He shrugged. "If my guess is right, not talking hasn't done you any favours. You're not going to get what you need from Abbie if you make this about sex. You're both too comfortable with physical intimacy and terrified of any other kind."

I blinked at Josh's casual wisdom. "When the fuck did you get so enlightened?"

He laughed. "I've been where you are, and I've learned a few things this past year. If I remember correctly, you were the one who helped me get past my shit and admit that I loved Emily in the first place."

"I never said I loved Abbie."

Josh grinned and shot me a wink. "You didn't have to."

22

WILL

THE LOFT WAS dark and silent when I let myself in around midnight. I did what I always did, which was check on Seb asleep in his bed, then do the same with Abbie upstairs. She was curled up on her side tonight, her long lashes resting on her cheeks, her long blonde hair tumbled about in tangles on the pillow. I collected the baby monitor from the bedside table and paused to get another look at her, releasing a sigh of regret that I'd been such a dick today. None of this was Abbie's fault. It was my own for spending the entire stretch of my twenties living in a way that proved all her assumptions about me true.

I glanced at the grainy image of my son sleeping alone in his room. Will Kidd: reckless, irresponsible, unreliable. And fucking egotistical. Abbie hadn't rejected *me*. She'd rejected the entire concept of monogamy. Of marriage and a family and a traditional life. Only I could take her philosophy and make it personal.

Soaking in the sight of her one last time, I tiptoed downstairs, stripped off my clothes, and squashed my long frame onto the sofa. I punched the pillow once or twice, hoping that would make me feel better enough to rest, but I couldn't get comfortable. I tossed and turned to find a position that wouldn't twist my back before checking the time, but only twenty minutes had passed. I finally started to doze off when I spun to the left and hit the floor, landing on my shoulder heavy enough to send a jolt of pain spearing into my neck.

"Fuck!" I flopped onto my back and stared up at the dark ceiling, too exhausted to even bother pulling myself up onto the couch again.

"Will?"

Abbie's whisper floated down to me from the top of the stairs.

I lifted my head, but the loft was dark enough that all I could make out was a shadow. "Yeah?"

"I heard a bang. Are you all right?"

I dropped my head back to the rug with a dull thud. "I'm fine," I muttered, closing my eyes. "Just fell off the sofa. Again."

There was a long pause before she replied. "You want to come up?"

"You're not sleeping on the couch, Abs."

"No. I mean, we can share the bed. There's room for both of us."

I smiled without humour into the darkness. "What about the line?"

Silence again, then the quiet creak of Abbie's footsteps moving away from the stairs.

I was a fucking arsehole, and no level of fatigue or frustration could excuse it. I lay there a moment, hating myself, before I stood, picked up the baby monitor, and dragged my feet to the stairs. I needed to apologise.

Just as I set my foot on the first stair, Abbie reappeared. I looked up at where she stood on the small landing, wearing my shirt again. Her long legs practically glowed in the ambient light of the loft, and her hair was loose, but this time the sight did nothing to my cock. My heart, however, swelled too large for my chest.

She reached out a hand, and I climbed the next few steps to take it. She led me to the bed, and I had to laugh when I saw it.

"Not so much a line as a wall," she explained with a grin, pointing at the pillows she stacked along the centre of the mattress. "But it should keep us honest for a night."

I let out a quiet laugh, then lifted her hand to my mouth and kissed her palm. "Thanks, Abs."

"Don't mention it."

I set the monitor on the side table, pulled back the covers, and sank onto the bed with relief. It was so fucking good to have the soft, familiar surface underneath me. I turned to burrow into the pillow, and Abbie's coconut scent overwhelmed me. I inhaled deeply, letting the comforting fragrance lull me into the kind of sleep my body desperately needed.

Movement on the other side of the pillow wall indicated Abbie was under the covers now, too. I wished I could reach over and take her hand again. My fingers crept closer to the pillows, but I didn't go any further. My eyes started to drift shut, but a few minutes later, I was still unable to sleep.

"Hey, Ellison?" I whispered.

"Hm?"

"You awake?"

She hummed again in reply.

"I'm sorry about today."

The mattress shifted as Abbie rolled towards me and moved the pillow between our faces out of the way. She tucked her hands underneath her cheek, and her honey-brown eyes glinted in the dull streetlight streaming in through the window.

"You want to talk about it?"

I turned to mirror her posture, my head resting on my bent arm. "I don't know."

"Okay."

We stared into each other's eyes, saying nothing until the words tumbled out.

"I don't like that your parents think I'd date you and let you sleep with other men. I hate that they think I'd be with other women when I was lucky enough to have you."

A crease popped up between her eyebrows. "Will—"

"Is that the kind of boyfriend you think I'd be?"

She closed her mouth with a snap and blinked, but she didn't reply.

"Forget it." I snatched up a pillow and rebuilt the Great Wall of Abigail.

"Don't be like that." Abbie yanked the pillow away again. "You took me by surprise, that's all. I had to think about it for a second."

I rolled onto my back and stuck my hand underneath my head. "There's my answer, I guess."

"If you'd let me *finish*... I had to think about it because I've never given much thought to the type of boyfriend you'd be, just like I've never worried much about the type of girlfriend I'd be. I've always assumed it wasn't in the cards for either of us."

"Okay." I chewed on my bottom lip and stared into the darkness, the words coming easier if I didn't have to look at her. "So, if I asked you to consider it now, what kind of partner do you think I'd be?"

"A provider," she said without hesitating. "Someone a girl can lean on. You'd make her the centre of your world, and she'd never doubt for a day that's where she belonged because you wouldn't want it any other way."

I didn't mind the sound of that, and the corner of my mouth ticked up. "What else?"

"You'd be a little possessive in a good way. And protective. You'd think only good things about her, and you wouldn't let anyone say otherwise."

I spun around again, plumping the pillow under my head. I was starting to like this game. "And?"

"You'd make her laugh." Abbie grinned and shifted another pillow so she could poke my chest. "And you'd make sure she didn't take herself too seriously. You'd call her out on her shit, but you'd respect her even if you didn't always understand her. You'd ask smart questions that made her think about things in different ways. You'd see her potential, and you'd do everything in your power to make her see it, too. You'd move the Earth for her."

I pushed the next question past the catch in my throat, swallowing my apprehension with effort. "Would I be faithful?"

Abbie shook her head against her pillow, and my heart sank. But then she said, "No doubt about it."

Something broke open inside my chest, flooding the darkness with light. "Yeah?"

She chuckled quietly. "Yeah. When I imagine you in a relationship, I can't see you as anything other than a one-woman man."

"You know what?" I ran my hand through my hair and rolled onto my back again to hide my pleasure. "That doesn't sound too bad."

"No?"

"Nope." I exhaled loudly as today's anxiety and frustration seeped away. Fatigue rolled over me, and I let my lids fall close. "Thanks, Ellison."

"Hey!" She shoved at me gently. "What about me?"

I bit back a grin. "What about you?"

"Well, what kind of a partner do you think I'd make?"

I blinked at her and tried to keep my amusement from

showing in my expression. Amusement—and hope. "You think you'd want to be someone's girlfriend one day?"

She shrugged one shoulder and pulled at a loose thread on the corner of her pillow. "I don't know, but if we're playing this game, you have to play fair. If you had to predict what kind of girlfriend I'd make, what would you say?"

"Hm. You'd think about his needs before you thought about your own because that's the kind of woman you are, so you could only be happy with a man who took good care of you."

My eyes fell to where Abbie nibbled on her bottom lip, and my dick twitched.

"You'd defend him to everyone," I added, voice a little husky, "even if you disagreed and even if you thought he was wrong, but when you were alone with him later, you'd let him have it."

Abbie pressed her lips together, her eyes sparkled in the dark, and before I knew it, I was wriggling closer to the pillow wall.

"You'd do little things without him asking or even knowing about it, just to make his life easier. You'd believe in him even when he didn't believe in himself. You'd never stop flirting with him in front of his friends because you'd know how good it made him feel. You'd live in yoga pants because you know they drive him wild. You'd kill him with your cooking"—I laughed when she lightly punched my chest—"but he'd love you enough to eat anything you put in front of him and tell you it was delicious."

175

Abbie licked her lips, then whispered, "Would I be faithful?"

"Always."

Her lips curved in a small smile as her lids grew heavy. "Thanks, Will."

As I brushed hair back from Abbie's face, her breathing shifted into the slow, even rhythm of sleep. My own pulse eased as exhaustion won against my arousal, and I drifted off, thinking about the kind of boyfriend Abbie thought I would be. Her version of me made me feel more like a man than no amount of sex with other women ever could. Her version was exactly who and what I wanted to be.

"Anytime, babe," I murmured into the night. "Anytime."

23

ABBIE

SEB STIRRED BEFORE six a.m., and I switched off the baby monitor and crept downstairs, leaving Will asleep behind me. He always took the morning shift while I did afternoons with the baby but, given that this was the first time in more than a week he'd slept in a real bed, he needed rest more than I did.

Seb's cries cut off when I opened the door and let a little light flood in from the first glimmers of sunrise. When he saw me leaning in to unzip his sleep suit, his face brightened with his beautiful baby grin. This kid was sunshine in a onesie, all smiles and giggles—unless he was hungry, of course, and he'd be ravenous first thing in the morning. Working fast, I changed him and set him in his bouncy chair while I fixed a bottle and pulled a little pot of stewed fruit from the fridge to add to his baby breakfast cereal.

In the early morning quiet, it was impossible not to think about last night's conversation. We had talked about *maybes* and *one days* and *what ifs*, but Seb had changed something in Will—or maybe the little boy had given Will a reason to embrace a different part of himself—and if I'd never let myself acknowledge that side of him before, I had no choice but to face it now. I'd always told myself Will wasn't the kind of man who would commit to one woman, but I didn't believe that anymore. Maybe I never had. Maybe it was a lie I told to protect myself, and it made me wonder if I'd been holding onto a version of me I'd outgrown.

I was snuggled up on the couch, giving Seb his bottle, when Will's footsteps sounded on the stairs. He yawned as he pulled a hand through his hair, mussed from his pillow, and I ran my gaze over his hard, bare chest, the carved planes of his torso, the long lines of his shoulders and arms. He'd put on a pair of shorts, and I was disappointed he wasn't still in the boxer briefs he wore to bed last night. Those left nothing to the imagination.

He came directly to us and leaned over the back of the couch, brushing Seb's head with a light kiss. "Good morning, little guy."

Seb smiled around the bottle's plastic teat, and warm milk leaked out the sides of his mouth.

Will tugged a lock of my hair. "You didn't have to get up this early. I would have woken for him."

I shrugged one shoulder and smiled down at Seb. "You were due for a little more sleep, and I don't mind."

Will straightened and stretched his arms over his head, highlighting the tight, toned lines of his abdomen. "Coffee?"

"Hm?" I dragged my eyes up to his. "Oh, yeah. Thanks."

He tweaked my nose with a smirk, and I rolled my eyes, but what point was there pretending I didn't like looking at him? We'd well and truly crossed that line.

No, not crossed. Moved.

Ha. I didn't know if I believed that anymore. Not after the conversation last night.

"Josh was at the bar last night, and he asked if I wanted to surf this morning." Will's glance darted to the wall clock. "They're probably already out. Think this is a good morning for Seb's first sandcastle?"

"Uh, yes!" Seb drained the last of his milk, and I set the bottle on the table before sitting him upright on my knees. "You hear that, little man? You're going to see the ocean today."

I beamed at Will, who approached me with a smile on his face and a cup of coffee in his outstretched hand. "I'll pack a bag," he said.

Twenty minutes later, we were walking along Main Street towards the beach, Will with his longboard under one arm, an umbrella in its carry case slung over the other shoulder, and towels in his hands, me with Seb in a little swimsuit and hat strapped to my chest plus a bulky bag of supplies on my back. It was a short distance from the loft to where the best swell was rolling in, but as we crossed the road and headed down the sand, the weight I carried grew heavier. Huffing and puffing as the warm sand slipped and squeaked underneath my bare feet, I threw a quick look at Will, burdened as much as I was, and burst out laughing.

He looked at me with a curious expression. "What?"

"Look at us! We're loaded up like pack mules."

Will grinned and adjusted Seb's little cap to get a look at his face underneath the brim. "Seb looks like he's enjoying himself, so I'd say it's worth it."

"I didn't say it wasn't worth it, but I never thought we'd be these people."

Will winked. We angled towards the lap of the sea on the sand until the water was kissing our ankles, then continued north to where we'd spotted the boys in the ocean, bobbing on their boards at the back as they waited for a solid set. I put my head down so the brim of my visor better blocked the bounce of the sun off the sand and powered ahead. The beach was quiet, and we had our pick of places to set up, so I dropped my bags and laid out a couple of towels as Will dug a spot to stick the umbrella. After freeing Seb from his carrier, I sat in the shade with the baby between my knees and pulled out the infant sunscreen, applying it to his nose, cheeks, and legs.

Will set his board upright in the sand with a grunt, then collected Seb from the towel as soon as I'd finished with the SPF. "What do you reckon we introduce the little guy to the ocean before I join those bozos in the back?"

"Yes! Let's do it."

Excitement fluttered in my chest as I jumped to my feet and peeled off my T-shirt and shorts to reveal my bikini underneath. Baby's first saltwater swim was a big moment for parents around here, and I skipped ahead a few years to picture Seb signing up for the Nippers program at the Valentine Bay Surf Life Saving Club. The idea of being there with Will when Seb reached that milestone made my heart space open with pride.

We waded into the water until it was waist deep, with Will holding Seb tucked protectively against his chest the entire time. When the cool water tickled the baby's toes the first time, I tensed as he drew up his legs and snuggled in closer to Will.

"Maybe it's too cold?" Will mumbled, and he dipped a little to sweep Seb's legs into the water.

Seb squirmed, and we exchanged a concerned look.

"Let's try once more," I suggested, "but if he's not feeling it, I'll take him back onto the sand and get him dry."

Will nodded as he curled his large, tanned arms around Seb and sank with him into the water. Will kept his eyes on me, watching for Seb's reaction in my own, and when the baby blew a happy raspberry and smacked an open palm on the surface of the water, I gave Will a grin and two thumbs up. Seb seemed much happier with Will's body heat against him, and he began to kick his legs. I pretended to scold Seb each time he splashed me, which only made his little arms and legs flap harder.

When we were thoroughly wet, and Seb's giggles had morphed into whimpers, Will curled the baby up towards his face and blew a soggy raspberry on his tummy. It was

SAMANTHA LEIGH

a move that usually got us a bout of gutsy giggles, but Seb squirmed and pulled away.

"I think he's had enough," Will announced. "Let's dry him off and get him something to eat."

I tweaked Seb's little toes and dragged my legs through the water in the direction of the sand, Will keeping pace beside me. "I was just about to suggest the same thing."

Under the umbrella, with Seb dry and playing with a squishy plastic toy, Will picked up his board and took a couple steps towards the water before pausing and turning his head. Salty paths of water dripped from his hair down the back of his tan neck, travelling the lines and dips of his muscled back.

"I won't be long," he assured me. "And I'll keep an eye on you. Just stand and wave if you need me to come back in."

I rolled my eyes and lifted Seb's arm to imitate a wave. "Go. Have fun. We're totally fine here."

I watched as he disappeared into the ocean, arms flexing as he set the board on the water and stretched his long body on top of it then paddled with practiced form past the swell.

I sighed and ran my hands over Seb's soft curls. "Your daddy is a beautiful man," I told him. "More beautiful since you came into his life, if you can believe that."

I dug around in the bag of baby stuff and pulled out a container of cooled, steamed broccoli florets, then handed one to Seb. Among the stack of parenting books Will had delivered to the loft a few days ago was one about a feeding strategy called baby-led weaning. Soft broccoli was one of the suggested finger foods for babies Seb's age, and much to both Will's and my shock, he'd loved it at first taste.

Making sure Seb was securely wedged between my thighs and against my stomach, I leaned back on my hands, dropped my head back, and took long breaths of salty air. That expansive feeling across my chest, the one that felt so much like pride for Seb, was still there. It triggered a sense of presence I'd only ever been able to find on the yoga mat, but whenever I closed my practice, that hard-won contentment faded away. I didn't know what was happening exactly, but I was certain it was fleeting, so I took careful notice of the way the sun felt on my upturned face and internalised the vibration of the morning, hoping I could recreate it after it disappeared.

A spray of sand hit my leg, followed by something—or someone—tripping and falling onto my ankles. My eyes flew open, and my arms circled Seb protectively, drawing him closer to me and turning his face from the flying sand. "What the—"

"I'm so sorry!"

A harried-looking woman ducked under the umbrella and picked up the tiny girl who had tumbled over my feet. She brushed the sand from her chin and smoothed the hair back from her eyes as the young girl twisted away and demanded with wordless wails to be put back on the ground.

"It's her first time walking on sand, and she's so independent that she won't let me hold her hand. She has to do *everything* herself." The woman gave me the kind of smile that said *you know how it is.* "Are you all right? She didn't hurt you, did she?"

I flapped my hand and offered the little girl a smile. "No, not at all. She's a cutie."

"Like a hurricane is cute." The woman snorted affectionately and deposited the girl on the sand. She immediately squatted down to get a better look at Seb, who offered her his half-chewed piece of broccoli. I plucked it out of his grip before our little visitor could accept it.

"That's sweet, buddy," I said with a laugh, "but not exactly hygienic."

The woman chuckled and shook her head. "Say hello, Sienna."

The little girl mumbled something nonsensical, and Seb babbled something in return.

I crossed my legs and sat up straighter, shifting Seb to the front of my ankles so he could continue his conversation. "How old is she?" I asked, nodding at Sienna.

"Fifteen months." Sienna's mum dropped to her knees with a tired sigh. "And yours?"

Maybe I should have corrected her and said Seb wasn't really mine, but it would have made the conversation awkward.

"A little more than six months."

"And he's on finger foods already?"

"Uh…" Uncertainty made my heart skip. She made it sound like I'd done something wrong. Had I misunderstood the information in the books? No, I was sure I had it right, and I'd made Will read about it, too, so we could agree on ways to expand Seb's diet. There was no reason to doubt myself about this.

Before I could answer, Seb swiped another floret from the container and brandished it at Sienna.

"Seb." I removed it from his grasp. "Stop trying to feed her."

The woman laughed. "It's okay. If your son can get my daughter to eat something green, I'll pay you to visit us every night at dinnertime."

I smiled politely, distracted by the way my heart pattered at this stranger assuming I was Seb's mother.

"So, whereabouts are you guys from? I know it's not Valentine Bay. This town's not small enough to hide a kid this cute."

The woman accepted my compliment with a smile. "We're just passing through on our way to Sydney."

"Ah." I nodded. "Well, welcome."

"Thanks." She smiled at Seb, who was accepting Sienna's face-pats with equanimity. "He's a cool kid."

I smiled and dropped a kiss on his head. "He is."

"Well, I'm sure you've heard it all before, but if you can get through the first six months, you can get through anything. I don't know about you, but those were the toughest for me."

Unexpectedly, the image of Heather walking down Will's hallway flashed through my head, and I experienced a pulse of sympathy for what she might have gone through raising Seb on her own for the last half a year. I hadn't spared much thought for the woman who abandoned this sweet little boy, and the few I did hadn't been too kind, but something about the way Sienna's mother tried to connect with me over our shared challenges had me revisiting my judgement. It was followed by a stab of guilt that I was lying by omission about raising Seb myself.

"I, uh—"

"Sienna!"

The woman tugged the little girl away from Seb, who was now cluelessly wearing a broccoli floret hat. I laughed as I pulled the vegetables from his curls, and a surge of love bubbled up in me. Seb was just so darn perfect that how and why he came into our lives didn't matter much to me. I wouldn't have changed anything about the way things had turned out.

Sienna was apparently tired of her game, and she stormed out from under the shade of the umbrella. The woman jumped to her feet.

"It was nice talking to you," she said as she walked away. "Have a great day!"

"You, too!" I called as she followed her determined little girl down the beach.

I scooped the broken bits of broccoli into the little box, put it out of Seb's reach, and offered him a sippy cup of water instead. He grinned and swung the cup at me before depositing it in the sand.

"Did you hear that, little man?" I asked. "That lady thought I was your mama. What do you think about that, huh?"

Seb babbled and waved his arms, which I took to mean he didn't think it was a terrible idea.

And neither did I.

I looked out over the water to where the boys were not surfing but sitting out on their boards and shooting the breeze. Will happened to be facing the shore at the same time, and he waved his arm over his head to say hello. I waved back with a weird kind of pressure building in the part of my chest that had been so open and clear a few minutes ago. And if I couldn't articulate to myself what that meant, I was a hack who shouldn't be on the yoga mat.

The kind of peace I experienced that morning only came with alignment. It was the result of knowing I was in the right place at the right time—that I'd found something that fit. That I belonged. I rubbed my sternum and breathed into the discomfort.

All the years I'd spent looking for myself in my practice, and I'd found her while sitting on the beach with a baby in my lap and the man I loved smiling at me from the ocean.

24

WILL

I OPENED THE front door to the Valentine Bay Council Chambers and moved aside so Emily could step out onto the street before me. I'd just wrapped up a one-hour grilling with the tourism committee—Emily had been there in an official capacity as the Bay's tourism photographer and social media consultant, as well as The Stop's marketing manager—and we walked in tense silence until we'd cleared the next corner.

As soon as the council building was out of sight, I drew to a stop and faced Em. She stared up at me with wide green eyes before a smile broke across her face.

I burst into relieved chuckles, then scooped her up and spun her around as her laughter sounded in my ears. Even better, my back barely twinged when I did it, and my shoulder was almost as good as new. I hadn't spent another minute cramped on my crappy sofa since the night Abbie invited me to sleep beside her wall of pillows, which meant I'd had four nights of comfortable rest—and four nights of Abbie sleeping close enough to touch if only I was brave enough to try.

I set Emily down on the pavement and ran a hand through my hair. "Holy shit. That was the most painful hour of my freaking life."

Emily grinned. "You nailed it. I don't think anyone in that room was expecting you to be so prepared."

I shook my head and released a shaky breath. "I wasn't. I came up with half of that stuff on the spot."

"Well, you wouldn't know it. The committee is thrilled with the work you've done, and your commitment to this project has earned their confidence. I'm not just saying that, Will. You were impressive today."

"So were you." Emily waved away the compliment, but I wasn't having it. "Seriously, Jones. You had my back in there and I appreciate it. Thank you."

Her cheeks glowed, and her smile widened. "You're welcome, Kidd."

I checked my watch. Abbie was teaching her first baby yoga class at the church hall, and it was due to finish in half an hour. There was work for me to do at the bar, but I could spare the time it would take to walk the long way back to Main Street, picking up Abbie and Seb on the way.

"Can I walk you home?" I asked Emily, knowing her place was on the route to the hall.

"That's very chivalrous of you," she teased.

I graced her with the smile that set off my dimple, and her lips twitched. "I have an ulterior motive. I'd like to go over a few things from the meeting if you can put up with me for another few minutes."

"Of course. What do you want to talk about?"

"Some of the social media stuff. You know I've always been comfortable leaving The Stop's account in your hands, but I don't quite understand how the poker tournament factors into things."

"Right." Emily shifted her bag on her shoulder as we set off up the street. "The Salty Stop has a much larger following than the official Valentine Bay account, so I intend to schedule a few collaborative posts between the bar and the tourism committee. Does that sound okay?"

"Sure."

She cast me a sideways look. "Some of them will need to be themed around the Valentine's Day Festival." I winced, and she rushed to add, "I'll keep it classy and on-brand for the bar. I promise."

"I suppose it's unavoidable, and I trust you."

Em beamed. "Thank you. I also want to increase the volume of content we're posting on your pages from now until the poker tournament. I'll be at the event taking pictures and managing the live feeds, and I'll do my best to include branding for The Stop and the new brewery in all the content, but you're still the draw card for The Stop, so I'll have a camera in your face more often until this whole thing is over."

My stomach lurched as Emily unwittingly broached

the subject I needed to address. Her observations were an almost exact echo of Josh's comment earlier in the week about how half my business came from women wanting to get into my bed, and I'd snapped at him at the time, but he was right. It had played on my mind for days until I'd made a decision that I knew was right for my personal life but might not be best for my business.

"How do you think my marketing would adapt if I wasn't front and centre on social media anymore?" I asked.

A line popped up between Emily's eyebrows. "What do you mean?"

I grimaced as I tried to articulate my thoughts in a way that made sense. "I mean, I'm not comfortable being the playboy bartender anymore, and I want to take The Stop's social media in a new direction."

Emily pressed her lips together and folded her arms over her chest, frowning at the path as it disappeared under her footsteps. "Did I do something wrong?"

"What? No! God, no. Em, you've made magic on socials, and my business wouldn't be nearly as successful as it is without your genius. I'm so grateful for all your work, but... things change, right? I don't want to be that guy forever. I've been given a chance to make this town see I've got what it takes to be a success. I've got Seb now, and I want him to be proud of his dad. Then there's Abbie—"

"Abbie?" Emily looked stunned. "What about Abbie?"

"Nothing." She looked at me askance and I rolled my lips to stop a grin. "Let's just say living with Abbie has helped me see what kind of man I want to be."

Emily's mouth tipped up at one corner. "Smooth."

"That's my middle name."

We drew to a stop out front of Emily's apartment building. "We can always rethink marketing strategy for The Stop," she assured me. "There are a hundred different angles we can take, but I don't think switching gears right now would be smart. There's too much at stake with the tournament and the festival and announcing the new brewery, and we don't want to confuse the messaging. Are you comfortable keeping things as they are for a while longer—at least until we get past Valentine's Day—then we can put our heads together and devote the time required to be smart about this?"

My shoulders dropped as tension leached from my muscles. If Emily had insisted Will Kidd stay "open for business" to keep The Stop from going under, I'd have had to insist we find another way, even if it meant taking a hit to my income. My father had always put a quick buck before his family, was always chasing another dream or running another con and promising it would be the last time, but I didn't want to be that kind of man. Seb needed me to be more than that, and so did I.

I gave Emily a hard hug. "Two more weeks? I can do that. Thanks for understanding."

My step was lighter on my way to surprise Abbie at her class. Things had been good between us. Like really good. We hadn't come right out and talked about us, but we'd settled into a routine that twelve months ago would have sent us both begging for our next hook-ups. We hadn't said as much out loud, but I'd started to enjoy the domesticity of our life at the loft with Seb, and I believed Abbie did, too.

There might still be a line of pillows separating the two of us at night, but the real boundaries between us had shifted. And the way Abbie looked at me when I handed her a coffee before she had to ask, or I cuddled with Seb in the minutes before bedtime, wasn't the same as the way she looked at me before. It was softer and more open, and it made me hope that the line she insisted we keep between us might not be there for much longer.

25

WILL

———

I LET MYSELF into the old hall behind the church at ten minutes to the hour, not knowing what to expect inside. The small foyer, with its rickety timber table piled with pamphlets and magazines, was empty, but a door stood ajar at the opposite end, and meditative music played on the other side of it. A baby squealed, then someone laughed, and I hesitated. I was curious enough to want to peek, but the proper thing to do would be to wait outside for the class to finish. I'd taken two steps back when Abbie's voice reached my ears, and before I knew it, I was standing at the open door and looking in.

There were about eight women on rubber mats arranged around the room, each one with a baby, though they were all different ages. Most were at least as small as Seb, some younger. One or two were old enough to crawl away the moment their mothers moved into a different yoga position. One kid made a game of it, darting away at every chance, only for his mother to latch onto an ankle and slide him back. The purity of his belly laughs made me smile.

And there, at the far end of the room, stretched out on her back with Seb draped lazily along her torso, was Abbie. Her eyes were closed, and she had her arms wrapped around the baby, one palm moving up and down his back in soothing sweeps. They looked so at ease together that I found it hard to swallow, but I couldn't look away, so I crossed my arms over my chest and leaned against the door frame to watch.

"Okay, everyone." Abbie's voice was smooth and melodic as she opened her eyes to give Seb a grin, shifting him to a seated position on her hips and bending her knees. "Let's move into bridge pose with the baby on your pelvis. Press into the soles of your feet and lift your hips, holding onto baby nice and tight to keep him safe."

With her grip on my son, Abbie raised her hips and relaxed down again, smiling and murmuring to Seb the entire time. She completed a few more reps, directing the class to do the same in that pretty, calming voice she never used around me before moving into another position. This one set Seb stomach down along her raised shins, "working the core muscles", as Abbie explained to her students. They held this position for a short spell, Abbie swaying her legs forwards and back a little after noticing that Seb seemed to enjoy it. Abbie's eyes never left his, not for a second, and she never stopped smiling. In fact, she *glowed*.

The lump in my throat wouldn't go away, only now I had a weird catch behind my ribs, too, making it hard to take a full breath. I pushed away from the doorjamb and rubbed my open palm over my chest.

I didn't get many opportunities to watch Abbie with Seb, and never without her being aware of my presence. We'd fallen into a routine where we tag-teamed the baby duties, which meant when Abbie was with Seb, I was working and vice-versa. Other times, the three of us were all together, or Seb was sleeping. I trusted Abbie with my life, and I'd seen enough to know Seb was always safe in her care, but I'd been too distracted and too exhausted to give any thought to whether the two of them had formed any kind of bond. I'd been too busy worrying about the kind of parent *I* needed to be that it didn't occur to me that with all the time they spent together, these two would develop a closeness, too. On some level, I probably didn't think about it because Abbie had never been open to children in general, but watching them now, I realised my mistake.

Abbie loved Seb. Anyone watching them now would see that as clear as day, and Abbie loving my son only made me love her more.

Abbie instructed the class to stretch out on their mats and settle their babies on their chests, and as they moved into a deep breathing exercise, I backed away from the door and sank into one of the chairs lining the far wall. I needed deep breathing exercises, and by the time the class was over and the last student had filed past me, my head was clearer. But something had shifted on a cellular level, and there was no undoing it now.

Abbie walked through the door pushing the pram, her rolled-up yoga mat tucked under one arm, and when her eyes fell on me, her face lit up in a way that decimated me. "Hey, you. I thought we were meeting you at the loft."

Her eyes traced my face, and whatever she saw there made her expression fall. "Oh, no. The meeting was awful, wasn't it? Shit. I'm so sorry, Will, but I'm sure we can figure out a way to get those stubborn old bastards off your back." She grimaced and shifted her yoga mat. "I don't know how, but—"

"No." I stood up and took a step closer, running my hand over the top of Seb's soft curls as I passed him on my way to Abbie on the other side of the pram. "The meeting was fine. Better than fine. They're really happy with the way things are going."

"Oh." Her forehead furrowed with puzzlement. "Well, good. So, you came down here to check out the class?" The line between her brows deepened, and she nibbled her lip before asking, "What did you think?"

I took another step towards her. "I only caught the last few minutes, but you looked great up there."

Her shoulders dropped, and she grinned. "Of course we did." She reached down to pick up Seb's hand and rubbed the back of it with her thumb. "Did you hear that, Seb? Daddy came all the way down here to see you in your first yoga class."

Abbie glanced at me from underneath her lashes, her pink lips twitching because she knew what the word

Daddy in her mouth did to me, but I wasn't playing games anymore.

In three long, measured steps, I closed the distance between us and plucked the yoga mat from her arm, setting it against the wall.

She looked once at the mat, then at me. "What's going on?"

Slowly because I wanted to remember this, gently because I wanted her to know I meant it, I cradled Abbie's head in my hands, took one more step to remove the final bit of distance between us, and kissed her.

I felt her intake of breath as her muscles tensed, but I wouldn't let myself pull away. Nerves couldn't get the better of me now. I moved my mouth over hers, capturing her top lip first, then the bottom. Beneath my fingers, her jaw began to move, and triumph flamed in my blood.

Hesitantly at first, she met my nips and sweeps with the gentle, nervous touch of her soft lips. I brushed my mouth back and forth, breathing her in as much as I tasted her, then went back to kissing her, greeting the warm, wet tip of her tongue with mine when she offered it to me. Her hands skated up over my hips and sides, to my shoulders and down my arms, where she circled my wrists and didn't let go. The warmth of her skin felt like coming home, and we melted into the first kiss we were always meant to have.

Abbie drew back to rest her forehead on mine and closed her eyes. She clung to my forearms like I was her lifeline, and the corner of her mouth lifted a little, but when a single tear leaked onto her cheek, fear stirred in my chest.

I'd fucked it up.

"Hey." I brushed the lone tear off her cheek with a sweep of my thumb and tilted my head to tickle the tip of her nose with mine. "Was it that bad?"

She huffed out a laugh. "No. It was… perfect. It was the kind of kiss people write books about."

I inhaled deeply, then released a breath that took my apprehension with it. "But?"

Abbie shook her head with small, fast movements. "This doesn't only move the line, Will. It—"

"Erases it?"

We stood pressed together at the forehead, the chest, the hip, the toes, my hands cupping her face. She opened her eyes and gazed up at me, bit her lip, and nodded.

I was overcome with a rush of emotion for this woman—for the girl she used to be, for the person she was now, and for the way we'd grown up together not only over the years but in the last couple of weeks—and I was done tiptoeing along a fucking line that neither of us wanted. We were stuck because Abbie had been the one to draw it, and she didn't know how to take it away, but I was going to make that decision now—for both of us.

"Good," I replied, and her eyes widened. "I don't want any more lines between us. I'm done pretending."

Abbie pressed her eyelids closed, and her fingers tightened around my wrists. Her voice was barely audible as she asked, "Pretending what?"

"That I don't love you."

Her eyes flew open so wide it showed the whites all around her honey-brown irises, and I could almost feel the panic coming off her in waves—or maybe that was the vibration of my own heart beating at a hundred miles a minute. We were so close, and I couldn't screw it up now.

"Will—"

"Stop."

I drew back so I could duck my head and hold her gaze. Her throat bobbed with an uneasy swallow, but she nodded in small motions that told me she understood what I was trying to do here, and her grip on my forearms tightened.

"I know you're scared," I said, "and I get it. I'm freaking terrified, but I want to do this anyway. I want to give us a shot." I shifted my hand to drag a thumb over her bottom lip, watching it pull at her skin as if I could shape the words I needed to hear. "Tell me you feel the same."

Abbie inhaled deeply, and her eyes grew glassy. My heart, which had been ready to beat right out of my chest a moment ago, suddenly stopped altogether. The whole world came to a standstill as my question sat between us.

When her answer came, it was delivered in a shaky whisper. "I do."

The pulse of my blood beneath her fingertips sputtered as I asked, "You love me?"

Her mouth tipped up on one side. "I love you."

My heart took off again, and an exhilarated laugh bubbled up from deep inside my chest. Abbie grinned up at me with pink cheeks before she slid her hands into my hair and dragged my mouth back to hers.

This kiss was nothing like the first—desperate instead of patient, demanding instead of sweet. I wrapped my arms around her waist as she sagged against me, and I claimed her the way I'd always wanted to. Years of desire exploded like fireworks between us, all oxygen evaporating as I breathed in nothing but the coconut scent of her skin. Opening her lips with mine, I sought the stroke of her tongue with insistent sweeps of my own, and when her hands clutched at my shirt hard enough to pinch my skin and a needy whimper vibrated in the back of her throat, my dick thickened fast. I groaned and kissed her harder.

"Will," she muttered, turning her head. I rained open-mouthed kisses along her jaw, down her neck, and across her collarbone. Her fingers dug into my shoulders, and with a reluctant moan, she pushed me away. "Not here."

Not here? I'd forgotten where *here* was. The church hall foyer with my baby boy tucked into his pram just a few steps away.

Reason brought me crashing back to Earth. I stepped back and ran a hand through my hair, chest heaving as I caught my breath. "Right. Not here." Stepping to the side, I glanced into the pram to make sure Seb was okay, and his little face turned up, totally unaware his old man was pawing a woman just out of sight. "Not here. Not now."

Abbie cleared her throat and picked up her mat, which I promptly took and slung over my shoulder before scooting ahead of her to hold open the door. She set her hands on the pram and wheeled Seb through, her chest stained with mottled pink and obviously avoiding looking at me, so as she passed, I lowered my head and whispered in her ear, "But soon."

26

ABBIE

———————

WILL AND I tried to keep things normal on the way home, but I hadn't felt butterflies like this since I was a kid. We talked about Seb and the bar, and I steered the conversation away from anything that touched on the state of my studio and apartment in too much detail. In every pocket of silence, Will gave me a sidelong look and knowing smirk that made my stomach flip. It was almost like we were teenagers again, and as eager as I was to take our relationship to the next level—the memory of his husky voice whispering "but soon" in my ear gave me goosebumps all over—I wasn't against enjoying the extended tease. I'd missed out on this when I was growing up. Flirting with boys without any intention of going all the way. There'd been a stretch of time when "no" hadn't been part of my vocabulary, and all the "yesses" made every encounter less special. I'd given up on ever feeling butterflies again after the one and only time I believed in them. That was when the guy made me feel worthy, then told everyone how quick I'd been to give it up for him.

We arrived back at the loft just as Will was due to open The Stop, so after a quick shower and change—and another kiss that had me struggling to stand—he was out the door, and I finally had the space I needed to take a full breath and get my head on straight.

That morning had been... unexpected. Our first real kiss. Our declarations. The way Will claimed me, but not in a sexual way—or at least, not *only*. He knew I was scared, but he was too, and in some weird way, that made this whole thing less terrifying. Will wanted us to take a chance on this *together*. That morning's kiss opened my chest and dissolved the apprehension I wore wrapped around my ribcage. With three little words, that niggling feeling that something wasn't right evaporated like it never existed.

Plus, I could now confirm that Will was an excellent kisser. Like, knees-buckling, sigh-inducing, panty-ruining *excellent*. And thank God, because no matter how good a man was with his penis, I'd never survive if he didn't know what to do with his mouth.

My afternoon with Seb passed like any other, but Will had arranged for us to have an early dinner with Lori and Ray at The Stop that night, so instead of making Seb's dinner using the pots of vegetables in the freezer, I dressed him in something cute and made my way down from the loft.

Slipping into the bar using the private side entrance, I was surprised to see my parents sharing a table with Lori and Ray in the middle of the room. I paused in the doorway with Seb on my hip and watched the foursome for a moment. Though they'd always been friendly, Lori was more than fifteen years younger than Mama. Ray was closer to ten years younger than Dad. Yet they were drinking and laughing together, and it warmed my heart to see my parents so relaxed and happy.

While they were deep in conversation, I took the opportunity to skirt the edge of the room and sidle up to the bar to let Will know I'd arrived. It was a little busier than might be expected for the middle of the week, but that was a good thing. Will had created a sought-after venue, and as his social media profile climbed, so did his profit margin. He didn't see me straightaway, so I hung back to appreciate my man at work. He was a natural charmer, and though I'd never say so out loud, Will, in his element, reminded me so much of his father. He'd had the dimples, too, the roguish charisma that made his social feeds jump off the screen and drew people to him like moths to a boyish flame. People like the trio of attractive women hanging over the bar, trying to get his attention right that minute.

A flare of jealousy burned hot and fast in my stomach, and the muscles in my jaw started to ache as I watched the girls flirt outrageously. I was somewhat soothed by the sight of Will on his best behaviour, but even with his dimple dialled down to one, Will Kidd was more than capable of sexual mass destruction.

One of the girls sensed my eyes, and her smile slipped as she glanced my way. Will followed her gaze, and when his eyes landed on me, I was the one who got his megawatt grin. As the pretty young things picked up their cocktails and walked away from the bar, disappointed that they hadn't got what they really wanted from the man they'd come all this way to see, I couldn't stop the juvenile surge of triumph knowing Will was now mine.

"Hey, you two." Will dropped his towel on the bar and met me on the other side, holding out his hands for Seb. The baby practically threw himself out of my arms, and Will chuckled as I handed Seb over.

Without something to hold, I stood there awkwardly, and a flutter of nerves had me licking my lips. Was I supposed to kiss him hello or put an arm around him? Did I give him space while he worked and maintain a professional distance? I tried to think about how my friends behaved around their boyfriends, but they were all so comfortable with the public displays of affection that I couldn't recall how things had been in the early days of their relationships.

"You're going to chew through that bottom lip if you're not careful," Will commented. "What's the matter?"

I released my lip from between my teeth. "I'm wondering what a good girlfriend would do when she greets her sexy bartender boyfriend at work."

"Ah." Will's blue eyes sparkled as he leaned in a little, but then his brows drew down and he straightened, and his expression grew sheepish. "That's something I wanted to talk to you about. I spoke to Emily this morning about The Stop's social media strategy, and I told her I was done with the playboy reputation."

Surprise and pleasure warmed me from the inside, and I rocked forwards on my toes. "Really? Like, you did this before you picked up Seb and me from the yoga class?"

His mouth tilted up on one side, but then he rubbed the back of his neck. "Yeah. And although she's totally on board, she suggested that it might be smarter to wait until after we've wrapped up the tournament and announced the launch of my new brewery. There's too much going on right now to throw another announcement into the mix."

"Oh." I dropped back onto my heels and crossed my arms, eyes falling to the floor to hide my disappointment. "That makes sense, I guess, and Emily knows what she's talking about." I lifted my chin and tried to grin. "But don't think I won't be having a quiet word with her later about this."

Seb squirmed. Will shifted him to the other arm, but his eyes remained on mine, and they were alight with sincerity. "I'm done with the flirting, Ellison. I promise you that. I'm done with the casual sex. I'm done with everything that made Will Kidd the most reliable lay in Valentine Bay. I want to tell our friends and family about us straightaway, and I can't wait to make you mine in every way." Arousal leaped in his gaze, and I audibly swallowed. "But we might need to wait a little while longer to start mauling each other over the bar."

A vision of Will taking me on the long timber counter after everyone had gone home flashed through my mind, and I nodded distractedly as I played the picture through to its delicious climax.

I crossed my legs and squeezed my thighs, and Will gave me a knowing smirk. Why should I care what the world knew—or didn't know—about me? What mattered now was Will's success and getting him through the biggest month of his career—of his life. If I needed to keep my hands and lips off him in public for a couple of weeks, I was prepared to do that. We could make up for it when the doors were closed.

Forget the days of foreplay and the extended tease. I wasn't an inexperienced teen anymore but a grown woman with needs.

"But public mauling will be on the menu eventually?" I teased.

"Hell, yes. After the year we've spent watching our friends practically mating in the streets, we've got some payback to take care of."

I pretended to groan, still distracted by the throb between my legs. "You are *so* right. Those girls have tortured me with their satisfied glows for long enough. It's past time to give them a taste of their own medicine."

Will wriggled his eyebrows. "I'll happily help you write a prescription."

"When?" I blurted out.

"Desperation looks good on you, Ellison."

I shoved his shoulder as I rolled my eyes, but my heart

beat erratically, and I had to take a deep breath before starting again.

"What I mean is, when are we going to find time for mauling, public or otherwise." I nodded at Seb in his arms. "Between this little guy, my classes, your hours behind the bar and working in the warehouse, we don't have a lot of time. And Will, I don't want our first time to be…"

Will nodded, eyes sweeping up and down my body in a way that made goosebumps spring up as though he'd brushed his fingers over me and not just his gaze.

"It won't be rushed," he promised. "And it won't be bad."

I cocked a suggestive eyebrow. "Oh, I know it won't be bad."

Will shook his head with a chuckle. "You're right. I don't know why I said that." His mirth faded, and he dipped his head to breathe in Seb's baby scent. "But you have a point. As much as I love this little guy, he's not going to make it easy. But don't worry. I'll figure something out."

"So…" I grimaced. "It might still be a while?"

"Afraid so. But I promise you this…" Will leaned in until his lips brushed the shell of my ear. "I'm worth the wait."

His hot breath over my skin made me shiver. "Do you think the ego trip works on me, Kidd?"

He pulled back and smirked. "I know it does."

I tried to smile, but I was a little off balance with the way my nerves continued to flicker in my middle. I wasn't scared of sex, and I certainly wasn't scared of sex with Will. Was I?

"Thank you," I murmured.

Will gave me a puzzled look. "For what?"

"For not letting things get awkward between us."

Will winked. "Never going to happen. So, Stephanie will be here to man the bar for me any minute. Do you want to take this rugrat over to the table, and I'll join you soon?"

I glanced over at our parents, who had not only spotted us but were staring across the room with no attempt to conceal their impatience—or their curiosity.

I sighed. "Fine, but do *not* leave me alone for longer than I need to be, okay? I have a feeling there'll be a few questions tonight."

"And I'm happy to answer all of them."

"For someone who's never been a boyfriend before, you're pretty good at it, you know?"

Will's smile took on that arrogant tilt that made me want to rip his pants off and knock the edge off his ego all at the same time.

"I take it back," I quipped. "There's still work to do."

His eyes sparkled with amusement as he gave Seb a kiss on his forehead, and I clapped my hands in Seb's direction to coax him away from his dad. Unexpectedly, because he'd never done it before, Seb threw himself at me the same way he'd lurched towards Will, and I caught him with surprise. An overwhelming surge of adoration made swallowing difficult. My eyes darted to Will's, and there was no missing the way they shone with satisfaction.

27

WILL

———

"I COULDN'T EAT another bite." Ray stretched back in his chair and patted his flat stomach appreciatively. "Noa outdid himself tonight."

Mum gave Ray an affectionate look, and not for the first time, I offered up thanks that she'd found a way to get over my dad and take a chance on someone else. I liked Ray. He was my mother's total opposite—sensible where she was sensitive, grounded where she was flighty, realistic where she was a dreamer. He'd come on the scene when I was well into my twenties, so he'd never tried to take a father-figure role in my life, but I never wanted that anyway. All I cared about was my mother having someone in her life who loved her enough to stay.

I wiped my mouth with the napkin on my lap and dropped it onto my empty plate. Noa made incredible food, and I'd insisted everyone order what they wanted on the house. Across the table, Mr Ellison finished off his third helping of double chocolate mud cake with an indulgent moan. Abbie shook her head with mock embarrassment, and when I tweaked her knee under the table, she shot me a look that said, *what are you doing?* All I could do was grin, but instead of moving away, I shifted my hand northwards and rested it on the inside of her thigh. Abbie rolled her eyes a little, but she crossed her legs to trap me there.

The whole dinner had been a good time. I'd joined not long after Steph arrived to relieve me at the bar, taking the seat next to Abbie's and pulling it in extra close. Everyone noticed my move, as well as the way Abbie widened her eyes at me, and you could almost see the pain it caused our mothers not to ask what it all meant. I had every intention of letting everyone at the table know that Abbie was finally my girl but dragging it out for an hour or so was fuck loads of fun.

"This cake is delicious," Arthur commented, setting down his fork. "Perhaps I could get the recipe?"

I shook my head and put on a regretful face, taking care not to move too much. It was inching towards Seb's bedtime, and he was curled up in my arm, sucking on the ear of his favourite stuffed bunny as his eyes drifted closed. The warmth of his little body against my chest and the subtle smell of him on my shirt were the kinds of comforts I wondered how I'd gone so long without. "Nice try, Mr Ellison. Noa's food is a trade secret. I'd be out of business if people could make this stuff at home."

Arthur gazed wistfully at his empty plate. "I suppose you're right."

"But I can get him to box up a couple extra slices for you to take home if you like?"

He brightened like he'd never heard a better offer, and Nancy *tsked*. "You don't need all that sugar, Arthur."

"But I'll take it," he said with a grin.

"So," Mum said after Noa's server had cleared our dishes away, "we've waited all night for one of you to tell us what's going on under the table there, and nothing. William, sweetheart—you're forcing me to make this awkward."

She exchanged a loaded look with Nancy, and at the smug looks on both their faces, it was clear they had it all figured out. It wasn't hard. If I'd sat any closer to Abbie tonight, I'd be in her lap. And there was a time or two that she'd brushed my hand and hadn't tried to hide it. She'd eaten off my plate, too, now that I thought about it, although we had done that in the past.

I was beyond ready to lock this in, but I wanted to give Abbie one final out. I shot her a questioning look that she read like a book. *Can I tell them?*

She lifted one shoulder, a secretive half-smile on her mouth. *Better you than me.*

I winked at her, making her lips twitch. "Abbie and I would like you to know that we've made things official. We're now exclusive." I met Nancy's excited eyes, wishing I could express that as momentous as this felt for her, it was nothing to the way things were clicking into place for me. I extracted my hand from between Abbie's legs, laced my fingers through hers, and gave it a squeeze. She returned it, holding on tight and not letting go. "Seriously."

213

"Oh!" Mrs Ellison clapped her hands together under her chin, tears swimming in her eyes. "I'm so happy. I knew this would happen. I knew it!"

"Calm down, Mama," Abbie muttered, but spots of pleasure had sprung up in her cheeks.

Mr Ellison reached over the table, and I had to drop Abbie's grip to shake his hand. Then he wrapped an arm around Abbie's shoulders and dropped a kiss on her temple.

"I'm happy for you, Pumpkin," he said.

"Thanks, Dad."

Mum stood to give me a hug, which I returned as best I could without disturbing Seb. Nancy clung on for a lot longer than my own mother, and I let her, and then Ray tried to get his arms around Abbie and me both. When the congratulations were done, I scanned the room quickly to see if anyone had noticed, but we hadn't made enough of a fuss to cause a scene.

By the time I sat down again, Mum and Nancy had their heads together on the other side of the table, and when Abbie, Arthur, and Ray were seated too, our mothers straightened in their chairs and stared ahead blankly—the giveaway look of two women who were keeping a secret.

I was in too good a mood to be suspicious, and my amused glance bounced between them. "What's going on? You're up to something."

In my arms, Seb whimpered, waking a little and twisting as he searched for a more comfortable position. I juggled him into a new position as Abbie reached over and stroked his back, and he quietened down with a line between his brows.

"It's late," Abbie commented. "Maybe we should take him upstairs and put him to bed."

I was halfway to my feet, all curiosity forgotten, when Nancy threw up a hand. "Wait!"

I frowned and sat back down as Mum set her hand over Mrs Ellison's and carefully settled it in her lap, keeping a hold on it as she said, "What Nancy means to say is, I forgot to tell you, ah, William, that the room for Seb at my place is all set up. Ray finished putting all the furniture together yesterday, didn't you, honey?"

"Sure did, and I can assure you, we spared no expense. Seb's got a whole new wardrobe over there. Toys. Books. A changing table that turns into a little tub for bathing. And though I first thought Lori went a little over the top with the decorating, even I have to admit that it all came together like a dream in the end. That room belongs in a magazine somewhere."

Mum beamed at Ray over Nancy's grey head. "Thank you, darling."

I didn't see what was so important about this news that couldn't have waited until I wasn't itching to get Seb into bed. And I'd only hired Steph for a three-hour shift, but if I moved now, I could put him into bed myself tonight, and I rarely got the chance to do that. After *that*, there might even be enough time to give Abbie another kiss she'd be thinking about all night.

I made a mental note to call Dylan soon and confirm

that not only did I know what I was doing but that I'd also successfully rewritten my and Abbie's embarrassing first kiss. He'd appreciate the update.

"Uh, that's great, Mum," I said, standing again. "I'll try to come by later in the week to check it out."

"Wait!" Nancy cried again.

Mum's face winced with the effort of keeping the other woman's hand in her lap.

I glanced at Seb. His eyes remained closed, but there was still that little frown on his face, so I dropped back into the seat, impatient to move but also a little entertained by whatever was going on here. I'd never known Nancy to be so on edge. "Yes?"

"Well, you see," Mum went on, "I was thinking that tonight might be a good night for Seb to have his first sleepover." She nodded at the baby. "He's already had his dinner, and it's late. I could take him home—I have a car seat and everything—bathe him and give him his bottle, then put him to bed."

Her offer stirred up a flurry of emotions I wasn't prepared to feel. "I don't know..."

Give my son to my mother for one night? He'd be safe and probably have a great time, and he'd only be a few blocks away, but a few blocks wasn't as close as the next room. I was determined to be a good father, and good fathers didn't hand over their babies for no good reason, did they? I pressed my lips to Seb's soft curls, wondering how I could feel so resistant and so desperate at the same time. As much as I tried not to look directly at her because this was my decision to make, my eyes strayed over to Abbie, and she appeared as conflicted as I felt.

Fuck. How shitty of a parent would I be to take Mum up on her offer... then drag Abbie upstairs and fuck her into tomorrow?

Flip side of that coin—how lousy of a boyfriend would I be if I *didn't*?

Mum's expression took on a pleading look. "I've missed my grandson, and I know that sounds silly, but I want to spend more time with him. Get to know him a little better. Give Seb a chance to get to know me."

Nancy nudged Mum with a short, sharp elbow, and Mum closed her eyes to take a deep breath before she focussed on me again. "And the last few weeks have been challenging for everyone. You two must be exhausted. You need time to yourselves, to rest and, uh...

"Get to know each other better," Nancy offered.

"*Mum!*" Abbie shifted uncomfortably as she glanced at her father.

So did I, my heart beating so hard it hurt because it wasn't hard to read between the lines, and the message clearly said, "We're giving you two time alone to make this *really* official." But Arthur had tactfully picked up a menu and was reading it with great concentration, so I averted my gaze and took his attitude to mean it was smarter to play dumb.

"Oh my God," Abbie muttered beside me, raising her fingers to her forehead and turning her head so she could lower her voice. "This is the most blatant fix-up in the history of parental interference ever."

"What?" Mum assumed an offended posture. "Are you telling me I can't take care of a baby for one night? It's not even twenty-four hours. I can bring him home after breakfast unless you'd like to visit in the morning, Nancy? We could put him in the stroller and take him to the park."

"You bought a stroller too?" I asked in surprise. At the same time, Nancy replied, "Oh yes, I'd love to."

Jesus. I wished this didn't feel so much like an ambush. It was hard to think with five pairs of eyes staring at me. But I didn't have time to consider this with a cool head, and all I could do was look for an answer in Abbie's eyes. She met my expression with raised palms as if to say *the decision is yours*, but I knew her better than that, and the message in her gaze screamed, "Hand that baby over now, and let's go do bad things in the dark."

Okay. Maybe I was projecting.

Fifteen minutes later, I was securing Seb in the back of Mum's car and handing over the baby bag with a long list of instructions that went some way to settling my unease.

"Bath, bottle, and straight to bed," I told her. "He might wake anytime between midnight and two a.m., but then he should sleep until six. There's a pot of applesauce in the bag, and he'll have that for breakfast after his formula. Do you have a highchair?" I frowned, wanting a reason to call this whole thing off just as badly as I wanted it to go off without a hitch. "Look, maybe this is a bad idea."

"We have a highchair." Mum reached up and set her hands on my shoulders, squeezing them before she rose on her toes to press a kiss on my cheek. "It's normal to be nervous. It's what makes you a good parent, and I hate to break it to you, but it never gets easier. Never."

It was a simple thing to say, but the idea that my anxiety was proof that I might actually be doing a good job eased the tension across my chest. Mum must have felt my muscles loosen because she gave me a pleased grin and dropped her hands.

"Seb will be fine," she said. "More than fine. He's going to have a great time with his grandma."

"Hm." I rolled my lips against a smile. "You'll call if there's a problem? I don't care how late it is. I'll come right over and get him."

"I'll call."

"You promise?"

"I promise."

Abbie stood with me on the lamp-lit street out front of The Stop as we watched Mum pull her car away from the kerb. I waved as they disappeared, and Abbie lifted my hand. Her thumb moved in tight circles over my skin.

"You sure you're okay with this?" she asked.

I had to think about it to make sure my answer was an honest one. "Yeah. I want what's best for Seb, and that means family. That kid deserves all the love in the world, and I like the idea of Seb and Mum having a close relationship. He's lucky to have a grandmother like her."

"Agreed. Lori's a special woman."

The heat of Abbie's body suddenly registered against my skin, and the possibility of an entire night alone with her stretched out before me. I let my eyes roam over her face, and my skin prickled with heat as she caught her bottom lip between her teeth.

"What do you say I ask Steph to work the rest of my shift tonight?" I whispered.

"What do I say?" she murmured, eyes dark and distant as she was distracted by thoughts of her own.

I fought a smile as I moved close enough for her nipples to brush against my chest. "Mm-hm. What do you say?"

Her gaze dropped to my mouth, and I hoped to God she was imagining what I might have in store for her over the next twelve hours because nothing she could come up with would ever compare. "I say yes."

28

ABBIE

WILL ASKED ME to wait for him while he squared things away with Steph, but it was only a few minutes before he met me at the side door that led into the private hallway outside the bar, where the staircase took us straight up to the loft. He pulled me through and closed the door, and suddenly, we were alone, but just as those pesky nerves started swirling again, he paused and retrieved his phone from his pocket.

"One moment, okay?" he murmured.

I nodded, curious and a little anxious as he fired off a text, then frowned at the screen until a telltale *ping* announced a reply.

He turned the phone to show me the screen, and my heart expanded at the picture of Lori holding Seb in his new bedroom. "He looks happy," I observed with relief.

Will tucked his phone into his back pocket. "He does— and safe. So now I can do this."

I stumbled back as Will slid one hand into my hair and pinned me against the wall. The hard heat of his body made contact with my thighs, my hips, and my breasts, and I barely had time to lift my chin before he'd cupped my face and captured my lips with his.

The kiss was insistent, and I opened my mouth at the swipe of his tongue, meeting him stroke for stroke. Arousal coiled in my core, and a moan escaped my throat as I ran my hands over his back and down to his arse, cupping and yanking him against me while I rolled my hips against the thick length between us.

Will groaned and pulled back, breathing hard, and his hand became a fist in my hair. "I'm so close to fucking you against this wall, but that's not how our first time is going to go."

I closed my eyes and nodded. As loudly as my body screamed to be filled up by him, neither of us wanted to look back on this night and remember a quickie in a barely private hallway. He dropped his forehead to mine, and when our breathing had slowed, he kissed the tip of my nose, took my hand, and led me upstairs.

As we made the short walk to his front door, I had to mentally pinch myself. I was kissing Will. I was about to have sex with him. Things had shifted between us after the incident in the bathroom, but we hadn't gone far enough then that there was no coming back from it. Sex, on the other hand...

Sharing my body never came with such significance before, and although my friendship with Will could and would survive anything—including sex—it was my heart on the line here. Was I ready? The swirling nerves and desperate throb between my legs aside, the answer was yes. So much, yes.

Will fumbled with his keys when he tried to unlock the door, and his exasperated grunt was equal parts adorable and reassuring. He was nervous, too. Once we were inside, he threw his keys onto the dining table, pulled out his phone and left it there too, then took my bag from me, looping it onto the coat rack near the door. Something that wasn't there before hung in the air between us and we stood in the almost dark, staring at each other. My heart raced, and so many thoughts ran through my head that I stopped trying to separate one from the other. I didn't have to think right then. I just had to be.

Moving slowly, Will walked over and picked up my hand. Setting a finger under my chin, he tilted my head back and touched his lips to mine. The reverent brush of his mouth made everything tingle, and I melted into him, arching my back as he bent over me, letting him hold me up as my muscles turned to water.

When he pulled away, I let my eyes float open, and he was staring down at me with a serious expression. "I want you to know something," he murmured.

Nothing in me was afraid of what would come next. "Okay."

"I've never had sex with someone I loved before," Will confessed.

I blinked against the sting in my eyes as his words sank into me like saltwater into sand. I loved that he was being so honest, even though it clearly cost him something to do so.

Will collected my other hand in his and twisted his fingers through mine as if he thought I was going to run away, but that was never going to happen.

"That makes me sound like an arsehole, I know, and I wasn't sure if it was a good idea to tell you, but I needed to say it before we... Look, tonight is the first time I'll be with someone I love, and..." Will tossed his head and huffed out a dry laugh. "I'm nervous, Ellison. I know that sounds stupid, but I am."

My lips curved in a small, relieved smile, and the butterflies darting around in my middle got faster. "I'm nervous, too."

Will cocked an eyebrow, and one corner of his mouth lifted. "Yeah?"

"Yeah. This is *you*, Will. This is *us*." I squinted up at him with a crooked smirk, wanting nothing more than to put him at ease. "We both know I'm going to be good at this, but the pressure's really on for you to perform tonight."

His smile widened, and his dimple danced, and I inhaled sharply as he tugged on my hands, pulling me against him so his hard cock pressed into my stomach. "That's not what I meant, and you know it."

I swallowed and got serious, giving his fingers a hard squeeze. It was my turn to return his trust with a confession of my own. "I've never been with someone

I loved either, and I don't know what that says about us other than maybe we're both as bad as the other."

Will ran his gaze over my lips. "Or made for each other."

"Or that," I whispered.

"I'm glad that my first time is going to be with you," he said.

A smirk pulled at my lips. "I've never been with a virgin before."

Will's eyes twinkled in the dull light. "I'm trying to be serious here."

"Oh, right." I stretched up on my toes and brushed the tip of his nose with mine. "I'm glad my first time is going to be with you, too."

Will groaned and leaned in so his lips hovered over my upturned mouth, but then he pulled away and stepped back. "Can you give me a minute to…" His eyes darted up to the loft and away again. "I just want to get the things ready."

He dropped my hands and ran his through his hair. Nervous Will was very cute, and as much as I wanted to ask what he was up to, it was more fun to let him have his secrets.

"Sure," I replied, pressing my hands to my middle to try and soothe the flutters. "It'll give me a chance to freshen up."

I took my time in the downstairs bathroom to give Will the space to do… whatever it was he needed to do. I helped myself to a spare toothbrush, reapplied a little of my coconut-scented body lotion, and twisted my hair into a loose braid. I was a twitchy bundle of nerves and arousal, so I sat on the edge of the tub and did a short breathing exercise.

When I finally stepped out into the loft, Will was waiting for me at the bottom of the stairs, and any calm I'd collected in the last fifteen minutes left the building.

Jesus, he was beautiful in his dark blue jeans that hugged his hips just right, the tight black T-shirt straining around his arms, that freaking smile that had always frustrated me because I couldn't call it mine. He stretched out his hand, and I practically floated to him.

"You ready?" he asked.

I pressed my body against his and kissed him on the lips. "You have no idea."

The notes of slow music reached me first. Will guided me to the top of the stairs, and when we reached the landing, I discovered that he had turned off the lights and arranged flickering candles around the room. The windows positioned high in the lofted wall, usually too far out of reach to bother pulling the curtains aside every day, were open, and a cool breeze floated in with a sparkling patch of the starry night sky.

I gasped. "It's so pretty. You didn't have to do this."

"If I'd known this was happening tonight, I'd have done a lot more."

Will took me over to the bed—he'd changed the sheets—and we stood beside it. There was an awkward pause, and Will dropped his head back with a moan. "I feel like a fucking clueless teenager."

Perhaps he wanted to make me laugh, but I couldn't. He was trying so hard to make this special, and that was nothing to joke about. Instead, I looped my arms around his waist the way I'd always done and pressed my cheek against his broad, familiar chest. Inhaling the soothing scent of him, I sighed and closed my eyes and said something out loud I'd never even admitted to myself. "I wish we were teenagers, Will, then you'd really be my first."

Will's arms came around me, and he rested his chin on my head. "I can't be your first, babe, but I'm going to be your last."

An automatic rise of panic flared, hot and fast like it was gasping for its last breath. Then, with my next exhale of breath, it flamed out. All it left behind was excitement for what came next.

"I like the sound of that."

29

ABBIE

—————

WILL'S HAND BRUSHED my jaw, I offered him my mouth, and we sank into a kiss that erased the world around us. His fingers tickled my stomach as they played with the hem of my T-shirt, and I raised my arms in the air so he could peel it off my body. The path of his fingertips left goosebumps on my skin.

His lips fell on mine again, and the kissing didn't stop as I did the same with his shirt, pushing it as high as I could up his hard torso and outstretched arms before he had to help remove it completely. I skated my fingertips over the exquisite lines of his chest. Will's dark nipples tightened as I brushed over them, and I smiled when his breath caught in his chest.

His hands grew gradually more demanding as he took a handful of my hair and tilted my head so he could lick his way down my neck and over my collarbone, my bra straps falling off my shoulders as he worked. The warm trail of his tongue made my pussy pulse, and I began to knead at his bare torso with my fingers and palms, lightly scratching my nails over his back and running a desperate fingertip inside the waistband of his jeans.

A strangled groan sounded in his throat as Will unhooked my bra like a pro and tossed the flimsy lace aside before bending down to capture one aching nipple with his mouth. I dropped my head back with a relieved moan as he lapped expertly with his tongue and palmed my other breast with firm, confident pressure.

My core ached to be filled, but when I set my hands on his pants, Will swept my legs out from under me, knelt on the edge of the mattress, and laid me out before him. My heart raced as he towered over me, his eyes and hands never leaving my body.

"I've been thinking about this for too many years not to enjoy you the right way," he said, and my pussy throbbed as he unzipped my shorts, dragged them down my legs, and threw them across the floor. "Now relax and let me show you what it's like to be fucked by someone who loves you."

Will set one knee on the bed and paused to stare down at me, like he wanted to remember every detail of this moment for the rest of his life. The light in his eyes made it hard for me to breathe, and I felt exposed in a way I never had. No man had ever looked at me this way, and I didn't know enough about myself to realise just how much I deserved it.

Even if Will and I walked away from this bed right now, he'd already given me something I'd never had. He'd made me consider that maybe I was worthy of this kind of love after all.

Will blinked as if remembering where he was, then stretched out beside me and covered my pussy with his hand. The heat from his palm had me arching my back because I wanted him so damn badly, and he responded by covering my neck and chest and stomach with soft and slow open-mouthed kisses, happy moans sounding in his throat and his large hand cupping me with torturous heat.

Every touch of his lips built on the one before it, and when I tilted my pelvis to ask for friction where I needed it, he tugged my panties to the side and ran two fingers through my soaked folds before sinking those fingers deep into my core.

I cried out, wanting nothing more than for Will to reach places I'd never been touched before, so I arched higher at the pressure, spreading my thighs to invite him deeper.

"I know, babe. You needed this so bad, didn't you? You needed my fingers inside you." I nodded shallowly, eyes hooded, as he kissed along my neck and over my chest. When his hot mouth sucked on my nipple the same time his fingers curled inside me, I gasped.

"Jesus fucking Christ. I must have thought about this a million times," he murmured, skating his mouth between my breasts and down my ribs until he swirled his tongue around my navel. "But nothing could have prepared me for how good your pussy feels on my hand."

His dirty talk drove me wild, and I pulled his face to mine, searching for his mouth and sucking his tongue greedily when I found it.

Will tongue-fucked my mouth as he applied his thumb to my clit, rubbing small, tight circles over it until I was on the edge of orgasm. My core clenched, and I whimpered and lifted my hips to beg for more, but Will pulled away, smirking and dragging his fingers from my body. He brought them to his mouth and licked my arousal straight off them. I watched, panting and flushed and squirming with the desperation to be touched.

"And you're such a fucking tease, aren't you, Abigail?" Will ran his fingertips over my twitching skin with a smug smile. "Giving me that taste of your sweet pussy the other day, thinking you'd won some kind of competition? All you did was make an addict out of me, and now I'll never get enough."

He slid off the bed and dropped to his knees on the floor, and I quivered at the vision of his head between my thighs. He reached for my panties and gently dragged them down my legs, then with his eyes glued to my bare pussy, he set one hand on each of my knees and opened me wider.

"You're so fucking beautiful on your back," he murmured, hooking my knees over his arms and yanking me to the edge of the mattress. "On your back, open like this, and soaking wet. Only for me."

I always imagined Will had a dirty mouth, and he did not disappoint. I clawed at the sheets, wound up by his words as much as his touch.

"Only for you," I echoed in a breathy moan.

His hands stroked the insides of my thighs before his head dipped down, and I cried out as he dragged his tongue up my centre before latching onto my clit and giving a long, firm pull. I tossed my head back and bit back a moan because it had been so fucking long since I'd felt a man's mouth between my legs, and this was Will.

Oh God, I could already tell this orgasm was going to be so fucking good.

A satisfied rumble escaped his throat as my pussy fluttered on his tongue. Will wrapped his arms around my hips and pulled me against him like he couldn't get close enough, and he ate me so hard and fast that my vision started to blur. His arms tensed, and he pulsed my body against his face in short, sharp motions, his fingertips digging into my flesh as his tongue thrust into me. My core contracted, and I tangled my fingers through his thick hair and ground into his mouth, crying out as hot wave after hot wave of my orgasm ripped through my body. It was so freaking intense that actual fucking tears leaked from my eyes.

I let the last pulses roll through me, sinking into my first real orgasm in months and pretending that I wasn't the kind of girl who cried when she came. And I wasn't—until now. When I opened my eyes, Will was on his feet, looking down at me with his jeans undone at the waist and a heated but satisfied look in his eyes.

He reached down and wiped a bead of moisture from the corner of my eye. "That's my girl."

I was a traitor to women everywhere because I turned my cheek into his hand and basked in his praise. *I was his girl.*

I stretched my arms up over my head and feigned a yawn because somewhere deep down, I was still me—and I was nowhere near done. "Guess I got what I needed, so I can go now."

Will growled and knelt on the mattress between my knees before lifting my hand and cupping it over his swollen cock. "You sure one little orgasm is all you came for?"

I lifted one eyebrow as I sat up and hooked my fingers over the waistband of his underwear, yanking them down just enough to let his hard-on spring free. Up close and personal, Will's dick was nothing short of perfect. Tall, thick, straight, throbbing with veins and glistening with a drop of pre-cum at the tip. Arousal fluttered low in my stomach as I stroked his length with a featherlight touch. Will inhaled sharply and dropped his head forward to watch as I wrapped my hand around him.

I swirled the pad of my thumb over the bead of moisture on the crown, then sucked it off my finger.

"No," I told him, gazing up at him from underneath my eyelashes. "*This* is what I came for."

30

WILL

I HISSED IN a breath as Abbie's cool, slender fingers brushed the length of my cock, then dropped my head and breathed past the urge to come. I desperately wanted to do tonight right—take my time and worship her body the way she deserved—but I also wanted to fuck her hard enough that she wouldn't walk tomorrow without remembering my cock between her legs. I couldn't have both right then, but I had every intention of going again tonight. And in the morning. And every chance I got for the rest of our lives.

I'd seen her almost every day for the last ten years wrapped up in skin-tight yoga wear that left nothing to the imagination, and yet the sight of Abbie spread out on my sheets in nothing but her skin felt almost forbidden.

This was the girl who never said yes to me, who never wanted to ruin what we had with sex, and here she was—

open, vulnerable, wanting. Letting me in on all her secrets. And when she gazed up at me with hooded, hazy eyes all soft and dreamy from her orgasm, the last of my nerves faded away. I knew beyond any doubt there was nowhere else either of us was meant to be.

"No more lines between us," I told her as I reached over to the side table to retrieve a condom from the drawer. "No more walls. No more distance."

Abbie leaned back on her elbows and widened her legs for me. "No more."

Her gaze dropped to my dick, and a thrill shot through me at the way her pink tongue ran over her bottom lip as she watched me roll on the condom. I stretched over her, guiding her back down to the bed, and bent my head to her chest again. Her tits were small and perky, the way I'd hoped they'd be, and just enough to fill my palms.

She was sensitive, too, and my blood jumped again as I took her nipple between my teeth and flicked the peak with my tongue, and she gasped and moaned in response. I wanted to spend forever making my girl feel good.

I settled my hips between her legs, rocking a little as I willed myself to slow down, but the need to sink into her hot, snug centre was overwhelming. And when she reached between us to rub the tip of my dick between her slick folds, then guided me to enter her, the last of my resolve evaporated.

But I wanted this to be good for her. Our first time couldn't be fast and manic. I had to do better than that, so I held my breath and eased into her, one inch at a time, my heart beating wildly in my chest and my lungs refusing to exhale. Sweat beaded on my forehead as her muscles stretched to accommodate my cock. Beneath me, Abbie closed her eyes and hung onto my arms, accepting me with pretty little moans that made me feel like a fucking king.

Finally, I was buried all the way, and I dropped my head, committing this moment to memory. This was Abbie's heat pulsing around my dick. Abbie's fingers clawing my arms. Abbie's hips rolling against mine. I never thought she'd give this to me, and I'd never have this moment again. I wanted to savour it. Every—single—second of it.

Abbie ran her hands down my back to my arse, pulling me against her to make sure she had all of me. My groan was pained as she circled her pelvis against me almost lazily.

Her teeth bit on her bottom lip as she moaned, "God, you feel so good."

I couldn't believe this was real.

Grunting because I was so fucking hard for this woman, and it would have been so easy to lose control, I slid in and out of her with deep, slow strokes, paying attention to the play of emotion on her face, the arch of her back, the pressure of her fingers digging into my glutes. I met the tilt of her hips with the base of my cock, giving her clit the friction it needed, then licked the droplets of sweat from her collarbone because I already missed the taste of her on my tongue.

"Harder," she panted as I moved in and out of her at a pace that tortured us both. "Faster. Please, babe. Faster. Harder."

I only moved a little quicker as I tried to keep it romantic, but after another few long, slow thrusts, Abbie shoved her fingers through my hair and yanked my head back hard enough that my scalp stung.

"I appreciate the effort you're putting in, and I promise I'll tell everyone about your superhuman stamina, but right now, I just need you to fuck me. Hard."

Jesus. She was something else. Something perfect.

I captured Abbie's mouth with mine and picked up the pace, slipping in and out of her wetness with a speed that we both craved. Abbie's muscles tensed, and her legs wrapped around me as the pleasure escalated, and I looped one knee over my arm to shift the angle so I could fuck her deeper. All my intentions to go slow and adore her with loving, reverent touches flew out the window while she cried out "*yes, yes, yes*" at every obscene smack of my hips against her thighs.

The connection between us grew frenzied as Abbie raced to the end, and I hung on for a respectable second place. Sweat slicked our skin and made the slide between our bodies more sensuous, and I was hanging on by a fucking thread as I got closer and higher, moved harder and faster, and begged for Abbie to get there. Finally, her pussy clamped down on me as she tossed her head back, exposing the long column of her neck and crying out with release.

The pulses in my body echoed the pulses in hers as the throbbing pulled us under, and the seize-and-release of our muscles set us trembling and gasping at the same air.

When I opened my eyes, Abbie was smiling lazily underneath me. She was flushed with a pretty pink mottle from chest to cheeks, and the braid in her hair was destroyed, hair damp and tussled and totally sexy.

She opened her mouth, but before she could say anything to drag us from this moment, I dropped my head and kissed her softly. When she snaked her arms up around my neck, I tumbled to the side and pulled her closer, my only want to make this kiss between us last forever.

Because this kiss was unlike any we'd had before and may ever have again. It was a moment in time we'd never be able to recreate, a new line in our relationship that separated "before" and "after."

This kiss felt like we were saying hello for the first time but also for the last.

31

ABBIE

"GOOD MORNING."

Will startled from where he stood in the kitchen, naked from the waist up and staring into nothing. I cleared the last step on the staircase from the loft and smiled almost shyly as he straightened. His eyes were bright and excited, his grin wide, and his dimple deep and natural. He looked like a kid who just remembered the awesome gift he got last night—and that there was still time to play with it today.

I was wearing Will's old Salty Stop T-shirt again. I could tell he liked me in it, but the soft, worn cotton was comfortable to sleep in. My hair was a mess from all the sex, my cheeks were pink from the warm bed, and my lips were puffy from all the kissing.

When I'd looked in the bathroom mirror, I was struck with wonder. I never dwelled on things the night I lost my virginity. I hadn't looked too hard at my reflection in case something about me had changed, something visceral that other people would notice. But today, I searched for differences—in my face, in my eyes, in my aura, and in my energy. I was lighter, I thought. I couldn't help the way my mouth curved up at the corners. The goddess in me was innate and undeniable, and for the first time, I embodied her in a way I couldn't when I found her on my yoga mat. I was happy.

Thrusting out my bottom lip in a dissatisfied pout, I strutted over and looped my arms around Will's narrow waist. He wrapped me up and kissed the top of my head, and I squeezed tight enough to make him grunt.

"Imagine my horror when I woke up to find the bed empty," I murmured against his bare chest before twirling the tip of my tongue around his nipple. His lungs expanded with a short, sharp breath, and I smiled against his skin.

I wasn't really bothered by waking up in an empty bed—we'd barely fallen asleep—but I liked to tease him. "I know you're new at this, but I think—I *think*—there's an unwritten rule that people in relationships must snuggle the morning after."

I squealed as he hoisted me up onto his waist, and I wrapped my legs around him, rolling my bare pussy against his hard stomach. I smirked as his eyes widened, and he spun and deposited me on the kitchen counter. Arousal throbbed in my chest and between my legs as Will widened my knees and yanked me against him, gripping my arse and holding me against his body, and I draped my arms around his shoulders.

He ran the tip of his nose across the curve of my neck, and when a ripple of goosebumps cropped up on my skin, he closed his mouth over them. "*We* are new at this, babe," he murmured, "and we can write any rules we want."

Will might be in trouble for skipping the snuggling part of our first night together, but he was very good at getting out of it. So good that it was in my best interest to find more things to be mad at just so he'd have to make them up to me.

"Fine," I said breathily, leaning back on my hands and opening my legs a little more so I could press my wet heat firmly against his abdomen. "Rule number one, you don't get out of bed until I'm done with you."

Groaning, Will kissed his way up my neck and across my jaw to my mouth. "Even if I've slipped away to make you breakfast in bed?" he mumbled against my lips.

I kissed him distractedly as I craned to look over his shoulder at the tray he'd prepared. Coffee. Cereal. Toast. Fruit. It was nothing fancy, but neither of us was exactly competent in the kitchen. With a family to take care of now, that might be something we needed to work on.

My stomach rumbled. Breakfast in bed and *then* snuggling was a brilliant idea.

"Oh, you're a good boyfriend, aren't you?" I cooed before tensing my arms and legs and latching onto Will like a koala. "Let's go."

He rolled his eyes as if he didn't like the praise —although, by the way his lips twitched, he totally did—

and pushed away from the counter, taking me with him. Glancing once at the breakfast tray, he left it there as he climbed the stairs with me nuzzling his neck. I covered his skin with soft, warm kisses, smirking at the twitch of his dick against my arse.

Will deposited me in the middle of the bed, and I reclined against the headboard, feeling all sorts of blissed out as he disappeared to retrieve our breakfast.

On some level, it was surreal, almost like our night together was so magical it could only have been a dream. On another level, being together physically felt just as authentic as any other time in our relationship. The sex was new, but we were familiar, like soulmates who'd lived a thousand times as lovers and were experiencing each other for the first time in this life.

Or maybe this was just what it was like to be in love.

When Will returned, he set the tray to one side and then handed me a cup of coffee before settling in beside me with a bowl of fruit on his lap.

I picked up a strawberry and popped it in his mouth. "How long do we have before it's time to pick up Seb?"

Will retrieved his phone from the side table as he swallowed, then sighed when he saw the time.

"Mum texted half an hour ago to say Seb was fine. Better than fine. He woke once during the night, has already had his breakfast, and was about to get a tour of the succulents patch in the backyard. I promised to collect him before his morning nap."

Will swept a regretful glance down my body, eyes

lingering on where I'd pressed my naked pussy against his side. "We've got about an hour. Maybe a little more."

He plucked a grape from the bowl and brushed it against my lips. I opened them to accept the fruit, then kissed his fingertips as I closed my lips around it. Will moaned and set the bowl aside. "What about you? Do you have classes this morning?"

"Mm-hm." I rested my head on his shoulder and ran my foot up and down Will's calf as he shifted his thigh higher between mine. I opened them wider, loving the feeling of his thick leg against my centre. "A session in the park this morning. A seniors' class at the community centre after that. And a baby class in the afternoon."

I stopped rubbing my centre against his thigh as nerves temporarily doused my arousal. I needed to ask him a favour, the kind I didn't want to be muddied with sex.

I turned to look up at Will. "Emily's coming along to the first two to take some shots for my website and socials, and I'd love to do the same for the baby class. I have consent forms for my clients, and Emily promised me she can angle the shots in a way that ensures the babies' faces aren't on camera, but I'd love to get some shots of me with Seb."

He frowned, and my stomach sank. Will hated social media, and he was so protective over Seb. I'd loved the idea when Emily pitched it, but I should have known it would make Will uncomfortable. I never should have asked.

"You can say no if you want to," I added. "It was just an idea."

Will curled his arm tighter around me and tucked me closer against his side. "I trust you, and I trust Jones. It sounds like a great idea, but maybe try to keep Seb's cute little mug off your feed."

Relief washed away the regret, leaving behind an overwhelming pride that Will trusted me with Seb.

I smiled slyly and fed him another strawberry. "Oh, Daddy. Would you believe I'm almost as protective of that little guy as you are?"

"You do that on purpose," Will growled as he set the bowl of fruit on the side table, followed by his coffee cup, then shifted down the mattress until he was kneeling between my ankles. "But I do believe that, and I appreciate it. Let me show you how much."

32

WILL

IF THERE'D BEEN Any chance of keeping my dick in my pants that morning, it went out the window as soon as she called me Daddy.

After transferring the breakfast tray to the floor, I lifted her shirt—*my* shirt—to expose her completely and skimmed my palms over her body, from her shoulders, over her tits, circling the pebbled buds of her nipples, brushing past her ribs, her hip bones, the crease of her legs, down her thighs, to her knees. Just as I'd pressed them open and was diving in to kiss my way to heaven, Abbie squirmed.

"Wait. Will—" she hissed as I nipped at her skin, then covered it with my mouth to soothe the ache. "We're in— We're in a rush."

"No, babe." I looked up and flashed my dimple. "There's always time to eat you the way I want."

I dragged my tongue up her slick centre, and she bent her knees, dropping them wider to grant me easier access. I growled, turned on by her confidence, and made a V with my fingers to spread her open before lapping at her clit. "I know I've said it before, but it bears repeating. You're the sweetest thing I've ever tasted."

She moaned and let her head drop back against the headboard. "That's quite the compliment coming from you," she mumbled.

I laughed and nipped her again, more gently this time, on more sensitive flesh. "You're going to pay for that, babe."

"Oh, no. I'm *t–t–terrified*," she whispered, and I laughed again.

I'd been told I was a maestro at this—her words, not mine—and I really fucking loved giving head, but Abbie's pussy was a nirvana I'd never experienced before. I teased her clit with languid circles before pulling it into my mouth. When she cried out, I worked my tongue a little faster and slid one finger inside her, waiting for a desperate whimper before I added another. I worked slowly, licking and sucking and sinking into her like I had nowhere else to be because although I had a hundred other responsibilities, I never wanted Abbie to doubt that she was at the top of that list.

"Feel good?" I murmured, and she gave me a frantic nod. "That's good, but I think my girl can take one more, can't you, babe?"

She moaned and squeezed her eyes closed but spread her legs wider and bit down on her bottom lip.

"Good girl," I whispered as I slid a third finger into her. I pulled back to watch my hand sink in and drag out of her over and over, my dick so hard I was about to hump the fucking mattress.

"Look at me, Abigail," I demanded as I increased the pace of my thrusts, making them rough and powerful, and she lifted her head. Her eyes were dazed and glassy, her hands clawing the sheets as her hips searched for release, and her pussy started to flutter around my hand. "Do you know how beautiful you are stuffed full of my fingers? Can you see how fucking turned on I am watching your pussy stretch for me, taking everything I have to give you?"

She nodded and rolled her head back before forcing herself to meet my eyes again.

"And after I've filled you with my fingers and made you come all over my hand, I'm going to spread those pretty lips and stuff your mouth with my cock. How do you like the sound of that?"

My girl moaned as her orgasm hit, her body tensing and shuddering as pleasure tore through her. I slowed the pace of my fingers and watched with awe as her arousal burst over my hand, and when she reached for me, I leaned in and kissed her hard and messy on her open mouth.

Our kiss grew slow and gentle until Abbie flopped back on the pillows and let her eyes float closed. "Mm. I could get used to this."

"I'm a big fan of this breakfast-in-bed thing," I agreed, dusting her collarbone with kisses.

I could get used to satisfying you like this, I amended silently. *Tasting you whenever I want. Being the only man to make you come.*

Abbie cocked one eyebrow, and a smile twitched her mouth. "Oh, me too. And now it's my turn to see if you're half as sweet as me."

She shimmied down the mattress a little, then propped herself up with pillows. I blew out a measured breath as she worked my pants down my legs, and I swallowed with anticipation as she guided me to straddle her face.

Another first. My dick between Abbie's lips. I wasn't sure I was ready for it.

My cock was close enough to her open mouth to feel her hot breath caress the tip. Her hands skimmed the front of my thighs, and just her touch wound me up so fucking tight. My heart raced hard enough I almost worried that an orgasm right now would kill me. But what was death? A blow job from Abbie meant I'd already died and gone to heaven.

"What was it you wanted to do, babe? Stuff my mouth with your cock?" Abbie gave my length a single stroke with her hand, then collected my pre-cum with a soft swipe of her tongue. I dropped my head back as she curled her hands around my arse and pushed my dick a little closer, greeting the crown with a soft, wet suck so fleeting I let out a strangled groan.

"I've waited years to get my lips on your dick, babe, and I'm really looking forward to this, so Will?"

I had to force the word past my mouth, and it still came

out cracking with lust. "Yeah?"

Abbie wrapped a hand around the base of my cock and licked her lips, desire setting her eyes alight. "Be a good boy and get a grip on the headboard. Show your girl who's boss."

33

ABBIE

─────────

THREE DAYS LATER, I stepped onto the porch of Jess's cute, renovated Californian bungalow, psyched to confess to my closest friends that Will and I were taking things to the next level.

I wondered if the girls would be sceptical about our relationship or if they'd believe me when I told them how much my life had changed in the last few weeks—and even more in the last couple of days. I'd fought it for so long that I was a little nervous about today, and it was hard to shake the old sense of shame I felt at the idea of people judging me.

My hand was raised to knock on the front door when it flew open. On the other side, Jess crossed her arms and tried not to smile as she swept her eyes up and down my body.

"You had sex."

Bitch stole my thunder.

"I—"

Emily popped out from behind her and thrust a mimosa at me. "Oh yeah," she agreed with a bright grin. "Look at that glow."

"About time!" Birdie shouted from deep inside the house.

This town was the world capital for gossip, and Will was in the running for Town's Biggest Mouth—Town's Best Mouth, too, if we were giving out prizes—but I wasn't mad. He'd done me a favour, and I was relieved I didn't have to broach the subject. Nobody liked hearing *I told you so*, especially me, and these girls had been teasing me about Will for at least a year.

I stuck my nose in the air and accepted the cocktail. "You guys are the worst."

Jess snorted and closed the door behind us as Emily gave me a hug. "You love us."

Rolling my eyes, I swung an arm around her shoulders and dragged her down the hall with a sigh. "God knows why."

Jess had invited the girls over to her place for brunch, and as I entered the open-plan dining space, I saw the table topped with pastries and fruit, coffee and berry frappes and champagne. Birdie raised her palm as I passed and I graced her with a high-five, while Tash handed me an empty plate with a quirked eyebrow and a side of smug.

Emily dropped into a chair on the other side of the table as Jess took the empty one next to me, and then all four of them sat in silence, watching me with bright eyes and lopsided grins.

Nobody ever accused me of avoiding centre stage, but right then, I would have happily bowed out.

It was weird to be on this side of the conversation. I'd spent the last ten years telling stories about one-night stands—everything from lousy lays and selfish lovers to all-night sex sessions and orgasms that left me comatose—but now my friends were asking for dirt on Will, and I didn't know how to give it. I'd never been vulnerable about a man before.

"So?" Emily leaned forward, hands clasped on the table in front of her, and her green eyes sparkled. "Tell us everything."

I scanned their faces and shook my head, huffing out a self-conscious laugh. "Oh, my *God*, you guys."

They squealed so loud I jumped, but their enthusiasm was the antidote to my nerves, and I blew out a relieved breath as the band around my solar plexus eased.

"But seriously," Jess said after shushing everyone. "We need all the details. Our boys are good for the headlines, but getting specifics out of them is like pulling teeth."

"And I don't believe it's only about the sex," Emily added. "Not with you two."

"It's not only about the sex," I agreed. "If that's all it was, I'd have slept with Will a long time ago."

"I don't get it," Tash confessed.

I transferred a croissant to my plate to give my fidgeting fingers something to do because although I was more relaxed, I was still uneasy about admitting my feelings. It was those old programs trying to take over, and I had to fight the impulse to put on a front. Playing up parts of my character and ignoring others had become second nature to me, but living a life that was aligned and joyful was more important than worrying about other people's opinions. And there was more at stake now than my pride. There was Will and Seb to think about. My responsibilities were bigger than me alone, and I was determined to own this choice as fiercely as I'd owned my others.

But it would take courage.

"I love him," I admitted, hesitantly lifting my eyes to gauge the response. Jess's grin grew wider as Emily bounced in her seat, but I ignored their excitement and focussed on getting the words out. "I've loved him for as long as I can remember, but we both had a lot of growing up to do before we were ready to make a real commitment—and sex, I'm sorry to say, is not a real commitment. I've been a plaything for a long list of men I never cared about, but I was never going to let myself be that to Will."

My friends were a picture of confusion and surprise, with a little sympathy thrown in. I didn't want any of that, so I went on as if I didn't notice it.

"Will already had plans to expand the bar and open the new brewery, but finding out he has a son really kicked him into adulthood." Wonder pulled at my lips. "You should see him with Seb. He's so sweet and so determined to be a good father to that little boy. And the way he's handled the boost to his business at the bar on top of this whole tournament thing, juggling all his responsibilities without dropping a ball—it's incredible. *He's* incredible. But then there's me…"

I glanced at Jess, and she frowned at my tone. All the girls were a little more subdued with me taking this so seriously. I pushed past the impulse to make a joke or poke fun at myself, anything to shift the focus. I liked a superficial spotlight, not the kind that shone directly into my soul.

"I had—have—a lot of things to work on, too. The first was admitting that the partying and bed-hopping stopped being fun a while ago. It doesn't fit anymore, and I've been hanging onto that version of me for all the wrong reasons."

"What reasons were those?" Jess asked.

"I've worked hard to own a narrative that I never asked for." I huffed out a laugh and shook my head. "Abigail Ellison: a man is for now and not forever, right? And don't get me wrong—I adore sex, and there are only a handful of nights I'd never do again if given a chance to do them over—but it felt as though I'd backed myself into a corner, and if I changed my mind about marriage and babies, everyone would roll their eyes or laugh or worse—tell me they told me so. They'd think I was an idiot."

Birdie snorted, and my head jerked up. Jess, Em, and Tash looked startled too. I don't know about the others, but I was surprised—and a little hurt. Birdie was the most like me in terms of her romantic history—Isaac had worked hard to break down her walls—and of all my girlfriends, I'd have bet Birdie was the most likely to empathise with my situation. Maybe even give me the best advice... if I could bring myself to ask for it.

"Sorry." Birdie threw me an amused glance. "But if falling for Will makes you an idiot, it makes me one too. And, well... I'm not an idiot. At least, not because I finally admitted I loved Isaac. Fighting him so hard even though I knew we were endgame? *That* was stupid. Working on my intimacy issues and staying in the Bay to give us a real chance? That was the smartest thing I've ever done, and I've done a lot of clever things."

Birdie threw me a wink, and I returned it with a grateful grin. If a bona fide maths genius could make the same mistakes as I had and still not think of herself as stupid, I could do the same.

Jess reached out and took my hand in hers. "Abs, I feel awful. I had no idea you felt that way."

"It's okay," I reassured her because other people worrying about me still made my skin feel too tight. "Neither did I until recently."

She gave my fingers a squeeze. "I'm sorry if I was one of those people who made you feel like you couldn't change, and I'm sorry you didn't feel you could talk to me about it. Maybe I didn't make it clear that you have my support no matter what. I only want you to be happy."

It wasn't my intention to make my friends feel bad, but Jess's apology soothed a wound I didn't even know was there, and I couldn't bring myself to dismiss it the way I wanted to.

"I know." I wrapped my arms around her and held her tight. "Thank you."

"I'm sorry, too," Emily said. "I just…"

"You just… what?" I prompted, laughing wetly as I wiped a tear from Jess's cheek.

Emily twisted her fingers together before she wailed, "I just always thought you and Will made the perfect couple!"

That made me laugh, in part because it was funny but also because it felt like the last thread of tension in the room had snapped. The conversation had turned a corner and taken me with it.

"Well, that's nice to hear," I said, "considering Will and I are officially together now."

"You are?" Tash asked with wide eyes.

"Yeah," I confirmed, and it felt good. "I mean, we're keeping it on a need-to-know basis for now, but we are."

Jess embraced me again, this time with a grin, and I hugged her back as Emily clapped her hands. Birdie and Tash tapped their glasses together in a silent toast.

Tash leaned over the table, and we all leaned with her. "Okay, so I have to know…"

Excellent. Here came the sex talk. I'd been tortured with glorious tales from these girls' bedrooms—and bathrooms, and workshops, and dark alleyways—for months, not to mention the disgusting collective post-coital glow I'd been forced to endure. This was my chance to get a little payback.

"What's it like to have a baby?" Tash whispered.

I straightened with surprise. "It's, uh… good?"

"Abs thought you were going to ask about the sex," Birdie murmured with a smile, and Jess chuckled.

"Oh." Tash blushed and self-consciously patted her stomach. "Sorry. I can't think about anything other than babies these days."

"No, it's okay." Thinking about Seb made me smile—then yawn.

I didn't want to tell Tash that the baby had woken up twice last night and three times the night before. I didn't want to tell her that he'd refused to eat his favourite breakfast that morning or that he hadn't napped for longer than twenty minutes at a time the day before.

Will had spent every spare minute sifting through parenting websites for answers—was he too hot or too cold, going through a growth spurt or developmental leap, or having tummy pains because a new food disagreed with his system—and if we thought parenting was exhausting in the beginning, it was nothing compared to the last week. But I didn't think Tash was hunting for horror stories, and Seb had been such a dream that it seemed unfair to talk about these small challenges instead of the good stuff.

"It's amazing," I told her. "I won't lie, it's challenging. Outside of my classes, I've barely had time on the mat for my own practice, and my hair is in desperate need of shampoo, but the way I feel about Seb is indescribable. I adore him."

"Wow," she replied on an exhale. "That's wonderful. And he's not even yours."

I flinched, and Tash's eyes grew wide. Panic painted her face as she reached across the table. "Oh my God, I'm so sorry, Abbie. I didn't mean it like that."

"Don't worry about it," I assured her with a smile that wasn't real. "I understand what you mean."

I swallowed the hurt because her comment was thoughtless, not cruel. And anyway, what had she said that was so wrong? Seb *wasn't* my child, and as much as I cared for him, it was probably nothing compared to the love of a real mother.

Like a row of dominoes, hard truths kept falling in my head. I wasn't Seb's mother. Will and I hadn't spoken about what was going to happen when the tournament and festival were over, but the plan had always been for me to return to my apartment as soon as it was repaired. The loft wasn't my home. Will's business wasn't mine either; it was his to grow and run and build. All his success was his alone.

I was growing attached to things that didn't belong to me.

"Is it something you think about?" Birdie asked. "I mean, if it's possible to love a kid that much even if you didn't carry him yourself?"

I shook off the dark thoughts and considered the question, but there was no hiding how I felt about that little boy.

"Honestly? No. I don't have anything to compare it to, of course, but Seb is Will's son, and maybe that makes a difference. I love that baby a little more every day, and I can't see there being a cap on that."

Birdie nodded thoughtfully as she helped herself to some more fruit.

"And it's hard to believe I'm saying this," Jess said with a grin that took any sting from her words, "but you really do look natural with him. Will, too. The change we've witnessed in the both of you is kind of breathtaking."

It was wild how good her words made me feel. Me— the woman who never wanted to have children. "Seb landing in our lives the way he did kind of forced the issue. Will was determined to do the right thing from the start, and all I wanted to do was support him in any way I could. I'm not sure either of us expected to fall in love with the little guy so hard or so fast."

"Any word from Seb's biological mother?" Emily asked in a quiet voice.

A pang of sadness stabbed at my throat, followed by a flare of insecurity. If it were up to me, I'd keep that little boy all to myself, but I'd seen the way Will struggled with his relationship with his own father, and I didn't want that for Seb.

"No," I replied. "Will has tried to reach out, but she hasn't responded. To be honest, I don't know what's the better outcome—Seb having a reluctant mother or having her disappear forever. That's something Will struggles with, too."

Jess nodded. She was the only one besides me in the room who knew Will's history. "That's understandable."

"Well, Seb is lucky to have you," Emily offered. "Will, too. I'm sure he appreciates your support. And to think if that pipe had never burst in your studio, and if your apartment hadn't been unliveable all this time, things might have turned out very differently."

The girls murmured their astonishment at how serendipitous this whole situation had been, and I bit my lip to stop myself from blurting out that I could have moved out of the loft after a few days if I'd wanted to. The only people who knew about that were the people at the insurance company and the contractors who had finished the repairs on my place almost two weeks ago—and that's the way it was going to stay.

"I guess the Universe had a plan for us," I agreed.

Tash's cheeks bloomed a brighter shade of red. "I have another question, if that's all right?"

"Oh, this one's about sex for sure," Birdie said around a mouthful of strawberry.

Tash laughed. "You got me. I have to know: how do you find time for it with a baby in the house?"

We chuckled with her, but four sets of curious eyes turned to me, and I basked in the attention. It was about time I had some stories to tell.

"Take notes, ladies, because this is important information that you're going to need one day." I wiggled my eyebrows and started counting off on my fingers. "Tip number one: grandparents."

34

WILL

———————

ABBIE'S ALARM WENT off early on Monday morning, and she rolled towards it with a groan. The motion also took her out of my arms, so as soon as the irritating *beep beep beep* was cut off, I reached out and pulled her back, latching on with my arms and legs to keep her between the sheets with me. Where she belonged.

I nuzzled the back of her neck and inhaled her coconut skin before mumbling, "Don't get up."

"I have to," she moaned, but she tucked her back against my middle, and I curled around her protectively.

Snuggling. It was kind of nice.

Abbie pressed her arse against my pelvis, and I greeted the soft warmth of her skin with the hard length of my cock. A lusty sigh dropped from her lips, and as her hips circled against me, I snaked a hand up over her stomach to cup her breast.

SAMANTHA LEIGH

Fuck, this was the life. Touching my girl in the hour before the sun came up. Tracing the slope of her neck and kneading the flesh around her hips while she wriggled against my dick.

My mind raced ahead, fantasising about what might come next.

I'd groan with pleasure as she slipped her hand between her thighs to stroke my cock, then guide me into her pussy. Sweating with restraint, I'd sink into her with thrusts so slow and deep they tortured us both. I'd pull back to watch my dick disappear inside her, reach around to play with her clit, bite her shoulder to stop myself from crying out as we came together, then pull out at the last minute and shoot my cum over those sexy little divots in her lower back...

Snuggling. It led to other things.

"I have a class in half an hour," Abbie said with a whimper as I circled my palm over one hard nipple before giving it a gentle pinch.

I nipped the soft flesh between her neck and shoulder, then applied my tongue to soothe the pain. "I'll be quick."

"Mm," she moaned, but she pressed her arse more firmly against my cock, and I rolled my hips in response. "We can't."

Skating my fingers down her side, I traced the line of her panties before dipping one finger under the elastic and following it around to her pussy. "Are you sure?"

"I—"

A wail sounded from the baby monitor, and my chin jerked up, eyes darting to the screen. Seb was awake.

I groaned and flopped onto my back as Abbie gave me a sympathetic smile. "Let's try again tonight."

After scrubbing my face with my open palms to rub away the sleep, I lifted one eyebrow. "Assuming you're awake when I get home—and I can stay awake long enough to finish the job."

She chuckled and leaned down to drop a kiss on my mouth. "Assuming that, of course."

I groaned at the painful swell in my dick as Abbie disappeared into the bathroom. It was freaking hard— pun intended—to find the time for sex. Here I was, living the fantasy of Abigail in my bed where I'd always wanted her, and most of the time we were sleeping, not fucking. The sex we did have was off the charts, and anticipation made the actual act a thousand times hotter, but we had to fit it in between all our other commitments. And didn't I feel like Father of the Year, wishing my kid would sleep an extra hour just so I could have sex? Maybe that was normal. And maybe I was an arsehole.

I stuck a hand under my head and stared up at the ceiling to give Seb a chance to settle himself back into sleep. It was only five a.m.—a full hour before his usual wake-up time—but he'd been off schedule the last few days. His naps were shorter, his appetite was unpredictable, and his moods were all over the place. I must have scanned a hundred different books and websites for answers, and they all said almost the same thing: this is what babies did. When I'd posted on a message board for advice, explaining that Seb was generally a solid sleeper who loved his food, other parents told me to take it day by day. Just ride it out and follow his lead, and he'd return to his old self in his own time. Hopefully.

I was feeding Seb his breakfast—or trying to—when Abbie kissed us both on her way out the door. "You've got that big meeting today with a potential investor for the brewery, right?"

A whirlwind of nerves I'd been trying to ignore made my abs clench. "Yeah. I'll meet him at The Stop around midday. Will you be back by then?"

Abbie nodded confidently. "I'll make sure of it."

The investor's name was Jason Maloney, and Birdie had set up today's meeting because she thought he might be a good partner for the brewery. Jason was in his fifties and a former world champion surfer who had leveraged his winnings and sponsorship dollars into building a successful investment firm. I'd idolised him as a kid, which only made today more nerve-racking, and he had a diverse portfolio that captured everything from underwear to restaurants to poker machines. That explained the connection between him and Birdie, whose family was in the casino game. Jason had signed up as the sponsor for her tournament next week, and when she'd casually mentioned that I might be looking for someone to invest in my craft brewery start-up, he'd been interested in hearing more.

Exhaustion was the only thing keeping my nerves in check. This guy was the real deal, and if I could convince him that I was made of solid enough stuff to make my business a success, I'd be able to use the cash to purchase the kind of brewing equipment I'd need to scale quickly, and not the smaller batch brewing machines I'd outlined in my original proposal to Birdie. This meeting was my ticket to the big time without having to wait in line for God knew how many years.

I gave up on spooning the apple cereal into Seb's mouth and set it aside so I could wipe his mouth and hands, and then I set him on his play mat. He protested immediately, and I scooped him up. He'd been much clingier the last couple of days, preferring to be held than spend time in his chair or on his mat. I told myself it was developmental, like the books said, but it concerned me.

Abbie frowned at Seb, then crossed the living room to give us one more kiss goodbye. There were faint circles under her eyes that I hadn't noticed before, and she looked at least as tired as I felt.

"I hope today's better than yesterday," she said. "If you can get this little monster to sleep for you this morning, you should go back to bed for a little while, too. Signing with an investor is a big deal, and you need to be on your game this afternoon. I should have time to pick up the groceries we need after my last class."

I grimaced, not at her comment about the investor—although she had a point; I'd missed his last call because I'd been busy between my girl's thighs—but at the flare of guilt in my gut. Not only was Abbie here because she had nowhere else to go, but she was also exhausted when she didn't need to be, and she still thought about me and Seb before herself. I didn't deserve her.

"Any word on your apartment?" I asked, shifting Seb on my hip as Abbie retrieved one of his toys from the floor and handed it to him.

"You trying to get rid of me?" she asked lightly, but there was an edge to her tone that I didn't understand.

"God, no. But I bet you'll be glad when you can sleep through the night again."

I didn't want to burden her with my worries about how I was going to do this parenting thing without her. The thought of managing my career and my son without Abbie made me sick to my stomach. I could do it alone—I'd find a way to make it work—but I didn't want to.

Abbie shrugged. "Sleep is overrated. And to answer your question: no. I haven't heard anything new."

I shook my head, too weary to entertain a brief, hot flash of frustration on her behalf and too selfish to not feel relieved. "I can't believe they're taking so long. I'm sorry, Abs."

"It's okay." She leaned in to kiss Seb on his fat cheek, then kissed me one last time on the mouth. "I'll see you in a few hours."

The morning was not better than the three before it. If anything, it might have been worse—or perhaps I had fewer reserves to deal with it. Seb refused to eat or sleep. I'd read that car rides and time in the pram could encourage rest for unsettled babies, and I spent two hours pushing him up and down the boardwalk just to get him to nap for forty-five minutes. It gave me the chance to make mental notes for my meeting, at least, but when Seb was awake, I didn't have the brain space to focus on both him and what I might say to Jason. I barely gave my meeting any thought at all.

By the time Abbie rushed in the door—at ten minutes to midday—we had just enough time to exchange a kiss and instructions for Seb before I rushed downstairs. I paused at the door to the bar long enough to sniff my armpits and run an apprehensive hand through my hair. I'd showered that morning, at least, and shaved the day before, but in another life, I'd have done more than check for deodorant to prepare for a moment as important as this one. At least I'd had the forethought to ask Steph to work the bar for a few hours so I could give Jason my full attention.

Jason showed up wearing shorts, but he was fit for a guy approaching his sixties, and he had an air of authority about him that only money could buy, so when I shook his hand, I made sure my grip was at least as firm as his. After lunch on the house and generous samples of my own IPA, I supplied him with a copy of the business report I'd put together for Birdie what felt like a lifetime ago, with a couple of tweaks that Birdie had helped me put together.

When Jason asked me questions, he seemed genuinely interested in the answers, and I was relieved that they came to me easily enough. It was all still in my head, just buried under the other crap I'd been dealing with these last couple of weeks.

"I'm impressed," Jason said, closing the business report on the table between us and leaning back in his chair. My heart raced as he added, "Your food's good, the beer's even better, and these figures are well-thought-out. Any chance I could get a look at the space before the tournament this weekend?"

"Absolutely. I'll take you around now if you've got time?"

He smacked his hands onto his thighs in a businesslike manner and pushed to his feet. "Let's do it."

35

WILL

I SPENT ANOTHER half an hour walking Jason around the old warehouse, picking our way through the stacks of tables, chairs, and random paraphernalia stacked against the walls. The building works and repairs were due to be signed off in the next two days, and then we'd be able to get started on setting up in time for the event on Saturday. Now that it was so close, I wanted the party to be over. I was ready for this part of my deal with Birdie to be done and for the next stage to begin.

Jason opened a box containing bright pink ribbons, then another packed with fuchsia balloons and pastel pink streamers, and he hit me with an amused eyebrow. "Interesting colour scheme you're going for here."

I tried not to roll my eyes. "Yeah. The tournament's kind of the opening event for the Valentine's Day in Valentine Bay Festival. We do it every year, but the poker tournament has taken it to new levels. Our local tourism council took charge of the decorating committee, so the riot of pink you're going to get in a few days is kind of out of my hands."

"Ah." Jason hid a smile as he dropped the streamer in his hand. "Can't wait to see it."

I ran a hand through my hair as we left the warehouse and re-entered The Stop. "At least this place will be safe from their clutches," I said, gesturing around the room. "The bar's always been something like a safe house for local cynics at this time of year. The lone protester against all that pink."

Jason laughed. "Sounds like you might be single, eh?"

"Oh, uh—no, actually. I've got a girlfriend and a six-month-old son."

It was hard not to smile, saying that to a stranger for the first time, but I managed it.

"No kidding?" Jason regarded me with an appraising look. "A girlfriend. A baby. A successful business and plans to keep growing? I'm impressed."

I hoped he didn't notice the way the tips of my ears burned. "Thanks, Jason. I appreciate that."

From the corner of my eye, I spotted Abbie with Seb in her arms, talking to Steph over the bar. Before I could wonder why she was here, I was taken by the impulse to show them off. "In fact, I'd love you to meet them if you can spare another five minutes."

"I'd like that," he replied.

I led him over to the bar and touched Abbie lightly on the shoulder.

"Abbie, this is Jason Maloney, the investor I was telling you about. Jason, this is my girl, Abbie. And this is Seb."

I reached out to take Seb from Abbie's arms, but he shied away and curled into her neck. It reminded me that Seb had been acting oddly for days, and my briefly forgotten worry returned.

Abbie pressed her cheek against the top of Seb's head as she offered her hand. "Nice to meet you, Jason."

"Nice to meet you, too." He ducked his head to get a look at Seb, but my son wasn't having it. Jason chuckled lightly. "Looks like he's not feeling social today."

"No." I shot Abbie a puzzled look. "It doesn't seem like it."

"This might be my cue to leave, eh?" Jason gave me his hand, and I shook it distractedly. "I've taken up enough of your time today, but I like what I see so far, Will. You've got a beautiful little family here, an exciting business, and you're clearly a man who cares about his local community, and I appreciate that. It takes guts and commitment to juggle your competing priorities, but you're doing it pretty darn well as far as I can tell." He nodded and clapped me on the shoulder. "Let's make time to catch up after the tournament and see if we can come to some sort of agreement. What do you say?"

I blinked in surprise, wondering if I'd heard him right, but when Abbie grinned at me, a slow smile spread across my face, too. I shook Jason's hand with more vigour than necessary. "Yes. Absolutely, yes. Thanks, Jason."

"No problem." He reached out for Abbie's hand and shook it as well. "I look forward to doing business with you."

With a kind of dazed wonder, I watched Jason walk away, following the shape of his back as he manoeuvred his way past tables of people enjoying a late lunch and a booth of twenty-something women giggling over cocktails until he disappeared out the door. Beside me, Abbie murmured quietly to Seb, and when the spell of the moment finally broke, I turned back to her with a mess of apprehension and exhilaration swirling in my middle.

"It sounds like your meeting went well," she commented.

"Yeah, it did, but we can talk about it after you tell me what brings you down here." I rubbed Seb's back and tried to coax him into my arms again, but he wouldn't come to me. "Is something wrong with Seb?"

A line popped up between her brows. "He just seems a little off. He didn't eat much at lunch and only slept for twenty minutes. I thought I'd bring him down for daddy cuddles, see if that would cheer him up." Her mouth twitched as she glanced up at me. "They always work for me."

I winked, but my attention was focussed on Seb. " I think he's happier with you."

"Impossible."

She lifted him away from her body and deposited him in my arms, and this time, he tucked himself quietly against my chest. I circled his little body protectively and pressed a kiss to his head. His skin felt warm under my lips, but no more than when he woke up pink-cheeked from a couple of hours under his bed covers.

Abbie sucked in a deep breath and let it out. "It's been a long afternoon."

"Yeah. I'm sorry about that." My gaze darted to Steph and away again as I weighed my options. "I'll ask Steph to stay a few extra hours so I can help you with Seb's bath and bedtime routine."

"That sounds good. Thank you."

"Are you hungry?" I asked, gently rocking Seb in an absent way that had become second nature. "Thirsty? Did you want to sit down?"

"I want to lay down," she muttered, but before I could reply, my phone rang.

I awkwardly pulled it from my pocket and saw Jason's name flashing on the screen. I showed Abbie, who looked as confused as me. We moved away from the bar and into the private hallway outside, and with a sinking feeling in my gut. I answered the call and put it on speaker so Abbie could follow the conversation.

"Jason?" I said, clearing the hitch in my voice as Abbie took the phone, and I shifted Seb to a more comfortable position. "Hi. Did you forget something?"

"I just wanted to ask if you were free tomorrow? I've got a contact in Sydney who might be able to help with the supply and installation of the brewery equipment, and he's got time to meet with us and step us through the options."

Fuck, I wanted to say yes. I *had* to say yes, didn't I? It wouldn't be a good look to knock back an offer like this from the man who wanted to invest in me and my business. But Abbie was obviously having a hard time managing Seb without my support, and there was still work to do for the tournament. I couldn't afford a day away from the Bay.

I looked to Abbie for advice, and she nodded almost violently. *Yes*, she mouthed. *Do it.*

"Sure," I agreed before I could second guess myself. "Sounds awesome. Thanks for setting it up."

"No problem. I'm heading back to the city now, so I'll have to meet you there first thing in the morning. Is nine a.m. all right?"

"Perfect."

"Good. I'll text you the address and the details. See you then."

Abbie ended the call and handed me the phone. I stuffed it away and met her eyes, taken aback by how overwhelming it was to see the admiration shining so brightly in them.

"I'm so proud of you, babe," she said. "You're fucking killing it. Just like I knew you would."

"Language," I admonished, but I couldn't stop the smile. I was fucking killing it. And I had to keep killing it, so Abbie kept looking at me like that.

Abbie scrunched her nose and leaned in for a kiss. "Required."

I pressed my lips to hers, then glanced down at Seb. He'd fallen asleep.

"Why don't you take him up to bed, and I'll arrange the schedule with Steph? It'll only take a minute. I'll be up soon."

"Good idea."

As I carefully transferred the baby to Abbie's outstretched arms, my phone pinged again. Before

I could retrieve it, it pinged another half a dozen times, and when I checked the screen, it was lit up with a bunch of social media notifications. Curious, I swiped and opened the first of a bunch of posts from people I didn't know, but my handle tagged in the captions.

"Oh, Jesus," I muttered, swiping through to another post and another, and one more. They were appearing quicker than I could open them.

"What?" Abbie craned her neck to peer at the screen, shuffling around to get a better view. "What's wrong? What happened?"

I opened another post, one with "Hot Daddy Will" stamped across a pic of me with Seb in my arms. I was pressing a kiss to his curls while standing at the bar not ten minutes ago. The pic had been cropped to exclude Abbie.

"Rude," she joked.

"You're not upset?" I asked, a little surprised—and disappointed. It's not like Abbie had any reason to be insecure, but a little jealousy might be nice.

She snorted. "Ah, no. You are a hot daddy, and I'm not looking my best today. Whoever posted that pic did me a solid."

"You're not serious." I ran my eyes up and down her body, appreciating the subtle swell of her hips beneath the tight fabric of her yoga pants and the midriff tee that revealed a smooth expanse of her flat stomach. "You're fucking gorgeous, babe."

Her small smile was pleased. "Language," she chastised.

"Required," I fired back.

I swiped through to another pic, taken a minute before or after the first, and wondered who in the bar had taken them, but then the caption made me forget all about that.

"Girls!" it read. "Prep your ovaries, don your prettiest panties, and get yourself to The Salty Stop pronto! Valentine Bay's sexiest bartender is now the hottest single daddy on the coast, and we are not okay. Look at this man! And he's even better in the flesh. (Trust us. ;) Pub address and opening hours listed below. First come, first served (if you get what we mean, and we know you do.) You're welcome. #whowillrailyou #daddywill"

A strangled sort of noise sounded in Abbie's throat, and I quickly shut off the screen. She was pissed. *I* was pissed. We didn't need this shit right now. Abbie, least of all.

"I'm going to find out who did this and tell them to delete the pictures," I promised, starting towards the door through to The Stop.

Abbie stopped me with a hand on my arm. "Don't bother. They'll be long gone by now, and what are you going to say, anyway? That you're *not* single, and they might as well be wearing granny undies for all the use their crotchless knickers are going to do?"

I paused and gave her an appraising smirk. I shouldn't have taken pleasure in her snark, but I was happy to be a dick this once because Abbie acting all territorial over me felt fucking fantastic.

"You jealous, Ellison?"

She snorted quietly. "No. I'm *tired*, Kidd. And I'm taking Seb upstairs, okay?"

"Okay." I flashed her the dimple, partnering it with a smug grin that made her eyes roll and her lips twitch. "I won't be far behind you."

The booth of women drinking cocktails was empty when I returned to the bar, which confirmed my suspicions that they were to blame for the little boost to my follower count. As I arranged for Steph to stay a few more hours and asked Noa to send up an early dinner for me and Abbie an hour before I was due back behind the bar, I hoped the social media storm would die down quickly. After all, it was little more than a single pic of me holding a baby, and what was so interesting about that? There was no way people were that interested in me, and it'd all blow over by the morning.

36

ABBIE

I PRESSED MY ear to Seb's closed bedroom door, and when his little mewling noises finally stopped, I tiptoed away like there was dynamite under the floorboards.

Please, please, let him sleep longer than twenty minutes.

Seb had been up every hour during the night, and we'd taken turns trying to settle him, but Will was shattered when his alarm went off at six a.m. He'd been anxious to drive the ninety minutes each way to Sydney and leave Seb and me to fend for ourselves for an entire day, but I insisted he go. It was too good an opportunity for him to skip out on, and it wasn't too much hassle for me to reschedule the two classes I was supposed to run that morning.

Now, it was past midday, and I hadn't eaten anything since dinner the night before. My stomach rumbled, the kitchen was a mess, and there were toys all over the floor.

Added to that, in the laundry room sat at least four loads of clothes and towels that needed to be washed, and I pretended not to notice any of it. Instead, I beelined for the stairs and the unmade bed calling me at the top. When I reached it, I crashed face down onto the crumpled sheets and closed my eyes. Twenty minutes. That's all I needed. Twenty silent minutes.

I'd almost dozed off when I remembered I'd left the baby monitor on its charging dock downstairs.

Fuck my life.

I dragged myself into an upright position and rubbed my eyes, then picked up my phone from the bedside table. It was lit up with notifications, but nothing from Will, which was the first thing I looked for. That was fine. I wanted him to concentrate on what might turn out to be the biggest moment of his career, and it was a boost to my confidence, knowing that he trusted me to hold down the fort while he was gone.

However, the incessant *ping ping ping* was more sinister than that. I'd set up alerts for Will's socials to keep track of how out of hand this whole #daddywill thing was going to get.

Extremely. *That's* how out of hand.

I wasn't familiar with jealousy, and I didn't particularly like how it felt, but reasonable thought was beyond me right now. Like, what was everyone smoking to make them this feral over one little picture of a man holding a baby? *My* man. As far as all these hopeless, horny women knew, Will Kidd was single, and if he'd been sexy

279

before—the blue-collar playboy with a dimple to die for and a reputation that had women lining up outside his bedroom door—now he had a baby, and he was fucking irresistible.

Single was his brand. Single sold tickets. Single was what kept his business afloat, and single was what half of the tourists this week expected to find when they got to The Salty Stop in Valentine Bay this weekend.

But he wasn't single. He was mine. And I couldn't say a damn word about it.

I swiped to open the latest post and was practically choking at the caption when the screen flashed with an incoming call from Emily. She'd been trying to reach me all morning, but I'd been too busy with a screaming baby to answer the phone. I probably should have let this one go to voicemail, too, because I was holding onto my sanity by a thread, and Emily didn't deserve to be on the receiving end of my rage.

Still, I hit the green button. "They've hired a fucking bus, Jones."

"Which bus are you talking about?

"There's more than one?"

"Sort of. Yeah. There's a bus bringing a bunch of people who used to live locally and now reside out of the area. They're using the tournament as an excuse for a reunion. You might even know some of them. It's kind of sweet. A real feel-good story."

I gritted my teeth. "That's not the one I'm talking about."

I could almost feel her wince. "I know. I know! I'm so sorry."

"A *bus*. The Daddy Will Fan Club—a fucking fan club!—have hired a bus to come check him out in two days. Did you see the bingo card?" I put the call on speaker so I could scroll through to the post in question—a hideously pink Valentine's Day graphic with a grid of perverse Daddy Will-themed challenges. "One: Slip him your number," I read. "Two: Get *his* number. Three: Peck on the cheek. Four: A five-minute kiss. Five: Hand job. Six: Blow job. Seven: Quickie at The Salty Stop. Eight: Panties on his pillow. Ugh."

I gagged a little but forced myself to read the last square. "Nine: Knocked up with baby number two." I put the phone back up to my ear. "This borders on sexual harassment, you know. I don't even want to think about Will's reaction when he sees this."

"I know." Emily's voice was subdued. "I'm as surprised as you are."

I sighed as the brief burst of energy leached out of me and was replaced with regret and bone-deep fatigue. "I didn't mean to snap at you, Jones. I'm sorry. This isn't your fault, and I'm just so freaking tired."

"But I feel responsible. It was my advice not to go public with your relationship until after the tournament."

I rubbed my eyes and fell back on the pillows. "Don't beat yourself up. It was good advice, and I'm not sure why I'm letting something this stupid get to me."

"If there were women taking bets on who'd be the first

to get their hand down Josh's pants on Thursday night, I'd be pretty pissed about it too."

"But it's not like this is new," I argued. Exhaustion had robbed me of all my filters, and I couldn't stop the words as they spilled out of me. I'd never been a sharer, but my thoughts weren't going to make any sense until I heard them out loud, and brain fog made it feel like Emily wasn't even there to hear me.

"Will's always had girls hanging off him, right? I know things are different, and we're together now, but I trust him. There's not a cell in my body that believes he'd screw me over with any of these girls. So why does all the talk make me itch like there are ants crawling under my skin?"

"Maybe…" Emily fell quiet as if rethinking whatever she wanted to say.

"Go ahead," I said with a sigh. "I can take it."

"Maybe you're experiencing what any woman would feel in your situation. Jealous. Frustrated. Invisible. A little taken for granted. But this is your first serious relationship, and these kinds of feelings are new to you. Is it possible you're not sure what to do with them?"

"Maybe," I agreed, though I wasn't sure I did. My thoughts kept circling around an old hurt, the one that told me I was only good enough to be another notch on someone's bedpost.

I covered my eyes and grunted. "Or maybe I'm just too sleep-deprived to have any control over my emotions right now."

"A few more days, and this will all be over," Emily

replied. "Will's never going to encourage the hype, and this kind of frenzy can't last forever."

"Another week like this will feel like forever," I muttered before shaking off the self-pity. I didn't like the way it fit. "But this kind of exposure is good for Will's business, and that's the most important thing."

Emily and I said our goodbyes, and because it made me feel better, I saved a copy of the stupid bingo card to my camera roll and marked off the squares that applied to me. Six from nine. Ha! Make me president of your fucking Will Kidd fan club, why don't you?

I set aside my phone and started to drift off before I remembered that I still needed to collect the baby monitor from downstairs. With a reluctant moan, I got to my feet and dragged myself to the kitchen, where I retrieved the receiver from the charging dock, but I'd only made it halfway up the stairs before Seb screamed loud enough to make the monitor useless.

Pulling in a deep breath as if oxygen alone could get me through the day, I blinked back tears and turned around, bracing myself for an afternoon of hell.

37

ABBIE

———

"HE WON'T STOP crying," I sobbed into the phone. "It's been over an hour, and he won't stop crying."

"Abigail?" Mama's voice was sharp with concern. "What's the matter? What's going on?"

I bounced Seb on my hip as I paced up and down the living room with tears streaming down my cheeks. I couldn't catch my breath. My nerves were shot. I still hadn't eaten or even bathed, my head felt stuffed with cotton wool, and all I wanted was fifteen minutes of silence and to sleep for a hundred days. Will's phone was either dead or in a zone with bad reception because my three phone calls had gone straight to his message service. I'd hung up before the tone because I didn't want to worry him, but I was starting to freak out.

"It's Seb," I replied. "He won't sleep. He won't eat. He won't let me put him down even for a minute, and he won't stop crying. I don't know what to do."

"Sweetheart, I need you to breathe and stay calm, okay? Everything is going to be fine. First, tell me, is the baby safe?"

The authority in her voice calmed me a little, and I released a shaky breath. "Yes, he's safe."

"Is he sick? Does he have a fever?"

"He feels warm to the touch, but he didn't have a fever when I took his temperature half an hour ago. Hang on. I'll check again."

I pressed a palm to Seb's forehead for the hundredth time. He jerked away and kept bawling as I rushed to the kitchen to fetch the infrared thermometer. I set the hand-held machine to his temple until it beeped, only this time, the reading flashed yellow instead of green.

"Oh, fuck," I whispered. "He's got a low-grade fever."

"Do you have any baby pain relief medicine in the loft?"

"Um." I closed my eyes and tried to think before spinning around and opening every cupboard in the kitchen. Seb wailed in my ear. "I think so. I don't know. I can't remember."

"All right. I want you to listen to me."

I didn't reply. I was too intent on locating the medicine and trying not to let Seb's cries wind me up even tighter.

"Abigail?" Mama snapped. "Listen to me."

"I'm listening."

"I'm coming straight over. When I hang up the phone, I'm going to call Lori and ask her to pick up some medicine on her way to the loft. Can you manage on your own for another fifteen minutes?"

I nodded as overwhelm bubbled up from my chest and into my throat.

"Abbie? Can you manage on your own for fifteen minutes?"

"Yes," I said with a breathless sniffle. "I think so."

"If you need a moment to collect yourself, it's okay to put Seb in a safe place, like his bed, and walk away for a few minutes, all right? He'll be okay, but it's important that you're okay, too. I'll be there as soon as I can."

Fifteen minutes felt like fifteen years, and I couldn't find the bloody medicine. I also couldn't bring myself to leave Seb crying alone in his bed, so when a knock sounded on the door, I opened it with a screaming baby in my arms and salty lines of moisture tracking down my cheeks. At the sight of both Mama and Lori on the other side, the gently leaking tears morphed into deep, defeated sobs, and when Lori reached out to take Seb, I released him with relief and collapsed into my own mother's arms.

"Oh, darling." Mama stroked my hair and soothed me with a gentle shushing sound. "It's okay. Everything is going to be okay."

The two women hustled me inside, and now that I wasn't alone, the high alert I'd been in all day suddenly switched off. I'd been running on pure adrenaline for hours, and the moment it cut out, I was on the verge of collapsing. Mama kept one arm around me as she and Lori moved to the kitchen, and I forced myself to pay attention as Lori took Seb's temperature again—the reading was still yellow—then measured out the correct dose of medicine. Once Seb had swallowed the liquid, Mama ushered me upstairs and into the ensuite bathroom. She glanced once at the pile of wet towels on the floor, then disappeared long enough to retrieve a clean, dry one from the linen cupboard.

"Wash your hair," she ordered. "Brush your teeth. Put on some body lotion. I'll make you something to eat, and then you're going to bed."

My stomach rumbled, and a hot shower sounded so good that I wanted to fall down crying, but there was a baby to look after, and Seb was my responsibility.

"I can't," I protested, trying to duck past her and slip through the door.

She stopped me with a hand on either shoulder. "You can and you will."

I was too damned tired to argue when Mama spun the taps in the shower to get the hot water running. She turned to leave but paused with the door half closed.

"Nothing can prepare you for just how hard the difficult moments can be, but you and Will don't have to do this alone. You've got nothing to prove to anyone, least of all to Lori or me. Let us help you."

I nodded wearily, but I was incapable of focussing on much more than the steam billowing from the shower and the stale milk smell wafting from my dirty T-shirt. As soon as Mama closed the door, I stripped off all my clothes and stepped under the water with an indulgent moan.

I did as Mama ordered, sudsing up my hair—twice—then dragging conditioner through the ends before running my razor over my legs and a loofah over my skin. By the time I'd combed out my hair, brushed my teeth, and applied body lotion, half an hour had passed, and I felt halfway to myself again.

When I stepped out of the bathroom, the only sounds in the loft were the quiet murmurings of the two women downstairs and the background noise of a children's program playing on the television. Seb wasn't bellowing anymore, and at first, I was too relieved to give it much thought, but as I pulled out a clean set of clothes, a heavy sense of inadequacy came over me, and I was tired all over again.

The hold I had on any sense of control slipped until I was holding on by my fingernails. Why had Seb settled for them but not for me?

I kept my eyes down and crossed my arms over my chest as I descended to the living room. The loft was unrecognisable. Seb's toys were packed away, the dishwasher was loaded and purring, and it sounded as though the washing machine and dryer were switched on as well. Lori held Seb in her arms, rocking him while he slept, and both Mama and she watched me approach with sympathetic eyes. My throat tightened with gratitude.

"I've made you a sandwich and a cup of tea," Mama announced as she gestured towards the dining table.

My hunger had graduated from nausea to a tolerable hollow feeling, but I sat without a word and took a bite. My gaze flickered to Lori and Seb, but I was too worn out to ask any questions yet.

Mama carried another mug of tea over to the table, then set a bottle of water down for Lori, and they both joined me. Neither one said anything, and I got the impression they were waiting for me to say something first.

I finished half the sandwich and most of my tea before I was ready to talk. I tucked my hands together between my legs and nodded at Seb, peaceful and content in his grandmother's embrace. "Guess you've got the magic touch, huh?"

Lori smiled at the baby fondly. "Hardly. I've got a full night's sleep behind me and the luxury of handing him back if things get too overwhelming." She lifted her eyes to mine, a crooked smile of commiseration on her face. "He's also got very swollen gums and at least two teeth ready to rupture any minute, plus he's had a dose of pain relief medicine that wasn't available an hour ago. So don't beat yourself up about this, honey. Seb's just been too uncomfortable to eat or sleep, and he didn't know how to tell you."

I dropped my head into my hands to hide the tears welling up again. I'd spent the last two days silently promising any god who would listen that I'd do *anything* for four hours of solid sleep, and I'd never felt so selfish as I did right then. The poor thing had been in fucking *pain*, and I'd been totally clueless. Worse than that, there'd been moments I'd been frustrated with *him* that I couldn't work out what was wrong——and, of course, it had never been Seb's fault.

It had been mine.

38

ABBIE

———

MY THROAT FELT thick, and the tears threatened to spill over. I was an awful, awful person. I also wasn't his mother, I reminded myself, and I didn't deserve to be. I wasn't mother material.

"I can't do this," I whispered into my palms.

Mama's hand landed on my arm, and she rested it there in silence until I raised my head. I met her burning eyes with my sore and swollen ones.

"Yes. You can," she said.

I shook my head and used a sleeve to wipe my nose. "I'm such an idiot. I was so cocky that first week. Everything seemed so easy. He was sleeping well, and he ate everything we offered him, and he was always smiling—like, always." I laughed dryly as I ran my eyes over Seb's sweet, sleeping form. "He made me forget who I was. He made me think I could do this, but I can't."

Mama brushed her fingers back and forth over my forearms, but Lori snorted quietly.

My head jerked up. "What?"

She shifted to redistribute some of Seb's weight, and he didn't even stir. "I must have said the exact same thing a thousand times over the years."

I blinked and waited for the punchline, but she only sat there and watched me with a curious mix of empathy and amusement.

"I don't understand," I admitted.

"William was a dreadful sleeper. I don't think I got more than two hours of rest at a time for at least the first three months, then no more than four at a time the six months after that. I was not in my right mind for most of it, but I was certain it was all my fault. Other mothers had babies who slept when they were supposed to, so how hard could it be? What was I doing wrong? Would the lack of sleep impact his development? Was I cruel to leave him to cry, or was I creating bad habits by cuddling him so much? I never did find answers to my questions because nothing worked until my boy figured things out for himself."

Lori turned to Mama. "How about you, Nancy? How many times over the years did you decide that motherhood was too hard and you were screwing everything up?"

Mama blushed. At first, I thought it was because of Lori's language, but then Mama dropped her eyes in a sheepish way and looked at me with something resembling guilt.

"I can't remember feeling that way with Abigail," she confessed. "I was a lot older then, and we'd been trying for her for such a long time that by the time she was born, I had a much better perspective on motherhood."

When Mama rolled her lips as if there was more she wanted to say, my stomach tightened with intuition. "But what about when you had Adam?"

The flush in her cheeks deepened. "That was different. I was very young, and your father worked long hours. I didn't have a lot of help, and Adam suffered from colic. He cried *a lot*." Mama's smile was rueful. "There were some days I might have given him back if there was such a thing as a baby return policy."

"Wow." A teasing smirk pulled at my mouth. "I can't wait to tell Adam about this."

Mama tapped me playfully on the arm, but she smiled, too. "Oh, stop it."

My amusement dissolved quickly. As comforting as all this was—and it did ease the dull ache behind my eyes a little—it was also unsettling. "So… why doesn't anyone warn parents about how hard it's going to be?"

Lori lifted her shoulders and dropped them again. "I think it's somewhat better now than back in my day. There's less stigma around mental health, for one thing, and more support available in the community. But I think it's a combination of things. Not many mothers are comfortable asking for help, and I don't know anyone who likes to admit when they're drowning."

"And we don't want to scare new mothers," Mama added. "We don't want them to fear what's ahead, and we don't want to assume that our experience will be their experience. Not all babies are the same, after all."

"And we don't want to sound ungrateful," Lori added. "Because we're not. We love our children more than life itself—and parenthood is a privilege, not a right—so what kind of parents would we be if we spoke disparagingly about these loud, messy, demanding, exhausting, beautiful blessings?"

She punctuated her words with a light kiss on Seb's forehead, and I continued to stare at his precious little face while I sorted through what they were trying to tell me.

Motherhood was hard for everyone.

"I think I know what you mean," I replied slowly, thinking back to my brunch with the girls. "Tash asked me what life was like with Seb, and I avoided saying anything that would sound like a complaint. I didn't want to add to the anxiety she already feels about becoming a mother, and I didn't want anyone at the table to think I wasn't happy."

Mama's hand stroked my arm again, and her expression grew sombre. "But *are* you happy, Abigail?"

Lori watched me with expectation, too, as though the question was asking more than what was said on the surface.

"I'm tired," I admitted. "Really tired. And it's hard to eat well when Seb's schedule is so unpredictable. I'm not usually bothered by mess, but it's impossible to get on top of things in this small space." I looked around the room again, marvelling at how quickly these two must have worked to put it into order. "Having it all tidied now is a huge relief. Thank you. I appreciate it."

"It's what we're here for," Lori replied.

Mama nodded in agreement. "Please let us help. We *want* to help, not only because you and Will are our children, and we want to support you, but we adore this little boy, and it makes us happy to spend time with him."

Unease fluttered low in my stomach. I didn't want to betray my boyfriend's trust by accepting their help without his approval, but I was suddenly certain that letting our family help us was the right thing to do.

"Will's pretty determined to do this on his own," I said carefully, watching Lori's reaction and taking care not to give offense. "He wants to be a good dad, but he thinks the only way to do that is by proving how responsible and committed he is to Seb."

Lori nodded, and I thought I saw regret in her eyes. "I understand, and maybe this is another one of those things I wish I'd done better. Thank you for mentioning it. I'll talk to him."

"At the right time," I added clumsily, then dropped my head into my hands with a groan. "I'm too tired to know if I've overstepped here."

Lori rubbed my shoulder. "You haven't overstepped. You've done what any loving partner would do, and you're looking out for my son. Thank you."

I lifted my head to give her a grateful smile, and Lori cocked her head. She had a contemplative look on her face. "Maybe things would be better if you moved back to your apartment or at least spent some of your nights there instead of here. I could stay here with Seb or take him to my place, and that way—"

"No!" Lori raised her eyebrows in surprise, and I lowered my voice. Fatigue made it difficult to keep my emotions in check, and I didn't like the reminder that I didn't live with Will and Seb at the loft. I hated knowing that none of this was mine. "I mean, I can't. It's not ready yet. Plus, the Valentine's Day in Valentine Bay Festival starts in a couple of days, and the tournament is this weekend. It's not the right time for me to leave, even if it was possible. So, I'll stay."

"Oh, well, in that case, we'll just make the best of the way things are."

Way to go, idiot. Nothing says "believe me" quite like incoherent rambling.

Mama squeezed my arm. "But Abigail, sweetheart, you didn't tell us if you're happy, and I need to know you're okay. No matter how old you are, I'll always worry. That's just what mothers do."

I set my hand over hers, and even though I could have put my head on the table and fallen asleep right then and there, I gave her a reassuring smile. Because, yes, I was happy. I adored this baby. I was in love with Will. And even now, feeling like I'd been washed and hung out to dry, I didn't want to be anywhere else. And that was starting to scare me.

"Yes, Mama. I'm okay. Tired and hungry but okay. And, yes, I'm happy."

She patted my arm once and nodded sharply. "Good. Now finish your meal and head up to bed. You're dead on your feet, and you need your rest."

"But—"

"No buts," Lori interrupted. "Nancy and I can take care of Seb for one afternoon. In fact, I think we insist."

Twenty minutes later, I was passed out in the bed I shared with Will, but not before wondering if I'd ever forgive myself for letting Seb down so spectacularly the last few days, then offering him a silent promise that tomorrow I'd do better.

39

WILL

I WAS A dick for agreeing to go to Sydney.

I'd met Jason in the city early in the morning. He took me to breakfast, and then we spent hours meeting with prospective suppliers and inspecting equipment lines. I'd been so absorbed by our discussions and exhilarated by his enthusiasm for The Stop and the new brewery I didn't even realise that when I silenced the incessant social media notifications by switching my phone to the *do not disturb* setting, I blocked incoming call and text alerts as well.

I'm ashamed to admit that I was so wrapped up in my own world that I didn't think to check in with Abbie until I was in my car on the way home. I slipped into the driver's seat and pulled out my phone, and her four missed calls catapulted my heart straight into my throat. I phoned her immediately, my pulse racing, and as I waited for her to answer, my thoughts drifted to my dad. I'd disappeared, just like him. I'd prioritised the wrong thing, the way he used to. I messed up the way he said I would.

I only took a breath when she answered on the fourth ring and reassured me that she was okay and Seb was safe and well. But I could tell everything was not okay. She sounded so wrecked that it was an effort to stick to the freeway speed limits in my rush to get to her.

To occupy my mind on the long drive, I tried to focus on the information Abbie gave me before we ended the call. Seb was teething, she said, which explained why he'd been unable to sleep or eat for days, but she didn't know he was in extreme pain until she'd broken down and asked our mothers for help. And as much as Abbie wanted to beat herself up about not figuring it out sooner—and on her own—I shouldered a hundred times more guilt.

I'd worried for days that something wasn't right with him, but I'd pushed aside my instincts because I was too busy dealing with the stress of the tournament. Then I'd prioritised my meeting with the investor instead of staying home with Abbie, which was where I needed to be. The only consolation was there was nothing seriously wrong with my kid... but what if there had been? I'd spent the better part of a day distracted to the point of negligence, and I couldn't stop thinking about the *what-ifs*. What if Abbie had been calling about a real emergency? What if I wasn't there for her or my baby when they needed me? *What if... What if... What if...* The thoughts made me nauseous.

I'd dropped a ball, but it was one made of glass when all the others would probably bounce.

The loft was quiet when I finally rushed in the door, and it made me pause. Seb was wondrously asleep in his bed, and Abbie was curled up on the sofa. My mother and Nancy had worked miracles in the place—there were piles of clean clothes folded and stacked neatly on the dining table, the kitchen sink no longer overflowed with dirty dishes, and it was possible to walk from one side of the living room to the other without stepping on something that squeaked.

Never in my life had I been so relieved to be home. Abbie got straight to her feet at the sight of me, falling into my open arms, and I heaved in a calming breath as I held her tight and breathed in her coconut scent.

"I'm sorry I wasn't here," I mumbled against her hair. "I'm sorry you had to deal with all this shit by yourself."

She sighed and relaxed against me. "It's okay—and I'm okay. I had a couple of hours of sleep this afternoon, so I feel like a new woman. But Will?"

Abbie pulled back to look up at me, and my eyebrows drew down with concern as Abbie blinked back tears.

"Yeah?"

"I think we need to talk about asking our parents to help more often."

I pressed my lips to her forehead, then sighed and pulled her more tightly against me. "I think you might be right."

She *was* right, but admitting it felt like admitting failure, or at least defeat. Seb was my responsibility, and he deserved a good father, but he deserved a large, loving family, too. My text messages to Heather continued to go unanswered, and I was still no closer to deciding if I was doing the right thing by trying to lure her back into our lives. I didn't want him growing up with the sense of abandonment I'd wrestled with all my life.

I was also fucking up on the boyfriend front. Abbie was wilting under the pressure I'd put her under, but it took a day like today for me to realise it. I was a selfish jerk, taking too much from her and giving too little, and I couldn't expect things to go on as they were. When Abbie and Seb burst into my life and my loft within an hour of each other, things moved too fast to step back and make plans we both felt comfortable with, but all that would change soon. Moving in together had never been in the plan, and she was only here because she had to be, not because that's what she wanted. Once the repairs on her place were done, and this tournament and festival were over, Abbie would move back to her apartment, and I'd have to let her go.

On top of that, I had to find a sensitive way to talk to her about the way this hot single dad bullshit was blowing up on socials. There was a freaking bingo card, for Christ's sake, and the entire mess was my responsibility. Maybe even my karma. Once a playboy, always a playboy, right? It's not that it bothered me—on some level, I could even see the funny side—but I didn't want it to upset Abbie. Imagine if the roles were reversed? I could never stand back and say nothing if a bunch of random men showed up in the Bay and started sniffing around.

Fuck. I couldn't wait until this festival was over and I could announce to the world that Abbie was my girl.

The only consolation was I wasn't screwing up on all fronts. The Stop was doing better than ever. Everything was on track for the tournament, and I had a real shot at lining up a big-time investor for the brewery. Birdie's loan was well and good, but if there were deep pockets willing to get more hands-on with business growth and development, there was no limit to what I could do with the place. And as anxious as I was about my relationship with Abbie and my capacity as a parent, I couldn't stop feeling excited about my career.

I just had to get through the next week, then everything would become easier. I'd have more energy to concentrate on being a better father and boyfriend. One week. That's all.

How hard could it be?

40

WILL

———————

THE VALENTINE'S DAY in Valentine Bay Festival officially kicked off the Thursday before the tournament, and my nerves were wound so tight I got barely any sleep the night before. My schedule was packed from the moment my alarm went off Thursday morning until I was due to close up The Stop at midnight—in fact, every day until Valentine's Day looked pretty much the same—but I'd been so focussed on making this week a success that any exhaustion was swept away by adrenaline, and I woke that morning practically buzzing.

Seb, thank God, had only woken once overnight. His temperament had improved now that we understood his teeth made him uncomfortable, and in addition to using medicine when required, Abbie had purchased an amber necklace for its natural analgesic qualities, and I'd picked up a half dozen freezable teething rings.

We packed them all into Seb's tote bag and handed them over—along with Seb—when Mum and Ray came to collect him early that morning. They'd offered to take Seb *a lot* over the festival period, and I couldn't say no. There was no way Abbie was going to be stuck in the loft when the biggest moments of my career were happening downstairs. She'd worked as hard as I had this month to make the tournament possible, and I wanted her by my side to share in the victory. I couldn't imagine doing any of it without her.

"Are you sure you can handle him on your own for twenty-four hours?" I asked.

Mum cooed at Seb, and Seb giggled back. "Of course, we can. We're looking forward to it."

"I'll swing by in the morning to see him, and Abbie will take him for a few hours in the afternoon so you can enjoy the festival over the weekend, but—"

"He's spending the next few nights with us," Mum finished. "We know, sweetheart, and we're thrilled about it."

I rubbed the back of my neck and questioned whether spending so much time working this weekend made me a better dad or a worse one.

Abbie gave Mum a kiss on the cheek, then did the same to Seb. "Will is going to be tied up most of the day, but I can make myself available if you need me to pick him up. Anytime, okay? Day or night."

Mum spared us both a patient glance as Ray hefted the bag over his shoulder and replied, "We will call if there's anything wrong, but Seb loves spending time with us, and you need to focus on the event. This is a big weekend for everyone."

Shifting Seb to her other hip, Mum stretched up to give me a kiss. "Let us help," she whispered.

I nodded slightly as she settled on her heels and offered her a tight smile. "Thank you."

Bottom line was that I trusted my mother with Seb, and as soon as I closed the door behind them, I was able to draw a little more air into my lungs and shift my focus to the next few days. More tourists in general, and the poker tournament specifically. It was finally here.

"I'm going to miss him." Abbie sighed as she strolled over to the window overlooking the side street below. She tweaked at the curtains and peeked out. "Ugh, the decorations are up. Come look at this."

I joined her and looked out the window onto layers of pink everywhere, but it was hard to whip up any strong feelings about it. I'd come to terms with the fact that this year, the festival was on steroids, and I'd been in enough planning committee meetings that not much of what I saw was a surprise. I had bigger things to worry about. And maybe all the Valentine's Day stuff didn't bother me as much this year because I had someone to share it with.

I checked the time on my phone and pushed aside a surge of disappointment that I didn't have time to take advantage of the empty loft.

Still, I could spare a few minutes to kiss my girl. I swept Abbie's long hair to the side and ran my lips over her neck. She dropped her head to the side and hummed happily as I swirled my tongue across her skin. My cock swelled as she wiggled her arse against my erection.

Pulse quickening, I picked up her hand, spun her to face me, and looped her arm around my waist before capturing her upturned mouth with my own. Abbie moaned against my tongue, and soon, her back was pinned up against the window frame, and she was opening her knees as I shoved my thigh between her legs.

"Putting on a show, are we?" she asked breathily, turning her head to glance out the window.

"Maybe."

There weren't that many people in the street, but I drew Abbie forward a little so I could close the sheer fabric curtains behind her, just in case. The thought of fucking her with an audience was a massive turn-on, but now wasn't the time. It was still hot enough to know that the shape of her body against the curtain would be slightly visible, so I pressed her against the fabric and slanted my mouth over hers, stroking my tongue with urgent desperation.

"I have to go," I mumbled between kisses, but I slipped my hands underneath her shirt anyway. I couldn't walk away without first having a little more of her. Pulling down the fabric of her bra to get to her nipples, I plucked at the hard peaks hard enough to make her moan.

And then her hips started to rock.

I hiked my thigh and shoved it between her legs. "Need something to ride, babe?" She nodded as her tongue slipped and glided messily against mine, and she rubbed her pussy against the hard muscle of my thigh. Blood rushed to my cock fast enough that I growled as I pinned her harder against the wall, and her fingers clawed into my shoulders as she hiked one leg over my hip and ground her centre against my thickening dick.

I fisted her hair, shifting the angle of her mouth so I could kiss her deeper, and Abbie whimpered, hips jerking faster. Her head dropped backwards, and the sight of her long, exposed throat drove me crazy. I grabbed onto her arse and yanked her against my dick, rutting like a teenager into the heat between us.

My hands were everywhere, palming her breasts then lifting her shirt so I could mouth her nipples. Latching onto her hips and encouraging her to ride me harder and faster. I pictured this moment with no clothes between us. My fingers sliding into her slick pussy. Lifting her up to impale her on my dick. Her long legs wrapped around my waist.

Curtain open, and everyone watching. No more questions about who I belonged to.

It was an effort not to come, but I was holding on until my girl got hers.

"Oh, Jesus," Abbie gasped as her nails dug into my arms. A pretty flush crept up her neck as her eyes rolled back in her head, and her hips slowed as she rode her orgasm to its end. I watched Abbie's climax play across her face. I'd never get tired of watching her come. She was so beautiful like this.

I let Abbie soak in the last tremors of her release, running my lips over her jaw and collarbone in featherlight sweeps. A small smile appeared on her mouth, and with her eyes still closed, she slipped her hands under the hem of my shirt.

Screw my schedule.

But as I reached over my shoulder to drag the thing off over my head, my phone rang. I considered ignoring it for the briefest moment, but it might have been about Seb. I was already reaching for it when Abbie said, "It could be important. You should answer it."

We untangled ourselves as quickly as we could, but not fast enough for me to answer the call before it was sent to my message service. I recognised the number as one of the suppliers for the poker tournament, and her message was to confirm a final delivery that morning. I sighed, knowing I couldn't do anything about my throbbing dick for hours.

"I'm sorry. I have to get downstairs to accept a delivery, then today is going to be hectic."

"That's okay. I've got two classes this morning and a few errands to run, but I doubt you'll miss me. The Will Kidd Fan Club just arrived."

"The *what*?"

Abbie cocked an eyebrow, and though she was trying to keep things light, her small, mocking smile was tight. She jerked her head in the direction of the street. "Your fan club. It's here."

My stomach dropped as I leaned past her to tweak open the curtain. "Ah, fuck."

A white shuttle had pulled up on the street outside The Salty Stop and deposited at least two dozen women onto the footpath. They wore dresses in various shades of pink, most of them short, and Valentine's Day-themed fascinators on their heads. None of them looked older than thirty-five, and as I watched, some pressed their noses against the glass windows of the bar, others pulled out their phones and started snapping selfies.

One spotted me looking down, and she squealed, an arm flying up to point me out to the others. I snapped the curtains closed and took a step back, chewing my lip uncomfortably. Emily had given me a heads up on what to expect, and if I only had me to worry about, I'd have cruised through this week without breaking a sweat. But hashtags on social media and a Will Kidd Fan Club were a lot to deal with when I had a secret girlfriend to protect from the fallout.

"I suggest you take the rear exit when you leave the bar tonight," Abbie suggested sweetly.

She was pissed, and I didn't blame her. I was frustrated, too.

I paced away, then back, weighing my options. Did I *really* need to follow Emily's plan to wait another week to announce my relationship with Abbie? I thought about the women downstairs and what their reaction might be if they realised they'd come all this way for nothing. I didn't even have any single friends to sacrifice in my place, and I couldn't predict the impact a mass rejection might have on the success of the festival—or my bottom line. But I *was* certain this situation made Abbie uncomfortable, and doing something about that might make me feel less powerless.

"Fuck it," I said. "I don't see any reason to wait until after Valentine's Day to tell everyone we're together. What will it matter now? Everything's in place for the tournament. The stupid festival has started, and nothing's going to stop it now. Why can't we just go public?"

The tension left Abbie's pinched shoulders. "And start a riot? Those women want into your pants, Kidd. Just flash them a dimple and take a few numbers. It costs us nothing and gives the women what they want. We need everything to run smoothly this weekend, right? No complications. No drama. No social media crises."

I shook my head. I didn't want Abbie to be right, but she was. "This is fucked."

She sighed and walked over to me, then looped her arms around my neck. "It's actually the most exciting thing to ever happen to you—not counting Seb, of course."

"Not counting Seb," I agreed, then I kissed her gently. "Or you."

I slipped my hands under her shirt and trailed my fingertips light enough over her skin to trigger a shiver, and then I set my lips against her ear.

"We're finishing this tonight," I murmured as my dick tented my pants again. The hard tip brushed against Abbie's thigh, and she snaked a hand between us to rub my length with her open palm.

"Jesus, woman." I thrust slightly against her hand. "You're making my life very difficult, do you know that?"

Abbie pressed her open mouth to my neck, sliding the tip of her tongue against my skin, and she moaned as my dick jumped in her hand.

"We're finishing this tonight," she agreed. "No doubt about it."

41

ABBIE

THURSDAY NIGHT WAS ladies' night at the bar. Not that it was planned that way, but it just so happened that the ratio of men to women at The Stop on the first night of the festival favoured us over them. And by *us*, I meant certain women of a certain age dressed to impress a certain bartender whose stock had risen considerably now that he was officially a smoking-hot single dad.

I went to a lot of extra effort getting ready that evening. I missed Seb, but I was looking forward to a few hours of alone time before a night out with my girls. I also had a surprise for Will, and anticipation vibrated under my skin.

I started my evening with a full hour of yoga. It was the first time I'd carved out that much time for my own practice in nearly a week, and the way it slowed my pulse and cleared my head made me realise how much I missed it.

I spent much longer than an hour in the bathroom. I wasn't the type to feel threatened by other women, but tonight, I wanted to walk into The Stop like I owned the place. I shaved, exfoliated, and moisturised so that every inch of my skin was velvety smooth and smelled like coconut. I washed my hair, dried it, and styled it with loose, beachy waves. I pulled out my sexiest dress—a short, tight, blue number that always made Will look twice—and applied a touch more makeup than I usually would, paying extra attention to my eyes and mouth.

After slipping on a pair of strappy heels and tucking a sparkly clutch under my arm, I made my way downstairs feeling like a million bucks.

I was a woman on a mission.

I was fed up with feeling as though nothing in my life belonged to me. Will's baby, Will's loft, Will's business and all the brilliant things that were going to come from this weekend… What claim did I have on any of it? None. But there was one thing that was mine, and though I couldn't shout it from the rooftops yet, I could beat these other women at their own game. It was a little juvenile, and some might call it petty, but I needed to blow off a little steam, and I couldn't think of a more satisfying way to do it than being naughty.

My life might have been unrecognisable from the one I was living a year ago, but my time in practice that afternoon had reminded me of something. I was still *me*. I didn't have to give up one version of myself and become another completely. I could embrace some parts of me while releasing others. It was okay to be more than one thing.

And tonight, I wanted to be a vixen.

A muffled hum of music and voices inside the pub greeted me in the private hallway outside, and when I stepped into The Stop via the side door, I was taken aback at the press of bodies. I paused to look around at the crowd and the live local band that played on a raised platform in the corner. Will had resisted even a single pink decoration on the inside of what was essentially his home, and I smiled as a lick of pride burst inside my chest. He'd worked so hard, and it had all been worth it.

I threaded my way through the people and headed straight for the bar. The wait for a drink was three people deep, but I joined the queue instead of cutting ahead. Jess, Em, and Birdie were probably already waiting for me in our usual booth—Tash was at home with her head in the toilet—but the energy in the room was infectious, and I wanted a moment to experience it alone. There was an almost tangible buzz, a cyclone of sideways glances and whispers and flirty shouts among the women around me, and it was kind of a turn-on knowing that nearly everyone here wanted Will, but I was the one in his bed.

As I waited in line, an attractive woman squeezed in beside me. She was at least five years older than me, maybe more, and she spared me a nervous smile as my eyes cut her way. Her dark hair was perfectly curled, her lips were cherry red, and she wore shiny black pumps with her tiny shorts.

My head lifted, then whipped back towards this woman's feet. Not any shiny black pumps. New season patent leather Louboutins. I'd never seen a pair outside a store window, and they were the most gorgeous things I'd ever seen.

The woman gave me a side-eye before glancing down at her outfit. "What is it? What's wrong?"

I winced at having been busted checking her out. "Nothing! You look great. I was just admiring your shoes."

"My shoes?" She twisted her ankles as she checked them herself. "Oh, right. The Louboutins."

"Did you forget you were wearing them?" I joked.

She smiled hesitantly. "Sort of. They're new."

The woman turned her eyes back towards the bar, and I scanned her profile distractedly as I wondered if she were here for Will.

Her eyes slipped my way again, and her brows drew together. "What is it?" Her fingers flew to her mouth. "Is my lipstick smeared? Shit! I don't wear so much usually, and never a colour this dark. Do you have a mirror?"

"No. Your lipstick is perfect. I'm sorry. I don't mean to stare. I was just wondering how many of the women here tonight are hoping to meet Will."

"Oh." She shook her head with relief, and her shoulders dropped. "All of them?" Her laugh was light but self-conscious. "My friends dragged me here for a Galentine's Day long weekend, and this is the first I've heard about Hot Daddy Will. I'm not usually the kind of girl who joins man hunts, but they thought it might be fun."

Someone behind us snorted, and we both turned around. A young blonde woman who barely cleared my shoulders blinked up at me, rolling her lips as she tried not to laugh. I arched one eyebrow, and she whispered something behind her hand to a friend. That friend's eyes darted straight to Miss Louboutins before she burst into giggles.

Miss Louboutins' cheeks bloomed red with embarrassment, and before I knew what I was doing, I'd stuck out my hand to the shy brunette trying to get into Will's pants. "I'm Abbie."

She gave my hand a puzzled glance before the corner of her mouth twitched, and she slipped her palm into mine. "It's nice to meet you, Abbie. I'm Liberty."

A few people ahead of us moved away with drinks in hand, and the line moved a step closer to the bar. The crowd shifted enough to give me my first glimpse of Will for the night, and my pulse sped up while desire coiled low in my belly. He was so sexy behind the bar. Always had been. Hands moving competently, dimple flashing, and eyes dancing, totally in his element.

"I think that's him," Liberty whispered, pulling her phone out of her Burberry pouch. Burberry. She opened Will's social media profile, and her glance bounced back and forth as she compared it to the real thing. "He's better looking in the flesh, don't you think?"

"Much," I agreed, adoration fluttering behind my ribs as heat pulsed between my thighs.

Liberty swiped through her feed and pulled up the digital bingo card that had been circulating on socials.

I thought about the copy I'd saved on my own phone and the aggressive crosses marking off the six items that applied to me.

"Have you seen this?" Liberty asked, angling her screen towards me. "I wonder if anyone will get lucky this weekend."

"I'm sure they will, but it won't be you," said a venomous voice behind us, followed by the sounds of someone trying not to laugh.

I spun slowly to face the nasty blonde who had snorted earlier. She was hanging off her friend and vibrating with her own cleverness. On closer inspection, it was obvious they'd already had a few drinks, so I reined in my temper and crossed my arms.

"You think you're in with a shot?"

"Oh, I know I am." She stumbled forward as if to share a secret. "I've been here since lunch, and he's already pulled me aside twice."

I smiled tightly, both irritated and amused by this girl's delusions. "Good for you. I'm sorry. I didn't catch your name."

Her smile was both condescending and intoxicated. "Tiana."

"And what did you and Will talk about when he *pulled you aside*, Tiana?"

"He told me he prefers... *blondes*," she replied, casting Liberty a disparaging look.

Liberty crossed her arms over her chest and turned to face the bar again. That was the smart, mature thing to do, but I couldn't help myself.

"Blondes, huh? Guess I'm in with a chance, too. Don't you think?"

Tiana narrowed her eyes, then fished her phone from her pocket and sloppily scrolled through to her camera roll. "I noticed your friend there has her bingo card ready. Poor thing has some catching up to do."

She tilted the screen my way, showing that she'd crossed off two of the pink squares.

42

ABBIE

I RAISED MY Eyebrows. "You've exchanged numbers, eh? I'm impressed."

Tiana flicked her hair over her shoulder and shared a victorious look with her sidekick. "He practically *begged* me for my digits. I said it was only fair to swap." Fingers dragging across her phone screen, she opened up a contact listing named "Daddy Will" and flashed it at me. The number attached did *not* belong to Will, and I bit the inside of my cheek to stop myself from bursting into laughter.

"Efficient work," I congratulated her. "So, what else do you think you'll check off tonight?"

"I'm going straight for the blow job."

I nodded slowly as my teeth cracked with the strain of keeping a straight face. "Skipping the pleasantries. Nice."

Tiana tucked her phone away and shifted on her feet, obviously discomforted by the fact nothing she said pushed me off balance. "What about you? Are you playing the game?"

I let my lips tip up on one side and shrugged lazily. "I haven't decided yet."

The queue started to move again, and I turned to face the bar, putting my back to Tiana and standing shoulder to shoulder with Liberty, who looked as though she wished she'd never come to the Bay. I nudged my shoulder against hers. "Don't let one awful person ruin your night," I said in a low voice.

Liberty nodded, but she still seemed uncomfortable.

We reached the front of the line, but Will was busy at the other end of the bar. When Steph saw it was me waiting to be served, she shot me a wink and moved up to the next customers, leaving space for Will to move towards us. He grinned when he saw me, but before he could open his mouth, I stuck out my hand.

"I'm Abbie," I announced. He cocked an eyebrow but took my hand, shaking it with amusement. "And this is my friend, Liberty."

I elbowed her to indicate she should shake his hand, too, and she did, but she gave me a bewildered look first as if she couldn't believe my audacity, and it greatly improved my mood.

"Nice to meet you, Abbie. And you, Liberty. What can I get you?"

"A pitcher of your famous bottomless margaritas, please," I said. "And four glasses."

"Coming right up."

As soon as Will's back was turned, Liberty threw me a look that screamed *oh my God* and I gave her a conspiratorial nudge. When Will came back with the drinks, he set them on the bar, and I tapped my card on the payment terminal.

"So, Will. I was wondering if you wouldn't mind doing me a little favour?"

"Uh." He knew me too well, which meant he could tell I was up to something, and the hesitation in his expression was too cute. "Depends what it is, I suppose."

"It's Liberty's birthday today. Any chance she can get a happy birthday kiss?"

"Like…" Will shot me a loaded look. "On the cheek?"

I smirked at how adorable he was and because he'd unwittingly suggested the perfect kiss for tonight's purposes. "On the cheek would be perfect."

"Sure." He turned to Liberty and flashed a dimple, then leaned over the bar towards her. "Happy birthday, Liberty."

She tilted her body in his direction, and her eyes were wide as he dropped a chaste peck on her cheek. Around us, a few girls squealed. Others groaned. There were murmurs and hissed whispers. Beside me, Liberty's cheeks were pink, and she was trying hard not to smile. I turned my head to look back at Tiana, who had her arms crossed and was throwing daggers at my back.

I picked up my drink order, not bothering to hide my smile. "It was good to meet you, Liberty. If you're going to the poker tournament this weekend, make sure you ask for me, okay?"

Dreamily, she lifted her hand to the cheek Will had kissed. "I'll be there."

"And Will," I added with a wink, "I'll be in my booth. Send over something yummy when you have a minute, will you?"

He grinned at me, not the flashy thing he saved for the flirting he did over the bar. A real smile that made his cobalt eyes shine and his dimple dance in a way I'd come to realise it only moved for me.

I wound my way through the crowd, an oversized jug of margarita mix in one hand, the stems of the other glasses expertly arranged between my fingers in the other. I passed Josh, Logan, and Isaac on my way across the room. I lifted the jug in a silent "*cheers*" as they huddled around a small high top near the band, damp schooners of beer in their hands, and they raised their drinks in reply.

When I reached the booth Will kept reserved for the crew, Jess, Emily, and Birdie were seated on the smooth leather seats, each with a glass of wine in front of them.

"Put that swill aside," I demanded, dropping the heavy pitcher onto the tabletop as Jess relieved me of the glasses. "The margaritas have arrived."

"Finally," Birdie mumbled, pouring for herself and taking a gulp as she topped up the other glasses. "I've been dreaming about these for days."

"I noticed the boys on the other side of the room," I commented, pretending to be annoyed as I slid into the booth beside Jess. "I thought this was supposed to be a girls' night?"

"They all had the night off," Birdie replied, nowhere near contrite enough for my liking. "What were we supposed to do with them?"

"Give them chew toys, top up their water bowls, and leave them at home?" I suggested.

Jess's eyes rounded. "Abbie!"

"Ooh, you're mean tonight," Emily said, dutifully accepting a margarita.

I downed half my cocktail in one gulp and rolled my eyes apologetically. "I didn't mean it. I just met a couple of Daddy Will groupies at the bar, and one of them was particularly painful."

Birdie leaned forward on her elbows. "Tell. Us. Everything."

I laughed. "It's just so ridiculous, isn't it? All these people here for one guy, all because he's good-looking and a *single* dad."

Emily winced. "It'll all be over soon."

"I know." I fished out my phone and opened it to the bingo card. "Have you seen this? They've created a Valentine's Day bingo card with Will as the prize."

The girls craned their necks to check out the image.

Jess shook her head and sat back. "That's gross. Can you imagine men doing this to a woman? I don't get why anyone thinks this kind of thing is okay."

"It's grotesque," I agreed.

"Does Will know about it?" Emily asked.

"Yes, but he won't talk about it. He thinks ignoring it means it doesn't exist. Man logic."

"Hm." Birdie pinched the screen to zoom in on the squares I'd defaced with violent crosses. "Looks like you're winning."

"What was that?" I asked absently.

"Exchanging numbers," she noted. "A kiss. A couple of obscene but generic sexual favours. Quite frankly, Abs, I'd be disappointed in you if you didn't have at least six knocked off this list."

"Six or seven, give or take," I mumbled, switching off my phone and putting it back in my clutch.

Emily's eyes narrowed, and Jess's lips curled into a smile.

"What are you up to, Ellison?" Jess demanded.

I raised my eyebrows innocently. "I'm not up to anything."

"Liar."

Birdie's eyes twinkled. "Wasn't one of the tasks on that card *a quickie at The Stop*?"

I shrugged and took a sip of my drink. "I can't remember."

Emily's big eyes grew wider as her head whipped around at the crowd. "You wouldn't! Not tonight. It's too busy, isn't it? Oh my God. You would. You totally would. Where? And when? Do you need us to cover you?"

Birdie chuckled as Emily blushed, and I had to laugh as well. Tiana swanned past our table, raising an eyebrow at me that hardened my resolve, and I slipped out of the booth.

"No time like right now, wouldn't you say?"

I left Jess, Emily, and Birdie giggling behind me and made my way to the bar. It was immature. It was petty.

Some might even say it bordered on hostile. But I never wanted to be one of Will's many women, and now that we were together for real, I couldn't even stake my claim— at least not in a traditional sense. But when had I ever wanted to be traditional?

As I put my plan in motion, a rush of confidence burst through me. I liked this part of me—the risky, naughty, unconventional part that broke the rules. I could love one man and care for a child, *and* I could have sex in the back of a bar because it was thrilling and provocative, and it made me feel good.

And if I couldn't tell these women that I was Will's girlfriend, I could still make something clear in language they'd understand. Hot Daddy Will was mine.

43

WILL

———————

LOGAN APPEARED OUT of nowhere, tapped me on the shoulder, and spoke into my ear. "Abbie needs to see you."

I glanced at him, but I was mid-pour, the woman on the other side of the counter was mid-pout, and the noise made it hard to make out his words. "Huh?"

He jerked his head to the rear of the bar, and as soon as my customer sighed with resignation and walked away with her drinks, he shouldered me aside. "Abbie told me to cover you. She needs to talk to you or something. She's gone out back."

"Now? What does she need?"

This was the busiest night I'd ever had at The Stop. I'd been working non-stop for more than eight hours, running on fumes and kept upright by adrenaline, and there was no time to take a break, but if Abbie was pulling me away at a time like this, it had to be important.

Logan held up his palms. "Don't ask me. I'm only the messenger. She said not to make her wait."

He leaned over the bar to better make out the next person's order before straightening and pulling out a white wine glass. He'd worked at The Stop before, so he knew how things operated, and I didn't mind leaving him to hold down the fort for a few minutes.

Confusion led to concern. Was something wrong with Seb? I pulled out my phone, and though there were no missed calls or texts, it didn't relieve the anxiety. Nothing seemed to ease the constant hum of apprehension in my body these days. If I wasn't concerned about Seb, it was the bar or the future of the brewery, which had to wait until after I got through the tournament, of course. And if it wasn't one of those things keeping me up at night, it was Abbie. Not always in a bad way—I'd take sex over sleep any day—but I wasn't kicking goals in the boyfriend department either.

After quickly washing and drying my hands in the little sink behind the bar, I disappeared into the kitchen.

Noa looked up at me with surprise. "Need something, boss?"

"I'm looking for Abbie," I said, looking around. She obviously wasn't there. "Did she come through a few moments ago?"

"Not that I noticed."

I considered going straight to the loft to see if she was there, but Logan specifically mentioned that Abbie was waiting for me out back. "That's okay. She might be in the service hallway."

If Abbie was waiting for me in a stuffy old corridor, something had to be wrong. There was nothing back there but a dark, narrow hallway ending in a tiny office that I used as a storage room, which meant whatever she had to tell me, she needed to do it privately.

I hurried through the kitchen and stepped into the hallway, then closed the door behind me and switched on the light. I scanned the long space. Abbie waited at the furthest end with her back against the storage room door, arms crossed, and one leg bent so she rested her foot on the door. She wore a tiny blue dress that I'd always admired and heels that made her bronzed legs look a mile long. Her hair fell in soft, sexy golden waves around her face. I was convinced she got more gorgeous every day.

I drew close enough to notice a tiny smile on her full, painted mouth, and when I didn't sense urgency or agitation from her, my own anxiety receded enough that my dick twitched with appreciation. I slowed my pace to appreciate the view as she brought her margarita to her mouth, leaving a kiss of red lipstick on the glass.

"Logan said you needed to see me," I said, closing the distance and setting my hands on her hips. "Is everything all right? There's nothing wrong with Seb, is there?"

She hurried to swallow her sip of margarita. "I texted your mother ten minutes ago. Seb is divine, as always, and already asleep for the night."

"I appreciate that. Thank you." I skimmed my palms over the fabric of her dress, the tension and tiredness from a day spent run off my feet slipping away. I sighed and dropped my forehead onto hers. "It feels good to stop for a few minutes. Thanks for dragging me out of there."

Her free hand ran up my back, the familiar warmth both comforting and arousing. She hummed as I dipped my head and kissed her, sweeping my tongue against hers and toying gently with her lips. She tasted like salt and tequila and *her*.

"Mm," she moaned before pulling away, then she collected the front of my shirt in a tight fist and yanked me closer. "My intentions aren't honourable here, Kidd."

"Oh, yeah?" The memory of what happened against the window that afternoon flashed through my head, and I grinned. "Here to finish what we started earlier?"

"You might say that. I've got a score to settle."

"A score?" I set my palms on the door on either side of her head, caging her against the rough timber, and smirked at the fire in her eyes. "What kind of score?"

"There's a woman out there telling everyone you gave her your number."

My heart jumped into my throat. "The fuck? I didn't—"

Abbie set a finger to my lips. "Shh, babe. I know. I'm not here to ask for explanations. I'm here to cross a square off my bingo card so I can shove it in that girl's smug, insufferable face."

My fingers flexed on the door, muscles cording up my arms. "I'm sorry about that. It's fucking ridiculous."

Abbie cast her eyes to the ceiling, but there was irritation beneath her casual facade. "I know. It's madness."

"Yeah, it is." I dropped my eyes, too ashamed to look directly at her, as I said, "It wouldn't have bothered me at all a year ago, you know? I might have even played along because a guy who encourages that kind of attention for so long can't decide to grow up almost overnight and expect everyone to forget his past." I lifted my gaze. "I'm sorry you have to deal with this, Abs. It's not fair."

Her brows drew down as she listened to me, and when I was done, her grip on my T-shirt grew tighter.

"I'm not going to be one of those people who finds a boyfriend and gets boring, okay? We're used to having fun, and that's not going to stop because we're only having fun with each other. Do you want to play the game or not?"

Fuck. I loved this woman. I loved her strength and her confidence and the way she always found a way to return to centre and take me with her.

I darted in and nipped her bottom lip, and she used her fist in my shirt to hold my mouth to hers, kissing me like she had something to prove, stroking and sucking and grinding against me until we pulled away breathless.

I slipped my fingers into her hair, wrapped my other hand around her jaw and tipped her head back against the door with a soft thud. My heart raced with lust and exhilaration. "I want to play," I husked.

Her mouth turned up on one side, she turned the doorknob, and we stumbled into the storeroom.

44

WILL

———

I SLAMMED ABBIE against the door on the other side, the taste and feel of her heightened in the dark. My dick was rock hard, straining against my pants and pressed against Abbie's soft stomach as I swept my lips softly over her cheek, then my tongue across her jaw. Her empty cocktail glass dropped to the carpeted floor as she grabbed onto my shoulders.

"Is my girl thirsty?" I whispered.

My hands roamed over her body, lifting her skirt just enough to trace the curve of her arse with my fingertips.

"Yes," she replied breathlessly.

Her head tipped back, and her chest heaved as I slipped a fingertip under the edge of her panties. My heart pumped as I traced a path between her arse cheeks, then back around to the smooth, wet sides of her pussy. I groaned at how soaked she was for me.

I played between her legs with one hand, teasing her clit and slipping my fingers through her wetness, and lifted the other hand to curl around the curve between her neck and shoulder. I brushed my thumb over the hollow of her throat before pressing a soft kiss there.

"Does my girl need more tequila?" I murmured, skating the tip of my nose over her jaw as I pulled her little dress up to her waist, ran my thumb into the dip beneath her hips, and tugged her panties down to her thighs.

She nodded wordlessly, shifting to loosen her underwear and letting it drop to her ankles.

"Are you sure?" I asked, falling on her neck and running my tongue over her salty skin. "Or does my girl want to swallow my cum?"

Abbie groaned, and I had to hold her upright as her knees buckled.

"Guess there are things you haven't heard after all." I smirked as my ego grew three sizes bigger. "What kind of boys have you been fucking all these years, Ellison?"

Abbie made wordless, needy sounds as she sought the hard ridge of my cock with her naked pussy. I tilted away from her, and when I was satisfied that she could stand on her own, I left her there to retrieve a bottle of expensive tequila from a box along the wall.

Switching on the dusty old lamp perched on the office desk I never used, I stopped to look at Abbie, panting and pantiless against the closed door, dress hiked up around her waist and her underwear still looped around one heeled ankle, lipstick smeared, eyes bright with lust.

This was what made Abbie who she was. So sexy and self-assured that she had no problem making herself vulnerable for me. She'd shed so much of her old self these last few weeks—we both had—but Abbie was still a bad girl at her core, and I didn't need to be rid of Will the playboy altogether. The reminder that we could still be those people with each other was exactly what I needed right now. Abbie was what I needed—now and forever.

My cock throbbed painfully, so I undid my pants, pulling it out and giving it a firm, much-needed stroke. Abbie's eyes dropped to my crotch, and her tongue ran over her lips. I let my mouth tip up as I cracked the lid on the tequila, then sauntered towards her, bottle dangling by my side.

I ran the rim of the bottle over Abbie's bottom lip, and her tongue darted out again, tracing the glass. I watched, dick pulsing and blood racing, as I pushed it harder against her mouth, forcing the neck past her teeth until two inches had disappeared between her lips.

It was sexy as fuck, almost as good as watching my cock disappear between those perfect lips.

I pulled it back out. "Can you taste it?"

"No," she whispered.

"Open your mouth," I ordered. "And keep it open."

I lifted the bottle, and Abbie widened her lips to accept a shot straight from the bottle. I set my hand over the delicate bones of her jaw and tilted her head back. Her eyes flared as I set the bottle to her lips and dribbled a little of the sweet, smooth liquid into her upturned mouth.

It was messy. Abbie's throat worked as she swallowed, and as her lips closed, a trail of liquor slipped from the corner of her mouth. I dragged my tongue over it, across her jaw and chin, finishing at her lips and taking her mouth in a slow, sensual kiss that had her moaning against my tongue.

"Jesus, Abigail," I said. "I could spend forever listening to you moan just like that."

Snaking my free hand between us, I dragged my knuckles through her folds, grinding them against her clit as she groaned and jerked her hips.

"You got your cocktail," I said, removing my hand and sliding it back up her body so I could curl my hands over her narrow shoulders. "Now it's time to swallow my cock."

I applied a little pressure, and Abbie dropped to her knees.

It wasn't the first time I'd fucked Abbie's mouth, but I hadn't seen her like this. I reached down and pulled her dress down enough to expose her tits, then set a palm against the door as she took the tequila from my other hand, set it carefully on the floor, and dragged my pants a little further down my thighs. When she wrapped a hand around the base of my erection, I dropped my head back and breathed loudly through my nose, but when I felt the first flutter of her tongue against the crown of my cock, my head whipped forward again because I didn't want to miss the sight of my dick sinking between her thick red lips. She looked up at me with wide, eager eyes, and her cheeks hollowed as she sucked.

"Is it wrong for me to love you like this?" I grunted. "On your knees for me."

She shook her head and pulled harder on my cock, cupping my balls with one hand as the other gripped the base of my dick, and my last thread of control snapped.

With one hand braced on the door and the other tangled in her hair, I fucked her mouth hard. She dug her fingernails into my glutes, encouraging me to pump faster as she gasped and gagged, her choking noises and watery eyes making me feel as much a hero as they did the bad guy. Abbie opened her throat and took me deeper, her tongue stroking and her hand squeezing, and electricity sparked in every nerve ending of my body. Carefully, I slipped my hand into her hair and guided her head in a rhythm that felt good but not so manic, giving me a chance to not blow too soon. She slowed, bobbing on my cock as I watched her with wonder.

My girl.

I wanted it to last, but as the pressure of my orgasm approached the point of no return, Abbie pulled off my cock with a wet pop and pushed against my thighs. I thumped my fist against the door with a groan and put every effort into not shooting my load over her pretty little face.

"Wait," she panted. "I can't— I can't put a cross on the card unless this is a quickie." She looked up at me. "We need to fuck the old-fashioned way for it to count."

I growled and wrapped my hands around her upper arms, yanked her to her feet, then spun her around, shoved her forward, and folded her over the desk.

"It's your lucky day, babe. This is going to be the fastest quickie in the history of sex bingo."

She laughed, but I wasn't joking, and if she was insisting we finish this *the old-fashioned way*, I was going to have to dig deep if my girl was going to come on my cock. I breathed evenly as I fumbled a condom from my wallet, eyes on Abbie's pussy as she spread her legs for me, her arse tilted high in the air, her heels showing off the taut, toned shape of her legs.

I forced myself not to be rough as I palmed her arse, then ran my fingers over her core to be sure she was ready for me. She was so wet, her sex dripping onto my fingers as I circled her clit, and she shifted her legs a little wider to give me more room to work. I was already coiled so tight that the sight of her pink, swollen pussy was a special kind of torture, and I knew I wouldn't last long inside her. I pumped two fingers in and out of her centre until she fluttered against my skin, then I dug my fingertips into her hips as I lined myself up.

"Fuck, you feel so good," I muttered, pushing a single inch of my cock into her core, sweating with the effort of not going any further. I looked down, unable to resist the sight of her pussy stretched around my cock. Fucking torture. "Are you ready?"

"If you don't fuck me soon, I'm going to die—or kill you."

I drove into her with one hard, desperate thrust. Abbie cried out as her fingers curled over the edge of the desk, her bare skin shimmering in the dull golden glow of the lamp.

"Are you okay?" I grunted as I gently rocked my hips.

"It's good," she said, tilting her hips as her breath hissed from between her teeth. "So fucking good. Don't stop."

"Thank fuck."

My pelvis slapped against her skin as Abbie pulsed to meet every thrust. I reached around to play with her clit, and she grew wetter, flattening herself against the desk, thighs trembling and hips rocking. I worked my fingers harder as my thrusts grew manic, then folded over to sink my teeth into Abbie's shoulder as she screamed, her body trembling and pussy clenching around my dick in hot, pulsing waves.

Finally. With my girl satisfied, I gave into my own climax, releasing deep inside her until my thrusts slowed and grew shallow.

"Jesus fucking Christ," I muttered as I collapsed onto Abbie's sweat-soaked back.

She released an exhausted chuckle. "Amen."

It took a few minutes of heavy, laboured breathing until we were both upright again. I pulled out and found some paper towels, and by the time I'd cleaned up a little, Abbie was sitting on the edge of the desk, legs crossed at the ankles. She'd pulled her dress up over her breasts and down to her thighs, but there was no hiding what we'd just done. Her cheeks were flushed, her lips were swollen, and her hair had a freshly fucked look that I couldn't wait for everyone in the bar to see.

I zipped up my pants and strolled towards her. My muscles were beautifully loose, but the change in my body was about more than the physical release. It felt good to be *me* again. Just me. Not a father. Not a business owner or someone important in the local community. Not even a boyfriend. It felt good to fuck like sex was the only thing worth doing well.

"Maybe I can ask the Daddy Will Fan Club to come up with a bunch of bingo cards," I suggested as I straddled Abbie's thighs and stroked her face. "As much as I love the bar and Seb and calling you my girlfriend, I don't think I'm ready to give up *all* of my bad boy ways."

Abbie grinned. "If that means I get more of this, you have my full support."

I gathered her against my chest and kissed the top of her head. I wasn't sure there were many other women out there who would be secure enough to view my history with women as a pro, not a con. For a moment, I felt guilty that my promiscuity made me more desirable to women while Abbie's reputation had been a cross she'd had to bear. One she'd embraced and made her own, but not one she'd chosen, and it had caused her a lot of pain over the years.

But nobody knew Abbie's history better than I did, and as far as I was concerned, every moment of her past was a layer that made her the beautiful, brilliant, resilient woman she was today. I was proud of her, and I was going to do everything in my power to make her proud of me, too.

There was one thing I was curious about, however.

"Are you really going to mark this off your bingo card and flash it around out there?" I asked.

Abbie's eyes sparkled as she drew back far enough to look up at me. "Abso-fucking-lutely."

45

ABBIE

DID I SHOW that girl the cross on my bingo card?
You bet I did.

46

WILL

THE NEXT MORNING, I woke up with Abbie's panties on my pillow.

47

ABBIE

WILL AND I stood side by side in front of the full-length mirror in his bedroom. He was stupid sexy in a black and white tux, his hair slicked back, and his cheeks smooth and splashed with a cologne that made me want to wrap my legs around his face. I looked fantastic, too, in a silver silk floor-length gown, my hair pulled back in a sexy tail, my lashes extra long, and my eyes dark and smoky.

"Whose idea was it to make this thing black tie glamour?" I asked, running my hands over the slippery fabric and enjoying the feel of it on my skin.

"Birdie's."

"She really is a genius."

Will frowned at himself in the mirror and tweaked his narrow tie, then brushed his hands down the lapels of his jacket and twisted side to side. Suddenly, his focus shifted, and when his blue eyes swept over my reflection in the mirror, his expression darkened.

He slid an arm around my waist and pulled me against his side. "Damn, you look good, Ellison."

I leaned into him and smiled. "*We* look good."

Will dropped his hand from my hip to run his palm over my arse, and his eyebrows shot up. "You're not wearing underwear."

"I can't have a visible panty line in this dress!"

He growled and nuzzled my neck. "I'm going to be hard all night thinking about you walking around with your pussy bare."

I watched myself in the mirror, my mouth stretching into an evil grin. "No bra, either," I added, then squealed when he nipped my shoulder.

"You're a fucking tease, but you're going to pay for it later."

I arched an eyebrow at him in the mirror. "I'm counting on it."

He released me and tugged at the sleeves of his jacket, then fiddled with his tie again. I loved every version of Will. I loved the one who was cocky and confident, like in the bedroom and behind the bar, where he knew exactly what to do and how to do it well. I loved him as a father, witnessing his transformation into the provider and protector he always wished his own father could have been. And I loved him as the boy I'd known all my life, the one who blushed when his voice began to crack but who never wore a shirt in summer.

Yet, standing there now, I think I loved uncertain, nervous Will most of all.

"Tonight's going to be great," I assured him. "You've been planning for weeks. The run sheet is scheduled down to the minute. You've hired more than enough help to cover the crowds at The Stop so you can focus on Birdie's event. And Seb is having a wonderful time at his grandma's house."

A line popped up between Will's brows. "I miss the little guy."

My heart palpated at the thought of Seb because I missed him like crazy, too. We'd spent all morning with him that day and the day before, but the festival was in full swing, and the crowds at The Stop hadn't slowed since Thursday. It had been forty-eight hours of complete madness.

"Perhaps we should have bought him a little suit and tie and taken him with us?" I reimagined the reflection of Will and me with Seb in a baby-sized tux tucked into the crook of Will's arm. The thought made me all warm and mushy inside.

"And give him a few dollars' worth of chips?" Will quipped with a cocked brow. "Set up his highchair at the high rollers table?"

"Why not?" I fidgeted with an earring to be sure the clasp was attached securely to the back. "Kid's got to learn some time."

Will returned to his reflection, unnecessarily yanking at the bottom of his jacket. "Yeah. Right."

Checking the time on my phone before dropping it into my little purse, I gave my outfit a final once-over in the mirror, then turned towards the door. "It's show time, babe."

When he didn't reply, I touched his arm. "Babe? It's time to go."

"Yep, okay." Will fiddled with his tie again. "I'm almost ready."

I dropped my head to the side and regarded Will with concern. Perhaps this was more than just nerves. I twisted my fingers into his and led him over to the edge of the bed.

"Come sit with me for a second," I said.

He dropped down beside me and then stared at his open palms in his lap.

"Will?" I asked gently. "What's wrong?"

He sighed and shook his head. "It's been a month, hasn't it?"

"Yeah." I rubbed his back in soothing circles. "There's been a lot of change, and you've managed it so well."

He huffed out a dry chuckle. "Have I? Seb's spent as much time with you and my mother as he has with me, maybe even more. Doesn't make me feel like much of a father. At least, not a very good one."

My heart broke for him, and I wished he could see what I did. "Oh, babe. You're doing a wonderful job, especially given the circumstances. Once this weekend is over, you'll have a lot more time for daddy duties."

He cast me an amused sideways look.

"What?"

"Nothing." He dropped his head again. "Have you had any news on your apartment?"

I drew back, caught off guard by his question. "I, uh… No," I lied. "Nothing yet."

He nodded. "When this weekend is over, we need to work out what comes next because I know I haven't been the best boyfriend, and I've leaned on you a lot these last weeks with Seb. You've been amazing, and—"

"Babe, it's okay." Anticipation bordering on apprehension stirred in my middle. Was Will going to ask me to go—or did he want me to stay? I was surprised by how badly I wanted it to be the latter, and a flutter of fear had me changing the subject before he could suggest I move back to my apartment. "We can worry about all that later. You've worked hard to get to tonight, and you deserve to enjoy the moment. Look at what you've achieved! This is your chance to celebrate. This whole town is so proud of you, Will. Your mum and Ray, my parents, our friends. If Seb were old enough to know what an incredible man his dad is, he'd be proud of you, too."

Will twisted his head to look up at me, and his eyes were those of a little boy. I blinked back tears.

"*I'm* proud of you," I whispered.

An odd sense of foreboding washed over me, that familiar but uneasy sense of waiting without knowing for what, and I tried to tell myself it was a natural reaction to this conversation—the anxiety of not knowing what Will wanted for our future, the discomfort of spending hours away from Seb, and the pressure for tonight to be a success. But I wasn't fooled. This feeling was different. I knew this feeling. Change was coming.

Will took hold of my hand and kissed the back of it, and we left for the party.

48

ABBIE

———

BIRDIE HAD SAID it was a poker tournament, but it was so much more than that.

Will offered me his elbow on the stairs down from the loft, and I took it with a sense of pride. The way he led me through the hall and onto Main Street, his stride long and strong like he was more confident with me on his arm, put a warm glow behind my heart space. A public appearance like this didn't make our relationship official. If this last month between us never happened, he was still my best friend, and I still would have walked into this event by his side.

Every storefront on Main Street—aside from The Salty Stop—was covered in balloon garlands and flowers and paper lanterns in riotous shades of pink to mark the Valentine's Day in Valentine Bay Festival. Next to The Stop, the old warehouse had been covered in hundreds of twinkling lights and temporary wrap branded with the tournament details. The Salty Stop was listed as a sponsor, and I squeezed Will's bicep, hoping he'd understand my excitement and awe.

He spared me a small, sideways smile. "Impressed?"

"Speechless," I replied, gazing up at the building.

"That'd be a first," he muttered.

I elbowed him in the ribs, and he grunted. "Save that mouth for the bedroom, mister."

Will smiled, and his dimple popped. "Yes, ma'am."

At the entrance to the warehouse, red velvet ropes corralled the incoming guests as tall, buff doormen checked people off via glowing tablets. Will moved past the queuing guests—from what I could see, none of them Valentine Bay locals—and went straight for the head of the line. I was born for the VIP treatment, but when people began to whisper and take his photo, I tried to pull my hand from the crook of his arm. I didn't want to complicate things for him tonight.

"Don't," he murmured, grasping my hand and holding it there. "Don't let go."

I gripped him tighter as the warm glow in my chest burst into fire. The bouncers at the door recognised Will on sight, nodding as they pulled back the rope to let us through.

"I had no idea this event was going to be so elaborate," I said as we moved into a makeshift coat room. Music and conversation filtered through the dark, heavy curtain between us and the warehouse space. "Guest lists and tuxedos and velvet ropes. Why didn't you tell me?"

"It was meant to be much simpler to start," Will replied, stopping to straighten his jacket. "But Birdie was open to hearing a few of my ideas, and things kind of escalated from there."

Now, it was my turn to be nervous. I glanced at the curtain, wishing I could see through it. What had he done? More importantly...

"But Will... *Why*?"

Will lifted his eyes to mine, and we exchanged an entire conversation in just one look. He knew what I meant. *Why* had he made things harder for himself than they had to be? *Why* did he want to prove himself tonight of all nights, with so many people watching and so much at stake? *Why* did he feel the need to prove himself at all?

And I knew his answer. He did it to prove to himself that he could.

I swallowed the lump in my throat and blinked back tears before they spilled over and ruined my mascara. It was almost impossible to tease apart the maelstrom of emotions swirling through me. I was sad for the little boy Will used to be and heartbroken that he had to go to such extremes to feel that he was worth something as a man. And so ridiculously proud that he'd pulled it off.

I took his hand and held it tight. "Are you ready to make your fashionably late entrance?"

"Yeah." He took in a fortifying breath. "I am."

Will pulled back the curtain, and I gasped.

The official theme was "Monte Carlo Casino," and everyone in the room was dressed either in a black tux or glamorous gown, but it didn't end there. The space was cavernous. Dark curtains covering every wall and strings of tiny white lights hung at half the height of the ceiling neutralised its impersonal, industrial feel. Four large, round gaming tables had been cordoned off in the centre of the room, set aside for the poker tournament and allowing plenty of space for foot traffic and spectators to gather around and watch. Elsewhere were a roulette wheel, a craps table, a blackjack table, and a barrel for raffle tickets. Each was complete with a black-vested dealer. Servers circulated with trays of champagne, and a buffet table loaded with food was set up at the rear of the room. The air was thick with jazz music, conversation, and the smell of whiskey and canapes.

"Will!" I turned my wonder on him. "This is unbelievable. Why didn't you tell me about any of this? It looks like so much work. I could have helped. I could have—"

"I wanted it to be a surprise." He shrugged like it was nothing, and I pretended not to notice the pale red flush creeping up his neck. "And it was something I needed to do on my own."

I pressed my arm against his, the only show of affection I could risk with all the cameras pointed his way. The lump in my throat grew thicker. "I know I already told you this, but I have to say it again. I'm so freaking proud of you."

"Don't think I'll ever get tired of hearing you tell me that."

His smile was small and self-reflective, but then his head jerked up, and he grinned at someone across the room.

I followed his line of sight to our friends congregating around the blackjack table. They looked ripped from a photo shoot, the men model material with their broad shoulders, styled hair, and sexy suits. The girls were a rainbow of style in elegant dresses and sky-high heels, each one a goddess. I was a bucket of love today, and my heart felt too small to hold all the affection I had for my crew.

I gave them all a full-armed wave, which Emily returned with gusto, and I laughed before pulling a funny face, eyes crossed and tongue poking out to the side.

"Jesus," Will groaned, tugging me forwards. "You can take the girl out of the small town, but you can't take the small town out of the girl."

"You love it," I teased.

Will sighed dramatically, mouth twitching with the urge to smile. "I suppose I do."

We reached our friends, but as I opened my mouth to declare that each one of them looked sexy as fuck, Josh and Isaac shifted a little, revealing another surprise behind them.

"Adam!" I screeched as I flung myself into my big brother's arms.

He laughed and put his arms around me, squeezing me tight enough to make me grunt. "Hey, Little Bug."

I pulled away but held on tight to his arms, admiring his black suit and the dusting of silver in his hair. "What are you doing here? Why didn't you tell me? Does Mama know?"

"Will invited me, and I felt a little guilty after missing the family reunion—"

"You did not," I joked, though it was totally true.

"You're right. I didn't, but I did miss my sister, and Mama's been hounding me to visit for months. It was time."

"Months? You haven't been back to the Bay in years. Oh! Have you met Emily?" I pointed at the little woman with short dark hair in a stunning green dress hanging off Josh's arm, then swung my finger around to Luca and his wife. "And Tash? She and Luca are having a baby soon. Oh! And Birdie moved back to town a few months ago, though you're probably too old to remember when she spent summers here."

Adam chuckled. "Slow down, Abs. I've been here for an hour already—enough time for the guys to introduce me to anyone I don't already know *and* lose a hundred dollars on the craps table."

I gave him an accusing look, which was hard to pull off with how badly I wanted to smile. "Sounds like you're actually having fun, Dr Ellison."

"It's a good night," he agreed. He reached past me to shake Will's hand. "It's nice to see you again, Will, and congratulations. You've done a spectacular job here."

Will shook his hand. "I appreciate that. Thanks."

We stood talking and sipping champagne for a few minutes before Emily excused herself. She was technically on the clock tonight as the Bay's promotional photographer and Will's social media guru, and she explained that she had to take some official pictures and update Will's accounts, boosting the relevant hashtags and commenting on the guests' live feeds.

As much as I would have loved to attach myself to the man of the hour all night long, it soon became impossible. Everyone wanted a little of Will's time, and after baring my teeth through half a dozen propositions from women playing bingo instead of blackjack, I gave Will space to work the room alone. He wasn't happy about it, but he understood that witnessing that shit wasn't fun.

It was actually rewarding to watch him from a distance. Will oozed sex and charisma and seeing him gently rebuff the constant advances because I was the woman he wanted turned out to be unexpected foreplay.

Gradually, the mood among his groupies shifted as, one by one, they walked away disappointed. He always gave them a smile and a dimple, but no was no after all, and nobody was able to tempt him. And, of course, there was that rumour on social media claiming someone had crossed off the *quickie at The Stop* and *panties on his pillow* squares on the viral Will Kidd sexy bingo card. It had been the virtual equivalent of a cold shower for a lot of the hot, horny women swarming around the Bay.

What a shame.

And it wasn't only the Will Kidd Fan Club who wanted a piece of him. At least a quarter of the party was made up of locals who looked sweet but uncomfortable in suits and dresses that might never be worn again after tonight. They hugged him and took his photo, and he rewarded their support with his trademark dimple. Watching him in those moments made me so happy for him.

When Rick Talbot, President of the Tourism Council, approached Will about an hour after we'd arrived, I tensed and floated a few steps closer. If Mr Talbot said a single degrading thing to Will, I was going to personally rearrange his toupee. But the older man smiled and warmly clapped Will on the back, then asked him to pose for a picture taken by the official event photographer.

Emily grinned behind her camera as she snapped away, and when the president moved on, she gave Will a proud thumbs up. Will looked a little shell-shocked—in a good way. Kind of like he couldn't believe how well the night was going or that he was the man responsible for it all.

I loved him like this. He was so fucking sexy. I shimmied as delicious tingles ran across my skin, and when Will caught me looking at him, he dropped his chin and raised one eyebrow like he knew what I was thinking.

I glanced down at my chest, and just as I thought, my hard nipples poked through the silver silk. So maybe Will did know what I was thinking after all.

49

ABBIE

THREE CHAMPAGNES LATER, I'd relaxed into the event. That scary first step into the room with Will had passed, and Will's nerves about how well—or not—his big event would go seemed to have dissipated. An end to the tension of the last few weeks was in sight. With Will deep in conversation with Jason Maloney—the would-be investor in Will's brewery business—I bled money at the gaming tables until my champagne flute ran out of bubbles.

"I need something harder than this," I announced. "Anybody want anything at the bar?"

"Cold water for me, please." Tash set another chip on the mat, crossed her fingers, and frowned at the roulette wheel. "And pretzels, if you can find any."

"Coming right up. Jess?"

"I'll grab another champagne when the tray comes around again," she said, glancing around the room. "But if I lose another dollar on this game, I'm giving up and trying my luck at the craps table."

"Noted." I offered a sloppy salute. "I'll be back in the flash of a trench coat."

I approached the bar with a polite smile for the bartender. He was dressed in the same uniform as the other servers from the catering company, and I didn't know him.

"Can I get an ice water, please?" I asked. "And a pink margarita? Thank you."

The guy checked his liquor stocks then gave me an apologetic grimace. "I need to get a bottle of tequila from the back. I won't be long."

I bit my lip to stop myself from smiling at the memory of fucking Will in the storeroom after he'd poured tequila down my throat. "No problem. I'll wait."

I leaned on the bar, humming happily, until a finger tapped my shoulder. Grinning because I assumed it was Will, I spun around—and my heart lurched painfully against the inside of my chest.

"Tristan," I gasped before turning my back to him and snapping my eyes onto the stacks of clean glasses and liquor bottles behind the bar. My heart was beating again, but it was too loud and too fast, and I wasn't sure if it was due to terror or rage.

"Hey, Abbie."

Tristan stood beside me—too close, close enough for our shoulders to brush—and rested his elbows on the bar. "Long time no see, eh?"

I hadn't seen this guy in almost ten years, and time hadn't changed him all that much. His hair was a little thinner, and didn't we all have a few more wrinkles around our eyes? But he was still tall and lean, still handsome in a conventional, predictable way.

And, apparently, he still made me want to throw up.

Rage, I decided.

"Yeah. Long time."

"You still living in the Bay after all this time? Fuck." He shook his head like he'd just found out I had a terminal illness. "That sucks."

"It's a much nicer place since you left," I replied. "What are you even doing here?"

He shrugged. "A few of the guys decided to revisit the old stomping ground for this poker tournament." He threw a contemptuous look over his shoulder towards the gaming tables. "Fucking waste of time. None of them got past the second round."

"Time to go home, then."

An ancient feeling of filth and shame burned the back of my neck, and I silently begged the bartender to hurry up so I could get away.

"Nah. I just won five hundred bucks at blackjack, so I might hang around a little longer."

"And the crew hasn't seen you?" I asked, and at his puzzled look, I added, "Josh? Isaac?" I swallowed. "Will?"

He snorted. "Not hard to avoid them. They're no smarter now than they were ten years ago."

No drink was worth this. "Well, I'd say it was nice talking to you, Tristan, but it wasn't. Bye."

I took a step to the side, and he grabbed my arm. "Where are you running off to, baby? You didn't give me a chance to tell you how good you're looking."

My heart did that painful jump again, and this time, there was an undeniable flare of fear. We were in a crowded room. He couldn't hurt me here, but my body didn't know that.

"Get your hands off me, arsehole."

He released my arm, raised his palms, and laughed. "Oh, still as miserable now as you were in high school, aren't you?"

"I'm not miserable, you moron. I'm furious. Now get the fuck out of my way."

He smirked as if my reaction amused him. "How about I buy you a drink, we go somewhere quiet and reminisce over old times?"

"Like the microscopic size of your dick?"

His eyes darkened, and he forced a chuckle as he touched me again. A light brush of his fingertips over my shoulder, then my cheek.

I don't know why, but I froze.

"Oh, you haven't changed, have you, Abigail?" he whispered.

Squeezing my eyes closed, I sucked in a breath through my nose. "Leave me alone, Tristan," I spat through my clenched jaw. "Just... leave me alone."

"Come on, baby. I didn't think you knew the meaning of the word *no*."

An arm shot out from behind me, shoving Tristan back three paces, and then a dark, broad back was blocking me from Tristan's view. A familiar scent enveloped me, and my stomach dropped with relief, knowing Will was there to protect me, but my heart still beat painfully hard in my chest. Adrenaline and fury and fear shot through my body like pulses of wild electricity.

"Will," Tristan said with an obnoxious laugh that told me he didn't sense the danger. "Good to see you, man."

Will took a step towards him, and though I couldn't see his face, the rage and possession in his voice sent a shiver up my spine.

"Touch her again, and I'll fucking end you."

50

WILL

AT THE EDGES of my vision, I noticed people stopping to look, but I didn't care. This was the scumbag who convinced Abbie to sleep with him when she was barely sixteen years old, then dumped her and laughed while he told every guy at school that she was easy.

Abbie retaliated with a rumour that Tristan had a tiny cock, and he'd graffitied half of Valentine Bay with the words "Abigail Ellison is a slut". Not satisfied that he'd hurt her enough, he made three of his mates tell the entire school that they'd slept with her, too, just to make sure the label stuck.

He left the Bay straight after high school, and his parents moved out of the area not long after that, but nobody missed them. If I'd known Tristan had bought entry to this event—*my* event—I'd have cancelled his ticket and scrubbed his name from the list.

And I'd never have let Abbie know how close he was to getting near her.

I'd punched him the day he told me he'd pressured Abbie to sleep with him, laughing like it was a joke, and that day was the only time I'd ever swung at another person. I was just a kid then, and it wasn't a good hit, but I was so fucking ready to take another shot.

"Ah." Tristan nodded like we were mates and I'd told him a secret. "I get it. You're fucking her, aren't you?"

Rage burst in my pulse, but I clenched my jaw and said nothing. Tristan tried to step around me, but I mirrored his body with my own. He wasn't going to touch her. He wasn't going to *look* at her. Not if he wanted to leave here in one piece.

Behind me, Abbie laid a hand on my back. "Will," she said in a low voice that only I could hear, "just throw him out, and we can get on with our night."

Somewhere in the crowd around me, I heard Luca and Josh trying to push through. Then Logan was laying a calming hand on my shoulder, but it only annoyed me, so I shrugged him off.

"He's fucking her," Tristan laughed again, then sighed theatrically. "About time. From what I hear, you were the only man in this town who hadn't."

Blood roared in my ears, and I lurched forward, grabbing the front of his shirt. "What the fuck is wrong with you?"

"Will!" Abbie tugged on my arm. "Leave it alone. Let's go."

Tristan laughed under his breath. "Thanks, Abs. I knew I could count on you. What do you say, Will? Let's just leave it alone, eh? Let me go, and I'll leave. Like I wasn't ever here."

It took effort to uncurl my fingers, but I was suddenly aware of phones being held up and pointed at me and Abbie's nails digging anxiously into my side. I loosened my grip and set Tristan down. "Get the fuck off my property."

"Sure, sure." Tristan dusted himself off, then waved to the crowd. "Just a little misunderstanding, folks. All sorted now."

Logan laid a hand on my back as he shook his head. "Fuck, Kidd. I've never seen you like that. I know he's a prick, but he's not worth it."

Tristan knocked into Logan on his way past, then flicked Abbie a derisive look. "Neither is she."

I spun on my heel, pulled back my arm, and slammed my fist into his face.

And fuck, it felt good.

51

ABBIE

"WILL! NO!"

Tristan staggered backwards after Will's fist connected with his face. Will shook his hand and winced, but there was satisfaction on his face as Tristan put a hand to his bleeding nose. Around us, people shouted and held up their cameras, and panic scratched at my throat. Will had to get out of here before things got any worse.

I tugged at his arm, but he may as well have been made of stone the way he stood there glaring at Tristan. I understood. Beneath my heightened emotions, I was ecstatic that the disgusting jerk got what was coming to him, but there was too much at stake to enjoy the moment.

"Come on, Will. Let's go," I begged, dragging on his arm.

He nodded without taking his eyes off Tristan, and with the way Will's jaw feathered with hate, I spared the creep a quick glance, too. Tristan scowled at the red stain on his fingertips, and when he lifted his head, violence painted his features. Will's arm tensed beneath my hand, and as Tristan lunged for him, Josh looped an arm around my waist and hauled me out of the way.

My back was turned, but the cracking thud of Tristan's fist landing on Will's face made me scream. Josh handed me over to Jess and Birdie, and they pulled me away. I fought against them as they wrapped their arms around me, frightened by the way Will was hunched over with his hands on his knees and then panicked at how he shook himself, straightened, and squared up to Tristan. Blood dripped from his mouth and down his chin, landing on the white collar of his dress shirt. I had to get to him. Touch him and run my hands over him and make sure he was okay.

I needed to get close enough to Tristan to kick him in the fucking balls.

But Josh, Logan, Isaac, and Luca were already there. Everyone was shouting, hurling insults and warnings and threats on top of each other. Josh and Logan held Will back, one of them on each of his arms, and Luca stood in the middle, keeping Tristan and Will separated with his outstretched arms. Isaac held Tristan from behind as the dickwad pretended to grapple against his grip. Coward.

I was peripherally aware of the press of bodies in a half-circle around us. The cloying scent of a hundred different perfumes mingling together. The heat of so many people confining us in a tight space. The loud murmur of talking and gasping and quiet questions. The cameras. But there was too much happening all too quickly for me to think past getting to Will.

I shoved against Jess and Birdie's iron-firm hold on me. "Will! Let it go!"

Tristan had stopped struggling enough that Isaac was now dragging him away from Will towards the back exit, and as Isaac yanked open the door, Luca took a shaken Tash into his arms. Will roughly shook off Josh and Logan and watched Tristan leave with pure hatred burning in his gaze. Jess and Birdie let me go, and I closed the few steps between me and Will like my life depended on it. He breathed heavily through flared nostrils, and I worried as much about the split in his lip as I did the fever in his eyes.

I reached up to run a gentle hand over his jaw. "Are you all right?"

Will jerked back from my touch. He had his back to the cameras, and he watched with a hard jaw as the rear door closed behind Isaac and Tristan. When they disappeared, the heat in Will's glare dimmed. Something disturbing passed over his features, a look of sadness or resignation or both.

I dropped my hand as apprehension replaced adrenaline in my body. The energy in the room was loaded with anticipation, and the voices around us grew quiet.

"Will?" I set a cautious hand on his arm. "Let's go up to the loft and talk. I can help you clean up."

He still wouldn't look at me, and my apprehension dialled up to alarm. It took effort to swallow.

"I fucked up," he muttered.

"No, you—"

"I fucked up!" Will glanced behind him at the cameras, then at me. "I can't do this. I have to go."

I watched him walk away with his head bowed, and the flutter of dread in my chest grew stronger. The crowds parted around him, and his long legs carried him across the room too quickly for me to pull myself together and follow him.

"Is he okay?" Jess asked beside me.

I wanted to say yes, but I couldn't. I didn't believe it.

"He'll be fine," Logan replied, but he didn't sound confident. "He just needs a few minutes to cool off."

Logan was wrong. I was more certain of that than anything else. I lifted the hem of my dress and took after Will, not caring that all eyes in the room watched me go. Will was in pain, and my place was by his side.

52

ABBIE

────────

WHEN I DIDN'T see Will on the street outside and couldn't find him inside The Stop, I ran upstairs to the loft and tried there. It was empty and dark, so I called him. It went straight to his message service, and my worry increased tenfold.

I changed out of my evening wear, threw on the first thing I found in my open suitcase, and then ran downstairs again. Before I could decide whether to go back into the party and ask the crew to help me look for Will or go it alone, Adam met me on the street outside. Concern etched his features.

"Is Will okay?" he asked.

I threw up my hands and tried to shake off my anxiety. "I don't know. I can't find him."

Adam rubbed my arms and scanned the dark street. "He can't have gone far. We'll find him."

The door to the warehouse opened, and a woman slipped out. She hovered there as if she knew me, and it took me a second to recognise her.

"Liberty?"

She approached hesitantly. "Hi, Abbie."

Adam's head swung back and forth. "You two know each other?"

"*You* two know each other?" I replied, surprise pitching my voice a little higher.

Liberty's mouth curved in a shy smile. "We just met," she said. "Adam bought me a free drink."

Even in my distress, I was pleased that my brother was having a good time. He was so dedicated to his work that he'd never had a relationship last longer than two years, and though I wasn't saying Liberty was the woman he'd marry, I was more hopeful about happily-ever-afters now that I'd found mine.

"Is everything under control in there?" I asked. I wasn't about to go in, but when I found Will, I wanted to be able to tell him that the night wasn't ruined.

"Birdie's on top of it," Adam confirmed. "It's almost like the fight never happened."

"Okay. That's good news." I nodded to myself as a little of my anxiety melted away. "Now I need to find Will so I can let him know."

"Any ideas where he might be?" Adam asked.

"One," I replied. I looked at Liberty regretfully, then back at my brother. I knew he'd be sober enough to drive— he never had more than two drinks at a time—but he was clearly enjoying himself. "I'm sorry to spoil your night, but I've had too much alcohol to get behind the wheel. Any chance you can drive me?"

"Absolutely." Adam turned to Liberty with an apologetic smile. "I'm sorry to cut the evening short, but can I take you to breakfast in the morning?"

Liberty's disappointment morphed into delight right before my eyes. I liked this woman. "Yes. That would be great."

I tapped out a quick text to Will while I waited impatiently for them to exchange numbers, then followed Adam to his car, where it was parked further down Main Street. We drove to our destination in anxious silence. I wasn't in the mood to grill Adam about Liberty—that would happen after I'd made sure Will was okay—and he knew me well enough not to talk to me when my head was someplace else. I kept my phone in my hand in case Will called, but he didn't.

We didn't have far to go. Turning the corner onto a familiar street and pulling to the kerb, we found Will sitting in the gutter in the dark outside his mother's house.

He looked so forlorn and lost, all alone in the dark, and my heart broke. He'd taken off his jacket and rolled the sleeves of his crumpled white shirt up over his forearms. His top buttons were undone, his bow tie loose and uneven around his neck, the blood stain dried and brown. His lip was split and swollen, but ironically, his hair was immaculate. He had his arms looped around his bent knees and was staring over the road and into nothing.

Adam switched off the engine, but I dropped my hand on his before he could unbuckle his seatbelt.

"I got this," I told him.

It looked as though he was going to protest but thought better of it and simply nodded. "Call me if you need a ride home."

"I will. Thank you." I glanced at Will, then back at Adam and grimaced. "Mama and Dad are going to hear about this before I get a chance to explain. See if you can do some damage control for me?"

Adam nodded again, but tension made the muscles in his sharp jaw flicker. "I'll talk to them, but I think they'll understand once I tell them Tristan was there tonight."

I sighed with resignation. Bringing up this part of my past would cause my parents unnecessary hurt, but they'd learn the truth from someone sooner or later.

I leaned over to press a kiss on Adam's cheek. "Love you."

"Love you too, Little Bug," he replied. "Now, do something about that man on the street there. Let him know he has family and friends here to help fix whatever he thinks is broken."

I waited until Adam had disappeared down the road before I lowered myself to the gutter beside Will. He didn't acknowledge my presence, which didn't hurt me as much as it made me ache for him. He was in pain.

"Whatcha doing?" I asked, gently bumping his shoulder with mine.

He picked up a stone from the road and turned it over between his fingers. "Waiting for a light to turn on inside so I can go in and give Seb his bottle."

An echo of his heartache reverberated in my chest. I never knew it was possible to miss someone as much as I missed Seb. Without him close, it was like being without a limb or unable to shake that sensation of having forgotten something important.

"Does your mouth hurt?" I asked.

Will shrugged. "A little."

I didn't take offence that Will wasn't in the mood to talk. It was rare that he fell into moods like this, but not unheard of. It used to happen a lot when we were teenagers, and his father was in town. I knew from experience that Will would open up when he was ready.

"Big night," I commented softly.

Will spared me a swift, incredulous look. "Big fucking disaster."

I looped my arm through his and dropped my head on his arm. I welcomed his frustration so long as he was talking to me about it. "No. Big fucking success with a little hiccup at the end." The thought of Tristan made my pulse surge with fury. "That sleazeball had it coming."

Will didn't reply and instead dragged his phone from a pocket and swiped to his voice messages. Selecting one marked "Jason Maloney", he hit play and put the message on loudspeaker.

"Will? This is Jason Maloney. I'm on my way back to Sydney, but I wanted to let you know immediately that

I'll be retracting my offer of investment in your bar and brewery. Given tonight's events, I'm sure you understand that it's no longer in my firm's best interest to pursue a partnership, and I've been advised to cut ties without delay. Good luck to you."

I blinked at the bright screen as the phone went silent. I couldn't believe what I'd heard. Jason *liked* Will. He was behind his business plan one hundred percent. He said it had the potential for huge gains over the next three years. They were excited about working together, and after one little punch, this guy was going to bail?

I tamped down the hurt I felt on Will's behalf. He needed support and a voice of reason now, not more fuel poured on this emotional bin fire.

Will switched off his phone before tucking it back in his suit pants. "Big. Fucking. Disaster."

"He's just one investor," I replied. "Just one option and nothing was put on paper yet anyway. There'll be other chances to pitch your business—"

"Not like that," Will cut in. "Not after tonight."

He dropped his head into his hands, and I stared silently at my fingertips. I wanted so badly to soothe him, but I couldn't find the right words.

"I knew I'd screw this up," he muttered.

The resentment in his voice alarmed me because it was so out of character. "You knew you'd screw *what* up?"

Will laughed. "Everything? I'm a lousy father who's barely seen his son these last three days and not much more in the last three weeks. And the only way I could justify spending less time with him and more time on the business and this stupid fucking tournament was because I told myself I was doing it all for him. To build something for *him*. To make *him* proud. And look at me. I've worked my arse off to achieve something I would have thought impossible a year ago, and I've blown it all. I'm sitting in the fucking gutter after knocking someone to the ground for touching my girl. What part of that sentence would make any son proud of his dad?"

An iron band snapped shut around my ribs and made it hard to breathe. Will wasn't blaming me for this, was he? Not directly and not intentionally, but he was clearly struggling with what happened as much as why, and I heard alarm bells.

I was going to ignore them. We just had to get through tonight, and tonight wasn't about me.

I dropped my head on Will's arm again and held on tighter. The urge to stop his fear was creeping into panic. "I mean, your girl's pretty pleased with you."

Will shook his head. "You shouldn't be."

The iron band around my chest clamped down harder. I straightened and pulled my arm from his. "What do you mean?"

He stared at the road between his feet. "I don't know how to be a boyfriend, Abs, and the more I think about how we got here, the less I understand it. We didn't really choose this, did we? You didn't choose it. You needed a place to stay while your apartment was unliveable, and I was too scared to be alone with Seb that I took advantage of the situation. You were stuck, and I pushed too hard, and we ended up here."

I blinked as my head spun and my heart screamed. Now was the time to confess that I could have gone home weeks ago, and I opened my mouth to say the words, but something stopped me.

What if I told him, and it made no difference? What if it made him mad? I couldn't tell him I'd manipulated my way into his home because, to start, I didn't think he could take care of a baby by himself, and then later, I didn't want to be without him or his beautiful son. How would he react if I told him I was as much invested in his success as he was, giving so much of myself to support him while he worked so damn hard to support a family that I thought included me? Would my dependency on Will make him stronger—strong enough to hold us up while we got through this rough patch—or would it be the thing that broke him?

53

ABBIE

———————

I WAS SUDDENLY aware of my vulnerability. I'd put myself in this position willingly with my whole heart because I trusted Will, but now I felt unsafe.

"What are you saying, Will?" I whispered.

"I don't know. I'm saying I love you, but you deserve better. I'm saying I don't want to lose you, but I don't know if I have what it takes to make this work. I'm sick of screwing everything up, and I can't let people love me if I'm only going to let them down. I know how that feels."

My mouth was dry, and it hurt to swallow. I knew he'd do this. I *knew* it. Sex, he could handle. My heart? I should never have let him have it. The danger of him breaking it had never really gone away.

I was a fucking idiot.

Will turned to look at me with tears in his eyes, and my heart broke all over again.

We were both idiots.

I picked up his hand with a sigh, threading his fingers through mine and kissing his knuckles. Before we were lovers, we were friends—best friends—and nothing would change that. Will loved me, but he had some work to do before he learned to love himself. Until then, I just had to love him enough for the both of us—even if it hurt like hell.

"Seb is what matters right now," I assured him. "He'll always be your number one priority. As for work, well... There are a few days left of the festival, but it'll all be wrapped up by Valentine's Day. The weekend crowds will thin out, and things will be more manageable from tomorrow on. When the dust settles, you can get your head on straight and make a plan."

I snorted, though it took effort to be so blasé. "Forget Jason Maloney. You had your heart set on landing an investor, but that kind of cash isn't the only way to make things happen. Go back to your original plan. Will it take longer? Maybe, but slower might be better. It'll give you more time to focus on Seb, who adores you. You could never let him down. It's impossible."

Will traced little circles on the back of my hand, frowning as his thumb moved around and around. A little of the tension had left his body, which told me he'd bought my act. "My dad let me down all the time. It happens, Abs."

"You are not your father," I replied fiercely.

"Yeah." He grunted and shifted his feet. "I know."

I could have pushed him a little more on that, but I had to get to the hard part now, or I might not be able to get through it. I squeezed his hand. "And as for us? You're right, things moved fast, and maybe it's smart to rewind a little. In fact, I had a missed call from the insurance company yesterday, letting me know my building is ready. Perfect timing, I guess. Things between us will be back to the way they used to be before the end of the weekend."

My heart thumped in my throat as I waited for his response. I hated myself for hoping he'd ask me to stay.

"Fuck." Will dropped his head. "I don't want you to go, but…"

My heart plummeted, and there was a painful pause.

"I have to," I finished with a crack in my voice.

Will met my eyes and nodded slowly. I had to go. Not to end us but to save us.

Behind us, a light switched on in the house, and Will cleared his throat as we both got to our feet. "That'll be the baby." He gestured to the front door. "Do you want to—"

"No." I lifted a hand and stepped back, then plucked out my phone and sent a rushed text to Adam, asking him to pick me up. I'd never needed to get away from a situation faster than I did right then. He replied straightaway with a thumbs-up emoji, and my breath hitched with relief. "That's okay. You go. You need time with your son, and I need to pack."

I need you to walk away now before you see me cry.

Will watched me with regret painted across his face. "It's after midnight, Abs. And there's no rush. It can wait a few days."

"It really can't," I replied with an unintentional snap of defensiveness, and I took a calming breath. "If I'm going to go, I need to go now. But I'm still here to help with Seb, all right? You've got work and the festival—"

"No. It's okay." Will's gaze drifted to the lit window and back again, his eyes shining with hurt. "You've already done so much, and you must be ready to get back to normal life. I'll ask Mum for help this weekend."

At that moment, I wasn't sure the pain would have been worse if Will had reached into my chest and torn out my heart.

"Well, I'd love to see him, so call me anytime."

Headlights appeared at the end of the street, coming closer until they stopped a few paces away.

"That's Adam," I said, and before we could hurt each other anymore, I slipped my arms around Will's narrow waist and pressed my face to his chest. His warm, familiar arms circled me, and his lips landed on my hair, his chest expanding in a long, even breath.

"Everything will work out in the end. You'll see."

I'd told him what we both needed to hear. I doubted either one of us believed it.

54

WILL

———

"NO, I UNDERSTAND, Mr Talbot," I mumbled into the phone, taking the wrath of the tourism committee president with all the grace I could muster. He was lecturing me like I was a child, and it was pissing me off, but a short temper was what got me into this situation, and it sure as shit wasn't going to get me out of it.

And, I reminded myself, I deserved it.

I was sitting at Mum's breakfast table in my crushed suit pants and blood-stained shirt, my busted lip sore even after a night with a bag of frozen peas attached to it. I'd crashed on the couch because after the night I'd had, I didn't want to be away from Seb, and it had been too late to take him home.

I'd watched Abbie drive away with a hollow sensation behind my ribs, regretting every word I'd said even though I'd had to say them. Shattered that she'd walked away from me when she could have stayed and fought.

Then I'd walked through the front door in my dishevelled suit and bloody face, and fucking cried like a baby.

It was a relief and a comfort when Mum hugged me and then deposited a warm, sleepy Seb in my arms. I managed to pull myself together for the twenty minutes it took to give him a bottle and return him to his bed. By then, Mum had made up the sofa for me. We sat there for an hour while I told her everything and then fell asleep exhausted.

How could it be that last night was only hours ago? It felt like forever.

Old Talbot was still raving on the other end of the phone, so I set it to speaker mode and placed it on the table, dropped my head in my hands, and closed my eyes.

Fuck. I was tired. Physically. Mentally. Emotionally. I'd begun replaying the last three weeks and rewriting the ending in my head. No grand plans to expand my business. No stupid agreements to go along with this Valentine's Day Festival bullshit. No buying the warehouse, no hosting a poker event, no boost to my social media profile and saying nothing when things got out of hand. No punching dickheads on camera, even when they deserved it. No keeping my relationship with Abbie a secret.

Maybe no relationship with Abbie, period.

Stifling a frustrated grunt, I rubbed the heels of my palms over my dry eyes and forced myself to stop rehashing the same shit. No matter how many times I thought about it, I couldn't bring myself to erase Abbie from my story. Or Seb. It hurt too much. A better man would be strong enough to let her go, and I so badly wanted to be a better man.

"We're in damage control, William," Mr Talbot barked. "The good name of Valentine Bay has been impacted by your reckless behaviour, and all the hard work that Emily has done to promote our Valentine's Day Festival has put us in the difficult position of having to address your actions to multiple media outlets. We're front-page news, young man, and not in a good way. I hate to say it, but I expected more from you."

I winced once at his use of my full name, then again at the disappointment in his tone. I'd let him down. I'd let down the whole town, and this wasn't the first call I'd had this morning. It was the first one I'd answered, and only after Mr Talbot had tried to get through three times. So many people had a stake in last night's success, and I'd disappointed each and every one of them. I wanted to hide out here for the rest of my life.

It took me a minute to realise the phone was silent and another moment to understand that Mr Talbot was waiting for me to answer him. For the life of me, I couldn't remember what he'd asked.

"Yeah, look," I mumbled, "I'm sorry about what happened. I, uh…"

Mum entered the kitchen with Seb on her hip, grinning like sunshine, and I smiled. One, because his cute little face always made me feel better, and two, nobody tells you that one of the best things about having a kid is having a non-debatable excuse to remove yourself from shitty conversations.

"Listen, Mr Talbot. I have to go. Seb just woke up, and he needs me. I'll, uh… I'll talk to you later."

Feeling like a dick—a relieved dick—I hung up without waiting for a reply.

I reached out to Seb, and he squirmed to get to me. Mum kissed his forehead before she transferred him to my arms. "He's missed you, sweetheart," she commented, moving past us on her way to the fridge.

I bounced Seb on my knee and let the comforting weight of his body and the smell of his skin soothe my exhausted nerves. "I've missed him too."

Mum spared me a cautious glance as she prepared breakfast for Seb. "I spoke to Dawn earlier. She had a lot to say about last night."

I huffed. "I bet."

"She told me that the party was going incredibly well until your altercation with Tristan. You didn't tell me that."

I grunted. "Doesn't really matter what happened before," I replied, "only what happened after."

I transferred Seb to his highchair and snapped a bib around his neck, then took the bowl from Mum's hands. After testing the temperature of the food on my wrist, I spooned a small portion of cereal into Seb's wide, eager mouth.

"You mean before the fight?"

"I mean, before I was stupid and reckless and completely cocked up my life."

Mum shook her head sadly. "I wish you wouldn't talk like that."

"It's the truth, isn't it?" I smiled at Seb, but it didn't erase the bitterness in my tone. "I caused a scandal all over social media and put the reputations of this community, the festival, and all our local businesses into question. I lost the investor who wanted to work with me on the brewery, and I'm in more debt than ever before. My son has no mother, and no matter how many pictures or updates I send her, she won't answer my messages, and it makes me so irrationally mad. Oh, and I was a lousy boyfriend because I took advantage of the only woman who saw the real me and loved me anyway, and when I gave her the chance to walk away, she took it."

Mum straightened and dropped her mug on the table with a dull thud. "What do you mean, you took advantage?"

"Fuck. That's not what I meant." I set down Seb's lunch and pressed my thumb and forefinger to my eyes. Now, I was swearing in front of my kid. "She showed up the same day as Seb, needing a place to stay, right?"

Mum nodded but looked confused.

"Abbie wouldn't have moved in with me unless she had to, and once she was there, she must have seen how badly I needed help. It's like that thing—what's it called when a kidnap victim wants to stay with the person who abducted them?"

Her eyebrows shot up. "Stockholm syndrome?"

"Yeah. That's it. Stockholm syndrome. Abbie moved in against her will. She got stuck helping me with the baby, and in time, she convinced herself she wanted to stay. She started to believe I had something to offer her.

Now she's seen the light."

Mum picked up her coffee and took a sip. Her alarm had shifted to amused patience. "Will, that's nonsense."

"It's not." I picked up the little bowl and concentrated on spooning mush into Seb's mouth instead of the nausea rolling through my middle. "Abbie never wanted us to be together. Did you know that? She fought it, and I pushed her anyway. And you know *why* she fought it? She knew me, and she knew I'd screw it up. I'm irresponsible. Thoughtless. Selfish. It's in my DNA, right? With a father like mine, I was always going to be a loser. Abbie's better off without me."

Only after I'd said the words did I realise what I'd done. I'd never criticised my father so plainly where my mother could hear me, and I didn't want her to know how much I still thought about my childhood or that part of me blamed her for my father's mistakes. I glanced at her guiltily.

Mum didn't seem upset as she shook her head. "Oh, Will. I love you, and I know this is going to be hard for you to hear, but honey—you're wrong. About all of it."

"I'm not wrong."

"Oh, you are. And as badly as I want to make you feel better right now, be prepared to feel a little worse first."

"I'm listening," I said, but I was thinking, *Oh, Jesus. What else had I done wrong now?*

55

WILL

"FIRST, I WANT to give you a piece of advice about parenting, which you are free to take or leave as you see fit." Mum smiled fondly at Seb. "Make a decision about his mother and see it through. Either sign the papers she gave you or call a lawyer and sue for shared custody. You can't bully her into his life, nor can you keep on begging. He needs stability and security, and without a legal framework in place, you're both vulnerable. You know all too well the pain of having a parent drift in and out of your life the way your father was in and out of yours. Don't be the reason Seb has to live with that too."

Her words hit me like rocks to the gut. Sharp and painful. This was the first time she'd acknowledged that my relationship with my dad was problematic, but her validation didn't reverse my hurt the way I'd imagined it would. I was too focused on what else she had to say.

I *had* been failing my son, and not because I'd been working long hours or missed the fact that he'd been cutting two teeth. He needed me to make a choice about Heather, and I'd come up with every excuse to avoid it. Each minute I left the parental rights forms unsigned put Seb's home with me at risk.

I gazed at my son with a mix of love and fear. I was his father, and he trusted me to act like it. This was one area of my life where I couldn't accept defeat or settle for the middle ground. I had to sign those papers.

Mum sighed as she toyed with the handle of her mug. "Don't make the same mistakes I did, William," she added. "It's easy to see, in hindsight, that I didn't always make the right decisions where your father was concerned. I loved him, and I let him set the rules for our relationship and our family. I should have been strong enough to set better boundaries and demand he be a stable presence in your life, but I didn't do that, and it hurt you. I should have done more to reassure you that aside from the blue eyes and the dimples and the charisma oozing from your pores, you have very little in common with your father. He swindled people. He was dishonest. He charmed his way into hearts and pockets, then bowed his way out without any care for the consequences. He would never have built up a business like you have. He could never have earned the respect of the people in this town the way you have. They'd never have given him the responsibility of hosting a major event in its name."

The bridge of my nose stung, and I swallowed to push away the catch in my chest. I never expected to hear this from my mother. I never imagined she thought about our past in such detail or had any regrets. She was too positive for that and too ready to believe in the good of the world. Her honesty put my search for validation into perspective. I didn't need her to take responsibility for my father, but I did need to know she understood.

"Thank you," I said softly.

Mum nodded once, then smiled with brighter eyes. "Don't give up, William. Nothing in life is unfixable. You're determined, you're honest, and you're a hard worker. Everybody knows this community is important to you. I think you'll be surprised at how much people adore you and how willing they'll be to forgive and forget *if…*"

Trepidation settled in my gut and maybe a little hope. "If… what?"

"If you own your mistakes, sweetheart. If you do what your father never did and never could. Take responsibility for your actions—the good as well as the bad—and be a good man."

She glanced at Seb as if to make a point, and that love and fear swelled again. It never occurred to me *not* to take responsibility for Seb. I was his father, for better or worse. I'd never give up on my kid.

Mum was saying I couldn't give up on my business, either. Or this town.

It wasn't too late. I could fix it.

That just left…

"And as for Abigail—"

"The thing with Abbie is complicated," I said. "I won't force her into a situation she never asked for."

I didn't say it out loud, but after Tristan's reappearance in the Bay last night, I'd compared myself to him. It wasn't the same—nowhere near the same—but wasn't Abbie compromising herself and her values because that's what *I* needed, not what she wanted? The thought made my skin crawl.

"You didn't, and you're not," Mum said.

I huffed with frustration, set the empty bowl aside, and helped Seb take a sip of cooled, boiled water from his cup. "Have you been listening to a word I said?"

She smirked. "Oh, yes. And I have some information that'll blow your odd little theory out of the water."

I rolled my eyes. "By information, you mean gossip."

"I say pot*ay*-to, you say pot*ah*-to."

Delivered in her American twang, that little phrase always made me smile, and the fact that I could do so now made me realise that, somehow, Mum's support had already shifted some of my gloom.

"Nobody says pot*ah*-to, not even Aussies."

She flapped her hand. "Can't understand a word you're saying at the best of times, sweetheart. Now, do you want to hear this information or not?"

I shook my head but said, "Go on, then. Shoot."

Mum took a slow sip of coffee, enjoying the change in my mood enough to torture me now.

"Her apartment was ready to move into weeks ago. As quickly as three days after the leak, or so I hear."

"Bullshit." I glanced guiltily at Seb, then lowered my voice. "Who told you that?"

Mum leaned towards me. "Dawn."

I scoffed. I should have known better than to get my hopes up with gossip. "She's got no idea what she's talking about."

"That's what I thought, too, at first. She told me she was donating another box of items for the charity sale—"

"Jesus, are we still getting ready for that?"

"Yes. Anyway, she slipped inside Nancy's house to drop off the box and accidentally overheard a conversation between Adam and his parents. You said he picked up Abbie last night?"

I frowned as the pieces came together. "Yes."

"Well, he took her to the loft, where she packed up a few things, and then he drove her straight to her apartment. She told him it's been ready for weeks, but she didn't say anything to anyone."

I was missing something obvious, but I couldn't see it yet. "But... why not?"

"Why do you think?"

I thought a lot of things. I hoped for even more. An odd, happy twitch pulled at my mouth.

"And before you start wondering if Dawn got her wires crossed, I called Nancy immediately afterwards to confirm the details. It's all true, William. Abbie's been living with you because she wanted to, not because she had to."

I couldn't stop the tug on my lips. "Do you think so?"

"I think the Universe gave that girl a reason to live in your back pocket, and she grabbed it with two hands."

I started to feel hopeful, but it wasn't that easy to forget the events of the last twenty-four hours. Especially the moments that hurt the most.

"But last night, when I said she deserved better, she... she agreed with me."

Mum *tsked* and shook her head. "Well, I don't know about that, though I find it very hard to believe. What I do know is that Abbie loves you, and she adores this little boy. What's more, you're doing her a disservice by assuming she didn't choose to be in your relationship. She's a strong woman, William. Smart and fiery and passionate, and she knows her own mind. If Abbie wanted things to stay platonic between the two of you, I have no doubt she'd have moved out the minute she could. But she didn't. She stayed."

She stayed.

And last night, I'd told her to leave.

I ran my eyes over Seb's face. This boy was my world, but Abbie was my everything, too. I loved her with every fibre of my being, and though it was different from the love I felt for my child, it was just as powerful. We'd been children together. Our love was built on years and years of respect and common ground, attraction and admiration, friendship and torment and everything in between. She was more than my best friend. She was my soul mate. And if I couldn't give up on Seb, then I couldn't give up on Abbie. Our little family didn't work without her.

"It's not too late," I said. "I can still fix this."

Mum grinned. "Yes, you can. But don't wait too long. I can hardly stand the wait."

56

ABBIE

I SAT ON my yoga mat at the front of my freshly fixed studio. Quiet music danced in the air. Candles flickered in the dim light. And my class was made up entirely of couples who had enrolled in my Valentine's Day in Valentine's Bay Partners' Workshop.

I wanted to be anywhere else but here. A deserted island. A jail cell. A convent. Anywhere.

I'd agreed to do the class weeks ago when Emily had persuaded me to try it at least once over the festival period. She argued it would be good for my business and socials, and it was annoying how the woman always made sense, but I never could have predicted that I'd have to facilitate a class for lovers less than twenty-four hours after mine had punched a guy in the face for me, then broken my goddamn heart.

It didn't help that I'd forced Jess, Em, Birdie, and Tash to sign up to give me moral support, which meant Logan, Josh, Isaac, and Luca were in the room, too. Instead of swapping amused smiles and silent jokes with my friends like I'd hoped we would, they threw me furtive looks of sympathy—when they looked at me at all. It was the same with the other locals in the class. Burt the Third was here with his wife. Dawn, who hadn't had a partner in all the time I'd known her, had dragged her teenage daughter along, and the girl's eye-roll game was on point. Dorothy March was at the back of the room with her new man, and though she was at least ninety years old, I was pretty sure her date was only in his seventies.

Another time, I'd have called Dot a cougar with a wink and approving grin. Today, I wished the floor would open and swallow me whole.

"Okay, everyone." Even my yoga voice, which usually came so naturally, was a burden today. "Let's move into a partnered breathing pose. Settle into easy sit position—legs crossed at the ankles or shins, whatever feels most comfortable to you—and rest your back against your partner's. Notice how your body moves as you breathe in and out, and pay attention to the feel of your partner's ribcage against your own. That's it. Inhale... and exhale. Very good."

I allowed five minutes for the pose and kept my eyes closed the whole time. I focussed on my own breath and tried to find a centre inside my emotions.

I was sad, but I was also mad. Angry at myself for ever getting into a situation that had the potential to hurt me. Pissed off that Will had encouraged my trust, then left me when things got rough, and that he'd given up on us so quickly. Frustrated because when I tried to define it, I couldn't put a name on what I'd lost. Will and I were friends again. He wasn't gone—we'd simply reset our relationship to default mode. We'd never been a conventional couple, and this wasn't a conventional break-up.

So, what was it all for? What was the purpose of the last month? What was the Universe trying to tell me?

I swallowed my self-indulgent overwhelm and opened my eyes. "Okay, class. This next one is great for spine mobility and detoxification. It's a seated twist, and all you need to do is—"

The door to the studio bounced open with a bang, and my chin jerked up just as everyone in the room turned to look backwards.

Will stood in the door frame with Seb on his hip, the light from the hall outlining his tall, strong frame. An overwhelming surge of joy and relief hit me at the sight of the baby, and my heart beat faster as Will's eyes searched for mine. He found me and took a few steps into the room before he stalled and looked around, then stopped.

"I, uh…" Will shifted Seb on his hip and rubbed his forehead. "I didn't know you had a class."

I'd forgotten all about my students the moment I set eyes on him, and I wanted to tell him to keep moving forwards before he ran again, but I was frozen.

"It's okay, dear." Dot was closest to the door, and from her seat on the floor, she set a hand on Will's leg. He glanced down at her, and the look she gave him was slow and deliberate, as were her words. "Do you need to talk to Abigail?"

His brows drew together before he looked back at me. "I mean, yeah. I do, but…"

Hope trapped the breath in my lungs, and my heart pounded for a hundred reasons. Love. Fury. Relief. With his eyes on me, Will took another few hesitant steps into the studio. Each one tangled my nerves a little tighter.

I wanted to touch him. I wanted to kiss him. I wanted to shout and rant and tell him he'd ruined everything, and then I wanted to make up. I was a freaking mess for this man. Me. Abbie Ellison. That's how I knew I was gone for him, as if there'd been any doubt. I couldn't keep up the act anymore.

"If you've got something to say, then say it," Burt ordered as he got to his feet. He helped Mrs Spies stand as well, then crossed his arms and scowled. "We're listening."

"You're listening?" Will swallowed and looked around the room *again*. I could see the moment he spotted Dawn, then the crew. His eyes grew wide, but then he squared his shoulders and stalked through the class, only stopping when he reached me. I stared up at him, searching for answers in his expression, until he extended his hand. My body vibrated with expectation as I took it, and he helped me rise. When we were face to face with the whole class watching, we stood looking at each other for a long moment. And as much as I wanted Will to say something that would fix what was broken, I didn't object to the limbo right then. I could spend forever with Will looking at me the way he was.

"Well?" Burt grumbled. "Get on with it."

Someone shushed him—Dot, I thought—but I didn't bother looking to be sure. Suddenly, I was all too aware of our audience.

"Maybe we should do this another time," I murmured.

"No." Will kept on looking at me like we were the only people in the room. "I don't want to hide anymore. I want everyone in this room to hear what I have to say."

I couldn't quite believe what was happening. Someone turned off the music, and we were enveloped with quiet murmuring. All I could see was Will and the little baby reaching out to be put in my arms.

Will's mouth tipped upwards on one side as he offered me Seb. I took him eagerly, pulling him against my chest and pressing my nose to his hair to breathe in his exquisite scent.

A missing shard of my heart slipped into place.

"Why are you here, Will?"

He dragged a hand through his hair as his eyes darted to something over my head. I knew it was the crew, and whatever he saw there gave him courage.

Will cleared his throat. "I came to apologise."

Breathe in, I reminded myself. *Breathe out.* "For what?"

"For pushing you away when I should have pulled you closer. For letting my insecurities get the better of me and for making big decisions in the heat of the moment. Decisions that impacted not just me but you, too." He gently smoothed Seb's curls. "And our family."

Bursts of anticipation fired inside me. "Our family?"

Keep breathing.

"Yeah." He took a step closer, capturing Seb between us and turning us into a tight little unit. I forgot where we were as Will's gaze traced my face. "I don't want to go back to the way things were before Seb came into our lives. I don't want to live without you. You are our family. This doesn't work without you. *I* don't work without you."

I bit my lip and battled the urge to throw myself in his arms and declare everything forgiven. I'd spent so many years denying how much I loved this man because I was certain he'd break my heart. I never believed I was strong enough to overcome the pain of loving and losing him. But I'd learned something this last month, something I couldn't have known without loving Will and Seb as fiercely as I did.

Love like we had was worth the risk.

"You hurt me, Will," I said. "You, of all people, know how difficult it was for me to let you in. I love you. You know that. But how can I trust you?"

He blinked, and his throat bobbed with a nervous swallow. "Abbie, please—"

"Speak up!" Burt called out from the side of the room. "We can't hear you back here."

"Give them a minute!" Dawn retorted. "We can compare notes later."

Will's jaw tensed as he ignored the shouting. "Nobody knows me better than you do, Abs. When everybody saw an immature playboy, you saw my pain—but you also saw my potential. I waited years to tell you I love you, but we both know I always have, which kind of makes the word mean less than I need it to right now. I appreciate you. I respect you. I admire you. I know I screwed up last night— Jesus, do I know I screwed up—but there's only one thing I regret. And that's turning away from you when you should have been the first person I ran towards. I know I'm new at this, but that's no excuse. You wanted to be there for me, and I wouldn't let you. I was too disappointed in my actions to be completely honest with you."

I could feel myself melting a little more at every word, but his confession at the end yanked me out of my hazy stupor. I always believed what we had was genuine. Real. Truthful.

"You lied to me?"

"No!" Panic rounded his eyes, and he grabbed at my hand. "I just didn't tell you the truth that I'm telling you now. I should have said this last night so we could work through the hard shit together. We could have talked all night and woken together this morning and faced whatever comes next as a team. I let you down, and I'm asking you to let me fix it. Please."

Will hadn't lied... but a cold realisation sank into my bones. I had. A little white lie that didn't hurt anyone but made it possible for me to pretend to everyone—Will, my parents, my friends, even myself—that I was living with Will because I had no other choice. I'd become accustomed to deflecting my truth, so I never had to be vulnerable. But I'd never found true happiness that way. It needed to stop. Now.

Every cell of my being begged me to do this privately, but growth came from uncomfortable moments, and I was tired of worrying about what other people thought of me.

"Will, I have something to tell you." I swallowed and shifted my fingers between his. "When I asked you for a place to stay, I didn't know how long I was going to be at the loft. But the truth is, my apartment was ready weeks ago, and I lied to you about it. At first, it was because I knew you'd never ask for help with Seb, and you needed it. Pretending that I had nowhere else to go seemed like the easiest way to force you to accept my help."

I chanced a look up at him. He didn't look angry—that was good—but his expression was serious.

"You were right. I needed help—more than I should have expected and taken from you, to be honest. If I hadn't been so stubborn about being a good father on my own, we could have relied more on Mum and Nancy, and you wouldn't have been under so much pressure. I feel like I took advantage of you, Abs, and I hate myself for that. I'm so sorry I put you in that position."

Shaking my head through the last part of his speech, I rushed to correct him. This was the important part and the hardest part to say out loud. "I said helping you was only the start of it. Three days in, I could have left, but I didn't want to. I used the flooding as an excuse to be near you—and Seb." I absently kissed the baby's forehead to hide the sting of tears. "Leaving felt wrong and staying felt right."

"It did feel right." Will cupped my cheek and softly brushed his thumb across my skin. His blue eyes grew soft even as his dimple popped with a little smile—the smile that was all mine. The one that made me feel like I was the only woman in the world. "I understand why you did what you did. And thank you for being honest with me, but... I already knew about your apartment."

"You— what? How? That's not possible. Nobody knew about my apartment."

Will looked a little sheepish. "It's not like I knew all along. Mum only told me about it this morning."

"Your *mother* told you?" I frowned, trying to follow the path backwards from Lori to me, then the only answer clicked into place. "*Adam.*"

"Yeah, Adam," Will confirmed, "by way of your parents—and Dawn."

I whipped around to get a look at the woman herself, and Dawn waved at me. "I only told one or two people, darling. I promise. Your secret's safe with me."

"Good to know, Dawn," I replied with affectionate sarcasm. I should have been upset that people were talking about me, but all I felt was relief about giving up one more charade. "Thanks."

Will watched me with hope in his eyes, then flashed me his get-out-of-trouble-free smile. "So, what do you say? Can you give us another chance?"

Something of my old fire rekindled deep inside. The heat of loving him so fiercely and the excitement of loving who I was when I was with him.

But also the burn of fear when I thought I'd lost everything. Fear that bubbled up as irritation.

I poked him in the chest. "Don't be cute, and don't give me the dimple, Kidd. That thing's not going to save you now."

He grinned because he'd won me over. We both knew it because this was the kind of banter we'd built our relationship on. "Okay."

"I've been thinking too, you know, and I've got some things I want to say."

"Can't wait to hear them."

"The first? Grow up."

Those eyebrows, arched with amusement, flew up to his hairline.

I narrowed my eyes because although I didn't want to fight anymore, I did want him to know that I was serious. "That's right, you heard me. Grow up. If I give you another crack at this, you are *not* going to do this to me again. You're not going to do this to *us*."

Will's humour dissolved under his solemn brow. "I know."

I nodded with satisfaction as the hurt and the fear of the last few hours sparked again.

"At first, I was going to go along with it, you know? I was going to let you flake out on me because I love you. I've always loved you, and I thought I could go back to loving you like I used to, but here's another truth."

I paused, glaring up at him, suddenly irrationally angry that Will didn't have as much faith in himself as I did. A warm flush spread across my chest, and I knew if I looked, the skin would be mottled pink.

"Uh, yeah?" he asked with trepidation in his voice and confusion around his mouth.

"Everyone fails sometimes! We all take risks that don't work out, and we all deal with shame at some point in our lives. That doesn't mean you're not worth something. It doesn't mean you give up. You fix it, Will. And if you can't, you learn your lesson and start again."

"Babe, I know. I'm sorry—"

"And what about what I've risked to be here?" I was on a roll now, and something I can only describe as Mama Bear Energy whooshed through my body. "What about the life I've been building? I love this little boy. I love him so damn much."

"I know you—"

"No more feeling sorry for yourself, Will. And no more shutting me out. It's time to—"

"I get it, babe, and if we can just—"

"And I'm not saying I'm perfect—"

"Maybe if we—"

"But we don't have to be perfect—"

"I know, that's what I'm—"

"We just have to be there for—"

Will slid his warm hand around my neck and slammed his mouth against mine. He kissed me, opening my lips with his own and tempting me with the tip of his tongue. I melted against him as someone carefully took Seb from my hip.

I looped my arms around Will's neck as he arched his body over mine. The kiss was warm and slow and so good, our lips dragging against each other, our tongues teasing until a round of applause sounded, whistles and catcalls and stomping feet bringing us back to the room. Will pulled away, and I laughed at the smile on his face.

He kissed my forehead as he gestured for Seb, and Jess darted in to hand him over. She gave me a fast hug before stepping away. Will pulled me against his side, and I lifted Seb's hand before meeting Will's eyes. The shadow of anxiety that had been present before had lifted, leaving nothing but love.

He set his mouth to my ear, and at the touch of his warm breath, goosebumps thrilled across my skin.

"So, is that a yes?" he whispered. "Do we give this another chance?"

"It's a yes," I replied. "So much, yes."

Will's arm tightened around me, and there was a moment among all the hooting and clapping that it was only us in that room. Only us in the entire world.

Just the three of us. Our little family.

57

WILL

IT WAS THE evening before Valentine's Day, and the festival was almost over. The events would officially wrap up tomorrow night with a revived round of flowers and decorations across town, carnival games, a night food market, and a jazz band in the park, but the crowds had thinned once the hype of the poker tournament was over. The tourism council had gone from pissed off and loud to pissed off and quiet, but that suited me fine. The only way to prove I deserved a second chance was to earn it, and the only way to do that was to apologise to the people I'd hurt and focus on The Stop, my son, and my girl.

Because Abbie was my girl now, and everyone knew it.

She moved back to the loft the night after we made up. Everyone in town was talking about it—thanks, Dawn— but we were happy.

Yesterday, I posted a pic of me, Abbie, and Seb on the beach on my socials and captioned it with the announcement of our relationship. I was past the point of caring about the impact of my marital status on my bottom line. If I'd learned anything these last few weeks, it was to give my energy to the things that mattered. But Abbie had been braced for backlash from the Will Kidd Fan Club. I'd pretended that everything would be all right but quietly believed she was right. I was ready to jump in and defend her against an onslaught of online bullshit… and then, it didn't happen.

Not counting one or two outliers, the online response was overwhelmingly positive. Everyone fell in love with Seb at first sight—no surprises there. Those dimples were going to get him into (and out of) a world of trouble. A bunch of women on my feeds were girl-crushing on Abbie, and her social followings jumped upward by the thousands after she shared that her secret to her luminescence was yoga (not sex, though that's totally what it was).

Bottom line, most people were happy for me. They saw something romantic in the roguish playboy finding his person and something viscerally satisfying in Abbie having the skills to tame me.

Hundreds of people asked if she was the girl who scored the quickie at The Stop. We neither confirmed nor denied.

I also signed and filed Seb's parental rights papers.

I woke up the morning after storming Abbie's studio with her wrapped up in my arms and the coconut fragrance of her skin in my nose, and it felt like I'd pressed a reset button on my life. I'd climbed out of a pit of self-recrimination and despair and into a world of love and possibility.

With twenty-four hours to go until I could officially put this year's Valentine's Day in Valentine Bay Festival behind me, I stood at the door to the loft and handed Seb to my mother for another sleepover. It didn't feel great having him spend the night away from me and Abbie, but once this week was over, it wouldn't happen nearly as frequent.

The door to the loft closed behind us then, and I turned to Abbie. She looked at me with a mischievous twinkle that I couldn't resist, and I pounced, throwing her over my shoulder roughly enough that she squealed before she laughed, then carried her up the stairs.

"I've been waiting for this since the moment I kissed you in the studio yesterday," I confessed as I laid her down on the unmade bed. "I love Seb, but being a father has got to be the biggest cock block there is."

Abbie chuckled, then propped herself up on her elbows as she watched me tear off my shirt and unzip my pants. Her eyes widened, and her tongue swept over her bottom lip. "I guess we're just going to have to get more inventive because I hope you know I plan to be a high-maintenance woman. I require access to your services at least five times a week."

"You'll get no complaints from me."

I dropped to my knees and tugged at her pants, peeling the tight material down her legs. "These make your arse look fucking unreal, but they're a bitch to take off."

"Got to make you work for it," she said with a chuckle before she collapsed onto the mattress.

I ran my nose up the inside of her open thighs, inhaling the scent of her, then pushed her knees further apart. Years of yoga had made Abbie's muscles firm and supple, and I leaned further on her legs, spreading her wider to give me full access to her dripping pussy.

Blood rushed to my cock at the first taste of her, and as I dragged my tongue up her wet slit and lapped at the moisture pooling at her centre, Abbie threaded her long fingers through my hair, twisted at the roots tight enough to sting, and ground her hips against my mouth. Her breathless moans and wordless cries spurred me to work harder, and I fucking got off on the way she bore down on my face, riding me with no restraint. So many women were shy about this sort of thing, but not my girl. I wanted her sex on my tongue, and she wanted me fucking her like this.

After she came screaming my name, I peeled the rest of her clothes from her body and removed my pants. I needed to feel her bare skin on mine, but when I covered her body with mine, she shoved me over onto my back and climbed on top.

I dug my fingertips into her hips and groaned as she straddled me, then took my dick and rubbed the tip over her wet centre.

"I don't know how I thought I could live without this," she said breathily as she slid onto my dick. I groaned and squeezed my eyes closed as I adjusted to the sensation of her snug walls around me. "I don't know how I thought we could ever go back to being friends."

"It would have been impossible," I agreed, moving my hands to her breasts and flicking her nipples with my thumbs. I gazed up at her lithe, powerful frame above me and rode another satisfying surge of *mine*. I'd reminded myself of that fact a lot today. It felt so fucking good. "But not because of the sex, right?"

"Well…" Abbie leaned forward just enough to tuck her feet underneath her arse, and in a twisty yoga move that made me sweat, she slipped her toes between my thighs and used them to cup my balls. I let out a strangled grunt, and then she began to bounce.

"Okay… *Fuck!*" I clenched my jaw and focussed on not blowing my load. "The sex is part of it."

Abbie laughed, but her eyes were closed, and moisture beaded across her chest as she rocked her hips over mine. She was so beautiful that I sat up just so I could wrap my arms around her waist. I held her against me hard enough to let her know I'd never let her go.

She hooked her legs around my waist and gripped tighter with her thighs. She rode me as we clung to each other, sweat mingling and our bodies slipping against each other, our mouths meeting messily in the middle as we breathed in the same air. She was mine, and I was hers.

"I love you," I told her as her climax hit, her pussy tightening around me and sending me over the edge.

I flew apart with her mouth at my ear and her voice ushering me into oblivion. "William Kidd. I love you too."

58

WILL

———————

I TOOK THE night off. Jess and Logan had organised a bonfire for the crew, and I didn't want to miss it. For the first time in a long time, I was relaxed enough to enjoy some time away from my work.

I held Abbie's hand on the way down to the bar to check things out before we went to the beach. I hadn't done a lot of hand-holding in my time, not with a woman who was my girlfriend, and I liked it so much I might never let her go.

The place was full, mostly locals, but also the kind of tourists we were used to seeing year-round. Couples, young families, and empty nesters who loved our town just as much as they did Valentine's Day. My regular cover band played on the stage, the smell of roasted garlic wafted from the kitchen, and the mood was upbeat but no longer frenetic. I preferred it this way.

"You got those drinks ready?" I asked Steph, pulling Abbie with me as I slipped behind the bar. I was looking for the oversized coolers I'd left in the kitchen to be filled with beers and bottled cocktails.

"Your boys came by and collected them about half an hour ago," Steph answered over her shoulder. "Told me to tell you to get your arse down to the beach as soon as you could."

"Noted," I said, but I moved further into the kitchen first, towing Abbie along. She came without protest, which made me feel awesome. "Noa? All good here?"

"All good, boss."

"I'm only as far as the beach if you need me, all right? Call if things get too busy."

Noa nodded with amused patience. "Will do, but if we can survive the number of plates we served this weekend, we can manage tonight just fine."

"And everything's all set for the food stall at the street markets tomorrow?"

"All set."

"Thanks for all your help, Noa." I clapped him on the back, then wound my arm around Abbie without dropping her hand. She leaned into me like it was the most natural thing in the world. "Not just for tonight and tomorrow or for this weekend, but also for your support with Seb—all the advice and the food. I appreciate it."

Noa grinned and pretended to wipe away a tear. "You're going to make me cry, boss."

Abbie chuckled as we said our goodbyes.

On our way to the front door, Abbie stalled as a woman stood from a booth and waved hesitantly at her. It took me a minute to recognise her as the woman at the bar the other night. The one who Abbie told me to kiss on the cheek.

"Liberty?" Abbie gave her a quick one-armed hug, which surprised me. I didn't realise they were close.

"Hi, Abbie." Liberty's eyes bounced to me and away again before she thrust out her hand for me to take. "Hi, Will. I'm Liberty Carmichael. We met the other night—"

"I remember." I shook her hand politely. "It's nice to see you again."

"I didn't know you were still in town. Is Adam here?" Abbie asked before she whipped her head around to look across the bar. "I thought he left for the city this morning."

"Adam?" I had no idea what was going on.

Liberty shifted on her feet and clutched her purse in front of her body. "Ah, no. Adam's not here, and he did leave for the city this morning, but, uh… It turns out that we don't live too far from each other, and we're going to have dinner later in the week."

Abbie squeaked and dropped my hand to embrace Liberty again, this time with a more enthusiastic hug that made the other woman grunt before she laughed and returned the embrace.

"Thanks," she said as Abbie let her go. I was stupidly pleased when Abbie collected my hand again. I preferred having her fingers twisted in mine at all times.

"We're just on our way down to the beach for a party," Abbie said. "Do you want to join us?"

"That's so nice, but I'm on my way home. I just wanted to drop in to talk to Will, actually."

"Me?" I looked at Abbie to see if she knew what this was about, but she looked as surprised as I was. Fuck. Had my little kiss on her cheek given her ideas? I was searching for ways to let her down gently when she spoke.

"Yes." Liberty's brows drew down. "Adam told me you've bought the warehouse next door because you have plans to build a brewery?"

I scratched my cheek, totally thrown off guard. "Ah, yes?"

"And he also told me that you lost an investor after what happened at the poker tournament the other night." I must have looked lost because she added, "After the fight, your potential business partner cancelled your deal?"

Heat crept up my neck, but this was part of owning my actions, right? The good and the bad. Facing the music. Admitting when I was wrong. Doing the thing my father was never able to do and being a better man than he ever was.

"He did."

Liberty nodded thoughtfully. "Well, I'm interested."

"You're... interested?"

I'm such an idiot because my head jumped back to the kiss again, and I assumed she was interested in *me*.

"You want to... invest in Will's business?" Abbie clarified.

"Mm-hm." Liberty opened her purse and pulled out a business card. I took it, and Abbie looked at it over my shoulder.

"Liberty's Angels," I read out loud. "What's this?"

"I'm an app developer," she said. "I create retail and consumer goods platforms, and my last app just sold for *a lot* of money." Liberty seemed to hear what she'd just said, and her cheeks turned pink. "It wouldn't have been possible without a seed investment, and I promised myself that I'd pay it forward if I ever had the chance. So, I've set up an angel investment firm, and I'm looking for start-ups who fit my ethos."

"And what's your ethos, exactly?" I asked. Surely, it wasn't to work with playboy single-dad bartenders who punched other men for insulting their girlfriends.

Liberty gripped her purse hard enough that her knuckles turned white. If I didn't know better, I'd have said she was nervous. "I want to work with good people. Decent people. People who are kind to strangers, love their families, work hard, and own their mistakes."

Abbie's eyes narrowed. "Did Adam put you up to this?"

"Adam?" Liberty shook her head. "God, no. I haven't told him about my money yet. But I will! It's just that…" She sighed. "Men can get a little… weird… when they find out I make more than them."

"Not Adam," Abbie reassured her, but then she frowned. "And if he tries any of that toxic bullshit, you send him my way. I'll kick his arse for you."

Liberty's mouth twitched. "Thanks." Then she looked at me. "So, will you think about my offer?"

I glanced at the card again, dumbstruck that securing money for my brewery was back on the table. I'd resigned myself to years of slow, hard work just to clear my debt and manage small-batch brewing before I'd ever be able to grow.

"I will definitely think about it," I replied.

Liberty smiled. "Good. My number and email address are on the card. And I've already got some ideas for your sales platform." She blushed again. "But we can talk about that later if you decide to call."

"I'll call," I assured her. "And thank you."

Liberty said her goodbyes, and I waited for the door to swing closed behind her before I spun to Abbie in disbelief. The grin on her face was wide enough to make her cheeks pop, and I swung her up into my arms, spinning her around as she laughed.

"I'm so proud of you, babe," she said.

"I think you had a lot to do with this." I read the card again, just to make sure I hadn't dreamed it. "Your kindness is what Liberty was referring to."

Abbie shook her head vigorously. "It was all you. You work hard. You own your mistakes. Just like she said."

It was suddenly hard to breathe, but I managed to choke out, "Maybe the lesson here is that we make a good team?"

Abbie grinned, and then she kissed me. "You bet we do."

We left The Stop and crossed Main Street, then set off for the bonfire stones at the end of the Bay. My phone rang, and after pausing to check the screen in case it was Mum calling about Seb, I flashed the screen at Abbie before holding the phone to my ear.

"Dylan," I said. "What's up?"

"Nothing much," he replied. "I just saw your post about you and Abbie, and I wanted to call and say congratulations. Guess your moves worked in the end."

I laughed as Abbie gave me a bemused look, and I winked at her. "Yeah, I guess they did."

"And Seb's a fucking cute kid, man."

"Won't argue on that."

"How did things go at the poker tournament?" There was an awkward pause. "Aunt Lori told me you had a big night."

"Yeah." I flexed knuckles that burned with the memory of connecting with Tristan's putrid face. "There was a fight."

"The way I hear it, he deserved it."

I shrugged. "He did, but I was a dumbass to do it on camera."

"Won't argue about that."

I huffed out a laugh and looked out over the horizon. The smell of smoke floated in the air, and in the distance, a bright orange bonfire licked at the purpling twilight sky. It created a picture I'd seen a thousand times over the years but somehow never got old. "And how are things over there? Izzy doing great things?"

"Izzy's a fucking ballbuster in a tutu," he said with a smile in his voice. "She's awesome."

"And the estate?" Things were tough for Dylan and his sister, Charlie, who had been running their family vineyard after their parents died. They had two other brothers and another sister, but only Dylan and Charlie had stayed on at Silver Leaf to keep the place running.

"It's, uh…" Dylan was quiet for a moment. "It's been better."

My good mood gave way to a pang of guilt. It was hard to be happy when people you cared about were in trouble, and recent experiences made me extra sympathetic to Dylan's struggles. I dropped my voice a little. "I'm sorry, mate. Nobody understands better than me."

"Yeah. Thanks." Dylan sighed. "So, listen. It's late here, and I've got an early start at the restaurant tomorrow. I was just checking in, and seriously, Will. I'm happy for you and Abbie. And the business stuff… that'll work itself out. You've got your boy, and you got the girl. That's a good life right there."

I glanced at Abbie again, and her impatient curiosity made me grin. I did have a good life, and Abbie and Seb made that possible. I bopped her on the nose to make her smile. "Thanks, Dylan. I appreciate it."

I ended the call as Abbie and I stepped onto gold sand, still warm from the day's heat, and we started towards the fire hand in hand. Eight shadowed shapes circled it, some standing, others sitting on driftwood logs, and I knew everyone so well I could pick them out from even this distance. Josh and Emily. Logan and Jess. Isaac and Birdie. Luca and Tash. All laughing and talking and drinking bottled cocktails and beers from the business I built.

I squeezed Abbie's hand and ran my eyes over her familiar features. I'd know those honey-brown eyes, those pale freckles, the wisps of golden curls around her hairline and the coconut scent of her skin anywhere. Dylan was right. It was a good life, and my girl was the reason why.

ONE YEAR LATER

WILL

———

I TUGGED AT the sleeves of my cream-coloured jacket, then fidgeted with the collar of my white dress shirt. It was almost sunset, so the air wasn't too warm, but I was hot. My heart thumped erratically, and every time I glanced at my watch to check how long I'd been waiting, it only ever showed another minute had passed by.

I wasn't nervous. I was impatient.

I stood on the beach under a simple timber arch draped with rippling ivory chiffon and wreathed with bouquets of pink and white flowers. The hum of the ocean was a familiar comfort, as was the endless blue sky spanning overhead. On either side of an aisle that Logan had constructed from lengths of distressed wooden planks were rows of timber chairs. About half of them were still empty, but they were filling up fast as the guests at my and Abbie's wedding trekked from Main Street. Josh, Logan, Isaac, and Luca ushered each person into a suitable position as I returned their congratulatory nods and abstractly noted how good they all looked. The women in long, flowing dresses and flowery hair pieces. The men in dress pants and shirts, most without jackets. No ties. No shoes. Kids in the kind of clothes they'd never wear again and would ruin the minute the ceremony was finished. Everyone in some shade of white or cream and muted pink.

I shifted and forced myself to breathe. Not nervous. Impatient.

Logan walked over and stood beside me, rolling his shoulders in a jacket that matched the one I wore, but the flower in his lapel was pink, not white. Beside him, Josh, Isaac, and Luca took up their positions as groomsmen.

"How are you doing?" Logan asked at my side.

"I'm good," I replied, though that wasn't the right word for it. I vibrated with anticipation, and there was a fluttering, empty feeling in my stomach—a hollow filled with butterflies as I counted down the minutes.

The celebrant arrived and shook my hand as she took her place under the bridal arch. To the side, a duo of acoustic guitar players began strumming a gentle melody, and I stared towards the enclosed bridal canopy set up at the end of the sandy aisle, where Abbie waited.

Romantic music floated around us as the last guests took their seats. On Abbie's side, the first chair in the front row was empty, waiting for Arthur to take his place. Next along was Nancy, then Adam with Liberty on his other side. I nodded at the man who was about to be my brother-in-law and shared a smile with his girlfriend, who also happened to be my new business partner. I hadn't rushed into anything this time, and we'd only signed on the dotted line earlier that week.

On the opposite side of the aisle, Mum and Ray sat in front with two vacant seats beside them. In the row behind were four of my five cousins. Dylan had the chair on the aisle, the best position to see his four-year-old daughter, Izzy, pass him as the flower girl. Beside Dylan was Charlotte—Charlie for short—with her warm brown hair in loose curls around her shoulders and her phone upright, ready to film. On her other side was Daisy. In her mid-twenties, with long hair dyed a striking shade of pastel pink, Daisy was the youngest of the Davenport siblings, and she looked tiny sitting there with Chord on her other side. Tall and strong with the athletic build of an NHL player—because he was; Chord played wing for the Calgary Crushers— I was surprised he'd made it here for the wedding, but Chord assured me he wouldn't have missed it for anything. The only person not here was Finn, but he was serving overseas in the U.S. military.

I was thankful they'd flown from California to be here. Aside from my mother, my cousins were the only relatives I had in the world, and I'd been excited to introduce them to Seb. They'd arrived two days ago, and Izzy had taken charge of him the second they met. The two had been inseparable since. It was fucking adorable.

Suddenly, the music changed, and I stood a little straighter. The guests turned in their seats to watch as the event assistants parted the white fabric of the bridal tent, and the first person stepped out.

I smiled politely at Tash, who was glowing in a billowy pale pink dress. She gripped a small bouquet of white flowers in her hands, and I glanced at Luca. His eyes were riveted to her, and when she passed Luca's mother holding their new baby among the rows of guests, Tash smiled. You could almost feel the mini-explosion of love between the three of them.

Birdie was next, also in a pink dress. Her red hair was braided and stuck with tiny white blossoms, and as she passed me to take her place at the altar, she threw a wink Isaac's way.

Emily followed, a tiny thing in another pink gown, white flowers in her hands. She blushed at the attention and cast Josh a shy look as she positioned herself next to Birdie.

Jess stepped out of the bridal tent and paced down the aisle towards us, keeping time with the music. I wish I could have said I paid more attention to her, but it was hard to even breathe, knowing Abbie would be next.

The fabric moved, and my heart lurched, but out slipped Izzy in her pretty white dress, with Seb hanging precariously to her hand. Izzy had a pouch of flower petals tied to her waist, and she threw these around with solemn precision as she clung to Seb's chubby little fingers with her other hand. Everyone cooed as my son and my cousin's daughter made their careful journey down the aisle, and I grinned. Seb was so freaking cute in his tiny cream-coloured suit, collared white shirt, and bare feet tripping over the sand. At eighteen months old, he was steady on solid surfaces but still struggled on the beach. Izzy kept the pace slow to accommodate him, and the serious look on her face was incredibly sweet.

As they approached, I leaned down to accept the little velvet box clutched in Seb's hand.

"Daddy!" He flung himself at my legs, and I scooped him up to give him a kiss before Mum took him and positioned him on the seat next to her. Izzy took the other one as Dylan reached forward and told her what a wonderful job she'd done.

The music changed again, and everyone rose to their feet. I didn't realise I'd shifted forward until Logan set a hand on my arm and pulled me back.

The event assistants drew back the canopy fabric, and the world stood still.

The dress was simple—strapless layers of delicate fabric that swirled around her legs and showed off her arms, her bronze skin glowing in the pink light of sunset. Her blonde hair was in loose waves down her back, and she wore a delicate wreath of white flowers as a crown. Her face glowed with joy.

Abbie was the most beautiful thing I'd ever seen, and it hurt to swallow. It hurt to breathe.

Her eyes found mine, and I lost my bearings, unable to break away from her gaze as Arthur stopped before me, kissed Abbie's cheek, and took his seat. I don't remember reaching for Abbie's hand, but there it was in mine, and now we were facing each other. The celebrant was speaking, and I was trying hard to listen, but all I could do was run my eyes over my girl's face. She was happy. She was perfect. And I needed someone to pinch me because how the fuck did I get so lucky?

"Abbie and Will have written their own vows for today," the celebrant was saying, and a swell of nerves scattered the fog in my head. "Will, would you like to go first?"

I cleared my throat and thought of the wadded-up piece of paper in the pocket of my jacket. I ignored it, just like I was about to ignore most of the things written on it. A page of rehearsed notes wasn't good enough. Not today, and not for this woman.

"Abigail." I cleared my throat as my nose tingled with the threat of tears. "We've known each other forever, but it's not the length of time we've spent together that makes the bond between us unbreakable. It's what we've shared over the years. Honesty. Heartache. Laughs. Love. I've spent a long time trying to prove to myself that I was worth something. I thought if I could just do enough, make enough, be enough, I'd be deserving of something good. I never dared to hope that *something good* might one day be you. You are my dream. My wish. My world."

Abbie gazed up at me, hanging on each word with a small smile on her mouth and eyes glassy with emotion, and my lips tipped up on one side.

"Three years ago, we were making secret promises and sneaky plans to avoid marriage forever because we're not the marrying kind, right?" Abbie laughed a little as a single tear escaped and dropped from her cheek. "But even then, babe, I knew that if I was going to grow old with someone, it had to be you. It was always you.

"And then Seb came into our lives, and my dreams changed. I watched you fall in love with my son, and I imagined raising a family with you. All my hopes for the future shifted to make room for this new dream, and now, nothing would bring me more happiness than building a life of love with you and our children. I love you, Abigail, and I promise to love you every minute of every day for the rest of my life."

A chorus of sighs rose up around us, and I leaned forward to kiss Abbie before I remembered there was an order to these things. Abbie bit back a smile and gripped my hands tighter as the celebrant invited her to recite her vows.

"Will. You are my best friend, and you've been my best friend for so long that I don't remember a time when you weren't beside me. Loving me on my good days and bad, always with a smile and hug when I needed it. Even when I didn't want you to. Even when I wasn't ready to love you back. I was scared for a long time. I didn't want to take a chance on us because I couldn't believe you might love me as hard or as fiercely as I loved you. I needed time, and you gave it to me without my ever having to ask for it. Thank you."

Her fingers tightened around mine, and I squeezed back. My heart raced ahead of my breath, thumping against my ribs, and I resisted the urge to gather her in my arms.

"A long time ago, you asked me what type of boyfriend I thought you would be. Do you remember?"

I nodded, and we shared a tender smile, recalling the first time we'd slept in the same bed, a wall of pillows between us.

"I guessed you'd be a provider, and you are." Abbie's voice grew quiet and croaky as she tried not to let emotion overwhelm her. I had to blink a few extra times myself. "I said you'd be a man your girl could lean on, and I don't know anyone stronger than you."

"What else?" I asked, and our guests laughed.

Abbie smiled through tears. "I said you'd be protective. A little possessive—in a good way. I told you that you'd made your girl the centre of your world, but... I was wrong."

My stomach flipped, and Abbie laughed. "You've given me so much more than that. You've trusted me to love and raise your son with you, and you've made us both the centre of your universe."

I couldn't stop the tear that tracked down my face or the warmth that sprung up in my chest.

"Some things are written in the stars," Abbie went on. "The Universe makes plans whether we like it or not, and our story was etched into the sky long before we knew our own truth. You are my destiny, William. You and that smart, sweet little boy over there. You are my future, and you always were. I love you, and I can't wait to keep loving you for the rest of forever."

Abbie leaned in this time, drawing my mouth towards her like a magnet, but the celebrant's voice recalled us to the moment, and we drew back reluctantly.

Our voices were strong and certain when we said *I do*. My hand shook as I slipped the simple wedding band onto Abbie's finger—the band I'd fantasised about more than a thousand times was now unmissable against her smooth skin. Her grip was sure when she slid the ring onto my hand, and I couldn't hold back a second more. I kissed her before the celebrant told me to do it, and cheers rose up around us as we were announced husband and wife.

I heard the words, and I kissed Abbie harder, folding her against me as I pressed her body against mine. I heard the words, and they sounded so true and so inescapable because there was no other destiny for us. No other way for us to live the kind of life that made us happy. We'd waited a long time to get here and worked hard to make it real.

Abbie was mine, and I was hers, the way we were always supposed to be.

ABBIE

WE STOOD AT The door to the loft, but after Will swung it open, he slipped an arm around my waist and pulled me back before I could walk through.

"What are you—oh!"

Will swung me up into his arms, and I laughed as I looped my arms around his neck, and he carried me over the threshold.

"I know I'm new at this," he said, kicking the door closed behind him and continuing up the stairs, "but I think—I *think*—a good husband is supposed to carry his wife straight to the bedroom on their wedding night, then stay up all night doing unspeakable things to her body."

"Mm." I brushed my open mouth along his neck, letting my breath caress his skin. "You should have put *that* in your vows."

He chuckled as he stepped onto the landing and set me on my feet. "How would that go? Something like, I promise to love, honour, and make you come every day for the rest of our lives?"

"That's a start," I replied as he spun me around to face the room. I gasped and looked around in wonder at the flickering golden light of candles everywhere—there had to be a hundred of them—and the pink flower petals strewn across the bed covers. Gentle music drifted from the speaker in the corner, and emotion caught in my throat as I recognised an acoustic version of our wedding song.

It reminded me of the first night we'd been together, and I had to blink back tears.

"It's beautiful, babe," I whispered as he led me by one hand over to the bed.

"Well, you wouldn't let me organise a hotel for tonight," he said, sweeping his fingertips over my arms so lightly it gave me goosebumps. "And God knows how long it'll be until we can take a proper honeymoon. I wanted this to be special. You're my wife."

A pleased tug pulled at my lips. "And you're my husband."

Will ran his eyes over my face and down over my wedding dress again. He'd been doing that all night, cataloguing every bead in the lace and crease in the fabric as if he never wanted to forget the way I looked. I never wanted to forget him like this, either. His hair messy and his shirt unbuttoned, the sleeves rolled up, and his eyes bright from a night of drinking and dancing with our friends and family. Smelling like sugar from our wedding cake and whiskey from the wedding toasts. Dimples popping only for me.

Will's hands travelled to my back, and his fingers played with the buttons on my strapless corset. He'd never get them undone without my turning around, but I let him fumble with them as I collected myself.

I had something to tell him, and it had been almost impossible to keep it a secret for as long as I had. Three days. A *long* three days. An even longer wedding reception. I'd been knocking back offers of champagne and margaritas all night, all the while hoping everyone else was too intoxicated to notice. I'd wanted our wedding day to be only about us. The wedding night, however, felt like the perfect time to tell the truth.

"Babe?" I said as Will pressed his mouth to the slope of my neck.

"Mm?"

"Do you remember the Valentine's Day Festival last year?"

He grunted unhappily but didn't remove his mouth from my skin. "I'd like to forget it."

I smiled and ran my hands over his muscled back, tugging on his shirt to release it from the waist of his trousers. "I think everyone learned a lesson, though, don't you think? The festivities were much more reasonable this year."

"They were," he mumbled before nipping at my earlobe.

"No buses with Daddy Will groupies this time," I commented.

SAMANTHA LEIGH

Will straightened and frowned. "I should hope not."

"You know what I was thinking about the other day?" I asked.

"Ah… no?" Will looked confused now, and I bit the inside of my cheek to stop a smile.

"That bingo card."

"The bingo card?"

"You remember." I stepped away to retrieve my phone from where I'd left it in the bedside drawer all night, then sat on the edge of the mattress while I scrolled through to the graphic saved in my camera roll. I flashed the screen at Will. "See?"

"Do we have to talk about this now?" he asked with a sigh. He dropped to his knees and plucked the phone from my hand, then set it aside. "It's our wedding night."

"I know."

Will kissed me, tilting my body back until I was flat on the bed. Then, he scooped up the layers of lace and tulle that were my wedding gown and disappeared underneath.

I giggled at the shape of his head popping up under the fabric. "Mrs Kidd! You're not wearing any underwear."

I giggled and opened my legs wider. "Surprise."

"Thank fuck I didn't know about this earlier." Will lifted my feet and set them on his shoulder. "I'd have been hard all day."

I moaned as he kissed the inside of one ankle, then the other. I could take one little orgasm before I told him, couldn't I?

Actually, no. I didn't think I could.

432

I ignored the coils of anticipation curling in my core and reached for my phone. Will caressed my calves as he worked his way north with warm kisses and lazy swirls of his tongue, and I breathed evenly as I swiped to open the screen and read aloud.

"Items number one and two. Slip him your number. Get his number." I snorted quietly. "I've had your number since we were thirteen. I crossed them off straightaway."

He hummed against the inside of my knees, and I ignored the throb between my thighs with some effort.

"Five-minute kiss," I said as my breath came a little faster. "The one at my first baby yoga class. Check. Hand job. Blow job. Marked those off a year ago, too. Quickie at The Stop. Do you remember that, babe?"

His head popped up, and I yanked at the fabric of my dress so I could see his face. His grin was cute and boyish. "Hell, yeah. That was fucking hot."

I shivered, remembering the way he'd poured tequila straight from the bottle down my throat and the way he'd licked it from my chin. "It was."

"Did it make your flick list?" he teased.

A laugh escaped me. "It's at the top." I glanced at my phone, even though I'd memorised every square on the pink grid. "Panties on your pillow. I did that, too."

Will massaged my inner thighs, his thumbs brushing tantalisingly close to my pussy, but he was invested in the bingo card now. "So that's what that was about. I didn't connect the dots at the time."

"Had to show your groupies who you belonged to, didn't I?"

"I suppose you did." He pulled me into a seated position and kissed me before checking my phone again. "Only leaves one square to go. Knocked up with baby number two." Will grinned, but his eyes pinched a little as his hands rubbed my arms anxiously. "What do you think about that? I know we haven't talked about when we'll have more kids or how many, but... I'm ready. I'd have a hundred kids with you if you'd let me."

I chuckled and snaked my arms around his neck. "Let's start with one, shall we?"

Behind his head, I added the final cross to the bingo card, then held the phone where Will could see the screen. His mouth twitched as his forehead creased.

"I don't get it."

Tears threatened to spill over again. I was only a few weeks pregnant, and I hadn't had any symptoms yet, but I'd cried more today than I had in the last ten years. It must have been the hormones.

"I'm pregnant, babe."

"You're... what?"

Will's eyes dropped to my stomach. It was still flat underneath the layers of gossamer and lace and tulle, and I chuckled.

"I'm pregnant."

His beautiful face split with a familiar grin, and though his dimple flashed, his eyes grew glassy. Then he kissed me. He held my face between his two hands, as gently as he'd hold glass, and kissed me. A slow, reverent connection that was careful and devoted and desperate all at once. It went on, a testament to what we meant to each other. Best friends. Lovers. Husband and wife. Parents.

Soul mates.

"Come on, Daddy." I tightened my hold around his neck, tipping backwards onto the bed and taking him with me. "Let's celebrate."

BONUS SCENE

———————

Will and Abbie's story doesn't end here!
Visit my website at samanthaleighbooks.com/books/
bonus-content or use the QR code to download
a bonus scene set ten years in the future...

UP NEXT: WALLFLOWER

He's the grumpy hotshot hockey player. She's too shy to look him in the eyes. He needs a live-in summer assistant and she's *perfect*.

Chord Davenport is the hottest, surliest man to ever slap shot a puck. He's given up everything to be the best—family, friendship, love—but he's about to retire as a legend of the game and that makes his sacrifices worth it.

Violet James wanted to be the next big name in bridal couture not a junior marketing executive for the San Francisco Fury hockey team, but her salary pays her dad's therapy bills and leaving him behind to chase a selfish dream would cost her too much.

When Chord hires Violet as his summer assistant, he's certain this pretty wallflower won't give him any trouble. But when she moves into the house he built on his family's California ranch, Chord can't take his eyes—or his hands—off her.

All he wants is to love her, protect her, satisfy her, and give her the courage to follow her heart. He didn't expect to feel a desperate need to become a better man.

In just one summer, Chord and Violet change each other forever, but will living their dreams be the very thing that tears them apart?

ACKNOWLEDGEMENTS

This is a pinch-me moment. My debut series is all wrapped up, saying goodbye to these characters is the very definition of bittersweet, and it's hard to believe we've reached the end. But we have! And I never would have got here without the love and support of a few special people.

Thank you to Dawn Alexander, Gina Salamon, Brandi Zelenka, Kate Farlow, and Stephanie Archer for your encouragement and guidance. Thank you to my beta readers, Callan, Heidi, Kasandra, and Nikki. A huge thank you to Mindy and my enthusiastic and always supportive ARC team, and buckets of appreciation to the wonderful creators of #AussieBookTok. Thank you to my LoveLeigh Readers group. And thank *you* for every review and every time you recommended my books to a friend, or posted about them on social media, or sent me a lovely message. I don't get to do this without my amazing readers, and I am so grateful for each and every one of you.

And last but never least, thank you to my family—my husband and my children. I love you.

ABOUT THE AUTHOR

Samantha Leigh is an Australian author of steamy contemporary romance. When she's not playing matchmaker in imaginary worlds, Sam is reading books with all the feels and all the spice. In the tiny slices of time she has between word wrangling, Sam likes to hit her yoga mat, go for walks in the bush or on the beach, continue her search for the perfect poke bowl, drown herself in coffee and hot cacao, and binge-watch nineties television.

samanthaleighbooks.com